iron
angel

Also by Alan Campbell

SCAR NIGHT
(VOLUME ONE OF THE DEEPGATE CODEX)

IRON ANGEL

ALAN CAMPBELL

THE DEEPGATE CODEX
VOLUME II

TOR

First published 2008 by Tor
an imprint of Pan Macmillan Ltd
Pan Macmillan, 20 New Wharf Road, London N1 9RR
Basingstoke and Oxford
Associated companies throughout the world
www.panmacmillan.com

ISBN 978-1-4050-9036-0 HB
ISBN 978-0-230-01605-7 TPB

1 3 5 7 9 8 6 4 2

A CIP catalogue record for this book is available
from the British Library.

Typeset by Intype Libra, London
Printed and bound in the UK by
CPI Mackays, Chatham ME5 8TD

Visit **www.panmacmillan.com** to read more about all our books
and to buy them. You will also find features, author interviews and
news of any author events, and you can sign up for e-newsletters
so that you're always first to hear about our new releases.

For Caragh

ACKNOWLEDGEMENTS

My sincere thanks to Simon Kavanagh, Peter Lavery, Juliet Ulman, and to everyone at Bantam and Macmillan.

CODEX EXCERPTS FOUND IN THE WRECKAGE OF RECLAMATION SHIP TWELVE

(FOLLOWS FROM REMAINING FRAGMENT BOFP, VOL. II, P. 783) . . .

The god of flowers and kni(*ves?*) could not kill this foe. He flew above the burning town of Skirl. And among the fire and smoke walked an arconite.

The corpses of [*illegible*] thousand Northmen filled the streets. And one hundred thousand more stood upon the backs of their [*unknown term; trans. – cold?*] brothers in order to reach the great winged demon.

They hacked the arconite with steel and burned it. But the demon (*laughed/howled?*) and walked among them and slew the Northmen. All the men of Coreollis came forth to fight, and the men of Brownslough and those of [*charred*]. One half of the (*handsome?*) god's men died beneath the arconite's club. The rest tried to flee. But the god of flowers and knives was wrathful.

[*following two lines charred/indic. collateral PF impact*]

Chains of bane were brought forth from [*unknown term; trans. – 'city of voices', see appendix 4a*] to bind the arconite's feet. It stumbled and fell and crushed many (*dwellings?*) in Skirl. But still it slew the warriors around it, for it would not return to Hell so easily.

[*Excised*] from Oxos came to poison the fallen demon. It would not die. [*Excised*] brought worms to devour it. It would not be

I

consumed. Slaves [*charred*] from the Riot Coast, and set about the beast with hammers and [*illegible*]. And after two moons the arconite had been pinned.

Even then they could not slay it, and so they buried it under the earth.

The god of flowers and knives brought forth a great rain to cleanse Pandemeria of [*excised*]. But in his castle he brooded, for his army had been decimated. And under the drowned earth, the arconite still breathed.

PROLOGUE

OBLIVION OR SLAVERY

Saltwater fog had engulfed the old galleon for as long as her crew could remember. The briny air had warped her joints and planking, eaten holes in her decks and bulkheads, and turned her interior into a dank, rotting hive. Everything creaked, dripped and groaned in the gloom. Even the throne upon which Cospinol sat had wasted, its once finely carved surfaces now reduced to so much mulch.

The old god was wearing his best armour, but the layers of hardened red crab shells had cracked and tarnished millennia ago and no amount of paint and glue had been able to restore the suit to its former glory. His wings slumped from his shoulders like the tattered grey and white sails this ancient vessel had once possessed. His eyes peered out through a bedraggled net of his own hair as he studied the axe in his hand.

'My Lord?'

This gradual corruption would be the end of him. Like the wooden axe handle in his fist, his vessel, the *Rotsward*, could only barely support her own weight. She simply would not survive another century. Her bones had atrophied, her skin had split, and now things moved through the dank spaces in her belly that had no right to be there. Cospinol lifted his eyes from the axe and listened for the patter of small feet.

'My Lord?' The slave girl kneeling before him clutched the hem of her smock. 'Your brothers are here.'

Cospinol made a dismissive gesture. A child sniggered in the passage outside the captain's cabin, and then a shadow darted past an open gap in the nearest bulkhead.

The old god raised his axe. 'This runt has been pestering me for days,' he growled. 'I intend to have the little bastard's head on a plate before they arrive.' He rose from his throne and took a step towards the source of the sound. Planks sagged under his shell-plated boots. Looking down through a hand-sized gap in the floorboards in one corner of the cabin, he noticed a much larger hole in the *Rotsward*'s outer hull. A small figure clambered through this and slipped out into the fog beyond, followed by a chittering mass of living red crabs. 'The boy is a damned spider,' Cospinol muttered. 'How is he able to climb *underneath* my ship?'

'He has hooks for fingers,' the slave girl said.

'Hooks? Since when?'

She shrugged.

The sea god grunted. 'This infestation is a conspiracy. The last thing I need is for my brothers to find such Mesmerist scum loose aboard this vessel. How do you imagine *that* would look?'

She made no reply.

'Those bastards might even try to supplant me,' Cospinol went on. 'They'll say I'm harbouring the enemy, then call a vote and have me expelled from my own dominion. They've been eyeing the Riot Coast for centuries, just waiting for an excuse like this.'

'The war in Pandemeria keeps them fully occupied, my Lord.'

Cospinol opened one of the cabin's rear windows and looked down upon the *Rotsward*'s stern and rudder. He could see little beyond the vague outlines of the scaffold that enveloped his entire skyship, the great floating nest of yards and ropes all wreathed in fog. A gull hopped along one of the timber spars and then took off, circling down towards the ground so far below the hull and scaffold, until it disappeared entirely in the grey mist. Cospinol could see nothing of the landscape down there, but he supposed the *Rotsward* must be drifting somewhere to the west of Pandemeria. 'Evidently not occupied enough,' he said, 'as they've left mortal generals in charge of their armies while they've travelled out here.' He closed the window again. 'Besides, what does a dead girl know about the war? You weren't Pandemerian, were you?'

She lowered her head. 'No, my Lord, I lived and died in Brownslough.'

The god nodded. 'Hafe's realm. I suppose you're one of the lucky ones. Just be thankful that Pandemeria is far from here, lass.' He wandered across the cabin to inspect the banquet table set under the stern windows: the white linen napkins, the silver platters, cutlery, goblets and candlesticks – all far too ostentatious for his simple tastes. He picked up a knife, wondering how his slaves had restored the blade to such a high sheen, before he then noticed a rash of black spots along one edge. Not even his best-kept silverware had survived the slow decay.

This endless fog was to blame, that dismal pall of brine on which Cospinol looked out every day, and which tumbled behind the windowpanes even now. Yet the god did not dare expose his vessel to the sun of this world.

Not yet.

His ruminations were disturbed by a thought. 'Where *are* my brothers? What's taking them so long?'

'My Lord . . .' The girl's chin sank even lower onto her chest. 'Your guests brought something overland with them. It is being hoisted up here even now. Your Lord brothers chose to pause and oversee the operation from the *Rotsward*'s yards.'

'What is it?'

'I do not know, my Lord. They found it in Pandemeria.'

Cospinol felt suddenly uneasy. Nothing good had ever come out of that war-ravaged land. Whatever Rys and the others had discovered would undoubtedly have some wicked purpose. He sighed and made for the door, beckoning his servant after him. 'Let's go and see it then.'

They left the captain's cabin and took one of the aft companionways up to the quarterdeck. From here Cospinol could look out across the *Rotsward*'s upper decks.

Fog wreathed the skyship on all sides. In Heaven she had been a square-rigged galleon made for salt seas – but her keel had not split waves in over three thousand years. Her mainmasts were missing: the tough oak had long since been cannibalized for vital repairs to other parts of the ship. Now her remaining tattered sails hung limply from the main starboard and larboard yards, far out beyond the ship's sides. To reach these, the *Rotsward*'s crew were forced to clamber like ants among the lattice of greasy beams around the hull – a perilous task in the ever-present fog – with nothing but sky between them and the ground so far below.

Work was under way amidships. Two of the crew were resting, exhausted, against the larboard winch handles, while six others wrestled a loaded net onto the deck. This net contained a spherical and dull-metallic object, like an oversized cannonball – and just as heavy, judging by the way his crew were struggling with it. Cospinol looked around for his brothers, but couldn't see them anywhere.

The *Rotsward*'s crew wore the same queer assortment of clothes they had died in. They had once been sailors on the seas below, hailing from Oxos and Meria and a dozen other human ports. Now their pallid faces evinced grim determination as they laboured to free the sphere from its net.

'What *is* that thing?' Cospinol mused.

A harsh laugh came from above him. 'It is the key to your freedom, Cospinol!'

The sea god turned his gaze upwards to see his brother Rys flying down to join him on the quarterdeck, his great white wings cutting through the fog. His mirrored steel plate gleamed like freshly minted coins, while the naked scimitar and many tiny blades in his silver belt shone with the brilliance of starlight. He wore a cloak of Battlefield Roses, as red as the bloody ground from which they had sprouted – and just as poisonous. The god of flowers and knives looked every inch the champion – and Cospinol hated him for it.

Then, from out of the misty sky behind emerged the others: Mirith, Hafe and Sabor. These three gods remained a respectful distance behind their elder brother: Hafe, obese and sweating under cauldrons of copper armour; dour, grey-haired Sabor in his dark suit of mail; poor mad Mirith in the motley of tin plates, leathers and garish velvets that Rys had given him to wear. It seemed that even their wings had grown to complement the stature of each god. If an ox could fly, its wingspan would resemble Hafe's; while Sabor had the look of a rook; and Mirith's wings were lopsided, and stitched with tiny bells.

Rys landed lightly on the quarterdeck. 'This floating gaol continues to amaze me,' he said. 'How do you keep it from completely disintegrating about you?'

Cospinol noted the insult in his brother's choice of words. Of all the five gods present, only Cospinol himself still lacked the power to leave his stronghold. This detail had forced the others to come here, and Rys would not be pleased about that inconvenience. 'The *Rotsward* is tougher than she looks,' he replied darkly.

'As are you, brother,' Rys said. 'You appear so frail one wonders how you are able to remain upright without assistance, and yet somehow you stand here before us, tall enough to be mistaken for an equal.'

The whole skyship gave a sudden lurch as Hafe landed with a mighty thump beside the god of flowers and knives. Sabor set

7

down lightly, a short distance further back, before Mirith landed with a clash of tiny bells and a whoop of glee.

Rys glanced over his shoulder and said, 'Don't feel disheartened, Cospinol, for I am now *surrounded* by cripples.'

'I am no cripple,' Hafe protested.

'This airboat pitches and shudders with every beat of your fat heart,' Rys remarked. 'Your very presence here is likely to send this whole sorry vessel crashing down out of the sky.'

The god of dirt and poison's face reddened. 'It's not my fault,' he grunted, 'that this ship is rotten. A flock of gulls could tear it to shreds.'

Mirith sniggered behind his hand, then gave a ridiculous jester's bow. 'But *I* am a cripple.'

'And a lunatic with it,' Rys agreed. 'Yet we find ourselves in this floating wreck partly because of your uncanny foresight.'

Cospinol's mood darkened further. He was about to respond, when a commotion from amidships distracted him. Rys's strange metal sphere had come loose from its net and rolled away, knocking a crewman to the deck and crushing his chest. The sailor wailed in agony while his companions struggled to roll the object off him.

'Be careful with that,' Rys yelled.

'Perhaps,' Cospinol suggested, 'they would be more cautious if you explained exactly what that object is. It *is* a Mesmerist weapon, is it not?'

'Much more than that,' Rys said. 'Come, brother.'

The god led the others down the quarterdeck staircase to the wide mid-deck, where the remainder of the *Rotsward*'s crew had freed their trapped comrade, and were now jamming blocks of wood under Rys's sphere to keep it from rolling away again.

Cospinol now saw that the sphere was comprised of ill-fitting metal plates, triangles and trapeziums loosely bolted together so that a network of gaps ran between them like the broken earth in a dry riverbed. The metal shone dully, like old pewter, yet each panel was heavily dented and scratched, as though the globe had spent much time rolling across rough terrain. A faint geometric pattern could just be discerned behind the scrawls.

Rys approached the globe and lightly ran a finger across the surface of one of these metal plates, as though tracing the outline of some obscure esoteric design. Then he pushed the panel inwards. It clicked once, and then sprung back out like a flap on its hidden hinges.

Behind the open panel was a face.

Cospinol stepped closer. The visage appeared human at first: an old woman with creased skin, a flat nose, and blind white eyes. But then her mouth opened to reveal a snakelike black tongue and three stubby yellow glass teeth. She gave a sudden desperate wail.

'Close the sphere! The sun burns us so!'

'There is no sun here,' Rys growled. 'Be silent, hag, until I give you permission to speak.'

Cospinol's eyes widened. 'You found a *witchsphere*?'

Rys nodded. 'My soldiers discovered it after the battle in Skirl. This *thing* had been observing the conflict for its master.'

'Menoa's dogcatchers will be searching hard for this object.'

'Let them search,' Rys grunted. 'It is far beyond their reach now.'

The hag inside the sphere cried out again. 'Traitorous dogs! We curse the sons of Ayen. We inhaled your blood in Skirl and in Pandemeria, and now we will exhale it in Deepgate. You have no more men to throw against us.'

'Silence!' Rys slipped a knife from his belt and plunged it through the open panel into the interior of the sphere. The hag screamed and spat blood at him, but the handsome god only twisted his blade and pushed it in deeper, until the wailing died away.

Wincing, Cospinol turned away from the gruesome sight. 'I see your talents of persuasion remain as keen as ever,' he said to his younger brother. 'But what did the witchsphere mean? How can the Mesmerists hope to attack *Deepgate*?'

Mirith giggled manically. 'All is not well on the other side of Hell.' His tin-plate armour rattled like beggars' cups as he danced away across the *Rotsward*'s deck.

Rys wiped blood and spittle from his face. 'Mirith is more astute than he appears,' he said to Cospinol. 'His madness masks a cunning mind.' He then faced the old sea god, his eyes grim, and said, 'Ulcis has been slain.'

So startling was this news that Cospinol actually laughed. 'Slain?' he snorted. 'A god slain? Impossible.'

'It is true,' Rys insisted. 'Mirith had a spy in Deepgate, a hell-walker by the name of Thomas Scatterclaw. He stole through the Maze to confirm this witch's tidings. Ulcis's death has left a second door to Hell unguarded. Now King Menoa's forces are gathering behind it.'

Cospinol hissed. 'But how could this have happened? How did our brother Ulcis become so lax?' he asked. 'How could he allow the Mesmerists to get a corporeal assassin into this world? How did they kill him?'

'*They* didn't,' Rys said. 'The god of chains died at the hand of his own daughter.'

'His daughter?' Cospinol stared at him in disbelief. 'He had a daughter? And he let her live?'

The god of flowers and knives nodded. 'His folly has put us all in grave danger. The battle at Skirl has decimated our forces. We cannot spare the troops necessary to halt a second Mesmerist incursion. The portal beneath Deepgate lies wide open, and the lands around the abyss are undefended. Ethereal entities are already rising from Hell and moving into the chained city under a veil of bloody mist. Icarate shape-shifters will follow soon, and then the full force of the Mesmerist horde will pour out of the abyss at their heels. They will corrupt the Deadsands as they have corrupted Pandemeria.'

While Cospinol considered this grim turn of events, Rys returned his attention back to the witchsphere. The hag inside was gurgling pitifully now, choking on her own blood. Rys closed the panel and then opened another flap on the top of the globe. A second hag peered out: a woman even uglier and more ancient than the first. Her single white eye lolled in a skull-like face as black as burned oak. 'Mercy for my sisters!' she cried. 'Let us return to Hell, son of Ayen.'

Rys grinned. 'When you have told my brother all you know,' he said.

'We have told everything,' the hag wailed.

'Tell *him*.'

The hag moaned. 'Our master is building a second arconite, even greater and more powerful than the first. Forged of bone and iron and leashed to the soul of a powerful archon, it will move in sunlight and walk freely across unblooded earth.' Her face twisted into a hideous sneer. 'It will crush the remnants of your armies like ants!'

Rys set about her with his knife. All the time the smile never left his face.

The handsome god was panting when he finally finished with the witchsphere. 'So far the Mesmerists have been confined to Pandemeria,' he said, 'simply because they cannot survive for long without drawing power from blood. In order to remain in this world, Hell's creatures must walk upon the red earth of battlefields, or upon land already saturated by Menoa's bloody mists. But these arconites . . .' He balled his fists. 'We could not *kill* the first one, Cospinol.'

'And when the second one leaves Hell,' Cospinol said, 'you will lose your hold on this world.'

'*We* will lose *our* hold,' Rys said.

But that wasn't true. Cospinol owned none of the wealth or kingdoms his four brothers possessed. He had been trapped in this rotting ship for three thousand years, wreathed in fog to hide himself from the destructive power of the sun. Only Ulcis, the eldest of all the goddess Ayen's sons, had been similarly trapped – hidden beneath the earth while he harvested souls to join Rys's army. But now Ulcis was dead, leaving Cospinol as the last of the gods to remain imprisoned.

'What has become of Ulcis's reservists?' he asked. 'The hordes he harvested from Deepgate?'

Sabor stepped forward. 'Their flesh is lost,' he said. 'The Mesmerists will have already used their blood for their own purposes.' Everything about the god of clocks was grey: his skin, his feathers, his hair, even his eyes. To read his shadowless expression, one required a degree of patient concentration. No wonder Sabor chose to wear black: a single item of coloured raiment might distract the viewer's eye and thus doom any conversation. Sabor continued in dull, authoritative tones. 'Yet the souls of his reservists remain in this world.'

Cospinol frowned. 'How?'

'Ulcis's daughter did not spill her father's blood. She merely displaced the essence of it.'

'She *drank* the fat sod,' Rys confirmed. Cospinol could not help but notice a glint of satisfaction light up in Rys's eyes. Should the mother goddess's sons ever reclaim Heaven, Ulcis's death left only Cospinol in line for the throne before Rys – a thought the old sea god found suddenly unnerving.

Hafe slammed a fist against his copper breastplate. 'You bastards do nothing but talk,' he boomed. 'When do we eat?'

Cospinol's slaves brought tray after tray to the captain's table: corpse crabs from Gobe Bay and steamed kellut from Oxos; squid and cuttlefish and bowls of pink prawns. The god of brine and fog had chosen the very best from his larders for this occasion, but now he had no appetite. While his brothers ate and chatted, Cospinol brooded in silence.

Ulcis was dead, his army lost, and his untimely departure had offered Menoa's hordes a second route out of Hell. Rys's armies had been decimated at Skirl. The survivors had retreated to Core-ollis in a desperate attempt to defend that stronghold against Mesmerist attacks from the Red Road. Even if the god of flowers and knives could spare enough of his troops to make a difference, would they be able to travel to Deepgate in time to halt this new incursion?

Cospinol doubted it. He began to suspect why his brothers were really here.

Rys spat at one of the serving girls. 'This food isn't fit for a dog,' he announced. 'Fetch us something edible. Bring us a bowl of the soulpearls your master hoards.'

She bowed and hurried away, without even a glance at Cospinol.

Mirith sniggered. 'Bowls of souls,' he said. 'Better than this filth. The dead can't cook.'

Hafe grunted in agreement without raising his face from the platter of eels he was devouring. Sabor glanced up at Rys, and then quickly back to his own plate, yet Cospinol noted the dark look of disapproval in the grey god's eyes.

Rys set down his fork. 'Your slaves are tediously slow,' he said to Cospinol, 'and your whole skyship stinks of corpses, gull-shit and brine. Tell me, brother, do you enjoy living in such squalor?'

'I survive.'

'But it's hardly a life,' Rys commented. 'Don't you tire of roaming the skies like a vulture, picking up the souls we leave behind? Wouldn't you rather sail a real ship upon a real sea? You must yearn to feel the sun on your face again, the wind in your hair. Would you not prefer to stand beside your own brothers as an equal?'

Cospinol said nothing.

The serving girl returned with a small bowl full of soulpearls. The tiny glass beads glimmered faintly in the gloom, while the whorls and loops etched into their surface seemed to writhe like threads of darkness. Cospinol tried to hide his dismay – he could not afford to thus squander so much of his hard-won power. Yet he dared not oppose Rys.

'Some real sustenance at last,' Rys said. He scooped up a handful of the priceless beads and tipped them into his mouth, before handing the bowl to Hafe. The fat god took most of the remainder for himself, then slid the container across the table to Sabor.

The god of clocks said, 'No, thank you.'

'You refuse power?' Hafe asked.

'It is not your power to offer,' Sabor replied.

Rys snorted. 'Sabor's quaint sense of honour will be the end of him one day. His own swordsmen actually slay wounded Mesmerists on the battlefield, rather than leave them to the slow suffering they deserve.' He nodded at Hafe. 'Cospinol can always fashion more pearls. Give the dregs to Mirith.'

Mirith lifted the bowl with both hands and upended it into his mouth. Then he giggled and shook his lopsided wings to make his bells chime. 'Even these souls taste like brine.'

'Enough!' Cospinol rose from his seat and glared down at Rys. 'I am the master of this vessel,' he hissed. 'And while you are aboard you will treat me with respect.' His thin chest heaved beneath his shell-encrusted breastplate. 'You speak of arconites and fallen gods, and a new threat to your forces from the west. Do you take me for a fool? You wouldn't have come here unless you needed my help. Yet you evade the question and continue to mock me at my own table.'

Rys scraped back his seat and stood up. He slapped Cospinol hard across the face.

The old god recoiled, his cheek burning with the blow. The slaves stopped what they were doing, and the ringing in Cospinol's ears diminished to a profound silence. Everyone was staring at him.

'Get out,' Rys said to the slaves.

They left.

The god of flowers and knives strolled over to the cabin windows and gazed out at the fog. 'I will forgive your outburst,' he said finally. 'I realize life has been hard for you here, Cospinol . . . trapped aboard this skyship, denied the freedom we four have won for ourselves.' He almost managed to sound magnanimous. 'But I am now prepared to help you change all that. We would like for you to join us as an equal – to have the honour of standing with us, shoulder-to-shoulder, against Hell's armies.'

How generous of you. Cospinol's cheek smarted. He felt bile rise in his throat, but he said nothing.

Rys went on, 'Only after we have defeated this Mesmerist threat to our lands here on earth will we be able to storm the gates of Heaven and reclaim our rightful inheritance.' He smiled. 'But you must prove yourself worthy first. This war with Hell threatens everything we have achieved thus far. Since our mother Ayen crushed our uprising in Heaven we have struggled back from the brink of oblivion. Our father Iril was shattered, the pieces of him scattered throughout the Maze. Do you think *he* can help us?' Rys shook his head. 'Iril's dissolution gave this upstart King Menoa the opportunity to claim the title of Lord of the Maze for himself.'

He sifted through a platter of shells, then wrinkled his brow in disgust. 'And now there is no more room in Hell. The Mesmerists must extend their bloody Maze into this world.' He gave a deep sigh. 'If Menoa's creatures win, mankind faces the same oblivion Ayen sought to bestow upon us.'

'And if you win,' Cospinol said, 'mankind faces slavery.'

'A kinder prospect, surely?'

Cospinol ground his teeth.

Rys stared at him for a while, then finally shrugged. 'After our victory, you can possess as many slaves as you like. Keep them alive for all I care. Just don't breed with them – don't make the same mistake as Ulcis. One demigod loose in our world is quite enough.'

'It was never *our* world,' Cospinol said.

Rys ignored this. 'Take your skyship to Deepgate,' he said. 'And seal this new portal before the Mesmerists can gain a foothold there. While our enemy's attention is focused on the chained city, the flow of demons into Pandemeria will cease. This will be the best chance we've ever had to attack the Mesmerists and drive them back into Hell.'

Cospinol gave a grunt of derision. 'You make it sound so simple, Rys. Yet you expect me to risk my life to secure your freedom, while I remain imprisoned here? What do you have to offer? A vague promise of solidarity between us? You'll betray me as soon as the Mesmerists are defeated.'

'You prefer oblivion?'

'If I am doomed to die aboard this ship, at least I'll die knowing that you have failed.'

The knives in Rys's belt glittered suddenly. 'But we intend to offer you the means to free yourself.'

Cospinol shifted his gaze between his brothers, looking from Rys's hard stare to Mirith's drooling grin; from Hafe's sweat-crumpled brow to Sabor's darkly serious frown. How could he trust any of them? Nevertheless he said, 'Explain.'

Now Sabor rose from the table. 'Ulcis had feasted for three thousand years,' the god of clocks explained. 'He had harvested enough power to leave his abyss, yet he was murdered before he could realize his escape. All the souls in his veins have now passed to his daughter, Carnival. Imbibing her blood would provide you with enough power to leave the shelter of the *Rotsward*.'

Cospinol felt his heartbeat quicken. Three millennia of souls just for the taking? If Sabor was speaking the truth, and Cospinol could capture this girl and harvest her blood, then he would be free of his prison at last. He would feel the sun on his face again.

'The witchsphere is capable of guiding you towards her,' Rys said. 'It is my gift to you.'

Mirith sniggered. 'Beware of lies, Cospinol.'

Rys wheeled on the crippled god, a silver knife already in his fist. 'Don't test me, Mirith. You rely too much on your fool's face to shield you.'

The crippled god jerked away from the blade. His chair fell back, striking the floor, and Mirith rolled backwards out of it, wings-over-heels. He squawked and came to rest on his rear.

Hafe boomed a laugh.

Rys turned back to Cospinol. 'Why should we betray each other when mutual cooperation benefits us all?' he growled. 'Seal the portal under Deepgate while we fight the enemy in Pandemeria. Kill the girl and use her power to shed this rotting carapace of yours. Then join us as an equal.'

An equal? Like poor Mirith here?

The sea god realized now how much his younger brother needed him. Rys's armies could not withstand an assault from a second arconite; he had no choice but to offer Cospinol the demigod's power in payment for his aid. 'The daughter . . . Carnival,' he said, 'she's already murdered one god, and she'll be vastly stronger now.'

'She's savage and untrained,' Rys continued. 'No match for your slave . . .' He gestured at the floor. 'What do you call him, the barbarian who drags this ship?'

'Anchor.' Cospinol barely noticed Hafe's guffaw in response to this. 'You suggest I use my slave as an assassin?'

'He is already an assassin,' Rys replied. 'How many has he killed for you now? A hundred thousand? Half a million?'

'More.'

Hafe chuckled. 'Half a million souls!' The god of dirt and poison thumped one fist against his huge copper breastplate. 'And you call me greedy? Goat's balls, this human slave has eaten more souls than the Maze.'

'Indeed,' Rys agreed. 'While we fostered legions to break free of Ayen's bonds and win our own kingdoms here on this world, our brother has invested the bulk of his power in one single mortal.' His eyes narrowed on Cospinol. 'And yet he himself remains weak, trapped here aboard his own airboat. It seems he has been feeding the choicest morsels to his pet.'

Cospinol's shoulders slumped. 'It's the weight,' he explained. 'The corpses . . . I take their souls, but the dead refuse to leave my ship. They cling to the rigging, masts and yards; they wander the decks and haunt my steps. I hack them off the gunwales, send them screaming to the ground below, but they always return. Each new cadaver slows the *Rotsward* further, and so my Riot Coast barbarian needs greater and greater strength to pull the ship behind him. I must give him his share of souls or else remain grounded and helpless.' He sighed. 'Ayen was clever in her choice of prison for me.'

'Our mother's cunning was evident in the design of all our gaols.' Rys flashed his teeth. 'Yet we four escaped ours long ago, while you remain here and starve.'

'I do not starve,' Cospinol snarled.

'But you are a prisoner.' The god of flowers and knives leaned closer. 'A slave.'

Cospinol's heart filled with despair. Rys was right: he was a slave, as pathetic as the hook-fingered boy who clambered through the rotting spaces of his skyship's belly. This floating wreck offered him no future. Yet with the Mesmerist witchsphere to guide him, he might find the power to be free of his skyship . . .

'I'll do it,' he said at last. 'I'll travel to Deepgate and seal the portal. I'll kill the girl and return to Coreollis.'

Whatever happened now, Cospinol had joined his fate to that of mankind: if he failed, he faced oblivion at the hands of the Mesmerists; while success would only bring him slavery under Rys's rule. To be truly free, he would have to defeat both his enemies and his own brothers.

Rys must have seen something in Cospinol's expression for he said, 'Do not think about betraying me, brother.'

Cospinol placed a hand against his stinging cheek. The decaying skyship creaked and shuddered around him. He sensed the impossible weight of the great vessel, the legions of dead clinging to its greasy timbers, and he envisioned his slave striding across the ground so far below, dragging it all behind him. If Cospinol could leave the *Rotsward*, then Anchor would also be free.

'Your barbarian is strong,' Rys said. 'But even he would be crushed under the tide of our combined armies.'

Cospinol allowed himself an inward smile.

You haven't seen the bastard fight.

PART ONE

THE DEADSANDS

I

MINA GREENE'S CIRCUS OF HORRORS

From the window of their tavern room, Rachel Hael watched a small flotilla of fishing skiffs jostle past a barge at the bend in the river. Gulls swooped around the clutter of boats, their cries like harsh laughter, or perched on yards and basked in the late afternoon sun. The larger vessel carried sandstone from the quarry at Shale, twenty leagues further up the Coyle. The skiffs were local and manned by louts with robbery in mind.

She had watched them use the same tactic on a Dalamoor palace barge yesterday morning. The Dalamooran captain and his men had been so busy yelling from the stern at the apparently hapless sailors responsible for the river jam that they'd failed to notice a small boy climb out of the water and steal inside the pilot's tent.

Now Rachel was watching a replay of yesterday's events. Amidst all the raucous confusion, the shouts and curses and steering poles knocking against hulls, nobody saw the young swimmer drag himself up and over the barge's stern bulwark. Once aboard, the boy moved quickly. He darted into the wheelhouse and emerged a moment later, stuffing a roll of paper into a waxed tube as he hurried back to the edge of the deck.

The captain's mercantile licence, Rachel knew. The thieves would ransom it back to him shortly after his vessel docked. And the captain would be forced to pay whatever fee they demanded or risk facing the Avulsior's justice on the killing stage – for the Spine had brought martial law to Sandport.

Faced with this new and rigidly enforced system of order, the local thieves and cut-throats had added blackmail and extortion to their list of crimes. Sandporters, after all, looked for profit in any situation.

The presence of so many temple assassins in the town made Rachel uneasy. She had abandoned her own leather armour for a gabardine and wood-soled sandals, even weaving beads into her hair in the local fashion, but her pale complexion and striking green eyes still drew inquisitive gazes from the men who inhabited this desert settlement. She was clearly an outsider here. Despite all her efforts, she still looked like a Spine assassin, the image of the very people who now hunted her.

Of course Dill could not leave the room at all, nor even show himself at the window. Rachel had been fortunate enough to smuggle him unnoticed into the heart of Sandport in the first place, but she could not risk exposing him now. She glanced back to the bed where her friend was still sleeping. He was lying on his stomach, his wings furled against his back like a thick feather cape, still wearing the tattered chain-mail vest that had once cost him his life. His sword lay on the floor beside the bed, its golden guard gleaming in the morning sunshine.

Down on the river, the barge was approaching one of the deep-water pontoons where two Spine Officiators waited to check its cargo. The captain gave the men a cheerful halloo. The temple assassins stood perfectly still in their black leathers, and did not respond.

Behind the harbour, the town of Sandport rose in tiers of brown adobe dwellings, like an amphitheatre built around the bend in the river Coyle. Over the cluttered houses and streets hung a thin pall of dung smoke, the smell of which almost masked the odour of boiled fish and crab from the harbour broth shops. A unit of Spine moved through the market crowds on Hack Hill, ignoring eager calls from the costermongers' stalls. Rachel took an involuntary step back from the window, before she stopped herself. The assassins were much too far away to identify her.

Three knocks sounded on the door, followed quickly by another two: a code Rachel recognized at once.

She went over to let the tavern proprietor in.

Olirind Meer carried a tray laden with a jug of water, some bread and two bowls of cold milk chowder, which he set upon a table by the window. A small dark man, he came from a small village – little more than a trading post – on the northeastern fringes of the Deadsands. His hair and eyebrows were raven-black and his skin was the colour of amarid bark: nomad blood. 'Another day without pay,' he said brightly, showing his small white teeth in a grin.

'And very much appreciated,' Rachel said with genuine affection. Meer had sheltered them from the Spine for almost a week now, although Rachel's coin had run out after the first two days. 'I will pay you back as soon as I'm able to,' she added.

'Pah.' The tavern proprietor dismissed her comment with a wave. 'You are welcome to stay here as long as you need to. Friendship means more to the Ban-Heshette than profit. Unlike these quick-fingered Sandporters, we repay our debts of honour.'

She had met Meer after the slaughter in Hollowhill, where she'd beaten a Deepgate Regular into a coma for what he'd done to the captured tribeswomen. One of those women had been Meer's wife.

'How is the angel today?' he asked.

'Much the same,' Rachel replied. 'Quiet, sullen, evasive. I think, in his own way, he's still struggling to come to terms with what happened.' She gazed down at his sleeping form. 'I'm not sure he'll ever fully recover.'

'Archons are resilient,' Meer observed. 'Have faith in Providence. The boy is sane, which is more than most people could have hoped for after a visit to Hell. He'll talk when he's ready to.'

Rachel was responsible for Dill's present condition. She had used angelwine to bring him back from the dead, plucking his soul back from the Maze, but then she'd pushed him to remember the experience. Her foolish inquisition had unearthed a horde of painful memories which now haunted the boy.

'You must not keep blaming yourself,' Meer said. 'There are too many other things that must concern you here.' He hesitated. 'More and more Spine arrive each day by airship. And they have offered a substantial reward for your capture. It is no longer safe for you to venture outside.'

The former assassin nodded. They should not have lingered in Sandport as long as this, but Dill needed food and rest, time to recover from his ordeal, and Rachel hadn't known where else to go. The Deadsands were brutally unforgiving to travellers, and the tribal villages still harboured resentment against those from the chained city. Olirind Meer remained one of the few people she could trust. The scarred angel, Carnival, had spat when Rachel had announced her intentions, and then deserted them without a word of farewell. Despite all the dangers they'd shared together, Rachel had not been sorry to see her former enemy go. Carnival was unpredictable and her intentions could still not be trusted.

'I have another room in the back.' Meer moistened his lips. 'It's a bit smaller and darker, not having windows as such, but it's cosier, and more . . . private. People will be less likely to notice you there, less likely to ask questions. I've already had a dozen enquiries about the availability of your current room. It's very much in demand among some of my better clientele, you see? They like the view.'

Rachel liked the view too. It allowed her to see who was approaching the tavern. Swapping it for a cramped, windowless cell lacked any appeal. 'Are we inconveniencing you here, Olirind?' she asked. 'I wouldn't want your business to suffer because of us.'

'No, no, no,' the small man replied. 'Business is fine. Don't concern yourselves with that. I was only thinking of your security.'

Yet Rachel had noticed a difference in Meer's attitude of late. As the days had passed, his light-hearted remarks had increasingly hinted at his fragile financial situation, his responsibilities to his regular guests, and how pleased he was to be able to offer his two stowaways the finest and most expensive accommodation on the south bank in repayment of his debt of honour. Rachel suspected he was beginning to consider that debt already paid. The steadily diminishing quantity of fish in the chowder he brought them each day suggested as much.

Nomad blood might run in his veins, but Meer had become a Sandporter at heart.

'Just a couple more days,' she said. 'Then we'll be out of your hair for good.'

The proprietor tutted. 'I wouldn't hear of it. Let the boy recover in his own good time.' Grinning again, he headed for the door. 'I shall continue to deflect persistent guests with the skills for which I have become famous. Enjoy your breakfast.'

'Thank you.'

Once he had gone, Rachel took one of the chowder bowls over to the bed and gave the young angel a gentle shake. 'Dill?'

The angel opened his eyes, and jerked away from her with a start. But then he seemed to realize where he was, and his panic subsided. 'A terrible dream . . .' he sighed, running a hand through his lank hair.

'The same one?' she asked.

He nodded. 'I dreamed I was this room. The walls were my skin and bones, the windows my eyes. My blood ran through wooden veins in the floorboards. My nerves . . . I could feel you walking through me and . . .' As he looked up at her, the colour of his eyes darkened from white to grey. 'Meer? Was he here?'

'He just left.'

Dill stared at his own hands for a long time. 'I dreamed of *him*, too.'

'The Mesmerist?'

'He was outside this room, outside *me*, but searching for a way in. I couldn't see him, but each time I peered out of the window I spotted something odd: a house that hadn't been there before, a new pontoon in the harbour, a crooked tree. Are there any trees in Sandport?'

'No,' Rachel admitted. 'And there aren't any trees out there now. It was only a dream.'

Her friend's nightmares had been consistent since his return from Hell. He dreamed of becoming the environment around him, whether it was a room in Sandport or a petrified glade or a sandy hollow in the Deadsands. And in each case the same shape-shifting figure waited nearby, disguised as a part of the wider surroundings. Dill had started calling him the Mesmerist, though he could not say why.

'You need to eat something.' She handed him the bowl, noticing now that it contained little more than milk. 'And we should consider leaving here soon. I don't know how much longer we can trust Meer.'

Dill looked exhausted. 'Where will we go?'

'As far away from the Spine as possible. The missionary ship, *Herald's Voice*, left Clune two weeks ago and should arrive in port any day. With Spine martial law now in place, it may well be the last temple ship to sail out into the Yellow Sea. The missionaries have a settlement in a village called Baske, one hundred and twenty leagues east of the Pocked Delta. If we can get the *Herald* to take us there, we'll be safe.'

'Would the priests shield us from the Spine?'

'They might shield *you*,' she said. 'You're a fugitive, but you're still an angel, and I can't imagine many of Deepgate's priests endorse the Spine's recent rise to power.' She thought for a moment. 'Yes, I'm sure they'd protect you.'

'But what about *you*?'

An airship droned somewhere overhead. Rachel listened to it for a moment, but was distracted by another, closer sound: a ruckus in the street outside. She went back to the window.

A gaily painted box-wagon, pulled by an ox, was rumbling along the wharf in front of the tavern. It had a red roof and yellow slatted sides, and boasted wheels with garish green and gold spokes. Emblazoned across the nearest side were the words 'Greene's Magical Circus: Witness all the fearsome horrors of Iril!' A crowd of people jostled around it, following its progress towards the centre of town. Rachel realized that it must have disembarked from one of the barges at the deepwater dock that lay out of sight around the harbour peninsula. Curious. Normally that dock was used exclusively by Deepgate's military to bring troops downriver from its outlying airship ports. Had the wagon originally arrived by airship? Or had it merely stopped to pick up cargo from one of the airship ports? Then she spotted a scrawled notice pinned to the rear of the wagon, and her breath caught.

See the slavering shape-shifting Maze demon here tonight!

The crowd of followers chattered with excitement. Groups of bare-footed children ran ahead of the wagon, shrieking and clapping and chasing each other. Rachel sat on the windowsill and watched as the wooden vehicle wound its way up the hill behind the tavern wharves and disappeared in the knot of lanes around Market Square.

Travelling magicians and freak shows were not unheard of in Sandport. So-called shamans and thaumaturges sometimes arrived from Clune and Dalamoor with a veritable cornucopia of disturbing objects preserved in pickle jars. Yet Rachel had never heard of anyone claiming to have possession of an actual demon before. A shape-shifter? The timely relevance to Dill's recurring dreams seemed too unlikely to be merely a coincidence.

'I'm going out,' she said to Dill.

But the angel had fallen asleep again.

By the time Rachel reached Market Square, the sun had fallen behind the low houses and the sky gleamed like gold fish scales. The wagon driver had almost finished setting up her sideshow in the centre of the square, where a rude stage of crimson boards had been erected beside the wagon itself. A small crowd had gathered on the brown flagstones around it, while others stood further back in the shadows of the surrounding houses. Flies buzzed around the fringes of the quadrangle, where fruit from the weekly market festered in the gutters and Sandporters sat on their own doorsteps and sipped fig wine. The wagon driver had evidently conscripted two burly men from the audience to unload a large crate from the rear of her vehicle, and she now stood to one side, petting a small dog cradled in her arms. As the crowd looked on, the two helpers manhandled the crate up some steps and onto the stage, under the woman's direction.

Rachel instinctively scanned the crowd of onlookers for likely pickpockets, before she remembered that she didn't have any money. Smiling, she returned her attention to the unfolding spectacle at hand.

The wagon driver was young and slender and wore her dark brown hair in thick curls which tumbled heavily over her narrow shoulders. Her oval face and dark eyes suggested Dalamooran origins, yet her skin was lighter than that of most northern desert dwellers. She wore a vibrant, if somewhat garish, rainbow-coloured dress adorned with beads of glass.

Once her helpers had finished positioning the box and stepped down, the woman placed her puppy on one of the wagon's running boards, and then turned and raised her hands to settle the crowd.

'Hello,' she called out in a cheerful voice. Her accent sounded Deepgate. 'My name is Mina Greene and I have come to Sandport to bring you magic, horror and wonder! If you are amazed by what you see here this morning, make sure to tell your families and your friends. And if what you see sickens or appals you, then tell them anyway. Just be sure to tell someone.'

A laugh from the crowd.

'And please return after dusk, for what you are about to see is only a little glimpse of my circus. I've travelled to the ends of the world looking for monstrosities, and later tonight I'll present them for your pleasure.' She sounded like a child reading from a script she had prepared. 'I've got ghosts and mazewights trapped in amber, and the corpses of unspeakable demons from the darkest depths of Hell, even the bones of gods and stone monsters from under the earth.'

One of the onlookers yelled, 'Yeah, we seen all that last year,' which triggered more laughter.

Mina Greene frowned and stamped her foot. 'Yes, the stitched-together things . . . the fakes. Jars of mermen and spider babies, the pickled oxen calves. You've seen it *all* here, haven't you?' She seemed to realize that she'd lost her composure, and made an effort to control her temper. 'But today I'm showing you the real thing – not tricks or lies, but living, breathing demons.' She ended with a dancer-like flourish. 'Behold the horrors of the Maze!'

She lifted the lid from the crate, then reached inside and fiddled with an interior clasp or lock. The crate's four side-panels fell away like opening flower petals, revealing the fleshy thing inside.

Rachel watched from the fringes, her face partially concealed by a silk scarf, as a gasp went up from the crowd. Several people backed away from the abomination on the stage. Then Rachel saw clearly what had caused the commotion, and she felt her stomach buck.

'This monster was captured in Deepgate four nights ago,' Greene called out. 'The Spine Avulsior allowed me, a humble show-woman and entertainer, to display it here so that I might make you aware of the true dangers of the Maze. Look at its limbs, see how it weeps and suffers. This is what happens to heretics and blasphemers.'

Had the Spine *hired* her to preach their message for them? Rachel wondered if Mina Greene believed a word of the Avulsior's lies, or if she'd just agreed to work with him in order to obtain this poor wretched creature.

It looked vaguely like a child, but Rachel could not see precisely how its twisted arms and legs connected to its torso. She couldn't even be sure it was human. Parts of it appeared to be fashioned from the same wood used to make the crate. It was like a knot of muscle and bone intermingled with white-pine joists. Watery, weeping eyes lolled madly in its hairless skull. Clearly it was distressed. A pitiful wail issued from its drooling mouth, and Rachel turned away in abhorrence and shock.

How could the Spine ever stoop to this?

Rachel began to thread her way back through the crowd. But the show was not over yet, for worse was still to come. Mina Greene lifted her hands again and addressed the audience. 'This horror, when left alone, tries to mimic its environment. You can see how it has copied the crate. It's like a seed that doesn't know which plant to become. Now watch closely.'

'No!' The thing on the stage wailed in a voice made thick by saliva. 'Please don't do this.'

Rachel glanced back to see Greene stooping over the creature and whispering to it. What she saw next stopped her in her tracks.

The creature's shape began to change. Its limbs grew longer while its head sank, like a bubble of pink mud, back into its neck.

As the crowd looked on in amazement, its torso swelled and split into two amorphous lumps. These then stretched and flattened, the skin darkening all the while. In moments, the creature began to resemble something else entirely.

Cries of disgust and alarm went up from the audience, and then suddenly there was complete silence. Nobody in the crowd uttered a word.

The thing on the stage had now finished its transformation. The hideous knot of muscle and bone had disappeared. In its place stood an ordinary wooden chair. Greene scraped it forward and then sat down in it. 'You all have these in your homes, right?' she said. 'Chairs, I mean, not demons. Well, don't try this with them.' She produced a knife hidden under the folds of her gaudy dress, then stabbed it into the wooden seat between her thighs.

Blood dribbled from the damaged seat and spattered against the stage underneath it, accompanied by an eerie sound, like the distant echo of a scream. Coming from the chair? The shape-shifter was still conscious?

'This is how demons are formed,' Greene said. 'It's a type of Mesmerism, and there are things in the Maze that use such techniques to mould your souls into any form they like.' She paused for a moment, and Rachel saw her glance at a small prompt card pinned to the side of her wagon. 'The Maze of Blood is aptly named,' she went on in an overly dramatic voice, 'for its halls and corridors exist as incarnations of living souls. The dead don't wander Hell; they are the bricks and mortar from which it is built.' She rose from her chair and made another flourish with her hands. 'Thus Iril is both the Maze and the shattered god who lives within it. Similarly, when this pathetic creature died, it became forever a part of the Maze – a living, breathing, *thinking* piece of Hell.' She paused, observing her silent audience. 'So, have you seen a show like *this* before?'

Rachel pushed her way out through the crowd and hurried

back to the tavern. With Spine agents about, she had risked much by attending such a public spectacle. The show-woman's words echoed in her mind. *It is a type of Mesmerism . . . there are things in the Maze that use such techniques to mould your souls into any form they like.*

Had the young angel been a victim of this unholy Mesmerism himself? And *what* had it done to him? She tried to shun gruesome possibilities, but the image of the weeping creature on stage gripped her imagination.

A part of the Maze – a living, breathing, thinking *piece of Hell.*

Walking briskly back through the darkening lanes, she dodged showers of fetid brown water thrown out of the doors of the mud-brick houses on either side, and she wondered how Mina Greene's demon had come to be in Deepgate at all. Wraiths and shades were known to haunt the darkest parts of that chained city, but those were ethereal, phantasms attracted by past violence and shed blood. Yet this shape-shifter had been corporeal. If it was truly what the show-woman had claimed it to be . . .

Perhaps the recent death toll had caused a larger or more permanent rift to open between the chained city and the Maze of Blood? After all, tens of thousands had died when Alexander Devon had brought his monstrous machine to Deepgate's doorstep. Rachel didn't much care what would become of the crippled city, for when she'd seen it last, it looked all but ready to collapse into the abyss beneath it.

'Miss Hael!'

The former assassin almost collided with Olirind Meer as he emerged from a side street. Sweating and dishevelled, as though he had been running, he now stopped short, clearly startled by her presence. 'What are you doing out here?' he enquired in tones which verged on panic. 'It's almost dark. Why aren't you in your room?'

'Keep your voice down, Olirind, please. I had to go out. There was something I needed to do.'

The tavern proprietor glanced behind him, then back at her. 'Quickly now,' he whispered. 'You must come back with me at once. There are Spine everywhere.'

With barely another look in his direction, Rachel strode on ahead of him. 'You can't afford to be seen with me,' she reminded him. 'I'll speak to you later.'

Leaving Meer standing bemused at the junction, she hurried on back to the tavern.

Dill was sitting on the edge of the bed, staring at his sword, when she entered the room. He hadn't even touched his bowl of chowder. 'I feel better now,' he said. 'I'm sorry I've been . . . distant lately.'

'We're leaving,' she said.

He accepted this decision without complaint. 'Did you discover something while you were out?'

'Only that Olirind Meer is a slimy, black-hearted wretch. I think he's just betrayed us.' She opened the wardrobe and took out the satchel containing her leather armour and knives. 'I met him out on the street,' she went on. 'He was hurrying back from the direction of the Avulsior's residence, and he did not look happy to see me.'

'Maybe he happened to be in that part of town on normal business, and when he saw you, he was just worried that you'd be spotted.'

'We've passed each other on these streets before, and he knows well enough to look the other way – nothing more than a passing glance between us. Otherwise he'd implicate himself if I was discovered.' She laid her leather vest and breeches on the bed, then opened the dresser drawer and began stuffing loose clothes into the empty satchel. 'But this time he didn't seem concerned about being seen with me. He even offered to walk me back to the tavern.' She snorted. 'He was far more worried that I wasn't safely here in our room, where he could—'

She stopped speaking suddenly, listening, then rushed across to the room door and turned the handle. The door remained firmly shut.

'Shit,' she hissed. 'Did someone come here while I was out? Dill, did you see anybody tamper with this, with the frame around this door?'

'I . . .' He looked helpless. 'I don't know. I was sleeping.'

'Get ready to fly. We're leaving right now.'

But just as Dill rose from the bed, the ceiling above his head collapsed in a shower of broken plaster. Something huge and metallic, like a spike, crashed down through the roof and embedded itself in the floorboards. Through the clouds of dust, Rachel spotted a trembling chain and a flexible tube leading back up through the hole above. Then she heard a low hiss and realized what was happening. 'Poison gas,' she cried. 'Don't breathe.'

Ferrets, Deepgate's aeronauts had called them. Fired from warship grapple guns, the huge iron spears were capable of delivering toxic gases more effectively into sealed buildings. They'd used them on the Southern Clearances to pump lime gas into an underground network of Heshette tunnels, killing thousands without ever having to land one of their warships. Even now such a vessel would be hovering overhead, pumping invisible fumes into Dill and Rachel's room. The gas leaked through holes in the shaft, while the barbs along its length could be detached and repositioned to determine more precisely how deeply the missile embedded itself into a building. The process to seal the door had been more subtle: a chemical solution painted on the inside of the frame designed to foam and swell upon contact with some silently administered catalyst vapour.

Rachel cursed her own foolishness and she cursed that bastard

Meer for his treachery. Why had she trusted him? Why had she trusted *anyone* in this godforsaken town?

The Spine had known she would hear their footsteps in the hall outside, and they had used her recent excursion to prepare this trap. And now they knew she must try to escape through the window. Hacking through the walls or floor would take too long.

Holding her breath, Rachel threw open the windows, then leapt quickly aside. The expected flurry of bolts did not appear in the ceiling above her. Were there *no* Spine in the street below? No crossbows trained on the tavern? What did *that* mean? She had not yet breathed and yet she was already disturbingly confused and disorientated. A poison designed to permeate the cornea? She turned towards Dill, but the young angel had already collapsed and lay sprawled on the floor beside the hissing metal missile.

She dragged him closer to the window, not knowing if he was already dead or not, yet desperately hoping that the lack of a secondary attack meant that the temple assassins had decided to take their quarry alive.

He was heavier than she expected. She noticed how much his wings had grown, what a broad wake they left in the dust-covered floor. And then she was forced to drop him and lean out of the window to take a breath of clean air. A whiff of poison gas reached her nostrils, and she gagged; she didn't recognize the toxin.

Something new?

From the effect that one tiny sniff had on her senses, it was more virulent than anything she'd experienced before. Sandport harbour swam before her eyes, a swarm of lights upon the dark river. She saw boat masts brawling, buildings melting into one another, the last blush of sunset. She heard the distant hum of an airship at high altitude.

They flew high so I wouldn't hear their engines, she thought. And then consciousness left her.

2

THE HAUNTED CITY

The Spine warship thundered over furrows of brown smoke clouds, her envelope flashing like a polished steel shield under the blue sky. In her wake came a flock of carrion birds: crows, eye-picks and blackgulls, all shrieking and feeding on the corpses suspended from the ship's aft deck and ballast arms.

She turned to starboard. Sunlight slanted across her gondola, granting the scrawls and abrasions in the metal hull a moment of crisp definition. Portholes gleamed dully like old men's eyes. Sandstorms had stripped her deck timbers of any varnish; had scoured the arcuballista, net and grapple guns down to their metal bones.

With her rudders hard to port and twin propellers blurring, the vessel turned until her bow faced east. Then she waited, her cooling engines ticking, while the crew moved inside to prepare their air scrubbers for descent into the turmoil below. Fumes tumbled under her gondola, curling around the feet of the hanging corpses and reaching across the empty decks, cables and rails – lingering, it seemed, at the locked portholes and hatches.

The ship's engines growled with a sudden surge of power. Elevators slammed back into dive position. Birds scattered, screaming, from the gruesome ballast. *Reclamation Ship Three* shuddered, purged air from her buoyancy ribs, and then sank into the boiling clouds.

Darkness engulfed the warship. Buffeted by turbulence, she rolled and pitched in upward-rushing eddies of smoke. Cables shivered and moaned under the stress; her envelope shook and creaked. Ten heartbeats passed, then twenty, and then a thin, grainy light suffused the air. Three whistles shrilled within the gondola. The sound of thumping pistons rumbled through her superstructure, as engines pumped hot exhaust back into the ship's exterior ribs. Her envelope swelled, slowing her descent.

She emerged in the amber twilight beneath a brooding ceiling of cloud, a hundred yards above the Deadsands, dragging corpses along like strung puppets.

Deepgate lay to the west, now half a league behind the airship. Torn and burning in a thousand places, the city hung in her surviving chains like a great blackened funnel over the abyss. Swathes of the League of Rope quarter had been reduced to a smouldering crust, or had crumbled entirely into the pit below, exposing further webs of chain. Ash skirled between the metal links. Fires raged out of control in the Workers' Warrens, in Ivygarths and Chapelfunnel, and on the fringes of the Scythe, where vast rents could be seen among the shipyards. Gases poured from ruptured aether vats and from the coalgas depositories around Mesa's chain, forming ochre and white layers between docking spines and buckled gantries. Trunks of black, red and silver smoke uncoiled from the Poison Kitchens, feeding the expanding clouds above, while the city below lay veiled in crimson vapours. The sun glimmered faintly, a copper-coloured smudge.

A camp had been built on the eastern curve of the abyss, where Deepgate's foundation chains met the desert bedrock and the surface pipes from Jakka curled over the lip of the pit. It was to this ad-hoc shamble of pulpboard shacks and bunkers that *Reclamation Ship Three* began to drift. Still with her stern facing the city, she relaxed the power fed to her twin propellers and allowed the howling gales to suck her into the low-pressure areas around the updraft. Orange sand fumed around her, battering and scouring her hull. The hanging corpses swung madly under her ballast arms.

There were no longer any docking spines available for use, but men appeared from bunkers and rushed over to guide the ship's grapples into anchor hoops fixed into the desert floor. In time she came to rest and was secured. Her port hatch opened. Nine Spine assassins in leather armour and sand masks disembarked: eight Cutters carrying light steel crossbows, and an Adept with a sword slung across his back. Their mirrored goggles reflected the burning city. Through the boiling dust, two of the Cutters carried the body of an angel towards the edge of the abyss, to where a wooden walkway dipped away into the district called the League of Rope. The Adept meanwhile dragged a manacled woman from the airship and threw her to the ground.

Rachel Hael spat sand from her mouth and glared up at the masked figure. He had an unusually rough manner for an assassin of his high rank. The process of tempering normally removed all aggression from an assassin, along with the bulk of his mind. These temple warriors killed more efficiently without emotional burdens or base human desires.

The Adept removed his sand mask, then pointed to a standpipe set alongside the walkway. 'Drink there,' he shouted above the howling wind. 'Water is scarce in the city, and you will have no more until we reach the sanctuary of the temple.' He tapped the mask against his hip, dislodging sand, then pulled it back over his head so that its copper grille again covered his mouth.

Rachel Hael staggered over to the water tap, her tattered gabardine flapping against her shins. She could barely stand in this ferocious wind, but she managed to crouch by Dill's insensate form and inspect him. 'He's barely breathing,' she said. 'He could die before we reach the temple.'

'His lungs reacted unexpectedly to the gas,' the Adept replied, his voice now muffled by the sand mask. 'Nevertheless, his death will be bloodless. We will then cast his body down to our Lord Ulcis.'

'This is madness.' She pointed down into the smouldering bowl of the chained city. 'Ulcis is dead. There's nothing left down there.'

The Adept's mirrored lenses surveyed the scene. 'Reconstruction is under way,' he said. 'Deepgate is as eternal as the abyss; it cannot be destroyed.' His pale fingers touched the tiny metal talisman fixed to his collar: the Knot of Ulcis, awarded only to the highest-ranking Church assassins.

Rachel had, until recently, owned a similar talisman. Her captors had demanded its return, but she had already sold it to buy food in Sandport. 'Reconstruction?' she cried in disbelief. 'Half the city is on fire. The Warrens, the Temple Districts – most of it has already fallen into the abyss, and the rest looks like it's going to follow at any moment. This city is not eternal . . . it's royally fucked. The League is little more than charcoal, and the temple . . .' She wiped dust from her eyes. 'Where the hell is it?'

'The loss of some support chains caused the Church of Ulcis to invert,' the Adept replied, his tone flat and emotionless. 'The bulk of the building remains intact, however, only now suspended beneath the city.'

Rachel snorted. 'And you're going to pull it back upright, are you? With what? Horses and camels? How will you forge new chains to keep it in place? Didn't you see what happened to the only machine capable of doing that? It's now lying at the bottom of that fucking pit!'

'The logistics do present some problems.'

'You don't say!'

At least one third of the foundation chains had snapped, or had pulled their anchors out of the abyss bedrock. Collapsing chains had shredded miles of ordinary homes. Gashes ran from the outskirts all the way down to the hub, where, through the billowing fumes, Rachel glimpsed a mound of huge metal rings and spikes. The base of the temple? She recognized it now. The great building had indeed flipped over entirely, and had punched a ragged hole through sections of Bridgeview, Ivygarths and Lilley quarters. Most of the other foundation chains had twisted over each other, buckling entire neighbourhoods for miles. Whole districts of townhouses had been compressed to rubble. Cross-chains punctured roofs, windows and walls. Bridges and walkways dangled like banners over the open abyss, while entire sections of the city hung from the sapperbane links like monstrous chain-wrapped pendulums. The only city quarters that didn't appear to be burning were those missing altogether.

Rachel therefore felt inclined to agree with her captor: the logistics involved in reconstruction would present some problems. Evacuating survivors would have been difficult enough, yet she saw no evidence that such an operation had been attempted. The newly constructed camp seemed scarcely large enough to hold a fraction of the population and, apart from the Spine who'd helped moor the airship, it appeared to be deserted.

Far below, a bright silver flash lit the area around the Poison Kitchens. The spreading fires had just claimed one of Deepgate's airship-fuelling vats, exploding a hundred tonnes of aether in an instant. A cloud of flames and debris mushroomed skywards into the smoke above the city. Tiny metal shards spun out over rooftops like a shower of stars.

A moment later Rachel heard the crack of that distant concussion, and the ground beneath her trembled. The walkway shook; its support poles rattled against the edge of the precipice and tugged at the massive chain anchor buried in the rock below.

Puffs of dust rose all over the hanging city as parts of Deepgate simply disappeared into the abyss. The gale seemed at once to strengthen and to wail in approval. Down beside the Scythe, flames leapt higher up one side of the Department of Military Science. Rachel took an involuntary step back.

'The incendiaries in the Poison Kitchens,' she shouted, 'you can't have had time to remove them all?'

'Fires and noxious fumes within the Department of Military Science have precluded retrieval,' the Adept said. 'The Poison Kitchens are inaccessible at present.'

'You haven't moved *any* of the stuff out of there?' She was thinking about those vast caches of poisons, chemicals and explosives that Deepgate's chemists stored inside that building. They barely had time to evacuate a quarter of it before Devon's monstrous cutting machine had reached the city perimeter. 'What about the workers?' she asked. 'There must have been six thousand people in that building when the Tooth attacked.'

'All dead.'

'Shit,' she said. 'You'd better hope they had the foresight to start dumping all that crap into the abyss as soon as the fires reached them.'

'Such action is forbidden by Codex Law.'

The mirrored lenses revealed nothing of the Adept's expression, but Rachel already knew his face would be devoid of emotion. Spine tempering had rendered him so thoroughly conditioned to serve the temple and the god of chains that he remained unable to reconcile himself to the loss of either. He would stay here in Deepgate until the very last chain-link snapped apart.

'Now drink,' he said.

While Rachel slaked her thirst, she considered their position. The Spine had declared martial law. Desertion was now decreed a crime against god, and therefore subject to punishment under

43

Codex Law. Even if she could prove to them that their god was dead down in his abyss, it wouldn't make much difference. The same tempering process that had peeled away their human desires had also ensured that their faith remained unassailable and inviolate. Rachel could not bargain with them. She had to hope for escape or intervention. And soon . . .

Flames had taken firm hold of the Poison Kitchens by now, and the metal structure looked more like a great steaming cauldron than ever before. White fumes hissed from the funnels at the apex, while thicker yellow-black smoke poured from a hundred windows and engulfed the surrounding warehouses, engineering yards and ship-berths.

The Adept motioned to two of his men, who then lifted the angel between them.

But then a gruff cry came at them from behind. Rachel turned to see six temple guards marching through the dust storm towards them. The men all carried pikes and wore heavy black-enamelled plate armour. Scratches in their steel suits indicated prolonged exposure to sandstorms. The guards' faces were hidden by scarves tied in the fashion of desert tribesmen, but Rachel recognized Clay's tattered cloak before the captain reached the party.

'Hold it there,' the big man called out to the Spine Adept. 'We'll take charge of these prisoners.' He stood panting for a moment, eyeing the manacles around Rachel's wrists, and then Dill's unconscious form. 'My pickets,' he waved a hand, 'saw the ship come in.' He exhaled and then sucked in another breath through his scarf. 'Hell's balls, I didn't expect them to bring you back so soon. The city's not safe – you'd best come with us.'

'We'd be glad to,' Rachel concurred.

The Spine assassins now stood in a crescent around them, their slim black figures stark before the umber desert. Deepgate's fires burned in their mirrored lenses. The Adept said, 'These are our prisoners, Captain. The temple guard no longer has authority.'

Ernest Clay gathered himself up before the other man, and yanked down his scarf, revealing his face. He looked angry. 'I've every right to interrogate them,' he said. 'They were out in the Deadsands for – what? – six, seven days? And another week in Sandport before you caught them. That girl's still got contacts up and down the Coyle. Chances are she'll have heard a lot more about our enemy's plans than you have.'

The assassin spoke from behind his mask. 'Captain,' he said flatly, 'your persistent interference in Spine affairs is becoming . . . inconvenient. I do not believe you intend to interrogate either of these prisoners. None of those you have gathered for questioning have, as far as we know, yielded useful reconnaissance. Nor have our captives ever been returned to us. Evidently you are trying to divert such people into your own camp for other reasons.' He paused, tilted his lenses to one side. 'Do you disapprove of our methods of punishment?'

Clay grunted. 'I don't care what you do with your captives. Just stick to your job, and I'll stick to mine. But it seems to me your torture cells are already full to bursting. We're doing you a favour by easing the burden a bit.'

'That may—'

'Besides,' Clay broke in. 'None of your new Cutters will speak to me. How am I to know what's happening out there if I can't question a few deserters?'

'Yet you invariably choose to interrogate the women and children.'

'Makes sense.' The captain scowled. 'We've bugger all food left, in case you hadn't noticed. Since you won't let us question everyone, we'll take the ones who eat the least.'

The Adept seemed to consider this.

'There might be a thousand Shetties a league from here, right now,' Clay went on, 'and we wouldn't know about it. We haven't been able to reconnoitre effectively since the sandstorms started. All this smoke around the city will bring metal scavengers and raiders all the way down from the Northern Steppes. We've already learned that they've been sniffing round the caravan trails for water and women.' He tipped his head at Dill. 'And he looks like he needs medical treatment. Don't you need them healthy before you start cutting into their brains? We have a doctor in our barracks.'

'Nevertheless,' the Adept replied, 'I cannot sanction the release of these two. The archon is temple property. This woman was a Spine Adept, and as such remains our responsibility.'

'Let me have them for a couple of days,' Clay said. 'I'll bring them back to you myself.'

'You have already reneged on similar promises, and then lied to conceal your deceit.' Another explosion in the chained city bloomed in the assassin's silvered lenses. Sand howled around him. 'Prisoners who you claimed had died under interrogation have since been discovered alive, hidden in one of the Codex bunkers. Such deception will no longer be tolerated.'

Clay winced.

'We are prepared to make allowances, Captain,' the Adept said, 'but do not take us for fools, and do not test our leniency.'

The captain paused. 'I'd still like to question the girl, if I may,' he said. 'If you've no objections, I'll accompany you to the temple.'

'As you wish.'

The group tramped down the steep walkway into the ruins of the League of Rope. Once they were below the lip of the abyss, the wind dropped noticeably. In the amber gloom down here, the air simmered with the heat of the recent fires. Ash smothered the walkway planks and crumbled away from the support ropes whenever Rachel gripped them. Agitated by the party's progress, the stinking dust soon engulfed them like a veil. The charred remains of shacks and platforms hung from the web of ropes on all sides, their vague dark shapes looking like insects cocooned within spider's silk.

Captain Clay matched pace with Rachel. 'We sprayed the whole neighbourhood with water from the Dawn Pipes to keep the fires here under control,' he said to her in a low voice. 'We were trying to preserve at least one route out of the city.' He pointed across the city. 'The Spine tried the same thing on the other side, but they didn't have enough water. So they sprayed those districts with effluence from the sewage pipes. Kept the fires from taking hold, I'm told, though I wouldn't want to go for a stroll there right now.' He grunted. 'Trust the Spine to ruin a perfectly good slum. I wonder what would have happened if the flames had reached the temple. Would they have doused it with water, or with—'

'Thanks,' Rachel said, 'for trying to get us away.'

Clay shot a glance at the Adept two paces ahead of him, then whispered quickly, 'The bastards have been tempering everyone who flees the city. It's martial law here now.' He shook his head. 'We do what we can, try to get the women and the kids out, but it's becoming more difficult. They don't trust us, and I sure as hell – goddamn it!' He tripped and lurched forward as a plank broke under his armoured boot.

Rachel caught him just in time.

Clay hissed. 'The whole city's falling apart. The temple . . . gods below, you should see it up close! It's hanging upside down like a god-damn stalactite. Every time I look at it, another spire or tower has fallen off. I don't know how it's survived for so long.'

'The stone and mortar came from Blackthrone,' Rachel replied, 'which makes them unnaturally strong. Devon once said that the mountain doesn't belong in this world. He believed it fell from the sky.' She shrugged. 'But, then, he was mad.'

'Rock and ore from Heaven?' The temple guard whistled. 'It's strong, aye, but not that strong. The rest of the building is going to fall sooner or later. You don't want to be stuck in there while you're waiting – I mean . . .' He looked peevish. 'I'm sorry, lass. We'd have got you away from them if we could. Our barracks aren't much – pretty crowded – and I wasn't lying about the food situation, but there's enough fresh water and we've a couple of priests on loan from the Spine. Nobody's comfortable, but at least the floor's not likely to suddenly fall away under our feet.'

His mention of priests struck her as odd: why would they need holy men in the temple guard barracks? 'It's not your fault,' she said. 'I should have foreseen this.'

'The *Carousel* brought us news of your capture, but it was sketchy. I heard they caught you in Sandport? They used a ferret?'

She nodded. 'They fired it from high altitude so we wouldn't hear the warship's engines. We were staying at Olirind Meer's tavern down by the harbour. I thought we'd be safe there for a while.' She shrugged. 'But I was wrong.'

Clay nodded. 'Sandporters,' he said. 'You can't trust those bastards. What happened to Carnival?'

'She abandoned us.'

'Sounds like her. Did you notice any Spine recruiters in Sandport?'

'They were everywhere.'

'They're keeping it subtle just now,' Clay said, 'disguising their recruitment drive as a form of law enforcement. You commit a crime, they drag you to the temple, break your mind and then enlist you as a Cutter. That's how it works here anyway. But they're becoming increasingly stringent, tempering folks for all manner of alleged sins. Soon there won't be anyone left in Deepgate but Spine.'

'I thought the refugee camp looked quiet.'

'Refugee camp?' Clay gave her a grim look. 'Hell, lass, that isn't a *refugee* camp. My people are squeezed into two barracks on the northern edge. The rest of the bunkers are full of books. The Spine have been moving Presbyter Sypes's library out of the city.'

Rachel's fists balled. 'They're saving the Codex?' she hissed. 'Why am I not surprised? They force the citizens back to the temple, and then save a pile of old—'

The sound of cracking, splintering wood interrupted her. To their left, a sunken mass of fire-blackened shacks collapsed in on itself, before crumbling into the abyss below. The walkway they were on lurched suddenly as a ball of dust rolled up out of the newly made gap beside it.

Rachel coughed, and squinted back through the dust. The two Cutters had dropped Dill's limp body like a sack and now stood over him, gripping the street-ropes for support. Fortunately no one had fallen. 'We'll be lucky to get to the temple at all,' she said, 'assuming it's still there when we arrive.'

The walkway dipped and rose as they followed a zigzag course through smashed acres of burned pulpboard and tin sheets, through nests of ash-black chains. The sound of pinging metal and cracking wood accompanied their footsteps, while deeper booms and clangs resounded from the industrial heart of the city to the northwest. The air grew steadily thicker and fouler as they marched onwards. Gusts of wind rattled the shacks around them, carrying the smell of airship fuel. Crimson and black clouds continued to unfurl across the heavens, now dappled in places with lozenges of yellow.

Beyond the League of Rope the party reached the more substantial districts of the Workers' Warrens. Most of the tenements here had already been gutted by fire; for the most part they were roofless and windowless: naught but black shells, empty but for pockets of rubble. Smoke drifted in greasy brown layers between them. Minnow Street and Pullow's Row had fallen away completely, leaving gulfs of dark abyss with tangled masses of chains and iron girders lining their banks.

The stink of soot pervaded everything. Rachel tasted it with every breath. It stung their eyes and gathered in the creases on Captain Clay's brow. Trickles of sweat left black lines down his stubbled jaw.

On Candlemaker Row the path narrowed and wove between great tumbles of stone that had once been glue stores and work-houses. Rivulets of milky gel had oozed from doorways and then set in hard pools which tugged at the soles of their boots.

Rachel glanced back at the Cutters carrying Dill. There was something almost mechanical about the way these lower-rank assassins moved, lacking the grace of their Adept Master. They even looked like automatons in their identical bug-eyed masks, their heads turning constantly as they studied the rubble on either side of the path.

Studied the rubble?

The Spine Adept stopped suddenly and raised a hand, sig-nalling his men to halt. Clay shifted position, taking a firmer grip of his pike, and glanced at the nearby shadows.

A peal of manic laughter came from somewhere close by.

Clay stared hard in the direction of the sound for a long moment, then relaxed his pike.

'What was that?' Rachel said.

'The Spine don't like us talking about them,' he muttered.

'Them?'

The captain shrugged. 'Manifestations,' he said. 'We've been seeing a lot of them since all the troubles began. They're drawn to the dead like flies, and we have streets full of corpses in this city. You'll be safer when we get to the temple.' He gestured towards the source of the laughter. 'Safe enough from them, at any rate.'

'Now I see why you need priests in your barracks.'

'Our guard dogs,' Clay explained. 'We've been allocated two of them – nice fellows but they've been really struggling just to keep these damned shades out. This perpetual gloom is bad enough, but it gets worse at night. Even the Spine won't dare leave the temple after dark without a priest to accompany them.'

'Have you noticed anything else unusual?'

'Like what?'

'Someone brought a demon into Sandport – a shape-shifter. She claimed it had been found *here*.'

The captain shook his head. 'I have seen nothing like that,' he said. 'But then I don't go strolling about the city if I can otherwise avoid it. What did it look like?'

'Like a chair,' she said, walking on ahead of the captain's bemused expression.

They smelled the Poison Kitchens before they saw the huge funnels and iron spines looming over the tenement rooftops. The bulk of Deepgate's fuel, coal and chemicals had been stored in the industrial areas around here. Now vast pillars of black smoke rose from the factories, warehouses and depots. Fires had ravaged this part of the district and still continued to burn in the north, bathing layer after layer of ragged brickwork in flickering orange light. Girders jutted like fossilized bones from broken walls and mounds of slag. Flakes of ash danced in hot breezes or fell upon chains and cobbles, accumulating in pale crusts that looked like snow but stank of fuel. Rachel's boots creaked in it and left faint red imprints behind. And from all around came the groans of heated metal.

The thoroughfares and humped bridges were stouter here than in most places, to allow for trade traffic to and from the shipyards, but all were totally deserted. Beyond their own party, Rachel had so far not seen another living person in Deepgate, though now she saw shadows moving everywhere.

'Best not to look directly at them,' Clay grumbled. 'I'll keep my eyes peeled for any chairs.'

Their Spine captors clearly had an intimate knowledge of the precise extent of Deepgate's destruction, for they frequently chose long and winding routes to circumvent obstacles and moaning crevasses. As the gloom deepened, shadows gathered in the shells of derelict buildings and peered out at them through the windows. The Adept lit a tarred brand and swung it around him, throwing harsh light over the nearby façades. The shades retreated, whispering and sniggering like children.

'Look there.' Clay pointed to a spot up ahead.

Rachel glimpsed a group of Spine moving through the ruins, their own torches winking in the deepening twilight. They were dragging heavy sacks behind them.

'Corpse duty,' the captain explained. 'They're out searching for bodies.'

'What do they do with the ones they find?'

'They add them to the pile at Sinner's Well,' he replied. 'You want to steer well clear of that place.'

She could not even tell when they finally arrived in Bridgeview, because there was nothing recognizable left of that ancient district. The street ended abruptly in a great hill of rubble over which they had to clamber. On reaching the summit, she saw that none of the old townhouses had survived. There was no Gatebridge spanning a moat of air, no esplanades or cobbled rounds, no winding alleys draped with silkwood walkways. A great snarl of twisted foundation chains had destroyed it all. Before them lay a wide expanse of open abyss, tapering off to a point several hundred yards to the east. In the centre of this gulf loomed the base of the temple itself, an island of iron spikes, rings and gantries. To Rachel's left, a flimsy walkway had been lashed to one of the few surviving sapperbane chains still attached to the temple.

But the sight below took her breath away.

She had known the building so intimately that this sudden change of perspective made her feel giddy. The temple's sheer black walls dropped far into the darkness below her, branching out into a mass of broken spires and pinnacles now looking like stalactites of stonework. Much of the structure had already crumbled into the pit, and yet the great bulk of it remained intact, held together by three-thousand-year-old Blackthrone rock mortar. The sight of it made Rachel stumble and clutch at the captain for support. It seemed so vast and improbable that part of her mind insisted that she was walking upside down, while the temple itself remained upright. Stained-glass windows burned in the walls, thousands of them, like jewels in the abyss.

'We must take the prisoners to the lowest levels,' the Adept told his Cutters. His lenses shifted between Rachel and Clay, then out across the abyssal gap towards the temple. The copper grille of his sand mask gleamed in the torchlight. 'And confine them in solitary cells.'

'Our holding facilities are overstretched,' one of the Cutters replied.

'Make space for them in the Rookery Spire.'

The other assassin nodded. 'What of those thus displaced?'

'Redemption.'

Rachel's heart felt like a hollow in her chest as she stared down at the vast black building with mounting despair. *Our holding facilities are overstretched.* Suddenly she realized why the city districts had been so empty. She understood now why all of the lights were burning in the temple, and a creeping horror stole over her. How many tens of thousands of people were interred there? She had lived with tempered Spine long enough to know how their broken minds worked. There were only two ways to cleanse a blasphemer of his sins: through either tempering or redemption by knife, rope and saw. Inside the temple before her, the torture chambers would be running with blood.

3

The Temple

They entered the temple via a near-vertical Spine conduit in what had once been the building's foundations. Flanked above and below by the Church assassins, Rachel and Clay clambered down a series of rungs bolted to its metal walls. She watched the captain's agitation grow as the circle of crimson sky gradually diminished above them. The big man seemed to become increasingly gruff and surly, cursing and muttering under his breath whenever his armoured boots or elbows clanged against the inside of the narrow passageway. He made almost as much noise as a blacksmith at his anvil.

For the first time during their trek, he seemed genuinely afraid.

With the help of a rope, the other Spine manhandled Dill down after them. To Rachel's great relief, she heard her friend moaning faintly at his mistreatment. He had regained consciousness at last.

The ladder terminated at a spherical antechamber from which a score of other tunnels radiated at all angles. An ancient aether light set into the floor gave a green cast to the sapperbane plates and rivets in the curved walls around them. When the Cutters finally lowered the young angel to the floor, Rachel rushed over to his side.

'Dill?'

His head lolled drunkenly but he didn't open his eyes or reply.

'He's breathing more easily,' she said to Clay.

'Good,' Clay said. 'I don't think your captors planned on sending for a doctor.' His gaze moved from the Spine Adept down to Dill's tattered chain-mail vest. 'It's all shit, you know – the armour and the gold swords they gave the temple archons. It was all just for show.'

'I know.'

'They shouldn't have lied to him.'

'Be silent,' said the Adept.

Rachel eyed the man's mask then turned back to Clay. 'Dill was never cut out to be a warrior,' she said. Her manacles clunked suddenly against the floor. The sapperbane panel had tugged at her iron cuffs with what felt like a strong magnetic attraction, but then immediately released its hold. 'That's strange,' she said.

'It's the sapperbane,' Clay whispered. 'It does all sorts of weird things. I never liked coming down here, not even when the temple was the right way up.' He paused, listened for a moment, then shook his head. 'These tunnels bend sound in odd ways. They say you can hear a conversation spoken in any room in the temple if you're standing in exactly the right place. Some folks even swear that you can hear conversations from the past.'

Dill gasped and threw his head back.

Rachel grabbed his shoulders.

He opened his eyes. 'Rachel? I smell poison.'

'You inhaled a soporific gas,' she said. 'But it's gone now. You're going to be fine.'

'No,' he said, 'they mean to poison us all and then bring their paradise to Earth. There's no more room for them in Hell. They are coming here.'

'Who is coming? Who are you talking about?'

'The Mesmerists.'

Clay shot an enquiring look at Rachel.

'Dill died,' Rachel explained. 'After we reached the bottom of the abyss, he was killed in battle. I used Devon's angelwine to resurrect him, but by then he'd already spent several days in the Maze. Since then he hasn't been able to explain what happened to him there. His memories are muddled, fragmented; they come to him only in nightmares.'

'Was what he said just then true?'

'I don't know.'

The Spine Adept removed his sand mask; his lifeless eyes now turned towards the captain of the temple guard. 'This conversation is illegal. I advise you all to keep silent.'

'Didn't you hear what the lad said?'

'The Maze is a place for sinners. Salvation lies only with our Lord Ulcis.'

Clay ignored him. 'Who are these Mesmerists?' he asked Dill.

'They whisper to the dead,' the young angel replied, 'and change them. They are making demons for the war to come. A red veil heralds their coming.'

'What war?'

'The war between Hell and Earth.'

The captain rubbed a big hand across his stubble. 'Fucking gods,' he growled. 'Ulcis offered slavery, and now Iril wants to wipe us out completely. You can't trust any of them.'

'Ulcis offers salvation,' the Adept said.

Clay punched him, or tried to.

The temple assassin neatly sidestepped the blow. Behind him, his men loaded their crossbows with bone-breakers, the heavy bolts they reserved for use in holy places. Their round stone tips could crush a man's skull without drawing blood.

'Clay!' Rachel warned.

But the captain's face had darkened with fury. He lashed out at his opponent a second time. He was quicker than Rachel expected him to be, much quicker than an old man in heavy plate had any right to be. But he wasn't nearly fast enough.

The Adept grabbed Clay's fist and turned it effortlessly against the force of the man's attack. Rachel heard bones snap in the captain's wrist. Clay roared in pain, and then threw himself forward, trying to use his own weight to slam the smaller man against the wall.

But the assassin flowed around his opponent's charge, almost lazily it seemed. He motioned to his men to lower their weapons, then drove a savage kick into the back of Clay's knee, one of the few weak spots in his armour. A second bone snapped. The captain crashed to the floor, his broad face creased in agony.

'That's enough,' Rachel cried.

'Not quite,' the Adept said.

'But he can't even get up to fight back.'

The assassin shrugged. He broke Clay's other knee with a second kick, then paused for a moment, studying the metal suit. Clay remained face down on the sapperbane floor panels, unable to turn over. He sucked in gulps of air through his teeth. 'Fuck . . . you,' he gasped. 'And fuck . . . your . . .'

'His armour is standard temple issue,' the Adept announced to his men. 'How would you seek to improve this design against ranged attacks?'

'Find and eliminate any weaknesses,' one of the Cutters replied. He removed his sand mask, revealing a youthful face with a high forehead and a weak chin. Bruises and needle-marks under his eyes indicated recent tempering. 'I would test all the joints for strength.'

'Then do so.'

The Cutter raised his crossbow and shot a bolt into the captain's neck-guard. The stone missile ricocheted off the metal with a hideous peal. Clay gnashed his teeth and groaned. The young assassin reloaded.

'Stop it!' Rachel yelled. 'You're just tormenting him.'

'Restrain those two. Bind the angel's wings.'

The remaining Spine surged forward, dragged Rachel and Dill to their feet, and forced them up against the wall. One of them produced a set of chain-and-burr cuffs, a torture implement like a short leash, and tightened them around the angel's wings, drawing them closely together behind Dill's shoulder blades. Meanwhile the young Cutter standing over Clay aimed down a second time. This time the bone-breaker struck the captain in the crook of his elbow. The big man howled and tried to push himself upright, but he could no longer move his broken legs. Four more bolts followed before the young Cutter finally stopped shooting. 'I don't see any weaknesses beyond the obvious gaps in the knee joints,' he observed.

'Give your crossbow and quiver to me.'

The younger man complied.

The Adept rewound the windlass, set the latch, and then selected a fresh bolt from the borrowed quiver. This missile had a yellow glass bulb full of oily liquid attached to its tip. 'Your mistake was to test only the efficacy of what you perceived,' he said to the Cutter, 'while failing to consider what was absent from the design altogether. These older suits lack fire-proofing.'

'No!' Rachel tried to break free from her restrainers. She struggled, every muscle in her body fighting against their grip, but it made no difference. She wasn't strong enough. The Adept aimed the crossbow down at the helpless man and squeezed the trigger.

The incendiary struck Clay's back and exploded, engulfing his whole body in crackling, spitting green flame. He screamed in agony as the burning chemicals trickled down through the tiny gaps between the plates of his armour. Rachel could feel the searing heat from the other side of the chamber.

'A productive lesson,' the Adept said, handing the bow back to the young assassin. 'Obstacles cannot necessarily be overcome by brute force. You must make yourself familiar with the entire breadth of your arsenal.'

He smiled, just for an instant, but long enough for Rachel to notice. Her eyes widened in surprise. This Adept had taken *pleasure* in murder. His stoicism was just a carefully maintained facade. Like Rachel herself, he hadn't been tempered.

They left the antechamber and Clay's charred corpse, and proceeded through a warren of interconnected metal tunnels. Aether lights set into the floors bathed each junction in soft green luminance, while leaving the passageways between shrouded in darkness. Eerie metallic tones with no determinable cause or origin haunted the spaces around them.

Their route gradually led them down into the temple itself. The sapperbane conduits gave way to passages constructed from cut black stone, and then finally to a lofty chamber with a sunken, bowl-shaped floor. Rachel did not recognize the place until she tilted her head, thus viewing the room the other way up. This had once been a hallway right below the Spine sleeping quarters. Smoke rose from cressets arranged along one side of the depression, and it hung in a thin blue layer over the heads of the nine assassins and their captives. The room also smelled vaguely of sweat. Shards of glass littered the floor, although there were no windows here. In the centre, a rickety scaffold had been constructed out of timbers and hemp: a series of ladders and platforms which rose twenty yards to connect two small doors positioned on either side of the flat polished ceiling that had once been the floor.

'Climb,' the Adept said flatly. His face still revealed no emotion, but Rachel now knew him to be a fraud. If he hadn't been tempered, why go to the trouble of pretending that he had been? His Spine masters would know the truth. Only the low-ranking Cutters would not be aware of his deception.

'Why aren't you tempered?' she asked him.

'All Adepts are tempered.'

She snorted. 'I'm living proof that they're not, and so are you.

You enjoyed what you did to Clay, didn't you? Torturing him gave you pleasure. My problem was always the opposite. I didn't particularly enjoy the messier aspects of my work.'

He stared at her, but his eyes betrayed nothing. 'Your Spine status was revoked,' he said. 'Indeed, you were never truly an Adept. You always lacked the ability to focus.'

This was the one Spine technique Rachel had been unable to master during her former training. The brutal process of tempering through torture and the administration of neural toxins vandalized an Adept's mind, destroying his or her ego, yet it also granted the tempered assassins mastery of their own physiology. Focusing enabled Spine to temporarily heighten their senses, and to push their bodies far beyond the limits of normal endurance. Such combatants were far quicker and stronger than normal humans.

Rachel had struggled for years to learn the technique, yet still her untempered mind had resisted. Every attempt at focusing had ended in failure.

Except once.

In the deep abyss under the city, the Spine technique had saved Dill's life. In that one desperate moment when she had most needed to become more than human, she had somehow succeeded.

'Climb,' the Adept repeated.

He led Dill and Rachel up the scaffold, and through one of the upturned doorways. The Cutters followed in a pack, their fingers never far from their weapons' triggers. One corridor led to another and yet another. In the loftier passageways, catwalks had been erected high above the floor to provide access to chambers on either side. Rachel glanced through doorways into tiny sleeping cells and vast training rooms full of sparring combatants. The sound of clashing blades and staffs echoed through the whole torch-lit maze.

At last they reached the Rookery Spire. There the Spine herded their two prisoners down a steep, spiralling slope within the upturned tower: following the underside of the main stairwell. It was a disorienting experience in cramped semi-darkness, a slip-sliding descent beneath steps cut into the roof. Rachel was forced to remove her wood-soled sandals and walk barefoot. She smelled sweat from her captors' leathers, an honest human odour at odds with their ghoulish faces and dead-eyed gazes.

Halfway down, they bundled Dill into one gloomy chamber, and then forced Rachel to descend another level before piling her into a second room and locking the door behind her. She fell all of eight feet in almost complete darkness, rolled over, and came to rest amid a pile of hard-edged debris.

When her eyes finally grew accustomed to the dim light, she was able to survey her surroundings. The cell had previously been a rough-walled chamber with a highly arched stone ceiling – the bedroom of a high-ranking priest, she supposed – before it had turned upside down.

The floor, once the ceiling, was a conical basin full of shattered furniture and dusty tapestries, dry rushes and broken porcelain, and the remains of fine furnishings that had come crashing down on top of an ancient iron chandelier. Her captors hadn't bothered to remove any debris, and little wonder with the temple so crammed with prisoners. 'Our holding facilities are stretched,' as Rachel recalled.

She got up off the floor and walked over to the window. A crimson mist wreathed the abyss beyond the glass and, looking up, Rachel could just discern the dark, cluttered bulk of Deepgate looming overhead, all wrapped in chains and illuminated in places by flickering firelight. Was this the red veil Dill had spoken of, or simply clouds of poison from the burning city? She was about to turn away, when a movement outside grabbed her attention.

Vaporous figures were rising through the mist, the ghosts of countless men and women. With arms outstretched they drifted upwards, their gazes fixed longingly on the city above. The nearest of them passed by only yards from the window, and she noticed that for the most part the men were dressed in the old-style suits and pudding-bowl hats once fashionable among Deepgate's wealthier pioneers, while the women wore layered frocks and carried parasols as protection against a sun which no longer shone upon them. They were almost translucent, as though formed of the red mist itself, but in their faces Rachel glimpsed terrible white eyes and lunatic grins.

Captain Clay had been wrong. Deepgate's apparitions were not born of the city's recent catastrophes. These shades had died a long time ago. And they were surging up directly from the abyss.

But why?

Dill hadn't been able to sleep. His wings chafed at their bindings and sent shards of pain up through his shoulders. He guessed the time to be well after midnight, so it ought to have been completely dark by now, except it wasn't. Dim blood-coloured light, filtering in through the huge multi-panelled windows, suffused the room, turning everything to hues of red. The folds of tapestries which had gathered in the floor depression looked like liver in a bowl. Cracks ran like veins through the surrounding stonework.

But Dill could not drag his gaze from the window. With a terrible fascination, he watched the ghosts beyond the glass.

Most of the shades appeared to be men and women dressed in queer, old-fashioned clothes, but occasionally Dill thought he glimpsed creatures with wings in the far distance, and massive, bulkier shapes rising through gloom. Whatever those were he could not guess.

He was so caught up in watching them that he did not at first notice the creature hovering immediately beyond the window, until a shadow crossing the glass alerted him.

This visitor was a tall, thin battle-archon in crimson chain-link armour. At his side he carried a serrated cutlass, and he wore an odd helmet shaped like the head of a hawk. His wings thumped languidly behind him, keeping the archon level as he studied Dill with deep red eyes. He was older than Dill, and handsome, yet with a cynical twist to his lips. At times his body seemed to fade into the mist outside and reappear again as though it was drifting between separate realities.

The battle-archon flew to the very centre of the window, and made an obvious sign that Dill should open it.

Dill shook his head. The Spine had already warned him against any such action. After all, priests had spent three thousand years blessing the temple's stone walls and stained glass to keep any unwanted phantasms out. Now this barrier against the ghosts in the abyss served the Spine better than any other. At night the Church of Ulcis was the safest place in Deepgate – or it would have been had it not been hanging upside down and inexorably crumbling into the abyss below.

The angel on the other side of the glass beat his wings impatiently and descended until his face was directly level with Dill's. He said something Dill could not hope to hear, then pointed insistently at the window latch.

Again Dill shook his head in defiance.

The stranger's expression twisted into one of disgusted frustration. For a heartbeat he faded, becoming nothing more than a swirl of red mist, before his body solidified again. He raised a fist as though to shatter the window, but stopped himself. His lips parted in a sneer, then he jerked a thumb towards the latch again.

Dill retreated to the back of the room, trying to ignore the window. Instead he feigned interest in the shattered furniture and tapestries piled up on the sunken floor.

By now the battle-archon looked furious. Lifting his cutlass with both hands, he held it up only an inch from a window pane, then he hovered for a minute, all of his attention fixed on just the sword. Slowly, he brought the blade forward against the glass.

Dill heard a tap.

The battle-archon grinned.

Morning finally arrived. As light filtered down through the chained city, the window of Rachel's cell turned a lighter shade of red. The mist thinned but did not dissipate entirely, yet the ghosts finally stopped rising from the depths.

The sunlight, feeble as it was, had driven the phantasms away.

Stained-glass panels before her depicted three scenes from the Deepgate Codex, each set one over the other: the fall of Ulcis from Heaven, the coming of the Herald, and the rise of Callis and the Ninety-Nine from the abyss. Now that the panels were upside down, Rachel could reach out and easily touch the image of Callis and his warriors, which otherwise would have been out of reach.

The door to her cell lay eight feet above what had now become the floor. The Spine would open it eventually, of course, if only to throw a bladder of water down to her. She studied the heaped debris that had gathered in the floor basin: broken furniture, cloth, smashed porcelain, and even an old iron chandelier – a cornucopia of potential weapons.

Rachel touched the window again. Thankfully this thin barrier of priest-blessed glass had kept her safe all night, and none of the apparitions had been able to enter her cell. But other parts of the temple had crumbled away before her eyes, and the great building would not survive for much longer.

She stood for a moment, thinking.

Tempered Spine felt no fear but they understood danger. They would not tolerate a threat to their precious temple. And if they wanted Rachel alive for tempering . . .

She made a sudden decision.

She picked up the leg of a broken chair and used it to smash the lowest pane, taking some pleasure in aiming directly for Callis's painted face. Broken glass fell away into the abyss outside, leaving a jagged hole in the middle of the pane.

A chill breeze stirred Rachel's hair. The phantasms would return at dusk. She had until sunset to find out if her terrible gamble had worked.

Carefully, she prised out loose shards of glass from the edges of the pane and arranged them in a line. They would serve as knives – too brittle to meet a Spine sword with, but deadly enough if they were thrown.

She first selected those shards with the best balance, and wound strips of tapestry around one end to make them easier to handle. This way she made six knives in all, although she doubted she'd get the opportunity to use more than one of them. Her first throw would have to be absolutely accurate. Next she used the chair leg to pound the smaller, less useful shards into a fine powder, which she gathered up into a makeshift pouch. Ironically, her Spine master had once taught her the efficacy of using such substances to blind an opponent temporarily. The chair leg itself she set aside to use as a club; if she ever escaped the room, it might be handy for close combat.

A scream erupted from somewhere overhead.

Rachel pocketed the throwing knives she'd fashioned, then stood up to look out of the window. The Rookery Spire had been the tallest in the temple, so now it naturally housed the lowest dungeon. The smooth black walls outside would be impossible to climb, but overhead, a clutch of spires – fingers of glassy stone and masonry – extruded like icicles. Beyond this, a black lattice of chains stretched on for miles, all wreathed in red fumes and silhouetted against an angry sky. In places spikes of orange light punctured the city, and constant dull booming sounds drifted over the abyss, as though the bones of the city were snapping one by one. And in a sense they were, for Deepgate was still crumbling into the pit. Showers of dust and debris rained down from the temple and its surroundings, stirring up clouds of grainy air. Looking down, Rachel saw that the roof of the Rookery Spire had already disappeared, and the stonework ended just twenty yards below her in ragged chaos.

A door to Hell lay deep in the abyss below this very city, in the darkness below Ulcis's palace. The god of chains himself had warned her of its existence. The things down there would tear you to pieces, he'd said. Had last night's phantasms found a way through this door? Were they refugees driven from the Maze?

Or advance scouts?

Rachel shuddered. The gloom down there was as darkly crimson as a well of blood. *They are making demons for the war to come,* Dill had said in the temple antechamber. *A red veil heralds their coming.*

A sudden, loud creaking sound came from behind her and, with a pang of dread, Rachel turned away from the window. A thin crack had appeared along the interior wall of her cell, just an inch above the edge of the floor, and now already five yards long.

Shit.

The spire was clearly breaking up.

A tremor convulsed the room. Broken furniture shifted, settling deeper into the sunken floor that had formerly been the ceiling. The crack widened suddenly to the width of a finger, and shot on through another five yards of stonework, instantly doubling in length. Now it stretched along two of the walls.

Rachel gazed in horror. So this is how it was to end for her? She would return to the abyss after all: one more skeleton on Ulcis's mountain of bones. And Dill, up in the cell above, would join her soon. A profound sense of melancholy struck her. The young angel had never shown signs of growing weary of her failure. But now? How could he forgive her now? She buried her head in her hands, exhausted.

And she waited.

Another rumble. The crack opened another inch, tracing a jagged line on a third wall as the mortar between its stonework split.

A sudden anger gripped Rachel. She rose and jumped up and down on the floor, stamping her full weight down, kicking the now useless pile of smashed furniture to one side. Why shouldn't it be over *now*? Why did she have to sit here and patiently wait for the end to come? Could she not at least be in charge of her own destiny?

Rachel picked up the chair leg she'd set aside in readiness and smashed it hard against the floor. Then she deliberately drove it deeply into the widest part of the crack, trying to prise the gap further apart. Nothing happened, however; the hanging tower would split under its *own* weight or not. Her efforts made no difference.

Suddenly she paused, breathing heavily, still staring at the piece of wood in her fist. Then she looked at the mound of debris . . . at the tapestries, at the broken furniture and the heavy iron chandelier.

Gods below, how stupid I've been!

Rachel moved quickly. She snatched up a corner of the nearest tapestry and dragged it clear of the pile. About two yards wide and twice as long, it depicted a battle scene of archons and heathens, like most of the others in the temple. The cloth was ancient; the weave thin, frayed and undoubtedly priceless. Good. Next she pulled out pieces of furniture, jagged panels, drawers, part of a bed, a chair-back curved like a lute, kicking most of this stuff aside. She needed something to use as a grapple.

The sound of rending stone drove her to greater urgency. Along the wall, the crack had widened again.

The chandelier! She grabbed at it and pulled, but it was secured to the floor by a yard of stout chain. She heaved, then let it drop again when it refused to budge. No time to mess with it. With the stout wooden leg in one hand, the U-shaped chair-back in the other, and one end of the tapestry bundled under her elbow, she rushed to the inside corner of the room, beneath the erstwhile door. She wedged the chair leg between the rough corner stones where the two walls met, four feet above the crack and the same distance below the door, then stepped back and kicked it securely into place. Then she pulled down on it, testing this makeshift perch with her weight. It moved a little, settling into the rough stonework on either side, then held firmly.

Another crack. The gap now traced a line around all four walls. At its narrowest, it was as thin as a hair, but closer to the window it was large enough to push a fist inside. The floor could fall away at any moment.

Rachel hooked the chair back over her wooden perch, then, still holding on to the tapestry, hopped up on top of it. She still had to fashion a rope, but reasoned that it was better to undertake that task while sitting safely above the disintegrating floor.

The weave parted with disturbing ease. It was almost rotten. Rachel considered fetching another tapestry – there were two more that she could see – but then rejected that idea. The floor had already become too dangerous to risk setting foot upon again. She'd have to make do with what she had. She separated the cloth into six long strips, which she then draped over her makeshift seat for fear of losing them. Next she plaited two lengths of rope from three strands each, tied them together, and then bound one end to the curved chair-back and the other to her perch. This would give her a long enough line to swing beneath the wall once the floor fell away. With a bit of luck she could then snag one of the stairwell wall sconces on the opposite side and pull herself up.

Until then all she could do was wait.

So she held the rope firmly, and waited.

And waited.

After several hours Rachel began to feel foolish. She eased herself forward, keeping most of her weight on the wooden perch, and pressed the toe of her foot gingerly against the floor. It felt solid, unyielding. Still gripping the rope, she carefully placed her other foot beside the first. Still no movement.

She then gave the floor a gentle kick.

Nothing alarming happened.

So she slid fully down from her seat and stood there, clutching the rope.

She jumped.

And then leapt again, bringing all of her weight down to bear upon the floor. The sound of her wooden heels striking stone resounded through the chamber, before the room settled to silence again. Rachel sighed deeply. She tied the rope around herself and sat down on the floor. It was already becoming very gloomy outside.

The Rookery Spire held together all afternoon. The crack in the wall did not lengthen and the floor did not fall away from underneath the waiting assassin. She watched the red mist darken further outside the window. Somewhere overhead the sun would be dropping low in the sky, casting the shadow of the abyss's rim over Deepgate. The ghosts would return soon, but now Rachel's cell had a broken window.

She tried calling out, but nobody came. So she watched the door and waited, flipping the glass-shard knife between her hands.

Eventually, a key rattled in the lock.

Rachel tensed. She'd have only one chance at this. The Spine would be wearing leather armour, which might be enough to deflect or break her fragile blade. Better if she aimed for the neck. If she could sever his carotid artery, death would come quickly.

The door opened.

Rachel lifted her arm to throw, but stopped.

A child stood in the doorway, a boy of about nine or ten, holding a water-bladder. He was painfully thin and pale, dressed in a sleeveless brown jerkin and breeches, a cheap imitation of a Cutter's training armour. His short red hair had been hacked roughly, probably with a knife, but it must have been beautiful once. Puncture marks and bruises marred his arms, evidence of Spine torture, and his eyes were as empty and haunted as any Adept's. He hardly seemed to see her. They had tempered him.

'You must not approach the door,' he announced in a high clear voice. 'I will throw you the water, and you must catch it. If the container bursts there will be no more water for you today.'

Despair swamped Rachel. She had a clear shot at the boy's neck. The glass blade remained steady in her hand, yet she hesitated. A child? Had the visitor been an Adept or even a Cutter, it would already have been too late to make a throw. But this boy obviously lacked the training and reflexes to react to this situation. He had been ordered to deliver water, and instructed on what to say. All he could do was obey.

'You must be ready to catch this,' he repeated, holding out the bladder.

Rachel felt the weight of the glass blade in her hand. She knew the position of the artery in the child's neck. In her mind she watched herself throw the dagger, saw it flash across the room and bury itself into his flesh. She imagined the jetting blood, the wet, gurgling sounds he would make as he fell. It would be an easy throw, over in a heartbeat. Then she'd be free, and able to help Dill.

The child had been tempered, hadn't he? He was one of them.

Rachel threw the knife.

★

70

Dill had not slept. The phantom battle-archon had remained out-side his window all night, tapping his cutlass against the glass. This simple persistence had evidently taken a lot out of the intruder, for his body had faded as the night wore on, becoming more gaseous and more insubstantial with each blow. When dawn finally came, the ghost had returned to the abyss, by then little more than a shadow of his former self.

But he had managed to make a crack in the window.

Dill studied the broken pane for the hundredth time, and with mounting apprehension. Shades should not be able to affect the physical world around them, and certainly not the blessed glass that protected the Church of Ulcis. In fact, no spirit had ever damaged the temple during three thousand years. Yet this dead warrior had managed a remarkable feat, seemingly determined to reach Dill at any cost.

But why?

And there was something else worrisome. Of all the ghosts Dill had seen that night, this armoured phantom was the only one to have now returned to the abyss.

Dill was exhausted, and the crimson mist outside was growing dark again. The chain-and-burr cuffs cramped and chafed his wings, sending jolts of pain through his shoulders whenever he moved. Broken feathers now covered the floor of the cell.

Time passed, yet nobody came to check on him, or to bring him food or water. Once he thought he heard a child crying out somewhere below him, but it might just have been a rook squawk-ing. He must have slept, because it was suddenly much darker. The tall windows shone dully, bathing his cell in a queer red radi-ance. Outside the ghosts were again rising from the abyss: more of them this time.

And then the phantom archon returned.

He floated outside Dill's room, his huge wings entirely filling the window frame. His body was solid, more corporeal again, and his eyes gleamed with malice. He raised his cutlass before the cracked pane and struck it hard.

The glass finally shattered.

Dill instantly heard a howl, like a powerful gale. The archon's form warped and faded until it became as thin as a plume of smoke. Curling and twisting, the smoke then began to flow through the broken window into the room. In a dozen heartbeats, the ghost had re-formed. His wings unfolded behind him, trailing wisps of red mist, and he stared down at the young angel with terrible eyes.

'You should have opened the window,' he said in a voice like leaves blowing through a forest. 'And that way saved us both some pain. This meeting has cost me dearly.'

Dill did not realize he'd been backing away until his own wings brushed against the wall behind him. He stammered, 'Who are you?'

The battle-archon's eyes narrowed. 'My name is Silister Trench.' He exhaled slowly, releasing drifts of red smoke from his nostrils. 'I am the champion of the First Citadel and commander of Hasp's archons.' He gave a small bow, and his hand settled on the hilt of his cutlass. 'I am your great-grandfather's great-grandfather, or something similar – the exact details of our family connection are not important. Needless to say, I am one of your ancestors, and your ancestors have need of you now.' He started towards the young angel. Crimson vapours rose wherever his boots touched the floor.

'Wait,' Dill cried. 'I don't understand. Why . . .?'

'I require your wings, your heart and your blood,' Trench said. 'My own form would soon fade under Ayen's sun, and yet I have an urgent message to deliver to one in your world.' He held out his gaseous hands and peered through them at the other angel. 'You see? This body is too insubstantial to survive here for long. It will only last long enough to provide a vessel to carry your own soul back to the Maze.'

Dill glanced frantically about for a chance to escape. Grinning, the battle-archon bore down on him, his intangible armour wreathed in bloody vapour. There was nowhere to run to. The young angel dropped to his knees and cowered.

'That's it,' Trench said soothingly. 'This will only hurt a little.'

'A foolish and desperate manoeuvre.' The Adept peered over the lath of his crossbow, as he aimed the weighty stone tip of a bone-breaker at Rachel's abdomen. 'You might have killed the child.'

Rachel looked up at him from the floor of her cell. 'He moved at the wrong moment.'

'Your skills have waned,' the other assassin remarked. 'Any ordinary Cutter could have thrown the blade more accurately.'

Her glass knife had caught the lad's ear, grazing him just enough to draw blood. If the Adept had known that this was exactly Rachel's intention, he might have been less dismissive of her skills. The boy had, of course, dropped the water-bladder and run back to his masters. Subsequently the Adept who'd brought her here had been forced to visit.

'Why do you pretend you've been tempered?' Rachel asked. 'Why keep up the facade?'

'I do not pretend,' he snapped.

She laughed. 'Are you so afraid of the procedure?'

'Be silent.'

'I used to yearn for them to temper me,' she said, 'but my brother wouldn't sign the consent forms. He did this to hurt me. He knew I couldn't cope with the strain of what my Spine masters expected me to do. I could never kill children. Yet you don't seem to have a problem with morality, do you?' Suddenly she thought she understood him. 'That's why you don't want them to temper you. The procedure would strip away your baser desires, deprive you of the joy you get from your work.'

'My master died on the night he was due to temper me,' he replied with a cruel smile. 'Quite suddenly, and inexplicably. With all the recent confusion, the destruction of the city, nobody thought to confirm that he'd actually carried out the procedure.'

'Bravo,' Rachel said. 'It couldn't have been easy to kill a Spine master.'

The man inclined his head. 'Over the years he had built up a resistance to every poison we stocked. I was forced to use less subtle methods.'

'I'm impressed. So what's your name? It isn't often I get to meet an Adept who actually remembers it.'

'Culver.'

'So, Culver, are you going to shoot me now, or take me away to be tempered?'

He lowered his crossbow. 'You'll go under the needles eventually,' he said. 'We need all the battle fodder we can get. Unfortunately we have rather a long backlog to work through.'

'A shame,' she muttered, 'because I'll be dead by tomorrow.'

Culver's hard eyes narrowed. 'Suicide is against Codex Law. Any attempt would be punished by—'

'By what? Death?'

He did not answer.

Rachel snorted. 'Save your sermons. I've no intention of killing myself. Look over there, corpse face.' She gestured towards the broken pane, the glass she'd smashed to make her knives. Already there were ghosts rising through the dark red mist beyond. It would only be a matter of time until one of them noticed and came to investigate. 'I'm afraid it broke,' she said. 'Quite suddenly and inexplicably.'

Culver cursed. 'You stupid bitch. Did you want to get yourself possessed? The whole room will have to be blessed now.' He dragged a hand through his short hair, thinking for a moment, before he looked back at her. 'Sod the waiting list,' he said. 'We'll temper you and the angel tonight.'

The long slow death of the soul by torture. It was almost a relief.

4

A MAN WALKS INTO A BROTH SHOP

Fog always brought more victims to the Widow's Hook. The damp grey air had filled the lanes around the broth shop for three days now, softening mud walls and wilting the eaves of gin dens and hovels until the whole neighbourhood seemed about to sink back into the wet brown earth. In such weather newcomers easily became lost in Sandport, and there had been no shortage of those recently: rich refugees who'd arrived by churchship after the chained city of Deepgate fell. Inevitably, some of these would wander into places they would have preferred to avoid. So when Jack Caulker heard the piper outside the Hook squawk out his warning medley, he leaned back on his stool, downed the last of his fishbeer and gave the nod to Hammer Eric by the door.

It seemed another stranger was about to venture inside.

They had robbed and murdered nine so far – if you didn't include the beggar woman who'd had nothing worth selling but her long yellow hair – and dragged their bodies down to the river for the crabs to pick clean. And still the victims came. Few of Sandport's barges or skiffs would risk sailing for Shale or Clune in this unholy murk, and so plenty of Deepgate's merchants and nobles had been trapped here. So many had been turning up at the Widow's Hook recently that Jack Caulker had been able to afford himself a room upstairs. Now he spent his nights in drunken stupor, swilling the finest fishbeers and raising a toast each time the fog bells rang out by the docks. By day he gorged himself on eel broth and chowder, while he waited for the next job. He was growing fat around the waist and fatter in his purse. It was a nasty, immoral business, but somebody had to do it, and Caulker had paid the Hook's proprietor a handsome sum to ensure that that somebody was he.

He scraped his stool back, shared a grin with his accomplice, stood up and froze on the spot –

– as the door opened to reveal the oddest-looking person he could have imagined.

The stranger blocked the doorway like a fifty-ton boulder, a half-naked giant with darkly painted skin. He wore brown leather shorts and little else, exposing more painted flab than Caulker would have thought possible for one man to carry. Some sort of enormous wood and leather construction engulfed his upper body: a flotation aid perhaps – for it seemed too sparse for armour.

As the giant ducked out of the fog and squeezed his great bulk inside the Widow's Hook, all conversation withered around him. Spoons slid back into bowls of chowder; half-raised cups were lowered. By the light of the cooking fires, Caulker suddenly saw what those closest to the door had already noticed. The fat man's body had not been painted: the colour was due to skin as dark as hull tar. His huge black fists were as big as mast-hammers, while his chest rose and fell like a deepwater swell.

But the rope was the strangest thing of all. A taut, arm-thick span of greased hemp stretched out from behind the man's shoulders, straight as a dock pole, and curved taut around the underside of the door lintel, where it disappeared upwards from sight. This wood and leather construction appeared to be a harness of some kind; this man must have been tethered to something outside the Widow's Hook, and something high up by the look of it.

'My name is John Anchor,' the stranger announced. 'I am told there is an angel's corpse here, yes?'

Nobody spoke. The regulars in the Hook were freshwater men: crabbers, river fishers and boat builders, a couple of barge pilots down from the Shale Forests, and few – if any – would have heard any whisper of the Gallows Fog before. But Jack Caulker, who had worked on missionary cogs before his cut-throat days, and had sailed to the Volcanic Isles, knew the legend well enough for the sight of this stranger to bring a furrow to his cynical brow. Temple sailors had spoken often of the Adamantine Man who walked across the ocean floors. A queer mist was said to accompany him: the Gallows Fog, which hid the floating hell he dragged across the world. Salt sailors feared such weather greatly, for east of the Isles, it was claimed, no ship could sail through such a miasma. All superstitious piss, of course, Caulker reckoned, yet Deepgate's seamen blamed every deepwater wreck on this Gallows Fog, and you'd be damned before you'd find one of them who'd sail a league beyond the Isles for fear of encountering it. Caulker studied the visitor with a mounting sense of wonder. Here was a man dragging a taut rope, and it had to be fixed to *something* outside.

But a skyship full of the dead?

Here? In *Sandport*?

Hammer Eric had backed away, the namesake weapon at his hip looking more like a toothpick now than a carpenter's tool, next to this tethered giant. Most of the broth-shop clientele had turned their eyes to Caulker; in their own small way they respected him. The cut-throat had been educated, he had travelled, and he knew how to handle himself in a fight.

It would do his reputation no good to let them see him spooked.

'Come in, friend.' Caulker raised his empty cup to the stranger. 'Merrigan Foley, the boss of this fine establishment, charges nobody nothing but a bowl of chowder to see the damn thing. It's there, plain as you like, on the wall above the counter.' He gestured over to where the bloody black corpse had been nailed up. A group of Ban Heshette goat herders had arrived carrying it two days ago, claiming to have discovered the boy in a ditch somewhere south of Deepgate. It was the temple angel, they'd claimed, and its wings had looked convincing enough for Foley to dip into his purse, though not nearly as deep as the desert folk had wanted him to. As curiosities went, it was rather pathetic: just a mess of tanned bones and white feathers pinned to a rude cross, barely even recognizable as an archon – not nearly as impressive as the shape-shifting demon that show-woman had displayed recently. Yet news of the angel had brought a steady stream of curious patrons into the Hook, for which both Foley and Caulker were glad. They'd even had a group of Spine take lodging here just to study the thing at their leisure.

John Anchor studied the gruesome exhibit for a moment, then frowned. 'The angel I hunt has dark wings,' he said. 'This is not her corpse.'

Caulker raised an eyebrow. The angel he *hunts*? 'Well, if it's angels and their whereabouts you're after, you've come to the right place. Nothing goes on south of Clune without somebody in the Hook knowing the meat and bones of it.'

This was not entirely a lie. The river men's gossip was as thick here as anywhere along the banks of the Coyle.

'Explain your problem,' he added. 'Sandporters are known for their generosity and their friendship to foreigners. If we can help, we will.'

John Anchor nodded. 'I seek a *scarred* angel.'

Caulker's brow furrowed. 'Carnival?' Folks said she had risen from the abyss when Deepgate fell, and then fled into the

Deadsands. Nobody knew for certain what had happened to her since, but that small fact need not affect the potential profit to be made here. The cut-throat was happy enough to sell rumours and lies, and he'd even embellish them some for an extra coin. He gave the stranger a smile and a knowledgeable nod. 'Aye,' he said, 'I think we can do business.'

The tethered man smacked his hands together and strode forward purposefully, heaving the massive rope behind him. Yard after yard of tough hemp scraped splinters from the underside of the door lintel. The timber creaked and bowed, under what must have been enormous pressure, then suddenly snapped. Smooth as a wire through cheese, the rope tore upwards through three feet of mud-brick wall above the door and then came to rest against a stout ceiling beam. This joist gave an ominous groan, but Anchor did not appear to notice the destruction behind him. He marched up to Caulker as though he had forgotten he was still tethered. 'Well met,' he said. 'I am a stranger here. Does salt have value in this land?'

The cut-throat flinched. Everyone in the place was staring intently at him now, and at this queer rope which stretched all the way from the back of the big man's harness to the creaking ceiling joist directly above the door lintel. 'Salt?' It took him a moment to regain his composure. 'You want to buy information with salt?'

Anchor frowned. 'It is good salt, from the Riot Coast.'

Caulker let his shoulders droop. He'd never heard of the Riot Coast, but the man spoke Low Coyle well enough to make him wonder if Deepgate missionaries had once been there. 'My friend,' he said with affected resignation, 'an exchange would be most welcome, I promise you, but I fear that salt would cast your homeland in . . . how shall I say, an ungenerous light. Salt is common here. Now if—'

'Pearls, then?' John Anchor suddenly beamed. 'You would like pearls? I have many.' He withdrew a bulging leather purse from his pocket and held it up. 'How many should I offer? One . . . or three? Six pearls? All right, ten.'

The cut-throat gave the purse a dismissive glance, while skilfully keeping the smile from his face. This was more like it. There had to be a pound of pearls in the newcomer's fist, and yet he'd whipped them out in full view of the Hook's patrons without a care. Big as the stranger was, he wasn't even armed. Why were foreigners always so ignorant of the simplest rules of life? And why were they always so bloody affable?

'Pearls?' Caulker feigned confusion, and then lifted his chin. 'Oh, yes, I see . . . those beads the fishwives sometimes wear? We find them often in little shells out in the bay.' He pretended to think for a moment while he exchanged another glance with his colleague by the door. 'Well, they're quite pretty, I suppose, and our women like their trinkets. A few sacks would—'

John Anchor interrupted him. 'This pouch,' he shouted out, turning to face the room, 'to any man who tells me where to find my quarry, a scarred angel. I have no more patience now.' He flexed his shoulders, and the rope behind his harness thrummed like an enormous lute string, working more dried mud free from the gash above the door.

Forty men yelled at once.

'. . . north into the Deadsands . . .'

'. . . west to Scarpa Well, but she . . .'

'. . . no, no, it was the chemist, listen!'

'. . . an angel, four of them and a hundred swords . . .'

'. . . Spine, you want. Sure as I'm sitting here . . .'

'. . . heard, but listen, she was scarred, black wings, brought down . . .'

'Too many voices!' Anchor boomed. 'Too much!' The room fell silent. 'One of you will now speak please. No more than one! I offer this pouch for the truth. You!' He shoved the leather bag towards a lean crabber in a frayed red shirt and patched breeks who was seated at the nearest table. 'You know where the angel is?'

The man moistened his lips. 'Aye, sir, she fled southeast, hunted by skyships. Poison arrows took her down near Cinderbark Wood. They hacked her up into little pieces 'fore she could recover from the drugs.' He extended a hand to receive his reward.

Anchor snatched the bag away. 'Dead?'

'Killed,' the crabber confirmed, still holding his palm out. 'It's true, I swear to Ayen. The Spine assassins got her, not two leagues away from where they grabbed this other one' – he pointed to the winged corpse on the wall – 'if the nomads told it true. There was an assassin captured with them, a deserter. The three were seen travelling together right after the temple fell.' There were many murmurs and nods of agreement from the Hook's other clientele on this last point.

Anchor grunted. 'An assassin?'

The crabber nodded.

'And where is she?'

'Why . . . she's lodging here now, sir.' Grinning, the man leaned back and put both hands behind his head. 'In this very house: top floor, last door on the right. The Spine took their needles to her, see? And numbed her mind. They came to claim the archon's bones, but Foley's been stalling them with his talk of all the refugees hiding around these parts. The assassins have been well busy of late, redeeming folks like they do. She's up there now with her Spine friends, and you'd best hire yourself a bunch of swords if you're thinking of speaking to her. Fifty men should do it. Happens I can get you just the fellows to do the job, for a small fee.'

'Here?' the giant asked. 'She is in this place? Now?'

'Spine don't like daylight, do they? They only come out at night, when there's redemption needs doing.'

Caulker understood the crabber's plan at once, and cursed him for it. Fifty men would make no difference. When the temple assassins lodging upstairs had finished hacking this big idiot and his newly hired help to a bloody mess, those pearls would be lost. No, the Spine weren't likely to give up such a treasure. He had to intervene now, get Hammer Eric to thump the stranger even as he left the Widow's Hook to recruit his sellswords. He gave his accomplice another secret nod, and smiled inwardly as the other man's hand slid down to his weapon. Salt sailors' tales of fogs and hellish skyships had little value here in the Hook.

But John Anchor did not turn and walk outside. Instead, he pulled a thin reed from his other pocket and blew into it. This rude flute produced no sound, or rather, none that Caulker could hear, for after a few moments he realized that Anchor had played a note not meant for human ears. From outside came a faint sound: a scratching, chittering noise that Caulker recognized from his midnight forays to the banks of the Coyle. The customers heard it too; already they were rising uneasily from tables, shifting gazes between each other and the open door as the sound grew more distinct. Caulker backed away; he had an idea what was coming.

Crabs!

Hundreds of thousands of the tiny red crustaceans poured into the room, all scrambling along John Anchor's rope and over each other. The hemp strands seemed to bubble and then drip with them as scores fell to the ground and then shot across the floor towards their master. Those crabs on the rope reached the big man first and surged over his shoulders and arms in a scarlet tide. Countless more scuttled across the floor, then swarmed up Anchor's legs and over his chest. In a heartbeat the giant was covered from head to foot in a writhing, clicking red suit.

Panic broke out. Customers yelled and shoved each other aside, knocking over stools and tables to get away from the tethered stranger and his pets. Cups, tankards and bowls fell to the floor and smashed.

Swarming with crustaceans, John Anchor marched towards the rear of the broth shop, where a steep staircase led up to the rented rooms on the upper floors. His rope swung after him across the room, gouging a horizontal slash through the exterior wall. Men scrambled aside to avoid the expanding line. For a moment Caulker gaped in shocked silence. Then he made a decision: a man in his position could not afford to abandon a bounty like this so easily. Somehow, the giant had summoned an army of crabs – but they were only *crabs*: each no larger than a man's thumbnail. He swallowed hard, then hurried after the stranger.

'Wait,' he cried. 'Anchor, wait!' The other man did not pause, so Caulker followed him up the stairs. 'These assassins are dangerous,' he said. 'Listen to me. There are five or six of them up there, all Spine Adepts and armed. Stop and hear me before they kill you. The worst is Ichin Tell, their master. They say he's butchered two thousand men and I've seen him murder nine here in Sandport myself. He denounced them as sinners and he didn't even bother to unsheathe his sword to take them down. Arm yourself at least.'

But the giant ploughed on up the stairs, dragging yard after yard of taut rope further inside the Widow's Hook. 'Thank you for your concern,' he said. 'But I must avoid bloodshed, even if attacked, or the souls of my enemies go to Iril's Maze. This angers my master, Cospinol, who wishes the souls for himself. Steel is therefore no good.' Red crustaceans boiled over his skin. Clumps of them kept falling to the floor, then flooded after him and scurried back up his legs. And still Anchor climbed. His rope rose with him until it pushed up against the innermost ceiling joist. Now the whole roof gave a mighty groan. John Anchor didn't slow, however. Once he reached the first landing, he turned to climb the second flight of stairs. Behind him, the rope skittered over the banister but caught on the corner post where the ground- and first-floor staircases met. The big man ignored it and kept on up the stairs still ahead of him.

Caulker struggled to comprehend this situation. What the hell was tethered to the other end of that rope? A skyship? Impossible – no man could hope to keep his feet on the ground against such a force, much less drag something like that behind him. But then what *was* pulling the stranger's tether skywards? The broth-shop ceiling was already cracking under the strain. To put so much pressure on a line as thick as this, the burden had to be unbelievably heavy or impossibly buoyant. Either way, how could Anchor heave such a rope up another flight of steps? The hemp would snag, or break . . .

. . . or tear the building apart.

A loud snap made the cut-throat flinch. The rope jerked violently as the banister corner post broke like a twig. Below them, the ceiling joists had begun to crack, and cries of alarm came from the broth-shop clientele. Caulker glanced back down the stairs to see a panicked crowd clogging the door, brawling to get themselves outside.

Clothed in his snapping red tide of claws and shells, the giant ploughed on up the second flight of steps. Caulker followed with mounting astonishment, cautious but curious now to see how much further Anchor could pull this huge rope. The whole building seemed to buckle under the upwards pressure. Could this stranger really kill six Spine? And would he be prepared to share his wealth for more knowledge?

'The assassins will have heard you,' he warned. 'Spine sleep lightly. It will be dark in their room, as they shun daylight.' He tried to think of something else helpful to say, some insight the big man might pay for. 'Don't underestimate Ichin Tell,' he blurted out at last. 'The man is a demon.'

Before Anchor reached the top of the second flight of stairs, the ground floor ceiling joists parted with a sequence of thunderous booms. Caulker watched the rope rip a vertical scar through eight feet of stairwell wall, and thump against the underside of the first-floor ceiling. He heard debris crashing into the room below. Crabs tumbled from Anchor's legs, then shot after him with renewed frenzy. But the big man didn't hurry. He opened the landing door and lumbered along the corridor beyond.

Breathless, the cut-throat scrambled after him. Anchor's strength seemed limitless – might he be a match for Ichin Tell? After all, Spine weapons and heads could be sold in the tribal bazaars; their poisons could be traded on the black market in Clune. Pearls or no pearls, Jack Caulker might still be able to make a handsome profit from this.

Gritty light seeped through a window at the far end of the passageway, illuminating four doors along the interior wall, which led into the Hook's rented rooms. The stink of old seafood clung to the plaster. Anchor marched on along the narrow space, dripping crabs and still towing his rope behind him. And when he reached a point halfway down the corridor, the joists supporting the second floor also began to break. The stressed hemp ripped through one, two, three beams, tearing a jagged scar right through the corridor floorboards. Splinters leapt like fleas. A deep moan came from the walls, and Caulker felt the building begin to list. The Widow's Hook was falling apart.

In his living armour, John Anchor arrived at the last door. He opened the door, and then stepped inside the Spine assassins' room. 'My name is John Anchor,' he said.

There was a heartbeat of silence.

And then Caulker heard a flurry of slaps, like steel striking leather. But any further sounds of combat there might have been were drowned out by a series of violent concussions from below. Anchor's great rope, which had so thoroughly sliced through the interior of the broth shop, abruptly severed the remaining joists. The taut hemp shot skywards, opening up the wall to the right, and sliced right through the roof. Caulker spied a crooked line of grey sky among flying rafters and spinning shingles before the entire building collapsed.

The cut-throat opened his eyes and groaned. His mouth and nose felt clogged with dirt. He sneezed, then winced in agony. Something heavy was pressing down on his legs. For a long moment he gazed up into the fog, dizzy and confused, wondering who had beaten him so badly, and whether or not he had been robbed. And then he lifted his head and saw that he was lying half-buried in a great heap of sodden timbers and impacted mud. Suddenly he remembered what had happened, and his head sank back into the rubble.

Hell.

Thank the gods he had been on the top floor, and not down among the brawling rabble below. He must have fallen all of two storeys, but at least the building had collapsed underneath him rather than on top of him. He was lucky even to be alive. Faint moans and cries came from somewhere amid the rubble below him. Gods, where was his purse? His money? Caulker fumbled for his belongings, then yelped as the back of his hand scraped against a protruding nail.

Slowly, the cut-throat heaved himself up into a sitting position and surveyed the scene. The broth shop had crumpled inwards, its innards ripped out by the giant's rope. Broken beams jutted from the mud-brown hovels on either side, while the collapsed floors slumped in a shallow valley between them. A heap of shingles and floorboards covered Caulker's legs, but he appeared to have escaped the worst of the falling debris. Only one of the heavier rafters had landed on him. He heaved it aside, ignoring the sudden ache in his shoulders and arms, and struggled to his feet.

John Anchor was busy further down the mound of debris, pulling timbers and sections of mud wall from the wreckage and tossing them aside. The crabs were nowhere to be seen. Now that the rope had ripped itself free of the building, it rose unchallenged from the harness on the giant's back and shot straight up into the muggy sky. Caulker's gaze followed it up, but he could spot nothing through the dense fog above.

The giant was humming a tune while he worked. Suddenly he let out an exclamation, reached down, and dragged something free – the corpse of a pale woman clad in leather armour. Anchor held the cadaver up by its ankle, frowned, then flung it down into the lane below as easily as if it had been a dead cat. Five more corpses had already been heaped there, all of them Spine.

Caulker picked his way down through the wreckage towards them. All of the dead assassins' heads appeared to be intact, he noted. Maybe this day wouldn't be a total loss after all.

Down in the lane, John Anchor joined him beside the pile of corpses and folded his arms across his harness. 'I wished only to speak with them.' He shook his head. 'Had they not attacked me, they would still be alive.'

Caulker examined the bodies. None of them had visible wounds. He turned one over with his foot and recognized it as Ichin Samuel Tell, head of Deepgate's temple assassins. Somehow, the Avulsior looked healthier dead. 'They must have been crushed when the building collapsed,' he said.

'No,' Anchor said. 'I think they would have escaped. This house is not so much to fall on their heads. They were quick enough, like little white cats.' He nodded solemnly. 'But not quick enough for John Anchor.'

'You killed them all?' the cut-throat asked. 'Before the building collapsed?'

Anchor looked suddenly peevish. 'They attacked me,' he grumbled. 'I meant them no harm. Do you think they were afraid of crabs?'

'I suppose,' Caulker muttered.

'No matter.' Anchor smacked his big hands together. 'Souls is souls, eh?' He flexed his shoulders, took hold of the rope which rose into the sky behind him, and began to haul it down towards him.

5

✝EMPERED

The final journey Rachel Hael would ever make through the Church of Ulcis involved much climbing up and down ladders. This had always been a place of echoes: of lofty hallways, passages and countless doorways which, since the building had flipped over, were now to be found high up in the walls, abutting flagstones over which the cassocks of priests had once glided. To provide access to chambers which would otherwise have been unreachable, the Spine had constructed a network of ladders, catwalks and scaffolds. Knotted ropes had been fixed in place to assist those who wished to ascend or descend the underside of stairwells. Rachel had to give the temple assassins credit for their unflinching persistence: they had created a labyrinth of hemp and boards within this crumbling stone shell. The insanity of it all both appalled and amazed her.

The original torture chambers had been extended to encompass the whole of the temple dungeons, a warren of low-ceilinged passages and dank grated cells. Evidently the Spine intended to swell their numbers on a grand scale, for tempering was under way in every dark and rusty corner. Torches blazed, fixed on rock walls. Shadows moved and convulsed behind iron bars. Screams echoed among the stone chambers. An atmosphere of sweat and pain suffused the place, so tangible Rachel could almost taste it.

Culver was having difficulty stifling his grin. 'The same master will temper both of you,' he said. 'He's one of the best, not many of his subjects die.'

'That's reassuring,' Rachel said. 'But where's Dill?'

'Oh, they've already started on *him*,' he said. 'My Cutters brought him up here an hour ago. He'll be nicely doped by now.'

An *hour* ago? Rachel tried to suppress a rising tide of fear. The whole excruciating process took days, sometimes weeks, and yet the earliest stages were often the most dangerous. Many Spine had been broken by the initial drug shock. She picked up her pace.

Pallets had been laid out in cells and passageways alike to accommodate those men or women who were undergoing the tempering procedure. Spine Masters in cowls and leather aprons strung with vials of poison moved silently through the dungeon, overseeing everything, while the needle work was carried out by acolytes. A fat priest in a red cassock murmured prayers while attending to a smouldering censer.

Culver dragged her before this man and said, 'Bless her.'

The priest turned from his censer. Without as much as a glance at Rachel, he pressed his sweaty fingers against her neck, and droned out a long, tedious verse. When he was finished, his bored eyes slid back to the censer.

'Now it's safe for you to bleed,' Culver remarked. 'For a short while, at any rate. The temple's full of cracks, and we can't have any ghosts coming in to sniff around you, can we?' Cradling his crossbow in the crook of his arm, he unloaded the bone-breaker and swapped it for a bolt with a wicked steel tip. Then, confident with this more deadly ordnance, he unlocked Rachel's manacles and shoved her roughly into a nearby cell.

Two pallets had been laid out at opposite ends of the floor. Three acolytes in blood-soaked leathers had already lashed Dill to one of them. They were crouching over him, busy doing something with his hands.

Rachel's heart clenched. But then something about him struck her as strange: the angel's eyes were black as hell. He wasn't scared, he was *furious*, kicking and spitting and gnashing his teeth, twisting and bucking against his restraints. Foam bubbled at the corners of his lips. Arcs of blood spattered the floor around him.

She heard a snap.

Dill roared in pain. The power and harshness of his voice struck an uneasy chord within Rachel. It didn't sound like him at all. Even *here*, in a Spine torture cell, she could hardly reconcile that voice with the angel she knew.

What had they done?

An acolyte muttered something, and then all three stood back. One of them, a small toothless old man, was holding a pair of iron shears. His sleeves were bloody to the elbows. Rachel gave an involuntary gasp.

God's below, they're not tempering him . . .

The Spine Master stood to one side, silently observing the proceedings, his pale hands clasped together in front of his greasy black apron. Hundreds of tiny pockets lined the front of this garment, each containing a vial of poison to be used in the tempering procedure. And yet none of it, it seemed, had been used. He pulled back his cowl, revealing a hollow face which tapered to a hornlike jaw. He looked remarkably frail, more like a skeleton than a man, his aged skin blanched and sagging under watery eyes.

'Why are you doing this to him?' Rachel yelled.

'It is most unusual,' the Master said quietly. His gaze flicked between her and the convulsing angel. 'The dogweed is having a milder effect on him than we expected.'

Dogweed was an intoxicant used to prepare the mind for tempering.

'So you decided to do *that* to him?' she hissed.

'There is evidence of mental schism,' the old man went on. 'His ocular responses are incoherent.'

The dead-eyed Adept who had escorted Rachel spoke up. 'A personality disorder?'

'I think not,' the Master replied. 'Such an illness would already have become evident in his youth. There is no mention of it in our records. Note the eyes . . .' He made a gesture. 'Their colour does not reflect the emotions we would expect to induce through the applied stimuli. It is a paradox, then, for the archon's consciousness is dissociated from his physical form, and yet he is clearly aware.' He thought for a moment. 'A second force of will may therefore be present: a confluence of souls in the blood.'

'He is possessed?' the Adept asked.

'Possibly.'

The angelwine! Rachel now thought she understood what was happening. When Dill had died in the abyss, she herself had used the Poisoner's elixir to resurrect him. The angelwine had contained a distillation of thirteen spirits taken from the Poisoner's victims. Could one of these have taken control of him now, forcing Dill's true consciousness down into the shadows of his own mind?

'This phenomenon must be investigated further,' the Master remarked to the acolytes. 'Remove another one of his fingers.'

'You will not,' Rachel spat.

Without turning, the Master added, 'And tie her down.'

Two of the acolytes came for Rachel, their faces as lifeless and pale as those of drowned men, while the third stooped over Dill again, brandishing his shears. At this Dill screamed and threw his head back, screwing his eyes shut. Culver moved back against the chamber wall. Dill's sword was still lashed to the Adept's belt, but he favoured the crossbow he now trained on her.

They had taken her glass knives, of course. She needed a new weapon.

Gods, I'm going to have to be quick.

She *focused*.

She had only managed this once before, but the Spine technique had already saved their lives in the tunnels under Deep. She had *focused* then to evade the scarred angel Carnival and to find her friend in utter darkness. And now she attempted to use the skill again, to sharpen her senses and speed the flow of blood to her muscles, to quicken her mind. To make herself fast. The other assassins would surely notice the momentary flicker of her eyes, and realize what she was trying to do. But then they also knew that she was untempered and therefore incapable of such a feat.

Their presumptions saved her life.

Culver hesitated for an instant before shooting his crossbow, but by then it was already too late.

Time stretched for Rachel. She was no longer breathing. She felt a sudden cool rush across her skin and then the deep, slow thump of her heart. At the edge of her vision the acolytes had stopped moving, as though the air had frozen around them. She could afford to ignore them for now. She considered the space between Culver and herself, glittering with suspended dust particles, and then she studied the glint at the tip of the man's crossbow bolt. Muscles were now bunching in his shoulders and neck; his irises dilated a fraction. His finger tightened around the weapon's trigger. She saw the latch rise, the bowstring and bastard strings quiver. A puff of dust from the strings, and the bolt flew forward out of its track.

Now she moved.

The pain of forcing her muscles to move at such reckless speeds wouldn't reach her for many heartbeats. She watched the bolt fly towards her, and snatched it out of the air. Then she leapt and drove the shaft up under Culver's jaw, forcing the tip into his brain.

She turned her head.

Behind her, the Adept was already dead. He would crumple to the floor in a moment. She had time to decide her next move. Could she take his crossbow and reload it while focused? Shoot it again? Doubtful. The weapon was too heavy to be handled at such speeds. She might break her arms in the attempt. Instead she ripped the bolt back out of the assassin's jaw and spun a kick towards the nearest acolyte. This man had not been combat-trained; his neck broke before he knew he had been murdered. The momentum of Rachel's kick carried her around. She went with it, crouching as she controlled the spin, moving her body to where she needed it to be. A gut stab with the bolt finished the second acolyte, but the shaft snapped in her hand.

Too fast.

Two opponents left. She had time.

But Rachel had underestimated the Master. She did not see his dagger until it flashed close to her face. She moved, but not fast enough to stop the blade nicking her shoulder. The wound would begin to bleed soon. The pain would arrive much later. Right now, the old man was focusing, moving at a speed equivalent to hers. Dust roiled sluggishly around him, disturbed by his blow.

He lunged.

Rachel was unarmed. She turned into him, seizing his arm, and drove her elbow into his chest. Vials of poison shattered in his apron. Now she dragged him round with her, throwing him off balance. Droplets of poison and fragments of glass spun away from him, all sparkling. She felt a jerk as his humerus popped out of his shoulder, then she turned him against the wall. *Not too hard.* She knew she had to judge the manoeuvre precisely. He was heavy; too much force and she would injure herself. The Spine Master had the advantage of experience, yet his old bones would break more easily. The increased speed that came with focus would work against him during such physical combat. He knew enough not to resist, but to turn along with Rachel – yet he had neglected to consider his proximity to the wall. His face left a bloody smear on the bare rock.

She had underestimated him, but not by much.

One acolyte left: the old man with the shears. Rachel turned to face him.

But then the cost of her exertions caught up with her. Her body could no longer continue to function at such an unnatural speed. It began to shut down. Time slowed for Rachel, and with it her heart began to quicken, and quicken more. A thundering pain rose in her chest. She fell to her knees, shuddering in agony as her muscles paid the price she had exacted from them. Her limbs burned, turned as limp and useless as sleeves of skin. Her head swam. She inhaled great gulps of rank dungeon air.

The old acolyte gaped at the dead assassin next to him. Then he stared at Rachel, then at the Spine Master, still sliding down the torture room wall. To his eyes, the battle must have been little more than a blur.

'You ghilled them?' he said, his toothless maw slurring. 'How did you ghill them?'

Had he genuinely never seen a Spine focus before?

Rachel gasped. She struggled to move, but found the effort beyond her, and collapsed instead. Drool trickled from her slack lips. 'I . . .'

'Stay where you are,' the acolyte said. 'I summon the Masters.' He hurried for the door.

Rachel balled her fists and tried to crawl. One lousy acolyte. He would spoil everything she'd achieved. She managed to drag herself two feet across the torture room, and then slumped back down in agonized exhaustion.

The acolyte was in too much of a rush. On a floor slick with poison and blood, he slipped, not badly enough to make him fall, but enough to make him stagger. From somewhere Rachel found a last reserve of energy. Yelling, she lashed out a kick. Her boot struck him in the shin – a feeble blow, but strong enough to unbalance her opponent. The man fell backwards, arms flailing, and his head struck the floor with a crack. His shears clattered away into the shadows. Rachel could hardly believe it. She forced herself to move, heaving her limp body across the wet floor towards the fallen man. The acolyte groaned. Then, dazed but unharmed, he tried to stand.

But Rachel had already reached him. She dragged herself halfway onto his chest.

'Wha?' The Spine torturer seemed confused. 'Let go of me. You stay.'

Rachel's lungs burned. The torture room whirled around her. She couldn't speak, and she lacked the strength to pin him down effectively. Her fingers scrabbled on the floor for something to use as a weapon. His shears? Too far away. There was nothing but fragments of broken glass and puddles of greasy liquid.

Poison?

She forced her wet fingers into his mouth, and heard him gag. Then she scooped up more poison and pressed it into his eyes. He struggled and bucked against her, crying out in agony. Again Rachel slid her hand across the floor, soaking her palm, and then smeared the toxic liquid across his lips, into his gums.

The whole world spun. Screams resounded through the torture chamber. Rachel couldn't tell if they were nearby or from far away. She felt the acolyte convulse one last time beneath her, before he finally went still.

When the pain passed at last, Rachel staggered to her feet. She retrieved the Spine Master's dagger and cut Dill's bonds. He'd had his eyes closed the whole time, but when he opened them she saw that they were still black with rage. Rachel didn't recognize who she was looking at.

The angel sneered, then lifted his mutilated hand and ran it roughly down the side of her face. 'Aren't you a pretty one?' he said.

6

†he ROtSWARD

Drawn from their houses by the sound of disaster, a crowd of fisher-folk had gathered in the lane beside the wreckage of the Widow's Hook. A few eager men were already picking through the damp piles of timbers, mud bricks and shingles, perhaps searching for valuables or survivors. Another small group stood muttering around the pile of Spine corpses which Anchor had dragged clear of the broth shop. But most of them, like Jack Caulker himself, waited in a breathless circle around John Anchor and stared up into the fog above.

The tethered man was pulling more and more of his huge rope out of the sky. Down and down it came, yards and then miles of it, until the lane was buried under coils of hemp and Caulker began to wonder if the stranger had been tethered to the goddess Ayen herself.

Anchor worked patiently, humming a tune, as if he'd done this a thousand times before. And still there seemed no end to that monstrous line. The giant drew down length after length of rope, flinging great coils of it onto the ground around him. Some of the hemp now appeared to be sodden and rotten, rimed with salt, and brought with it the heavy odour of brine. The crowd edged back-wards, uneasy. Caulker waited.

And waited . . .

. . . until the sky above Sandport began to grow dark. Something vast was descending over the town.

Now even those folks who had been eagerly sifting through the rubble stopped and peered up into the growing gloom. The stench of salt became acrid, like the odour from shrunken rock pools and rotting kelp. Caulker heard a warning bell clang wildly somewhere down near the docks, followed by another, and then yet another. Apparently Sandport's lookouts had spied something in the skies above their heads.

The cut-throat still could not spot any details in the unnatural darkness – a pall which now stretched far beyond both ends of the fog-veiled lane, like a thundercloud – but he sensed the air around him stir. Some of the fisherfolk let out cries of alarm, and suddenly those standing on the collapsed broth shop began to clamber hurriedly down from among the debris.

Caulker thought he heard noises far above, a sound which at first reminded him of squawking gulls. But then, as the giant continued to drag down his mighty rope, the cacophony grew louder and more distinct. Caulker realized he was hearing the wails and sobs of people: lots of them, some close by, others more distant; a chorus of suffering and despair which drifted down from the grey air and filled the streets of Sandport.

A broad grin spread across John Anchor's face. He began to pull with renewed vigour at his tether. His humming grew louder, as if he sought to drown out the cries of woe overhead. The sky darkened further, the stench of brine brought tears to the eyes. Caulker thought he caught a glimpse of something in the grey gloom overhead – something swaying. But before he could identify the object, it vanished again, swallowed by shifting mists. The fisherfolk were yelling in dismay now, backing away from the giant and his rope, their gazes still pinned on the lowering heavens.

Then Caulker finally saw what the stranger was dragging down from the skies, and his blood froze in his veins.

Out of the fog descended a great rope-tangled skeleton of wood. Like the rigging of an upended fleet of ships, the clutter of masts and yards formed a rude thicket of indeterminable width, breadth and height. Rotting, salt-furred timbers sweated moisture. Seaweed hung from dripping lines. As Anchor continued to drag the thing down, more and more of the poles and spars appeared amid the fog, until they totally filled the skies over Sandport. Yet Caulker realized that this scaffold formed only the lowest fraction of a far bigger vessel. The shadow of something solid and phenomenally huge still loomed in the mists above.

It had to be an airship.

Finally one of the longest masts punctured the rooftop of a nearby building, and the whole construction jerked to a halt.

Caulker's eyes widened. Among the rigging hung men and women and angels: a disparate army of warriors, suspended by ropes looped around their necks. Some were struggling and clawing at their nooses, their blue-black faces contorted in hideous anguish; others simply hung limp and moaned or wept. All wore corroded armour of unusual design; it was as though each suit had been forged in some different foreign land. Overhead, a knight in red rusted half-plate swung back and forth from a stout travis, gibbering and tugging at his noose, while above and to the left of him, a thin dark-skinned angel in a tattered coat of mail gazed up into the heavens from the end of its own rope. This pitiful creature had only one wing. Countless others depended from the yards around them, ranks of warriors and archons sheathed in rotting metal: in spoiled cuirasses, bucklers and mouldering brigandines, queer winged armets or dull half-helms. Steel ground against steel, and ropes creaked on timbers beneath the mournful sobbing.

John Anchor flexed his shoulders and let out a long sigh. He grumbled, 'Cospinol's ship is very heavy.' And then he laughed suddenly. 'One day I find a nice girl to give me a massage.'

Caulker dragged his gaze from the upended rigging and stared at the big man. 'Who are they?'

The giant shrugged. 'Soldiers, angels, demons.' He stomped a foot down on the rope, pinning it to the ground. 'Noisy crowd, eh? Always complaining and moaning. Unhappy because they are dead but cannot go to Hell.' He grinned and tipped his head at the Spine corpses he had pulled from the rubble. 'Now these white folks will come aboard. More nastiness for all. More complaining.'

'They're dead?' Caulker asked with a hesitant nod to the legions above, still unable to comprehend this hellish vision. 'But they're moaning . . . *screaming.*'

'Dead,' the other man said, 'but not . . . uh, not at peace. Souls still in this world, in Cospinol and inside me.' He slammed his huge belly. 'Very noisy.'

A terrible thought struck the cut-throat. 'You killed them?' he asked. 'All of them?'

Anchor looked uncomfortable. 'It is heavy,' he muttered, as if that somehow answered the cut-throat's question. Then he withdrew the reed from his pocket and blew another soundless note from it.

John Anchor's impossible skyship – if that was indeed what it was, for there had to be ten thousand interconnected beams in that scaffold overhead – had held the crowd enthralled, pinned by their own fears, but now the tiny red sprites which poured out of the fog above proved too much for them. The fisherfolk fled screaming. Caulker had a mind to run after them, but he fought this desire. He had not shied from these creatures before, and would not do so now. Let the river-sifters of Sandport cower behind their mud walls, but Jack Caulker had been a great salt sailor once, not a man to flee from skyships or crustaceans, and his instincts told him now that Anchor posed no threat. The

Adamantine Man hunted an angel. And he still carried a fortune in pearls.

Clicking and chittering, the crabs came out of the fog and scuttled down the greasy rigging. Millions of them converged on the giant's rope and then poured down it. When they reached the ground, they swept over the mounds of coiled hemp like a wave of blood towards the dead assassins.

'Six more souls for Cospinol,' Anchor grumbled. 'Six more pearls for his hoard.'

The cut-throat stood stock-still as the chitinous tide surged over his boots. 'Cospinol?' he ventured.

'My master.' Anchor tipped his head back. 'God of Brine and Fog, Pearlmaker and Pirate in Heaven. Ayen's Shipwright and Captain of the *Rotsward*. So many names, eh?' Then he grinned and lowered his voice conspiratorially. 'Crusty old bastard thinks them up himself and pays me to preach the word, but don't say this to anyone.'

The crabs now covered the dead assassins in a seething, bubbling mound. Red claws and legs murmured like hookfleas in a carcass. Caulker swallowed and turned away. 'Then this . . . thing is his *ship*?'

'The *Rotsward*?' Anchor said. 'Yes, it is his skyship. Used to be called the *Cleaver*, and before that the *Fist*, and once even the *Sally Broom*, after a woman.' The giant shook his head. 'Good pretty name, the *Sally*. I liked that name, but Cospinol is fickle. Never happy, always complaining. You think my real name is John Anchor? Ha! The name amuses Cospinol. This god lacks the wit to be subtle.'

Now a corpse-sized lump detached itself from the mass of crabs and slid over the uneven coils of hemp towards Anchor. When it neared the giant's feet, it rose, as if the dead body amid those crustaceans had been resurrected and was standing up of its own accord. Horrified, Caulker watched as the crab-enshrouded figure climbed up the harness on the giant's back and began to pull itself up the rope.

Anchor beamed at the cut-throat. 'You like crab?'

'I used to,' Caulker replied flatly.

'I like' – the big man clapped his hands together – 'Pandemerian crab salad with cuttlefish and sea jellies. Good for the heart, you know? Best food for sailors. You are a seaman, yes?'

'I was.'

By now the first red-covered figure had disappeared into the mist overhead, and a second clump of crabs had parted from the teeming pile and was inching closer to the giant.

'Ha!' Anchor exclaimed. 'I recognized you for a sailor. You have a stout heart. You know this land well?'

Caulker felt increasingly ill, but he managed a nod.

'Then you will help me find my quarry. My master's witchsphere lies to him, so he does not trust it to guide him now. We pay well for an honest guide. Many pearls . . . or salt. Salt we have in abundance.'

'Witchsphere?'

'Yes. You have them here? Evil things, always lying. This one has nine Mesmerist hags inside, so it never agrees with itself.' With a hideous rustling sound, the second red corpse stood and began to climb up the rope to the gallows waiting for it overhead. 'You will be my guide?' Anchor persisted.

A witchsphere? Caulker had no idea what Anchor was talking about. Yet evidently the big man needed help. No doubt he had also noticed the lack of any other would-be assistants in the lane outside the broth shop he'd just destroyed. Despite himself, Caulker moistened his lips and said, 'First let me see these pearls.'

Anchor retrieved the pouch from his pocket, and then rummaged inside it. He pulled out a tiny bead, sniffed it, then shook his head and dropped the thing back into the bag. Then he lifted out another, sniffed it again, and nodded. 'This is a good one,' he said, extending his arm to the cut-throat. 'In Oxos this would buy the death of a snake woman. In Pandemeria it might buy a blood-ship. Take it, but be careful, it is fragile.'

Caulker accepted the jewel. It was not actually a pearl as he had hoped, but rather a similar-sized bead made from glass. He held it up between two fingers and studied it. Intricate lines and whorls had been etched into the surface, and there seemed to be something glimmering inside: a weak, uneasy light.

'It is the soul of a powerful angel,' Anchor said. 'The archon once named Malleus Trench, brother of Silister who is Hasp's champion in Hell. Very dangerous warrior – but the soul is good for you, I think. You can eat it, yes? Make you big and strong like me.'

The cut-throat had seen enough of the world to recognize a scam when he saw one. This bauble was nothing more than glass, the light inside merely a trick of the engraving. He frowned. 'Really, my friend,' he said with a sigh, 'you'll have to do better than this.' With a snap of his fingers, he flicked the worthless trinket away.

The glass bead flew into the rubble of the Widow's Hook, and shattered.

A sudden roar compressed the air like a detonation. Caulker was thrown to the ground, his thoughts tumbling around him. He glimpsed shingles flying from the surrounding roofs, dust slough-ing skywards, shadows and blood-red crabs rippling at the edges of his vision. An explosion? Had Cospinol's skyship launched an attack? Overhead, the hanging warriors shook and gibbered and shrieked in their gins. Had John Anchor caused that unholy ruckus himself in some way?

But no, amidst the dust clouds, Caulker now saw a winged apparition, the spectre of an enormous battle-archon. Daylight bled through its heavy iron-plate armour and winged helmet. It howled, lifted a black blade as tall as a man, and brought it down upon the tethered giant.

Anchor stepped aside, avoiding the strike. His fists blurred as he launched a flurry of punches at the spectre's head and neck, but his opponent merely laughed. Anchor's hands had passed clean through the archon as though through smoke.

The archon's great sword burst apart like a cloud of black flies, but then re-formed and clove through the dust once more. Anchor was hard-pressed to avoid it. Yet avoid it he did, as purposefully as if it was a real blade. Could a ghost sword cause the giant harm?

Caulker watched in horror and fascination as Anchor lashed out again. For a heartbeat the big man's hand seemed to close upon the apparition's wrist and *grip* it, but then his hold on the creature dissolved and the archon was free once more. It raised its massive sword again . . .

. . . and screamed as daylight pierced its armour like flames through parchment. The battle-archon faded. A final terrible shriek resounded among the mud-brick houses, and then nothing remained but dust.

The big man stood motionless for a long moment. Then he examined his fist and sucked at a bleeding knuckle. 'The dead are tricky opponents,' he said to Caulker. 'It is like fighting a memory, or a nightmare. Not easy. We are lucky it is not night-time. Shades can only survive for a short time in daylight.'

He was smiling now. Something in that smile warned Caulker, for the twist of those black lips evinced none of Anchor's previous mirth.

'My friend,' the giant said ruefully, 'you have now sent the poor angel to join his ancestors in Hell.' He swept his gaze across the pile of mud and timbers. 'A door to the Maze will soon open there. Hell is coming now, yes? So we must go.' He sighed and squeezed the nape of his neck, then shrugged. 'Iril is Iril, and we do not interfere. But now you have a problem, I think. You owe me an expensive soul. You are – what is the word – undoubted to me.'

Caulker rose stiffly. 'Indebted,' he said.

'Good. Yes, this is what I mean. But come, let's talk more of this scarred angel and her companions. I will buy lunch: hearty food for sailors such as us. Crab salad, I think, with chowder and strong fishbeer.' He slapped his huge belly. 'You can recommend a good quiet place? A nice broth shop where we can speak?'

The cut-throat thought of all those restaurants, taverns and broth shops in the better part of town: the many establishments from which he'd been ejected for filching and cursing and fist-fighting over the years. And then he lifted his eyes from the giant, up the monstrous rope, past the seething red crabs and the climbing form of yet another dead assassin, to the creaking, gabbling wooden skyship which filled the heavens over Sandport.

'One or two places spring to mind,' he said.

7

The worst assassin

'Who *are* you?' she asked.

The angel's head lolled drunkenly, and Rachel was answered only with a mocking red grin. Dill had bitten his tongue during his torture. Except . . . this person wasn't Dill, she reminded herself. He leered at her through the young angel's eyes, but there was nothing in that savage expression which belonged to the friend she formerly knew.

Rachel blamed herself. She had given him angelwine, filled him with a cocktail of other souls which had now bubbled to the surface. But if Dill was still in there, she would pull him back.

'I asked you a question.'

The angel sniggered and spat a gob of blood on the floor. 'I think I'm intoxicated by your beauty,' he slurred. 'Or is it from the pain? I've not felt my nerves burn like this for a thousand years.' His tongue lolled over his teeth. 'It's quite something.' He tried to rise from the pallet, then collapsed back again.

'It's the dogweed they've given you,' Rachel said. 'Try to concentrate. Look at me. Who are you?'

'Who am I?' He fumbled for her breast, but she pushed him away. 'Who am I, you ask? Gods . . . who *am* I? I'm the scourge of every filthy Mesmerist? My message! Where am I?'

'You're in a Spine torture cell in the temple. You've been drugged.'

'Ohhhhh . . .' He shook his head. 'That means nothing to me. Come here, woman.' His bloody hands reached for her.

She slapped him away again. *This is useless.* She needed him lucid and able to walk without stumbling if they were going to get out of here alive. Rachel got up and went over to where the corpse of the Spine Master lay crumpled against the wall. Most of the poisons in the old man's apron had been smashed during their fight, but she still searched through them thoroughly. There had to be something she could use to bring the angel round. The Spine employed an extensive array of drugs during the tempering process, and not all of them were designed to disorientate and confuse the victim.

When she found the tiny green vial intact, she almost kissed it.

'Take this,' she said, trying to place the bottle in his hand. 'Just a sip.'

He waved his arms wildly in protest, and then gave her another wet grin.

She hissed. 'Open your mouth.'

'Open yours, sweetling.'

Rachel squeezed the angel's jaw hard, forgetting for the moment that the jaw did not belong to the person in the cell with her, and tipped a little of the clear liquid down his throat.

'Rrrrrr.' He screwed up his face and spat.

'There,' Rachel said. 'Now we might be able to have a proper conversation.'

She could see the drug working. The angel convulsed once, then gagged, then he sat up. He stared hard at her for a few moments, his black eyes full of loathing, then said, 'You'll pay for that.'

'I rather think you'll thank me for it. Who are you?'

'None of your damn business. Where is this place?'

'Answer my question and I'll answer yours.'

He snorted, but then he noticed the five Spine corpses strewn around the chamber and stiffened. Now he glanced back at her, warily. 'I am Silister Trench,' he said.

Trench? It was an unusual name, and Rachel did not think she'd heard it in Deepgate before. 'That's a start,' she said. 'There are a hundred things I need to ask you, Trench, but this is not the place to do it. I'll make this simple: if you value that body you're currently occupying as much as I do, then you'll come with me now. There are more assassins in this place than I can count, and they all want to stick needles and other pieces of metal into you.'

'And who are *you*?' he asked.

'I'm the worst of them.'

Leaving the temple was surprisingly easy, for there were so many newly tempered acolytes that none of them had yet learned who anybody else was. In the Spine leathers she stole from a supply room, Rachel looked like any other Adept. She was allowed to pass unchallenged. A cassock she snatched from one of the old priests' quarters served to cover the angel's blood-caked wings and his disfigured hands. No one thought to question an Adept leading a hunchbacked old priest out into the city. Of late the Spine had taken to travelling with priests for holy protection at night.

Dusk was barely upon them, but the roiling smoke clouds overhead brought darkness early to Deepgate. Rachel hesitated at the temple exit. The sky fumed black and crimson, and she could see yellow and green chemical fires burning in the east, sending torrents of silver sparks up from the Scythe. The sound of explosions rumbled over the city. Red mist veiled the ruins of Bridgeview and Lilley, and shadows moved silently among the chains.

The consciousness inside Dill tried to move the young angel's wings, and let out a gasp of agony. 'My flesh is bruised and raw,' he complained. 'My wings . . . Your ignorant assassins have damaged me.' The Spine chain-and-burr cuffs had bitten deeply into the muscles and tendons behind his shoulders.

'They're not *your* wings,' Rachel muttered as she stared at the burning city. Deepgate teemed with ghosts from the abyss, countless thousands of them. Shades capered among the twisted metal and rubble like wisps of living darkness. She half-heard sighs and shouts and cruel laughter: intangible voices hiding among the crack and rumble of stone, the creaking chains, and the roaring fires. Would that she had a real priest with her now. A holy man might keep Iril's shades at bay, protect them against the madness of the abyss. These phantasms would cajole and torment the pair of them.

And worse?

If she believed the priests' tales, then yes – much worse. The Church of Ulcis had gone to great lengths to protect Deepgate against Iril's influence. Yet here it was in the streets before her, undiluted and dangerous.

She could turn around and go back into the temple, a crumbling hive full of Spine assassins who might well have discovered her escape by now, or she could set off into that uncertainty stretching before her.

'Let's go,' she said.

8

✝o ask a god
one question

Gulliver Fank, proprietor and pot boss of the Canny Crab in Red
Menace Street, seemed decidedly reluctant to admit Anchor and
Caulker into his establishment.

'You have no tables?' the cut-throat asked again. 'None at all?
Looks quiet enough inside.'

Fank stood and fidgeted in the doorway of his shop. A rangy
old man with a loose neck and spotted hands, he worried at a
wooden ladle with a cloth while he spoke. 'Alas, no,' he said.
'Fully reserved this morning, sirs. It's the fog, I suppose.'

Caulker raised an eyebrow. 'The fog?'

Fank shrugged. He seemed determined to avoid looking at
John Anchor, or at the massive rope which struck skywards from
the big man's harness. 'The fog always brings more customers.
You know how it is . . . the sailors don't sail, civilian airships stay
grounded. Everyone's stuck in town, so our business picks up.'

'Well they ain't stuck in your place,' Caulker persisted, peering
over the other man's shoulder at the empty tables and chairs. He
was enjoying this. That bastard Fank had thrown him out on his
arse on more than one occasion and banned him the last time.
All for pilfering a copper-double tip from one of his tables. 'We
could take a seat, and move if anybody turns up,' he said amiably.

Fank failed to suppress a wince. 'I really am most terribly sorry, sirs. It is simply not possible.'

Anchor stood behind the cut-throat with his huge arms folded across his harness and a wide grin on his face. His eyes gleamed with mischief. 'Always this same problem for me,' he boomed. 'Never can find a table in good broth shops. Is my colour, yes? You don't like the dark skin?'

'Gods, no,' Fank said quickly. 'It's not that at all.' He rubbed briskly at his ladle, still avoiding the other man's eye. 'We have a . . . uh, policy regarding patrons bringing rope inside the shop.'

'Ah!' Anchor cried.

'Rope?' Caulker asked. 'Since when did you have a policy about rope?'

'Since this morning,' Fank admitted.

The giant smacked his hands together. 'No matter,' he said. 'Bring a table outside. We will sit in the lane. Two bowls of chowder, hot beans and bread, crab salad, cold fishbeers.'

Fank glanced up into the heavens, then seemed to shrink. 'Yes, yes,' he said. 'Chowder, beans, bread, and . . . yes, of course.'

Once the cut-throat and his guest had installed themselves at the hastily positioned table and had taken their first sips of fishbeer, Anchor said, 'Now, my friend, you are telling me that the scarred angel did not ever arrive in this town?'

'People would have noticed,' Caulker said evenly. 'Not much goes on in Sandport without the whole town finding out about it. When any decent-looking woman turns up, they post a notice on the board outside the Mudlark. And you're talking about an angel here, a witch who drinks the blood of innocents at darkmoon. Trust me, tongues would wag.'

He took another sip and continued, 'But she can't be far away. The Spine caught Carnival's two friends in Olirind Meer's tavern a couple of weeks ago, the same pair who originally left Deepgate with her. A temple warship destroyed half the building with a gas bomb just to get to them.'

'These friends . . . Where are they now?'

'The Spine took them back to Deepgate for tempering. They'll be locked in a temple torture cell by now.'

'Deepgate?' Anchor beamed. 'I had planned to make visit there also. There is a small thing I must do there for Cospinol.' He drained his tankard. 'So we go to the chained city and speak to Carnival's two friends. Maybe they know where she is hiding.'

Caulker hesitated. He didn't want to march into Deepgate if he could help it, not with all those poison fires burning out of control and the Spine rounding everybody up for tempering – not to mention all those ghosts which had taken to haunting the place at night. It would be better if he could dispatch Anchor somewhere out in the Deadsands. There were many dangers in that desolate wasteland, places where an unwary traveller might find himself in serious trouble. One such location had already sprung to mind.

Fank arrived with the meal. He hurriedly set a bowl of broth and salad upon the table, then disappeared back inside

'It might already be too late to speak to her friends,' Caulker said truthfully, eyeing his chowder. 'We don't know what the Spine have done to them. I reckon Carnival is holed up in the Deadsands somewhere, out of sight but still near enough to her prey.' More likely the angel had flown hundreds of leagues away by now, but he wasn't going to suggest this to Anchor, not when the big man had on him a pouch of genuine soul-infused jewels.

'The Deadsands? This is the desert between here and Deepgate?'

Caulker nodded.

'Good. We walk to Deepgate through the desert, all the time looking for Carnival. Killing two boars with one stone, yes?'

'Birds,' Caulker corrected. 'Two *birds* with one stone.'

Anchor gave him a puzzled look. 'Not in the Riot Coast. Tell me, Jack, you know these Deadsands well?'

'As well as any other man.' This at least was true: Jack Caulker had spent enough time robbing merchants in his youth to know all the old bandit trails and boltholes well enough. He wasn't overly fond of the sand itself, but could find his way between the occasional water springs if need be. 'Why are you hunting her, anyway?' He glanced up into the fog and then lowered his voice. 'What does your god want with *her*?'

The big man beamed. 'No need to whisper, friend. Cospinol hears everything I hear. But he never usually pays much attention, so it is no problem. My master wants this angel because she drank his brother, Ulcis.'

Caulker sputtered into his broth. '*Drank* him?'

'Yes, drank. Like a cheese.'

The cut-throat frowned. He was about to ask Anchor to expound, but then thought better of it.

The other man gave a roar of laughter, then slammed his empty tankard down on the table, rocking the bowls of chowder. 'She slaughtered half his army then drank him. What a feat! No wonder Cospinol seeks her. Her blood contains many souls.'

The massive rope on Anchor's back thrummed. The giant paused, his ear cocked towards the sound, and then leaned close to Caulker and whispered, 'He says I talk too much.'

'He's listening to us now?'

'Yes, you want to ask him a question? He will answer one question for you. Cospinol knows many things: the tides, the stars, why the moon circles the earth. He understands the hearts of men and why his mother, the goddess Ayen, closed the gates of Heaven. And he knows what the Mesmerists are planning. Sometimes he even knows things that have not yet happened, but mostly he's wrong about those.'

'Um . . .' Caulker blinked. What question to ask of a god?

He might not get a chance like this ever again. 'Well . . .' he said, thinking hard. 'Well, I suppose . . .' He rattled his fingers on the table. 'All right, then, how and when will I die?'

The rope trembled again. Caulker thought he heard distant shrieks and manic laughter from high up in the fog; he sank deeper into his chair. The question had been the first thing to come into his mind, but now he wasn't sure he really wanted to know the answer.

Anchor listened for a moment, then laughed heartily. 'Cospinol doesn't know the answer to this. Now he's angry. He says you asked the wrong question.'

Caulker felt somewhat relieved. 'Can I ask him something else?'

'No.' The big man bent forward again. 'Listen, friend Jack. You want to live a long time, yes?' He waited until the other man nodded. 'Good. I understand such a desire. Me, I have lived longer than any man on this world – longer even than this scarred angel I hunt. It is my reward for collecting souls for Cospinol,' he jerked a thumb upwards. 'But these days there are so many bad men. The world is rotten like an orange. Most up there are black-hearts, scoundrels and thieves. Wicked wicked souls. He shook his head, and his tone became serious. 'Cospinol knows I won't eat bad souls, so he feeds me only the good ones. Gives me more strength to pull his ship, you understand?'

Caulker nodded.

'But if I am to eat any souls, I must then kill *good* men.' He gave a deep and weary sigh. 'And I do not like to do this. I do not like it at all. I want to be free of this harness . . . this skyship. Is very heavy now. I want go back to the Riot Coast, make a farm and marry a woman.' At this, his eyes became a little distant, and he smiled sadly. 'So this one I hunt . . . this Carnival, very strong angel. The blood of a god in her veins. And enough souls to let Cospinol leave the *Rotsward* and walk free under Ayen's sun.'

'And if Cospinol is freed, then you are too?'

'This is the truth.' Anchor extended his big black hand. 'So we make deal? You lead me through this desert to Deepgate, help me find the one called Carnival, and I forget the soul you owe me. We become good friends. Agreed?'

What choice did the cut-throat have? He was indebted to a man who'd killed six Spine Adepts with his bare hands, and then brought a building down on top of them all. Caulker would have to lure Anchor into a trap before he could steal his treasure, yet even that prospect was beginning to lose its allure. If this floating god, Cospinol, really heard and saw everything, he might not look favourably upon the murder of his servant – not to mention his only means of locomotion.

Caulker shook Anchor's hand.

Gulliver Fank appeared and cleared away the bowls, stacking them against his chest, while still studiously keeping his eyes averted from the giant's rope. 'Can I get you anything else, sirs?' he muttered. 'No? I imagine you'll be keen to get on your way. May I say what a pleasure it has been to have you both here?'

'How much is the price for this meal?' Anchor asked.

'Two doubles, sir.'

'I have no coin,' Anchor said. 'You accept salt, yes? Good Riot Coast salt?' He scraped back his stool and rose, flexing his huge shoulders, then began to drag down his rope from the sky. 'It is up here somewhere.'

'No!' the broth-shop boss squawked. He waved his free hand frantically while clutching the tower of bowls with his other. 'I mean . . . please accept the meal for free – on the house, no charge. Really, it's the least I can do!'

Anchor grinned. 'Ah!' he exclaimed. 'Everywhere I find the same generosity! He is a good man this one, Jack Caulker. Without men like this I would go hungry for sure.' His huge chest heaved with laughter. 'Now I must make piss. Where is the privy?'

'Broken, sir,' Fank said. 'The drain is blocked.'

The giant's brow furrowed. 'Same problem everywhere.' He swept an arm to indicate the world at large. 'Bad plumbing, always bad plumbing. Same on Cog Island and the Merian Ports, Coreollis and Oxos. All the drains blocked. One day I find a plumbing man and ask him why this happens.'

Caulker couldn't decide if the giant was serious or not.

The broth-shop proprietor brightened a little. 'You could try the facilities at the Cockle Scunny,' he said, pointing down the lane and nodding eagerly. 'That place on the corner. I know the gentleman who runs it quite well, and he's just had his pipes overhauled. I'm sure he won't mind if you make use of them.'

'So be it,' Anchor said, turning to Caulker. 'Come, my friend, we go now.' He slapped his hands together and flashed his broad smile. 'I make piss, and then we go to kill an angel.'

9

ICARATES

Silister Trench, the soul in possession of Dill's body, remained surly and irritable during their trek from the temple, flapping his injured wings occasionally and moaning about the incessant pain in his shoulders. Rachel ignored him. She had other things to worry about. It was dark, they were in the Warrens, and the entire district was seething with the dead. Phantasms crawled through the shadows of derelict tenements all around them, half-seen figures in queer dark raiment. The air felt damp and had a vague red tinge to it, as though a fog of blood had settled upon the city. Faint voices drifted from the empty shells of buildings like the last bounce of an echo, but Rachel could not hear their words clearly. Sometimes she thought she heard growling, and occasionally sobbing.

A canopy of smoke blanketed the sky, its underbelly lit by colourful fires from the industrial districts. Angry red, yellow and black streaks fumed and tumbled between the towering silhouettes of tenement blocks. Now and then a concussion rang out, shaking ash from the chains on which the buildings were suspended. The air reeked of sulphur and fuel, and other bitter chemicals Rachel couldn't identify. She tried not to breathe in deeply, but her lungs soon began to sting.

They trudged up Lye Street, where the crumpled remains of

Barraby's watchtower stood silent and shuttered at the top of the hill, stark against the turbulent sky; then they turned left onto the narrow lanes around Farrow Wynd, scaling a heap of rubble and shattered barrels blocking Candlemaker Row. To the north, blue and green lights flashed across the heavens, followed by an upwards rush of dazzling silver stars, and moments later Rachel heard the boom and crackle of another poison cache exploding.

'What is this infernal labyrinth?' Trench asked.

'You don't remember?'

'Why should I remember?' he snapped. 'I've never been here before.'

'It's the Workers' Warrens,' she explained, but his ignorance didn't surprise her. The Master Poisoner, Devon, had taken souls for his elixir from all over the city. If this particular displaced soul had come from a noble family, he would scarcely have ever ventured down here. She watched him scowling up at the heavens, where the sky still churned with ash and smoke and tiny smouldering particles. Black shapes flitted through the widespread destruction around them.

Something odd then occurred to Rachel. Were the ghosts actually keeping their distance from them?

Deepgate's priests had long regarded phantasms as dangerous, there having been too many stories of citizens who had been possessed or driven to madness by such spectres. Yet these spectres seemed content to leave Rachel and Trench alone. She spied them constantly out of the corner of her eye, and heard their strange whispered chatter, but so far they had not ventured close.

Why?

Eventually the pair reached a granite and iron-link bridge which spanned a gap of thirty yards between Ivygarths in the north and Summergarden to the south. Flint pendulum houses surrounded them at all heights, all hanging cradled within a confusion of metal strung ropes below two massive foundation chains. A hard white deposit crusted everything; it creaked beneath their boots and formed pale clumps on the chains themselves. Rachel could almost imagine she was wandering through a winter forest. To the east of the bridge, a vast section of the city had fallen entirely from its foundation chains and sloped away into the red haze, suspended now only by the thinnest lacework of iron and cracked sapperbane. This, she knew, was the Taptack Acres, a district of Summergarden where tenements had been heaped one upon the other to house factory workers. On the opposite side, the nearest pendulum house hung directly from one of the links that still supported the bulk of this quarter. It was a dwelling of a style common among the industrial elite: in each case a vulgar mass of flint which tapered towards the top like a teardrop. Thin steel-link bridges connected the master's and the servants' separate doors to a network of intervening walkways which disappeared off into the gloom.

By now Trench was walking several yards ahead of Rachel, his cassock starkly black against the pale surroundings. Still grumbling and cursing to himself, he remained heedless of his environment – until a crossbow bolt thudded into the ground just two inches from his feet, and stopped him dead.

They were suddenly there among the pendulum houses: twenty or more assassins that Rachel could see, and only the gods knew how many more she couldn't yet spot. The crossbow, that weapon of choice for Spine, was naturally much in evidence.

How did they manage to get ahead of us?

Rachel cursed herself for not pushing on faster. The route they had been forced to take through the city had been tortuous, unfamiliar to her, yet the Spine themselves would be well acquainted with the extent of Deepgate's destruction. Now this exposed bridge made a perfect place for an ambush. If she tried to run, they would shoot her down before she covered two yards, and there was no chance of close combat here either. Resistance would only lead to their slaughter, but that may have been what the Spine intended all along.

A male voice called down, 'You have reached a place of redemption, Rachel Hael. Your journey ends here.'

She spotted her interlocutor as one of four Spine perched on the roof of the nearest pendulum house, sighting his weapon at her. Rachel braced herself, her muscles still weary from the strain she had put them under during that fight earlier in the temple. She doubted she'd be able to focus a second time quite so soon, and this time, anyway, the Spine would know what to expect. Nevertheless, she had little choice, and mentally she prepared herself.

A gust of air brushed her cheek, as though something had moved quickly through the air nearby. Somewhere far below, a chain creaked.

Carnival?

Rachel's gaze snapped to the source of the sound just as a violent tremor shook the bridge, followed by a mighty rumble of rock, as in a landslide. The entire granite deck pitched abruptly upwards, then slammed back down. Its chains groaned under enormous pressure. Rachel staggered, fighting to keep her balance. She heard the snap and whine of cables, then the hideous clamour of shrieking metal, and finally a series of vast booming concussions. The air clouded with white ash, as thick as fog.

And then silence, but for a shrill ringing in Rachel's ears.

She heard a voice: 'Remain where you are. There has been a disturbance.'

A disturbance?

Rachel coughed. Her eyes smarted. She could see nothing but churning clouds of sediment thrown up by the pitching bridge – which meant that for the moment her enemies couldn't see her either. The whole deck continued to rock in its cradle of chains. Trench was nowhere to be seen; for all she knew he might have fallen to his death. 'No shit,' she shouted back, to give them her position. 'Some sort of disturbance. I'm not going anywhere.'

They would be aiming now.

Her Spine training demanded that she flee, while she still had a chance of escaping from her foes in this murk. But they'd expect her to run, and would shoot ahead of her position. Instead, she took two steps backwards and sat down. Flying bolts whined through the air ahead of her. She heard them slam against the deck several yards away.

Now they would be reloading.

Rachel scrambled to her feet and ran. Vague grey shapes loomed around her, chains and pendulum houses suspended in the ashen murk. A darker shadow rushed by on her left side. She ducked, and sensed a large object dashing past, the air howling behind it. A storm of grit lashed the side of her face. She kept going, her eyes narrowed against the stinging dust.

A second barrage of bolts hit the deck behind her, though not nearly so many as before. But by then she was clear of the bridge: there were now cobbles underfoot. She found a doorway, pressed herself flat against it, and waited, listening hard.

Among all of the creaking and groaning metal, Rachel heard other, smaller noises: wet, ripping sounds, and the snap of breaking bones. At times she thought she heard a dull soft *whoomph* like the thump of wings. Something unseen was butchering the assassins. She didn't hear a single scream but, then, Spine never made a sound when they died.

Had Carnival returned to help her?

But when the clouds of sediment finally thinned, Rachel could see no trace of the scarred angel, merely a scene of utter devastation. An eerie silence hung over the bridge and its surroundings. She could see no sign of the temple assassins. Indeed, most of those pendulum houses in which the Spine had been hiding were gone, lost to the abyss, their broken support chains now empty and creaking back and forth in the dusty gloom. On the opposite side of the bridge, the Taptack Acres – that vast, already crippled district – had also vanished. Freed of their heavy burden, the mighty foundation chains which had once sagged under the strain of all those streets and houses now loomed overhead. It looked as if a storm had ripped through this broken quarter of the city, and then abruptly departed.

'Carnival?' Rachel called.

No answer.

Could those sounds of slaughter have been Rachel's imagination? Had the destruction been caused by nothing more than the parting of one weak but crucial support chain, a break which had sent a terrible shockwave through the entire district?

'Carnival!'

These silent chains offered no answers. Rachel glanced up at the pulsing, fire-lit sky and decided not to linger.

Trench had not gone far. In this warren of blocked and buckled streets he had chosen to flee down one of many dead-ends. Rachel caught up with him just as he was leaving the mouth of this same alley to retrace his footsteps. He was in no better mood than before: sour and scowling, his eyes as dark as murder. When he saw her he lifted his chin and glared at her with unmasked contempt.

'This wretched place will be the death of me,' he growled, jabbing a finger back in the direction from which he had come. 'There are already Icarates in the city!'

'Icarates?'

'Mesmerist scouts,' he said. '*Shape-shifters.* The city is infested with them.' He dragged the back of his bleeding hand across his lips, then spat. 'You must lead me out of here *now*. There's little time left.'

Rachel studied him carefully. 'Who *are* you?'

'Who am *I*?' His eyes flashed with arrogance. 'I am the champion of the First Citadel, commander of Hasp's archons.'

Hasp's archons?

Chill clutched Rachel's heart as she realized her mistake. The consciousness that now held her friend Dill had never been one of the thirteen souls in Devon's elixir, which meant that this *thing* could have come from only one place. The assassin felt her mouth go dry. 'You're from Hell?'

He smiled cruelly. 'The First Citadel is home to all angels who have died in battle in this world. My life ended nine hundred years ago in the service of your Church, and now I have returned to serve it once more. War has been raging in Hell for centuries, and our fortress is under siege. Many of us have already been taken by Menoa's forces to the Ninth Citadel, where our souls are *altered*, smashed apart, only to be changed into impure forms. I must deliver an urgent message to one of Ayen's sons before we are lost.'

'Where is Dill?' Rachel demanded.

Trench shrugged. 'He's in Hell. We merely required his body, not his soul.'

Rachel could only stare at Trench in numb shock. She had failed to protect the young angel on the mountain of bones down there in the abyss, and then brought him back only to witness his home and everyone he loved being destroyed. She had failed him again in Sandport when the Spine captured him.

And now . . .?

Now she had failed him in the worst possible way. Iril had reached out and claimed him back. Everything she'd done had been for nothing. She'd lost him all over again.

She grabbed Trench's shoulders. 'How do we get him back?'

Disbelief clouded the impostor's face. 'Do you have any idea who you are assaulting?' His voice dropped ominously low. 'I am a descendant of Callis, your own god's Herald. You will bow before me.'

'Ulcis was never my god,' Rachel said. 'I didn't bow before him, and I won't bow before you either.' She took hold of one of the angel's damaged wings and twisted hard. 'Now tell me how to get Dill back from Hell.'

Trench fought against her grip, clumsily, but his stolen body lacked the strength to resist. At last he stopped struggling. 'We share the same enemy, Rachel Hael,' he said evenly. 'Iril's Mesmerists threaten your world as much as mine. But if they are defeated, the archons of the First Citadel will try to release Dill and return him to this body. However, if I fail to find help, and the citadel falls, your young friend is doomed to suffer more than you can imagine. The Mesmerists remake souls into whatever form suits their war plan. Your kind might face Dill on the battle-field one day – not as an angel, but as a monster or a bleeding sword or a warship: a sensate hulk of iron without even a mouth to scream out in his agony.'

She slowly released the angel. 'Who are these Mesmerists?'

Trench flexed his wings and winced. 'They were once Lord Iril's elite,' he said. 'They rose to power after Ayen shattered Iril in the War Amongst the Gods. Menoa is their leader, a self-proclaimed king and one of Iril's former strategists. Since Ayen debased the Lord of the Maze, Menoa has assumed most of his former master's role for himself. Now he controls vast swathes of Hell.'

'But you opposed him?'

'The archons of the First Citadel have rejected this upstart king. We have been scouring Hell for the shattered remains of our rightful ruler, while Menoa gathered armies and crushed dissent. Yet many believe Menoa is already in possession of a piece of our shattered god, for he became too powerful too quickly. Now all who oppose him are changed.'

Changed? 'They're coming here?'

'One of their scouts is crawling towards us as we speak.' He pointed back to the lane from which he'd emerged. 'This is what awaits you if you linger here much longer.'

At first Rachel saw nothing, but then, slowly, she began to notice odd shapes in the ash covering the cobbles. Like two hands dragging themselves across the ground, trailing roots of fine white dust. They appeared to be moving towards Trench and Rachel.

She took a step back.

'It is a low-rank Icarate,' Trench said, 'a common shape-shifter. Yet it lacks enough strength to become the shape the Mesmerists have chosen for it.' He searched the ground quickly, then picked up a fragment of flint and hurled it at the two hands. One of the dust-shapes burst apart, then quickly re-formed. But now one of the hands looked darker and more angular, more like the stone shard Trench had thrown at it. 'There are probably hundreds of them around here, hidden among the chains and stones all about us.'

'Can you fly?' Rachel said.

Trench flapped his wings, then growled in pain. 'I can walk.'

'Then let's walk quickly.'

They hurried east towards the League of Rope, and the abyss rim of the abyss, as flashes of light pulsed across the horizon behind them.

10

GOODBYE to SANDPORT

Sandport's lights dimmed behind them as Jack Caulker and his companion reached the summit of the rocky bluff. On a clear night Caulker might have looked down to see a sprawl of mud homes slumped in an uneven bowl extending around the bend in the river Coyle, skiffs bobbing in its moonlit waters. But tonight the fog surrounding John Anchor and his master's skyship obscured the view.

The big man's teeth shone whitely in his dark face. His wooden harness creaked as he dragged the monstrous rope behind him, yet he seemed utterly tireless. 'It is good exercise,' he said jovially. 'To climb is good exercise, no?'

'I suppose so,' Caulker muttered. He was already feeling fed up, and he still had a whole sodding desert ahead of him. They hadn't even been able to stop for a drink, not after what had happened to the Cockle Scunny.

That broth shop had remained intact marginally longer than the Widow's Hook, although Caulker suspected that the building might have been saved from destruction altogether had the proprietor not threatened to summon the town militia as soon as Anchor showed his face at the door. The tethered man had marched in the front door, used the privy, and then left by the back door.

Men were probably still picking through the rubble of that building too.

Anchor seemed utterly unconcerned by the devastation he left in his wake. Indeed, he had remained cheerful during the whole incident, humming some halfwit sailor's shanty while the corpses piled up behind him. Caulker could well imagine what tomorrow's news yelled by the Sandport Criers would be.

At the top of the bluff, the murky air denied them any view of the Deadsands, but Caulker had seen the desert from this same point a hundred times before. To the west, the land rose and fell in waves of ash-coloured dunes, scoured in places down to the basalt bedrock or scabbed with thickets of brittle grass, scrub and ancient rock forest. A trail led north, following the river to Clune and the logging depositories there, while a second, wider route struck out directly west to the chained city of Deepgate. To keep traders well wide of the slipsand, cairns of glassy black rock had been built to mark this road, although the cut-throat could not even spot the first of them in the fog.

Caulker's hand kept returning to his shoulder, reaching for a pack that was not there. It felt discomforting to set out across the wasteland without provisions, but Anchor had deemed it unnecessary for his friend to carry anything. Whatever food and water they would need could be pulled down from Cospinol's ship in the skies above them. This thought did not help to improve Caulker's appetite.

Wreathed in fog, the two men thus set out upon the trail to Deepgate. Caulker winced to think of the sort of battle that lay ahead of his companion. Carnival had killed a god and stolen his power. And yet they'd sent a man to kill her – an odd, phenomenally strong man to be sure, but still only a man. Despite the open desert the cut-throat felt like he was trapped between two massive, inward-moving walls.

Behind them, the harbour bells rang out, like a celebration of their departure.

11

SOUR RAIN

'No,' Rachel said to Trench, 'the caravan trail is too dangerous by daylight. Spine are everywhere, hunting any refugees who attempt that route. And they're not the only ones. Rumours of Heathen attacks reached us while we were in Sandport. We must wait till dark and then head southeast.' She drew a line in the sand. 'Then we can cut east through Cinderbark Wood.' She hesitated. It was a dangerous route, but likely to be their best chance. 'From there we should be able to reach the Coyle without much fear of detection.'

Deepgate's expanding canopy of smoke throbbed overhead, a dark bruise streaked with toxic colours – orange, lime-green, yellow and red. Rachel and Trench had hidden in a sandy basin in the lee of an iron groyne, two hundred yards southwest of the Spine patrol routes and the abyss perimeter. Exhausted from their trek through the stricken city, and with only an hour till dawn, it had been pointless to continue across the Deadsands. Instead, Rachel had used the last of the darkness to sneak back into the perimeter camp, where she had searched for supplies for the journey ahead. Her foray yielded a satchel of labourers' rags, a field medical kit, a cord of pigskin, four flasks of water, and a serrated kitchen knife, which she secreted in her armour beside the dagger she had taken from the Spine Master in the temple.

Now dawn was here, and Rachel desperately needed to sleep. She sat in the shade of the groyne, tending to her companion's wounded wings. Red vapour was rising from the city like bloody steam. The low sun filtered through, turning the Deadsands the colour of burned skin.

'We must not delay,' Trench insisted. His scowl seemed to belong to an older face than that of the young angel he had possessed, yet his eyes burned as orange with annoyance as Dill's ever had. 'The Veil is growing denser. By nightfall the Icarates might have enough strength to regain their forms. Then everyone in Deepgate will die.'

Rachel pointed east, to where one of three churchships hovered over the Deadsands. 'They're looking for us. We wouldn't manage to cover half a league without being spotted. We don't have any choice but to remain here until dark.'

Trench's eyes darkened, and he growled frustration. Rachel studied those eyes for some sign of Dill, just a hint that her friend's soul might still be connected to his living body. Yet the harder she looked, the further her hopes diminished. Her companion was a stranger to her.

And so they waited there in the shadow of the groyne, taking turns to sleep or watch for patrols, while the sun glimmered like a weak lantern in the gloom. The chained city groaned, cracked and fumed behind them. Airships droned across the Deadsands in the distance, but their search soon moved away from the city.

Rachel slept in fits. Disturbing noises haunted her dreams: the distant explosions from the Poison Kitchens and the hideous twang and judder of overstressed chains became the sounds of war machines, things like huge insects and skeletal towers which shuddered and hissed jets of gas.

She woke sometime around noon to discover that the air quality had declined noticeably. A warm breeze sighed out of the abyss, carrying with it the stench of fuel. The heavens appeared angrier and more vivid than before. Fumes boiled in the blackness overhead, turning from clashing pinks and reds to fragile shades of yellow and silvery blue.

Trench had fallen asleep and rolled back onto his wings, reopening the wounds the Spine bindings had given him. Whatever regenerative powers Devon's angelwine had bestowed upon the angel now seemed to have departed along with Dill's soul.

Rachel pulled some lint from the field kit and cleaned the blood from her companion's wings, before wrapping a clean bandage around one of the deeper cuts. Trench woke, but did not resist her ministrations. When she had finished, he moved to the edge of the groyne and stared back towards the city.

Dark shapes flitted like windblown rags between the seething skies and amid the crimson mists now rising from the abyss.

'What are those vapours?' Rachel asked.

'It is the blood of the dead,' Trench replied. 'There is much power in blood, enough to sustain a soul in this world. And so the Mesmerists use it to stain the ground before their warriors set foot upon it. It feeds their armies. Without it they would wither and die.' He swept a hand across the vista before them. 'The Veil will spread until it covers all of this. When it reaches the sea the Mesmerists will make ships from blood and metal and souls.'

'Can we stop it?'

'Not while the portal beneath the city remains open.'

Rachel clenched her teeth. 'Ulcis warned us that he had built his palace over a gate to Hell.'

Trench looked surprised. 'You knew him?'

'I knew his daughter.' Rachel wondered where Carnival was now. Last night's ambush in the city had been thwarted by *something*. 'We once stood together above the gates of Hell.'

'*Gate* is the wrong word to use. The Maze exists in a separate reality from this one. Since Ayen sealed Heaven, the Maze has been growing, exerting a new pressure on this world. Now the membrane between the two realms is wearing thin. It is weakest in places where a great number of souls have poured into Hell – in battlefields, or in plague cities like Cog in Pandemeria.'

'The Church of Ulcis?'

'Deepgate's temple fed the god of chains, not the Maze. The portal under his palace was insignificant, no great threat to him or his Church.'

'But then he died.'

The archon nodded. 'And his death has allowed a glut of souls into Hell.'

A bitter taste filled Rachel's mouth. On Scar Night she had witnessed the death of the god of chains. In that dank cell at the bottom of the abyss, she had watched Ulcis's daughter feed. By killing her own father, Carnival had unwittingly damned the city to Hell.

Rachel tried to sleep again, but the foul mist creeping out of the abyss cloyed at her throat and filled her eyes with warm thick tears. Sleep, when it eventually came, brought nightmares.

A giant striding across the Deadsands towards her – a towering skeletal figure of bone and metal. Fireballs falling from the heavens struck the ground around it with the sound of pounding drums. Its grinning skull looming over her . . .

Trench was shaking her awake. The sky seemed much darker than before and the stench of decaying flesh filled her nostrils. She coughed and spat, tasting a vile film on her teeth. 'How long have I slept?' she asked. 'What time is it?' Her joints felt full of grit, her lungs heavy.

'Mid afternoon,' the angel replied urgently. 'The Veil is becoming dangerously thick. You were screaming in your sleep.'

'Just a dream,' she said.

'An unnatural dream. This air is not healthy.' He pointed east. 'Something has happened to the skyships.'

Far across the Deadsands Rachel saw three isolated pockets of flame.

'They came down,' Trench said. 'One after the other. I cannot explain it.'

Carnival? Rachel saw no sign of the scarred angel. But what else could have brought those airships down? The Heshette? It seemed unlikely. Deepgate's aeronauts always kept their ships well above enemy arrow range.

Then Rachel noticed the sands around her. Blue and green ash had drifted down and settled in soft bright clumps across a hundred yards of desert, like scabs of alien lichen. But this flora, when she disturbed it with the toe of her boot, stank of rotting metals.

A deep rumble rolled out from the chained city. Showers of white sparks rushed upwards from the burning city, sparkling against the vast dark columns of fuel smoke. 'The Poison Kitchens,' she said. 'Deepgate won't last much longer.'

'Then let us hurry.'

Trench got to his feet and unfurled his wings against the turbulent sky. For a heartbeat he appeared in silhouette – an angel wreathed in red smoke and falling stars – and then the sky behind him bloomed with white light.

Deepgate had exploded.

Rachel's head struck the metal groyne as a violent concussion slammed her backwards. Flames swam across her vision. She heard an explosion as vast and terrible as the death cry of a god – then nothing but a shrill whine. A fireball of unimaginable size was mushrooming over the chasm. Silver-white flashes in the sky bleached the surrounding landscape as the blast swelled upwards, sucking a vast column of white smoke and embers upwards in its wake.

She grabbed Trench and dragged him down behind the cover of the groyne.

Torrents of sand howled past the edge of the iron barricade. A furious rumble shook the ground. The groyne shuddered and groaned, then pitched over at a shallow angle.

Silence.

Through a thick haze of dust Rachel saw Trench crouching beside her. Grit pattered against her leathers. The air was opaque, a fuming cloud of white and pink, yet she glimpsed darker shapes in the sky above.

Debris?

It began to fall like hail. Shards of metal and lumps of stone thudded into the sand all around. Most of the pieces were small, no larger than a sword or a man's head, yet they struck the ground with enough force to kill. Something hit the iron barrier with a teeth-numbing clang. Rachel shoved Trench up against the leaning groyne, then crawled in beside him. The low barrier gave limited protection, with barely a foot of overhang under which to shelter, but it was better than nothing. There she waited while shrapnel pounded the desert around their makeshift shelter, raising puffs of sand and colourful ash.

Smaller objects pinged against their barricade, yet she felt deeper, more violent concussions through the ground. From somewhere came the screech of rending, ripping metal, the crack and crumble of stone – the final death rattle of a city.

How many minutes passed Rachel could not say, but the hail of debris gradually lessened and finally stopped. A deep silence fell over them.

She wiped sand from her stinging eyes. 'Shit. Are you all right?' What had the chemists stored there to cause such a powerful explosion? 'Trench?'

'I'm fine.'

Abruptly, the air grew cold. A chill wind blew in from the desert, towards them, like a reflexive inhalation in response to the outward force of the blast.

And it began to rain.

Gently at first, then with increasing vigour, the rain came down. Fat black drops of water churned up the desert floor, rattled against their iron shelter. Rachel covered her nose and mouth. The water stank, like . . .?

When she heard Trench screaming, she realized it wasn't water at all.

12

THE ROAD TO PANDEMERIA

After a while Jack Caulker began to hate the fog. It was damp, oppressive, gloomy, miserable, confusing, tiresome, frustrating and endless. He passed the time by thinking up more and more ways in which it annoyed him. How had Anchor managed to live within this gloom most of his life? Caulker had begun to despise the big man too. Anchor remained in high spirits, humming merrily as they marched across the Deadsands, a perpetual grin on his big, dark face.

Was the bastard actually human?

The wet grey murk blanketed everything but fifty yards of ground around them, making navigation through this wasteland treacherous. Twice already Caulker had been forced to retrace his footsteps to avoid pools of slipsand.

South of the caravan trail, the landscape dipped gently into a vast wet basin where poisoned water bubbled up through the sand in places. The whole area had been polluted by Cinderbark Wood, Deepgate's chemists' most hideous creation. Caulker planned to avoid the wretched place if at all possible. Besides, the majority of clean springs all lay on the northern side of the trail – each fed, it was said, by a subterranean river which flowed deep underground from Mount Blackthrone itself. On this route, all they had to worry about were Spine patrols and those occasional bands of

Heshette raiders who came down from the north to prey on pilgrims.

Having witnessed Anchor's combat skills in the Widow's Hook, a few temple skull-faces and heathen goat-fuckers would be the least of Caulker's worries. So when he heard riders approaching from the north, the cut-throat felt somewhat relieved. Some wanton slaughter might at least alleviate his boredom.

John Anchor called out to the riders before they could even see them – an action which did not disturb Caulker as much as the big man's reasons for doing so. Had the giant kept his mouth shut, the Heshette might easily have ridden past the two travellers in the fog. But Anchor's halloo made the horsemen change course at once. Sensible enough, Caulker assumed at first, for the giant needed souls to feed the god whose airship he was dragging around.

Except, as Caulker soon discovered, the Adamantine Man had not summoned these raiders to slay or rob them. His real reason for giving away his position beggared belief.

Six ragged warriors appeared out of the fog, clothed in sand-coloured gabardines and headscarves. They rode scrawny horses covered with tribal fetishes, the bones and feathers denoting their clan and their rank within it, and carried a motley assortment of weapons: mainly daggers and clubs, although a couple of men waved longer, curved blades.

'*Bara aresh*,' cried the leading rider. 'This is a bone road. You will stop and pay a toll, or you will bleed.' He stopped himself when he caught sight of Anchor's massive harness and the rope rising at a steep angle from his back. His thin horse reared, fetishes clicking in its mane. The rider controlled the beast easily, never taking his gaze from Anchor. He raised his dagger. '*Corras?*' he snapped. '*Arramon?*'

'I not understand this speech,' Anchor said. 'You speak the language of the Seven, the New Gods? This I know.'

'Your gods,' the Heshette warrior said in Low Coyle. 'Not mine.'

The giant beamed. 'I understand. Tell me, friend, where is the chained city? My guide . . .' He shrugged apologetically and gestured towards Caulker. 'He is good man, but confused by the fog, I think. We walk forward and then later we walk back. Always forward and back. Is better to walk forward all of the time.'

Caulker's brows rose. Anchor stopped merely to ask for directions? From these fucking savages? Had he no sense of the way of the world? That the Heshette had only asked for a toll was miraculous enough. Normally they just cut throats and took everything.

The warrior's dark eyes regarded the stranger through the gap in his headscarf. 'Northwest,' he said, pointing, 'for two leagues. Then the trail turns south and then west again. Why do you want to go there?' He glanced at the big man's rope again. 'There is nothing left but flames and poison.'

Anchor grinned. 'I am . . . how you say? . . . traveller.'

'A traveller?'

'From the Riot Coast. You know of it? Good blue lobster and fishbeer. Best in all Pandemeria.'

The mounted warrior let out his laughter suddenly and freely. Behind him, his men joined in. 'No, my friend,' he said, 'I don't know your homeland. But you are free to travel here in ours.' He sheathed his dagger, then cinched the reins around a knot tied in his mount's mane and dismounted. 'You must share bread with us, and tell us, please, what this queer rope is.'

'Rope?' Anchor glanced behind him. 'Ah, yes, sometimes I forget. I show you after we eat. Is only a small thing.'

And so Caulker found himself squatting beside a dung campfire close to the caravan trail, to share a feast of flatbread, camel milk and goat meat with a group of savages. The horseman who had first addressed them – a tall, lean man named Harranel

Ramnir – turned out to be their leader. In the clipped accent of the southern tribes, he introduced his men to Anchor and Caulker.

Caulker made a point of forgetting their names at once.

Under their headscarves Ramnir's savages all looked the same: hard, tanned faces and ragged beards. At first their uneasy gazes kept returning to the giant's rope but, as he did not seem inclined to speak about it, they did not press him. Soon the fire settled and the smell of roasted meat filled the air. Each of the Heshette had been pocked or scarred in some way by the poisons and diseases Deepgate's military had used against the desert tribes, as they explained to John Anchor when the big man asked about their wounds.

'For three decades they warred with us,' Ramnir said. He was about ten years older than his men, with a thin black beard, a long nose and intense dark eyes. 'We are Mer-Heshette from south of the bone road.' He pointed with the piece of flatbread he was chewing. 'The chained folk poisoned the springs, and drove us north into the nomad and Blood Heshette lands, where there is little grazing. Bad years. Many families destroyed. Those of us who survived the poisons starved when our herds died.'

'It is an evil way to make war,' Anchor agreed, shaking his head. His deep voice was full of sadness. 'Too cruel.'

A necessary way to make war, thought Caulker, as he ripped another piece of meat from a bone and chewed it slowly. Take out the women and children, and the savages can't breed. These people preyed on civilians, after all, Deepgaters and Sandporters alike. Watching them now, he felt nothing but disgust. He lifted his cup of camel's milk and drained it, hoping it might wash away the foul taste in his mouth.

'Once we have a war on the Riot Coast,' Anchor continued. 'Many years ago now, before the Mesmerists come to Pandemeria. Brownslough is the land to the north of us – a lot of mud and coal. We trade with them, fine, but they have only land around them. Trade not enough. They want our ports in Herrul and Oxos. So they come with an army.' He slammed his hands together, making the rope on his back quiver. 'Brownslough people not cruel, just stupid. On the Riot Coast our babies crawl, then learn to fight, and then to walk. You understand? Big mistake for Brownslough. They learn a hard lesson, then go back north, and we trade with them again. All good.'

'So many lands . . .' Ramnir said wistfully. 'I didn't know the world was so large. We Heshette have become so insular, so focused on the destruction of the chained city and those who persecute us. They say there was a time when our people wandered far across the world, yet now our hate won't let us look beyond the current conflict. If we opened our eyes, we'd see there's nothing left here.'

'Hate is poison,' the giant agreed. 'How many are you, all of your people together?'

The horseman sighed. 'Less than a hundred and fifty tribes left now. Perhaps six thousand people.'

Anchor grunted. 'It is not many,' he said. 'Come to the Riot Coast. We have enough land. We have big party, for a month or more. Six thousand, eh?' He thought for a moment. 'You can fish, no problem, and make homes. My people will help you build them. If you want you can have an island. We have lots of islands. Good hunting too – pigs, fowl, garren and bears.'

Ramnir smiled. 'A generous offer,' he said, 'but I doubt your people would welcome so many of us.'

'You don't know Riot Coasters,' Anchor replied, smiling again. 'Very hospitable. If I'm not there, you tell them John Anchor said it is fine for you to stay.'

Caulker felt physically sick. Was the black giant offering sanctuary to this rabble of scum? Surely Anchor must have another motive. Were the Riot Coasters cannibals? Would this month-long party involve a lot of fires and cauldrons? The cut-throat had heard of such things in his seafaring days.

The Heshette leader clasped the giant's shoulder, but said nothing.

Anchor was actually drawing a map now. Using his finger, he sketched out the outline of a coast in the hard sand. 'This is your land here,' he said. 'This is the Sand Sea, yes? The yellow waters. All this, all around.' A few feet away from this he drew some small round shapes. 'These islands we call the Tail of Smoke. Big mountains there, bad smell.'

The Volcanic Isles. Caulker recognized them from charts he'd seen. Deepgate's missionary ships had visited those islands.

'Now look here.' Anchor had drawn another coastline, at least twice as far away again as the Volcanic Isles, but on the opposite side of the ocean. 'This is Pandemeria. High Meria, here . . . Brownslough . . . and the Riot Coast.' He made lines in the sand, dividing up the continent. The last squiggle appeared to be a peninsula at the very southern tip of the land mass.

Caulker did some calculations. Pandemeria lay several hundred leagues beyond the furthest island to which missionary ships had sailed: on the far side of the Strakebreaker Sea, as it had come to be known after the loss of so many expeditions. The waters were said to be so wild and empty that most salt sailors feared to venture near them. Yet new lands meant trade, and profit. And if John Anchor had crossed them . . .

How had he crossed them?

Had his own god's airship carried him? Caulker wondered if Cospinol would accept another passenger – before the thought of begging a lift on such a gruesome mode of transportation made the cut-throat flinch. Boundless profit or not, he'd have to think about that one.

'You need ships,' Anchor said. 'Strong ships. Very dangerous seas here, and here.' He drew wiggles all across the Strakebreaker

Sea, almost dividing it in two. 'One time there was a great battle here, many ships sunk. Then Iril opened a big door under the water and something escaped.'

'A monster?' Caulker asked. He had been so caught up in Anchor's map, he had quite forgotten about the surrounding Heshette.

'No,' Anchor looked thoughtful, then frowned. 'More like a piece of Hell. Like something the Mesmerists would make.'

'The Mesmerists?' Anchor had mentioned them before. 'These people who came to Pandemeria?'

'They come to Pandemeria, but they are not people. Big problem with them in the east. You'll see them soon, I think. They will come here, too, now.' He looked sternly at Ramnir, his brow creased, and stabbed his finger in the centre of the first land mass he had drawn, to indicate the Deadsands. 'Big door to Hell opens, the Mesmerists come out. Same in Pandemeria, same in Deepgate. Much blood.'

The horseman met the giant's gaze. 'Why are you here, John Anchor? What is attached to the other end of that rope?'

Anchor gave a deep sigh. 'I go to Deepgate for two reasons,' he said. 'One: I kill someone. Maybe she is an angel, maybe a demigod, no matter. This part is easy. The other task . . .' He flexed his shoulders. 'This part is not so easy.'

Over the next hour he explained about the god whose skyship he dragged behind him.

'Cospinol will now try to seal the breach under Deepgate, but many things to consider, many dangers. It is a problem for you if my master fails. You have no other gods here, no great armies to fight the Mesmerists. Much of this land will become Hell, I think.' He nodded his head and stabbed his finger into the sand again, pointing to the distant land he'd drawn across the Strakebreaker Sea. 'If I don't come back from Deepgate, it is safer for you to find ships and go here.'

★

Poison and acid fell from the sky. This greasy, colourful rain spattered the Deadsands, hissing and smoking wherever it fell. It pummelled the clumps of blue and green ash, reducing them to smouldering mud, and it struck against the top surface of the leaning groyne under which Rachel and Trench were trying to hide. But while there was just enough space under the narrow shelter for the assassin to keep all but a few drops from striking her knees, it was a different matter for Trench.

Rachel tried to pull him under the iron overhang as much as she could, but it was useless. His wings were too large. There simply wasn't space for them under the metal canopy.

He continued to scream as the lethal rain burned his feathers and tendons.

'Just lie down!' Rachel yelled. 'There isn't room! We'll cover your wings with sand.'

The assassin tried to push Trench down while she scooped up sand and threw it over him, but he struggled against her. He was panicking, fighting her, oblivious to everything but his own pain. In blind terror, he shoved her out from under the groyne and tried to squeeze himself further into the gap where she had been. Even then he could not fit his wings in fully behind him. He wheeled around and tried to back up against the tilting barricade, but now his head and neck were exposed.

He screamed again.

Lying outside where Trench had shoved her, Rachel was fully exposed to the caustic downpour. Drops pattered against her armour, and the smell of singed leather filled her nostrils. She scrambled back under cover. A heartbeat later the piercing pains in her back and thighs told her where acid had eaten through to her flesh. She rolled on the ground, then shovelled more sand over her thighs.

By the time the rain stopped, the stench of seared flesh and feathers hung thickly in the air. Trench lay on the steaming ground, hissing quietly through his teeth. His wings – Dill's wings, Rachel reminded herself – now looked like black mulch. All of his feathers had burned away, exposing tattered skin full of black-rimmed holes and glistening white bone.

A vast plume of white smoke had risen above the abyss, and it now covered the sky like gauze. The darker red and black clouds had been torn apart and blown far across the wasteland. All around Rachel, the Deadsands hissed and shimmered in painfully harsh sunlight. Wisps of foul-smelling steam drifted from the tops of dunes, while shards of bright metal glinted where they had descended and lodged in the sands. All trace of the colourful ash had now been dissolved under the acid shower.

'I had forgotten what real pain was like,' Trench said through clenched teeth. 'I'm sorry for putting you in danger, Rachel Hael. I behaved shamefully.'

'Forget it,' Rachel replied. She knew there was nothing in the field kit to ease his pain. The Spine did not consider such drugs necessary. She could do nothing but watch him suffer.

Somehow he managed to stagger upright. Scraps of his chain-mail shirt slid from his back and shoulders, revealing swathes of blistered red flesh beneath. Pieces of skin fell from his ruined wings. 'The world has changed since I was last here,' he wheezed. 'What could have caused such an explosion?'

'Fuel?' she suggested. 'I don't know . . . Everything our chemists ever invented they stored in the Poison Kitchens.'

'The Veil has disappeared,' Trench observed.

She could hardly bear to look at him. Even now smoke continued to rise from globs of poison sticking to his eviscerated wings. Sunlight shone through the bloody fans of bone and skin. His face had paled yet his eyes raged darkly.

'Let us survey the damage,' he said.

They walked back towards the edge of the abyss. The angel limped slowly, painfully, but Rachel slackened her pace to match his. She was afraid to offer him support, afraid even to touch his seared flesh.

The journey took an age, but finally the pair drew near to the southern rim of the steaming chasm. To the east of them the tin bunkers of the reconstruction workers' settlement gleamed brilliantly, yet it appeared to be deserted. Rachel could see no trace of life in the dusty streets, only the metal skeleton of an airship, its polished ribs scattered over hundreds of yards.

At the edge of the precipice Rachel looked down and saw nothing but a pool of white smog. 'The city is gone,' she said.

'No.'

Then Rachel spotted chains. Amidst the rising steam, she saw the sweeping curve of one, two, and then four foundation chains. Between them hung a ragged web of smaller cross-chains, each supporting a score of houses and hanging bridges. A dark mass hunched in the centre of the pit, like an island floating in a sea of mist. 'The temple,' she said. 'That fucking thing just won't let go.'

Still hanging upside down, the great building had nevertheless survived the explosion. Tens of thousands of people would be trapped inside it, and now there was no way for them to escape.

Trench turned away, his wings hanging from his shoulders like a steaming cape. 'We must leave,' he said stiffly. 'Nothing has changed, and the Mesmerists will return soon.' He took a step, then stumbled and hissed through his teeth in pain.

Rachel smelled burning. 'Wait,' she said. 'Let me see your wings.'

'There is no time,' he gasped. 'My message . . .' He crumpled forward, landing on his knees in the sand.

Rachel examined him. 'The poisons are still burning you,' she said. 'You can't go on like this.'

'Then remove my wings,' he replied.

She just stared at him.

'You have a knife.'

'A *kitchen* knife,' she said. 'We should go to the temple guard barracks, we could look for—'

'I cannot delay,' he snapped. Then he sucked in a deep breath and steadied his temper. 'Forgive my outburst. These ruined wings are useless to me now, and amputation would seem to be the quickest and most practical solution.' He paused. 'Please use the knife.'

'Here?'

'Here.'

Rachel took two tourniquets from the field kit and wrapped one around the base of each of Trench's wings. She cleaned his flesh with alcohol, then forced him to drink most of the remainder of the bottle. She found a strap of leather for him to bite down on. Kneeling on the sand before her, he grunted and hissed through the corners of his mouth while she worked, but he did not move or cry out.

When it was done she doused the wounds with the last of the whisky and bound his stumps tightly in fresh bandages. She took the labourer's shirt from her satchel and eased it over his wounded shoulders.

Once more Rachel found herself heading into the Deadsands with an angel by her side. But this time, although her companion was here in the flesh, everything else had changed. The young angel's body had been possessed by one of his own ancestors, while her real friend's soul now resided in Iril's Maze: one more ghost among the endless dead. If he were ever to return, it would only be to discover that he would never fly again.

No Spine were about, but Rachel decided to keep to her original plan. The temple assassins would still control Deepgate's main caravan routes, and she did not know how many more airships were at large. They would head southeast towards Cinderbark Wood, travelling by night whenever possible, and hopefully reach Sandport in six or seven days.

Trench walked stiffly. The low sun cast a long shadow across the sands before him, but it was no longer the shadow of an angel. Now wingless and dressed in rags he could easily have been mistaken for a common labourer. He wore a grim expression on his slender face, and his eyes belonged to a much older person than the young angel he had usurped. But when he glanced at Rachel, she noticed a glimmer of the desire she had seen earlier.

He looked away suddenly. 'I have been dead too long,' he said. 'In Hell, pain and lust are nothing but memories. One can learn to control them, to forget about them. But the living are victims of their own blood.'

'Obviously you haven't spent much time with the Spine,' she replied.

He grunted. 'They too have changed since I was last alive.' He glanced at his wounded hands, at the bound stumps of his fingers. 'Tell me about my descendant,' he said. 'What was Dill like?'

'He annoyed me when I first met him,' she admitted. 'Deepgate's priests brought him up to believe the world worked in a certain way. They sheltered him from everything, even banned him from flying. It was only a matter of time before he rebelled.'

'And you helped him with that?' Trench asked.

She shrugged. 'I only did it to annoy the priests – to get back at them. In the end I realized he was the only thing they hadn't corrupted. I think they hid their own cruelty from him because he represented an ideal they could no longer recognize in themselves.'

'Was he a warrior?'

She remembered the way Dill had fumbled with his sword when she had tried to teach him to fight – he had been the most inept pupil she had ever seen. But then she recalled how he had stepped between her and Ulcis's army on the mountain of bones. He had even tried to protect Carnival. 'Yes,' she said firmly. 'He was.'

'Then the First Citadel will protect him for as long as it can. Hasp will not be disappointed. He welcomes the brave and punishes the unworthy.'

'Hasp?'

'Hasp was Ulcis's brother, and leader of the First Citadel. He has already taken a special interest in Dill.'

Ulcis's brother? A sense of dread crept up Rachel's spine. 'Why is your leader so interested in Dill?'

The archon looked at her strangely. 'Dill returned from Hell,' he said.

Some time later they reached the edge of a petrified woodland, at the summit of a high bank of dunes. Hard black branches rose up against the darkening sky before them. These trees had been dead for almost three thousand years, drained of life by the same force which had turned the landscape to desert when Ulcis had fallen to these lands from Heaven. The boles were as black and glassy as obsidian, in stark contrast to the soft white sands between. Rachel scooped up a handful of the powdery stuff and let it trickle away between her fingers; the grains glittered like crushed test-tubes.

Fumes still leached from the abyss and drifted across the heavens to the northwest. It may have simply been the sunset, but it seemed to Rachel that the vapours had taken on a reddish hue. Was the Mesmerist Veil already beginning to re-form?

They followed a meandering path through the stone trees. Twilight deepened, turning the sand underfoot from white to pink to maroon. Rachel heard the scratch of hookfleas and kisser-crabs under the sand, and watched for depressions in the ground. Yet her eyes kept returning to the canopy overhead. The branches came alive with twinkling lights as the skies darkened and the crystal thorns reflected the last rays of sunset. Soon the whole woodland seemed to shimmer under its own weight of stars.

Trench stopped to rest against the bole of a tree. His face

looked pinched and ashen. 'I keep forgetting that this is not my body,' he gasped. 'It has certain limits.'

'And your soul in Hell doesn't?'

He shook his head. 'A soul is ethereal. In Iril's Maze you are simply what you believe yourself to be. Your own mind decides the shape and limits of its form . . . within reason. Before the Mesmerists, most spirits simply resembled their original bodies. In Hell I appeared to be much the same as I had looked in life: an archon not unlike your friend, Dill, albeit somewhat taller and broader.'

'How did you die, Trench?'

He grunted. 'Carnival murdered me.'

Rachel closed her mouth.

'The Church sent me after her,' the angel went on. 'I was the second son born to my father, and thus expendable. I trained every day for twenty years, yet she still defeated me.' He looked away. 'But she had already feasted that night, and so she abandoned my soul to Hell.'

'I'm sorry.'

'Don't be. I got one good cut in. Not many can claim to have given Carnival a scar.' He stared into the trees for a long moment. 'I know she's still alive in this world somewhere. After I deliver my message, I intend to look for her.'

'And if you find her?'

He smiled and rose to his feet. 'I'll kill her.'

Soon afterwards they came across an unusual trail. Rachel's Spine training had involved extensive travel throughout the Deadsands, but she still struggled to identify the cause of it. She had never seen so bizarre a set of impressions. The sand between the stone boles had been disturbed by a much larger creature than a kisser-crab or a snake, something which had left a shallow, undulating ditch behind it. There were no footprints, yet the creature was evidently man-sized. It appeared to have crawled across the ground in a worm-like fashion.

The trail followed the route Rachel planned to take, which made sense as the only clean spring for leagues around lay in that direction. Looking back, it seemed to originate from a place near to where they themselves had entered the petrified woodland.

Had something crawled up there to get a look at Deepgate, and then returned the way it had come?

'Any ideas?' she asked.

'It's not any animal I know,' Trench replied.

They followed the trail to the opposite side of the woodland. Beyond this point the land sloped away to the east, north and south: a vast expanse of pale, rippling dunes and darker patches of scrub. Northwards towards Blackthrone and the caravan trail, a curious bank of cloud or mist smothered the landscape like a dim grey veil, almost as if another city was burning there.

Some trick of the weather?

Rachel turned her attention to the east. Across the horizon jagged the silhouette of the Shale Mountains, beyond which lay the Yellow Sea. Millions of stars crusted the heavens above. The river Coyle, a faint silvery line, wove across the plain below the foothills, although Rachel could not spy any of the river towns in the gloom.

Yet there were other lights.

Some leagues southeast of where they stood, a great phosphorescent patch covered the Deadsands. From this distance it looked like a town or perhaps a travelling festival, so garish were the colours. Shades of aquamarine, permanganate, yellow and ochre throbbed, shifted and bled together under the night sky. The trail they had followed through the petrified trees led down the slope towards it.

Trench pointed. 'What is that place?'

'Cinderbark Wood,' Rachel replied.

'Some form of sorcery?'

'Hardly,' Rachel replied.

'Then why does it shimmer?'

'Deepgate's chemists painted it with toxins,' she said. 'They conceived of the idea during the Southern Clearances. The stone trees were originally supposed to act as a warning to the surviving tribes, an aggressive display of the chained city's power. But it's also a trap for the unwary, for every branch and thorn down there is saturated with poison. One scratch can kill.'

'Might a cautious man walk through it without harm?'

'It's not that simple,' Rachel said. 'There are poisonous roots buried under the sand, and caches that leak toxic vapours. The dunes are constantly shifting within it, so trails soon disappear. Sometimes the trees are completely covered by drifts. You don't know what you're walking on. What might seem like a safe path is often perilous.' She wiped sweat from her brow. 'The chemists used the trees as a canvas, colouring their poisons while creating ever more devious ways to bring death to their foes. It became a proving ground, with each man striving to outdo the work of his peers.'

Trench unplugged his water flask and took a sip. 'We could skirt it?'

'We need water,' Rachel said, stalking grimly on ahead. 'The only clean spring for many leagues lies within Cinderbark Wood.' She glanced back to the north again, to the queer bank of mist hanging over the Deadsands, and frowned.

It appeared to be moving south towards them.

Caulker hated horses. They smelled as bad as the Heshette who rode them, and had less flesh on their bones than a bag of boiled knuckles. To make matters worse, he had been forced to share a horse with one of the savages. The cut-throat now perched on a skinny gelding, behind his bearded companion, wincing with every hard-boned step the beast took, while the horseman in front of him swayed easily in rhythm. This particular bastard seemed to have an unnatural fondness for horses. He was forever patting and stroking the beast's neck and mumbling to it in his heathen language. For all Caulker knew, the two were man and wife.

Anchor strolled up ahead, chatting with Ramnir. The Heshette leader was mounted, yet such was the giant's size that the pair of them were almost face to face. Often they glanced back at Caulker and spoke in whispers, and then Anchor's laugh would boom out in the fog, rolling back along the long line of horsemen. Since this morning, their ranks had swelled from six to almost thirty. The initial party had apparently been merely part of a larger group of raiders.

'Your master has a good heart,' said the horseman seated in front of Caulker. 'He boasts a cheerful spirit.'

'He's an idiot,' Caulker muttered. 'And he's not my master.'

Yet Anchor's fame was growing fast among the heathens. Ramnir had sent riders out beyond the fog to spread the word and beg news from other tribes. Each time the scouts returned, they brought with them more of these savages, curious to see the giant and his rope for themselves. Anchor welcomed them all with his big dumb grin.

In this way, scraps of news filtered in from the desert. A vast explosion had rocked Deepgate, spewing debris for leagues around. None of the tribesmen had ventured close enough to inspect the chained city, but the damage was rumoured to be extensive. The red mist which had enveloped Deepgate of late had dissipated – an observation which had greatly pleased the tethered giant.

The scarred angel's two companions had been taken to the chained city by airship three weeks ago. And one of them – the Spine woman – had since been spotted fleeing across the southern Deadsands with a labourer from Deepgate's workers' settlement. They were last seen heading in the direction of Cinderbark Wood, so Anchor had decided to make a detour south to look for them. Carnival herself had not been seen, and yet the apparently fortuitous destruction of three skyships the night before suggested she might still be in the area.

They made camp just before nightfall, to allow Anchor to discuss this last information with his master in the skyship above. The entire exchange consisted of muttered questions from the giant and unheard replies from the god above while Anchor frowned in deep concentration, but when it was over the tethered man made an announcement.

'It is no good,' he said. 'Now Cospinol is convinced that his witchsphere is lying to him. Always it tries to steer us away from the scarred angel, and warns of Heshette treachery. Always lies. The witches have been poisoned by Cospinol's brother, Rys.'

Caulker snorted. 'What makes you so sure it's lying?'

'It says we should trust *you*,' Anchor said.

The Heshette laughed, but the cut-throat only seethed and wrapped his blanket more tightly around himself. Hadn't Anchor himself lied to Caulker in order to lure him out into this wilderness? And what exactly had the giant been whispering to Ramnir about? Caulker noticed the way the other heathens looked at him, all shifty like they meant to do him harm. Well, Jack Caulker had no intention of allowing that to happen. He had taken to keeping a knife in his sleeve, and one eye always on the pouch of pearls in John Anchor's belt.

'Have your master send this witchsphere down to us,' one of the Heshette suggested. 'We'll roast it over an open fire until it decides to cooperate.'

Anchor shook his head. 'It is only a few Mesmerist hags,' he said. 'I think the gods have made them suffer enough.'

This false display of pity only increased Anchor's standing amongst his fawning crowd of followers, while the Heshette who had advocated torturing their enemy's agent was now shunned by his companions. Caulker felt his bile rise all the more. What did these savages know about the world?

And who *were* the Mesmerists?

The cut-throat had been able to gather just a little about them. From what Anchor had said, the Mesmerists appeared to be the ruling force in Hell, an elite group which now sought to expand the borders of their realm. Yet wasn't Lord Iril himself supposed to have complete authority in the Maze? Some even said that Lord Iril *was* the Maze – an even stranger concept. Could a god actually be Hell? Deepgate's priests had often spoken of an endless labyrinth of red corridors, like the network of roots beneath a tree through which the damned wandered. But what did those bastards know?

Caulker had begun to think of the Mesmerists as kings. It thrilled him to think that Anchor and his master were afraid of them. What sort of power could they wield? As he watched the heathens pack up their horses, he imagined the ground opening up beneath them. He imagined red warriors rising from the earth, and the tethered giant cowering on his knees before them.

Like every other Sandport crook, Caulker had always known he would end up in Hell. Deepgate's chains had never been for him, and he didn't subscribe to any of the heathen religions. The certainty of his damnation had even steered some of his decisions in the past. He had murdered, stolen and raped, and rejoiced in his sins.

And if he was bound for the Red Maze, then wasn't it better to be on good terms with its rulers? Once he was in Hell, the Mesmerists might reward him with far more than he could ever hope to steal in this world. He had valuable information to offer. If he could only beg an audience with them without first taking a knife to his own throat . . .

He again peered up into the skies above him, where Anchor's rope disappeared into seemingly endless fog. Whatever this witch-sphere was, it was clearly aware of him.

13

CINDERBARK WOOD

A wind from the south had now picked up; it blew sand around
their shoulders and into their faces, obscuring the trail they had
followed since the last stone forest. Rachel blinked and rubbed
her eyes, and for a moment the view ahead was blurred.

Drenched in phosphorescent toxins, Cinderbark Wood lit up
the eastern skyline like a festival celebration, its tangled branches
and boles *throbbing* with a furious mix of colour. To each hue
Rachel tried to apply the name the chemists had invented for their
individual creations: Hot-Mylase and S661, Sugarglaze and
Arkspot, Lemonbrine-4, Red-Seven, Deadeye and Lossus Green,
Asphyis-manganate and Crawling Peach. There were poisons to
blind and rot bones, toxins which hardened split flesh, rare psy-
chotropics extracted from lizard's skin and frogs, hog's livers and
anemones. Thorns glistened with black and red fluid, denoting
venoms or accidents stumbled upon in a lab.

Originally a proving ground for the Department of Military
Science, the trees had been used by Deepgate's chemists as a
canvas for their own imaginations. They had applied the caustic
tars liberally, leaving no twig or patch of bark untouched, till ultimately this had become their greatest work of art. One careless
touch might kill a man, or perhaps much worse.

For not all of the poisons were fatal.

The chemists had, of course, left the woodland's spring unspoiled. It was the only clean water for leagues around, as many desperate nomads had now discovered to their peril.

Rachel hesitated at the edge of the wood. Faced with its dazzling colours, she reconsidered her plan. They could probably reach the northern edge of the forest well before dawn, head north to the caravan trail, and find one of the Acolyte springs by tomorrow evening. But this would bring them closer to the Spine patrols, or possible attack from desert raiders. If they continued east they would reach a source of clean water in perhaps two hours, and then be clear of Cinderbark Wood before sunrise.

All they had to do was stay alert.

She turned to Trench. 'Don't touch *anything*, do you understand? Absolutely *nothing*! Most of the poisons in there are designed to be absorbed through the skin. And stay close to me, for there are other dangers.'

She was thinking about those caches buried beneath the sands, the jars of rotting chemicals deemed too virulent to keep in Deepgate's own fuming Poison Kitchens. Vapours regularly leaked from these hidden hoards and made colourful mists among the trees. It was a beautiful sight.

And so they walked into the vibrant hush of Cinderbark Wood. Overhead the branches clashed in a riot of pinks, greens, blues, yellows; a dizzying spectacle that resisted starlight and imbued the sands below with different, gentler hues. Something crunched beneath Rachel's foot, and she looked down to discover the tiny skeleton of a bird under her heel, its fragile bones polished by erosion. Scattered hither and thither were the remains of hundreds of others, too: their chalky beaks and claws, their wings reduced to delicate spokes. Some of the larger specimens she identified as sand-hawks, owls and vultures, but she couldn't put a name to the smaller remains. The sight of those unidentified birds, those tough little harridans of the Deadsands, filled her with a profound sadness. How many had been attracted to this false oasis from the sand and scrub only to meet their death?

Silister Trench seemed unaffected by this miniature graveyard. Instead, he appeared to be afflicted with a kind of awe. Like a scholar in a rare museum, he moved between the gaudy boles with his hands clasped to his chest – a posture less instilled by fear, Rachel suspected, than reverence.

This petrified woodland seemed largely impervious to the gales blowing beyond its perimeter. Only the tips of the highest branches shifted, glassy thorns tinkling overhead, and these tiny notes only heightened the deep sense of stillness. Rachel kept a hand on Trench's shoulder as she led him onwards, ever alert for sudden mists or exposed roots they might trip on. She looked for poisons she recognized, trying to fit hue and texture to the incongruent names the chemists had devised. One bowed trunk had been daubed in Whooping-Silver and spattered with purple Sirsic Acid ember. She saw Blood-Lime and EM9 on the bark of another tree, fused with streaks of Raven Stain, Rosemary's Throat, Blushlilly, Dogweed and Generic 120. Nothing but the sand itself, and the tiny skeletons, had been left unpainted.

There was no path to follow, no stars visible to keep them on course. She relied on gut instinct and those few memories she retained from her one previous visit here.

She'd been seventeen when the Spine had brought her back from Hollowhill for punishment. Her hands were still bloody from the fight with the Deepgate reservists, and now those hands had been manacled, chained to a line of Heshette pilgrims bound for the Avulsior's justice. None of the other prisoners would speak to her, despite what she'd done for them. Rachel didn't blame them. As a Spine Cutter, the most she could expect was a whipping, or to endure one of Devon's toxic dreams. The other captives, all Heshette heathens, were bound for Sinners' Well.

Seven leagues west of Sandport, the head Spine Adept had

announced they would take the path through Cinderbark Wood. His pale face had given nothing away when he'd told her why. They'd take the southern route, he said, away from the busy caravan trails, to spare Rachel her humiliation.

Four Heshette had died among the poisoned trees. The first man had rested a hand against bark when the party stopped to rest. His screams and bleeding eyes had prompted a second, younger warrior to attempt to flee. This boy – he had only been a boy, she remembered – had tripped over a root in his panic. His feet had been bare, his death violent and stinking. A third, a grey-beard at the end of the line, had breathed a lungful of pink air before the Spine Adepts had hastened the party away from the mist. The fourth had been a young woman, one of the maidens Rachel had saved from the reservists' tents. Weeping, the girl had wrapped her arms around a colourful trunk and refused to let go. The Adepts had carefully unchained her and left her where she was.

When the party finally reached Deepgate, Rachel never received her whipping.

Now Rachel looked at the physical form of the young angel before her, at the bloody stains on the back of his shirt and the ruined fingers he kept close to his chest, and her breathing became suddenly heavy. Where was Dill's soul now, she thought sadly. She inadvertently tightened her hand on his shoulder.

Trench glanced back at her, and quickly away again.

The night stretched on. Thorns chimed like memories. Further in, the woodland grew even denser. Low loops and snarls of branch had to be negotiated with care. Poisons glowed softly all around. Occasionally they were forced to alter course to skirt wandering mists or solitary spires of clear hot vapour, or thickets where the trees blazed like colourful fire. Chemical smells constantly assailed them, queer sulphuric odours which stuck to the back of Rachel's throat. Time seemed to move to a more solemn beat here, to belong to a different world entirely. Their footfalls were soundless as, unconsciously, they had both become light-stepped and adept at avoiding the skeletons underfoot.

It was Trench who found the spring first. The angel suddenly pointed through the wood towards a muddy hollow with a clear pool rimmed with red, white and lavender grasses. Silver fish, no larger than Rachel's thumb, hovered in its water. The tracks of small three-toed beasts pocked the mire. But there was another, larger and more familiar imprint, and the assassin stared down in wonder.

The queer trail they had followed previously resumed here.

Rachel instantly crouched down to inspect the wet earth. The imprints were clearer here: a shallow trench about the width of a person surrounded by other marks like scuffs. The tracks led off into the trees, becoming more insubstantial in the dry sand extending further away from the pool. She saw no foot- or hoof-prints. Whoever or whatever had come here to drink had *wriggled* along.

Quickly she filled their water flasks, then, after a moment's hesi-tation – the fish in the pool were alive, unchanged, therefore the water it contained should be fine – she took a sip.

'We're halfway through,' she whispered to Trench, offering him a flask, 'but there's still worse to come.' She eyed those strange wavy tracks in the mud again . . . wondering.

Trench drank and handed the flask back to her. While she refilled it, he found himself a safe place to sit. 'I think I recall this woodland from my previous life,' he said quietly. 'Long before Deepgate's poisoners changed it, my brother and I used to hunt here.'

'What did you hunt?'

'Heshette.'

Rachel stared at him coldly.

'You don't approve?'

'I've done worse,' she admitted.

He grinned. 'Crueller things happen on Earth than in Hell. Perhaps the Mesmerists are *afraid* of mortals. They can only reshape souls into things they understand – machines, simple demons. They cannot forge people.'

'They understand destruction.'

'Even a child knows how to destroy.' He sniffed suddenly. 'We should go. The air here is turning foul.'

Rachel noticed a cloud of pink gas drifting through the trees towards them. After a moment's thought, she decided to continue along the existing trail. It led in roughly the right direction, after all, and by stepping on already disturbed ground they would hopefully avoid any traps.

Barely two hundred paces further on, they came across a sight so unusual that for a heartbeat Rachel wondered whether she had succumbed to toxic hallucination.

A brightly painted wagon stood among the trees. It had yellow and green slatted sides, with red shutters and a red door, wheels with gaily decorated spokes. A tin funnel protruded from the roof. The long pole at the front had clearly been designed for horses or oxen, yet no such animals were anywhere in sight. Rachel recognized the wagon from her time in Sandport before she even read the legend painted across one side:

Greene's Magical Circus.

Beside the wagon a shack had been erected. If anything, it resembled a hand-puppet booth, but of much larger proportions, its planks all decorated with stars, rainbows and grinning faces. A hatch in the front of it had been lowered to provide an opening, through which Rachel could see a stage with a painted backdrop.

Above the stage dangled two man-sized puppets, each suspended by a number of ropes dangling from the top of the booth. They looked frail and cadaverous, yet with wild glassy eyes and the drooling lips of madmen. Each had been dressed in garish motley: a black-and-white striped suit with a red bow tie for the figure on the left, a puffy blue quilted jacket and green rubber boots for the one on the right.

The trail, Rachel noticed, continued around the other side of the puppet booth. She was just about to follow it, when one of the marionettes spoke.

'Is that you, Mr Partridge?'

The hideous thing was not a puppet at all. It was a living man.

'Mr Partridge? We have waited an age for you to return.'

The second puppet said, 'It's not him, Mr Hightower. I can see them from over here. It's not him, I tell you.' Slack-eyed and slack-jawed, he peered at the two travellers from the end of his rope. 'One of them appears to be an angel, although the wings beneath his shirt are naught but bloody stumps, the other one's a Spine assassin.'

'Why do you insist on taunting me, Mr Bloom?' the first man responded. 'You're becoming as bad as Partridge – and I find your choice of words vulgar.'

'I am not fibbing, Mr Hightower. Look, here they come now.'

Rachel and Trench walked around the front of the booth, until both of the living mannequins could see them properly. Both men hung limply, their arms supported by ropes at varying heights. Something about their bodies seemed odd to Rachel: they were altogether too *pliant*, and only their eyes and lips moved.

'My apologies, Mr Bloom,' said Mr Hightower. 'I see you have spoken the truth for once. She, over there, is indeed one of the Spine.' One of his eyelids twitched. A trickle of saliva fell from his chin and soaked into his blue quilted jacket. 'Tell me, Spine, have you seen our Mr Partridge? He's gone off and left us again.'

Rachel considered the trail. 'I suspect he's hiding behind the booth,' she said. 'Is he . . . in a similar condition to you?'

'Greene never strung him up,' said Mr Hightower. 'So the

lucky sod goes off wandering all the time.' His face creased in odd places. 'Unfortunately, he enjoys these bright poisons too much. He has now become an addict, and has no consideration for his friends. He abandons us frequently. When he *does* show up, it's only to mock us.'

'Do you mean Mina Greene?'

'That's her, the puppeteer. She went for a walk last week and never came back. I hope she stepped in something nasty. Now there are only the three of us, and Mr Partridge is hardly ever here either. It's tremendously dull for us. Would you mind terribly cutting us down?'

'Don't *ask* them to cut us down,' said Mr Bloom, managing somehow to huff. 'Now they know we can't get down by ourselves, it puts us at their mercy. You should have tricked them, Mr Hightower, by making them believe that cutting us down would be to their great benefit.'

'But it isn't.'

'I *know*, Mr Hightower, but they did not realize that.'

'Oh, I see.' Mr Hightower's gaze returned to Rachel. '*Would* you mind cutting us down? We'd be awfully grateful, and it would be to your enormous benefit to assist us.'

Mr Bloom sighed.

Mr Partridge, Mr Hightower and Mr Bloom? Rachel thought the names sounded familiar. She racked her memory. Where had she heard their names before? Suddenly her breath caught.

The Soft Men?

Were these the three scientists who had discovered angelwine, long before the master poisoner Devon had attempted to re-create their elixir? How did they get here? Hadn't the Spine removed their bones and . . .?

'They buried you,' Rachel said. 'The Spine buried you under the Deadsands more than three hundred years ago.'

'And Miss Greene dug us up,' said Mr Hightower. 'Six days

ago, it was. She claimed to be an entrepreneur. She cut our hair. And then she abandoned us, leaving that ragged little pup to guard her wagon.'

Rachel recalled the show-woman's pet dog from Sandport. It wasn't exactly much of a guard dog.

'Don't keep giving them information,' snapped Mr Bloom. 'Information is power – how many times have I told you that? Now they know who we are, and what we are, they'll be less likely to help us.'

'I thought you said knowledge was power?'

'It's the same thing, Mr Hightower.'

'Well, I don't see that it makes a difference,' said the other man. 'You're just being crotchety as usual.'

Mr Bloom harrumphed. '*You* weren't the one buried upside down.'

And on it went . . .

Rachel listened to their ranting for a while longer, and then interrupted: 'Where is Mina Greene now?'

'In Hell, I suppose,' said Mr Hightower.

Rachel and Trench exchanged a glance.

'Mr Hightower!' exclaimed Bloom.

'I don't care to listen to you any more, Mr Bloom.' The scientist's damp eyes turned back to Rachel. 'There's power in this forest, places where Hell bubbles up close to the surface. It's because of all the heathens who have died here – the sands have drunk a lot of blood, you see.' A strand of drool extended from his lip. 'Miss Greene is a collector of horrors, and she became quite animated when we explained all of this to her.'

'When *you* explained it,' said Bloom. 'You couldn't keep your mouth shut then, and you can't keep it shut now.'

Mr Hightower looked peevish. 'I thought she would let us go if she realized that there were more interesting specimens to be discovered nearby.' He stared down at the sand with a pitiful expression. 'But she didn't. She simply swanned off in the direction of a particularly nasty toxic cache to look for ghosts. She said she'd be gone an hour or two.'

'And this was six days ago?' Rachel asked.

'The whole forest is riddled with little holes into Hell,' said Mr Hightower. 'I suppose something terrible must have happened to her.'

'He's like this with the phantasms, too,' said Mr Bloom. 'He won't stop talking at them. And now they're so completely bored with him they don't even haunt us any more.'

'That's unfair, Mr Bloom.'

Rachel decided to leave them to it. She didn't have to go far to find Mr Partridge. He was, as she had suspected, lying right behind the puppet booth itself. Looking at his slack body, bundled into a black suit and white frilled shirt, she couldn't help but think of an oversized slug. Partridge had a shock of white hair and glazed eyes which looked in two directions at once. He was licking the red and black spattered root of a tree.

'I wouldn't do that, if I were you,' she said.

By moving in a series of jerking motions, Mr Partridge somehow managed to swivel himself around. 'This particular poison,' he said gruffly, like a schoolteacher reprimanding a pupil, 'happens to be one of my favourites. It helps me think clearly, while relieving the itching sensation in my backbone.'

'You don't have a backbone.'

'Are you *mad*?' he said. 'Of course I don't have a backbone.'

He shuffled back round and went on lapping at the root.

Rachel could not see how any further conversation with these men could improve her situation. All three of them were clearly unhinged. If these toxins couldn't actually kill Mr Partridge, then what did it matter if she left him to enjoy them? She shook her head, and returned the way she had come.

Hightower and Bloom were still – as she could hear – arguing with each other. 'They seem harmless enough,' Rachel said, step-ping down from the wagon. 'We should cut them down.'

Trench was staring at the two hanging men with contempt. 'What would they do then?' he grunted. 'Flap around the place like fish? Would that be any better than leaving them where they are? Once they leave this wood, someone will only find them and abuse them. They have no way to defend against that.'

'They want to be free.'

He shrugged. 'As you wish.' He helped lift each man down from the stage in turn, and Rachel severed their ropes. Mean-while, Mr Hightower and Mr Bloom did not stop arguing until their limp bodies were stretched out lying side-by-side on the sand.

'We are down, Mr Bloom.'

'I can see that, Mr Hightower.'

Both men's glances moved rapidly about them, as though assimilating the view from this new and strange perspective. Mr Hightower tried to move first. By flexing the muscles in his shoul-ders, arms and legs, he managed to squirm an inch forward. His hat fell off. 'Did you see that, Mr Bloom? I am mobile.'

'You are indeed, Mr Hightower!'

'Then let us race!'

'A *race*, Mr Hightower?' The other man sounded excited. 'Yes, yes, but to where?'

'To Mr Partridge of course. I intend to murder the scoundrel for leaving us to rot up there all this time.'

'Not before I do, Mr Hightower. Not before I do!'

With much exciting grunting and wriggling, the two Soft Men headed off, just like a couple of snails without their shells.

Their numbers had grown again since nightfall. In addition to forty or so riders, the Heshette raiders had now acquired a further dozen men on foot, three old hags who claimed to be seers, two dogs and a herd of goats.

News of a sighting reached the party when they were less than half a league from Cinderbark Wood. One of the outriders returned, his mount steaming in the fog, to tell them that he'd witnessed the Spine assassin and her companion entering the grove of poisonous trees.

Ramnir frowned as he addressed John Anchor. 'This woodland is a dangerous place,' he said. 'Deepgate's chemists went to work on it with every poison in their arsenal.'

Anchor shrugged his massive shoulders. 'It is no big problem for me,' he said. 'I don't die so easily.'

'Yet your rope might become entangled.'

'It happens often.' The giant gave him a huge grin. 'I just keep walking, no problem.'

Ramnir laughed and clapped the dark man on the arm. 'Then our elders and women will bring the livestock to the eastern fringes of the wood. But our warriors accompany you into the trees, John Anchor.'

Jack Caulker scowled. He didn't like the way these heathens had attached themselves so closely to the giant. They'd obviously seen profit in this situation and they'd stuck to it like bone glue. No doubt every one of them had an eye on Anchor's soulpearls. This display of jovial camaraderie they had put on for the giant's benefit was clearly faked. Now they were even going into Cinderbark-fucking-Wood of all places. Everyone who'd ever gone there had left it insane – if they left the cover of the trees at all.

Well, Caulker wasn't about to join them. 'We'll ride with the livestock,' he announced from the rear of his shared gelding. 'We shall be waiting on the far side in case the two of them get away from you.'

At this the remainder of the horsemen snorted and laughed,

and called him a coward. The rider in control of Caulker's mount laughed as loud as the others. 'Not all the livestock will miss this hunt, then,' he cried. 'I'm carrying one of them here on my horse. Did you hear it bleat just then?'

Caulker fumed. Where was Hammer Eric now, when the cut-throat needed some muscle to emphasize his point of view? These idiots would kill themselves in Cinderbark Wood. But he smiled gracefully. An idea had just occurred to him – a way in which he might change the situation to his favour. He swung his leg over the horse in order to dismount. But just at that moment his horse-man twitched the reins, urging their shared mount forward. Caulker lost his balance and fell clumsily, landing on his rear in the sand.

A chorus of laughter and hoots went up from the gathered Heshette riders.

The cut-throat scrambled to his feet, his face hot with rage. 'If any one of you is man enough to fight me,' he cried, 'then—'

A dozen blades rasped from their sheaths all around him.

Caulker felt the blood leave his face. 'Then I would obviously refuse,' he said quickly. 'The desert folk are not my enemies. We've shared fire and water, for which I am grateful. And if you're ever in Sandport, look me up so that I can return the favour.' He prayed that they *would*. Hammer Eric knew a dock official who collected Heshette ears. 'But it seems to me that we're facing a great deal of danger ahead. We're all weary after the long trek here, and a man needs all of his wits in Cinderbark Wood.'

'We are not *weary*,' Ramnir said, sheathing his blade. 'That trek, as you call it, was naught but a gentle excursion.'

'Then I admire your stamina as much as your generosity. But I'm a sailor, unused to horses and sand.' He stretched his legs and winced. 'My bones ache and my flesh is raw. I fear my presence will be a burden to you all.'

One of the Heshette spat.

'You are my guide,' Anchor told Caulker firmly. 'I need you with me.'

'You appear to have found some better guides,' Caulker retorted.

'But I like you, Jack Caulker.' The giant's smile now seemed to have a slightly sinister edge to it. 'We are good friends, and you are still . . . ah, indebted to me, yes? You would not break our deal?'

The cut-throat remembered the glass bead he had smashed – payment for services he had yet to provide – and he smiled as Anchor mentioned it now.

'John Anchor's generosity almost matches yours,' he said to Ramnir. 'He was kind enough to give me a soulpearl, a bead with the power to bestow great strength upon any man who consumes it.' Now he shrugged sadly. 'Foolishly, I broke the pearl.' He sighed. 'Such a waste of power is especially galling now. I think we'd all benefit from a boost to strength and endurance if we are to follow Anchor into the dangers ahead.'

He caught Anchor's eye and, for an instant, saw a shadow pass across the big man's face. *That's right. Not so willing to share your power with these heathen bastards, are you?*

None of the Heshette spoke. Several eyed the pouch at the giant's belt, then looked quickly away. The horses whickered. Finally Ramnir said, 'John Anchor has already offered us much. We do not need to be bribed with power.'

But Anchor beamed suddenly. 'No. Jack Caulker is right. I have souls aplenty, and any man who wants one is welcome to it.' He untied the pouch from his belt. Now the Heshette looked abashed. Not one of them would step forward.

Jack Caulker wasn't so modest. He reached into the bag and plucked out one of the glass beads. It glittered in the flat grey light, as though illuminated by an interior glow. 'I thank you, Anchor.' He popped the soulpearl into his mouth and swallowed.

Wild cackles of laughter assaulted the cut-throat's ears, as though the ghost of a madwoman had been let loose inside his head. His vision blurred and eddied and suddenly the view before him changed. He found himself standing before a parapet on the edge of a sickening drop, peering down into a fog-shrouded valley of green conifers. Great eagles circled in the air below him, drifting in and out of the mists. He smelled cold mountain air and pine needles. A gust of wind made him shiver – he was wearing a thin, floaty garment.

A *dress*?

But then two huge hands grabbed his shoulders. Caulker had just enough time to turn around and see a face he recognized – the massive wooden harness, the rope leading up into the heavens, and the thick dark lips split into a huge grin – before John Anchor shoved him out over the yawning precipice.

The cut-throat plummeted down towards the misty trees, his ridiculous dress flapping wildly about his ears – his screams now mingling with the feverish laughter of the madwoman in his mind. Green branches rushed up to meet him . . .

He hit sand.

Caulker opened his eyes to see John Anchor and a ring of Heshette riders staring down at him. A horse snorted nervously somewhere nearby.

Anchor grinned. 'You ate the soul of an old midwife,' he said. 'And you died her death at Rockwall Fortress.'

The cut-throat groaned. 'I died *her* death?'

'Yes. With Cospinol's soulpearls, you experience the soul's death. Now her . . .' He frowned, thinking. 'What is the word? Essence. Yes, her *essence* lives inside you.' He laughed suddenly. 'Makes you as strong as she was.'

Caulker's arms and legs were trembling; his heart hammered in his chest. The scent of that cold mountain still seemed to linger around him. 'It was horrible,' he said. 'You *killed* her. You threw her off a cliff.'

'From the Rockwall battlements,' Anchor admitted. 'Count Lat of Grenere asked me to dispatch this woman. So many infants had died in her care. All very suspicious.'

With some effort, Caulker rose shakily to his feet. He certainly didn't feel any stronger than before. 'I never want to experience that again,' he said.

'But you will,' Anchor said brightly. 'Her last thoughts are yours now. When you sleep, I think you will dream this death many, many times. It is a small problem with Cospinol's soul-pearls – these nightmares.'

Caulker felt sick, trapped, beaten. Of all the gods and archons and warriors the giant claimed to have in his horde of ghosts, why had Caulker chosen *that* soulpearl? *A murdering midwife!* Had Anchor *tricked* him? The thought of reliving that fall again and again filled him with despair. Would he ever sleep peacefully again?

The Heshette declined to take soulpearls for themselves. Indeed, they now seemed to carry themselves with a degree of righteous aloofness.

Caulker silently cursed them all. The more he thought about it, the surer he became that the big man had deliberately tricked him into choosing *that* worthless pearl. Anchor wasn't nearly as stupid and garrulous as he pretended to be. He clearly had some plan for Caulker – and Caulker didn't like that idea at all.

But if Anchor thought he could manipulate Jack Caulker, then he had seriously underestimated the cut-throat. Caulker hadn't survived as long as he had without good instincts, and he would now find a way to turn the tables on the giant.

The seed of a plan began to take shape in the cut-throat's mind.

The Heshette left their women, with their elderly folk, to steer the livestock around the eastern edge of Cinderbark Wood, while the mounted warriors accompanied Anchor and Caulker onwards directly towards the trees. Soon the snarl of phosphorescent branches loomed before them in the fog like a toxic dream. At the very edge of the forest, Anchor halted and addressed the others.

'I will go in first,' he said, 'and clear a path for the horses, yes?' He pulled up his huge shoulders then slammed his fists together, so the huge rope quivered behind his harness.

And then he marched headlong into Cinderbark Wood.

A small smile tugged at one corner of Jack Caulker's lips as he waited for the first poisonous thorn to bite the tethered man.

Anchor's rope snagged in the tree canopy above him, but he did not pay it any attention, dragging the rope onwards, further into the woodland. The petrified branches could only bend a little before snapping, showering down upon the big man like fragments of brightly glazed crockery. Anchor brushed this debris off his shoulders and harness, without any apparent concern, kicking the larger branches aside.

Caulker watched and waited. But the giant was unstoppable. He marched on into the fog, apparently immune to his toxic surroundings. His rope rent the canopy above him, snagging great colourful nests of branches, twigs and thorns before ripping them free.

Caulker jerked backwards, just as the Heshette horsemen spurred their mounts forward after the giant. 'Don't take us in there,' he hissed to the rider in the double saddle before him. 'You'll kill us both.'

'Where John Anchor goes, we follow,' the rider replied. 'Hah!'

His gelding picked up speed, and a heartbeat later they were inside Cinderbark Wood.

The twelve riders now formed a line, with Ramnir in the lead. The Heshette leader himself kept a sensible distance behind the tethered giant to avoid the debris falling from the canopy, but he was often forced to leave the giant's trail and choose a snaking route through the surrounding trees to avoid those tangles of painted stone which had already fallen. Countless twisted branches rose out of the fog, but the Heshette riders guided their horses skilfully through them.

Anchor crashed on through the wood, like a boar through a hedge, picking up pieces of the broken trees and tossing them aside. His hands and arms soon became stained with different coloured gels, yet none of the poisons had any apparent effect on him.

Had the toxic forest lost its potency?

Caulker was soon to find out.

The party had travelled less than a quarter of a league inside Cinderbark Wood before they lost their first rider. He was one of the Rook Clan nomads the party had picked up during the previous night: a willowy young man with cynical eyes, barely older than a boy, who rode a small tan-coloured mare. Led onwards by Anchor, the Heshette had reached the apparent safety of a glade, an oasis amidst the riotous colours where thick dark roots wormed in and out of the cool white sands. The nomad's little tan mare lost its footing in the soft sand and faltered, shifting two paces out from the Heshette column while it regained its balance. The beast's front fetlock brushed momentarily against a glutinous dark blue root.

The poison acted quickly and violently. From the saddle of his own mount, two positions further back along the line, Caulker watched in fascination as the afflicted mare suddenly reared. The young Heshette rider kept his seat while he fought to control his panicking horse. Somehow he managed to stop it from bolting, but nothing could be done to save the animal he rode. Tiny red blisters swelled on its fetlock, turning black and hard even as Caulker watched. An odour like spoiled meat filled the glade, accompanied by the sound of crisping skin. The bucking mare let loose a hideous scream. Its eyes wild with fear and froth spraying from its mouth, it spun around and then lunged drunkenly towards a dense thicket of pale lemon-and-peach-coloured branches over on one side of the glade.

Rather than leap free, the young rider remained in the saddle and tried to steer his mount away from the toxic trees. Hearing the commotion from his position at the far end of the glade, John Anchor turned and bellowed out a warning. He rushed forward to help the stricken horseman, but it was already too late.

Horse and rider plunged into the thicket.

The young Heshette's mount collapsed, and both horse and rider fell amidst the sharp glowing branches. Black blisters now covered most of the mare's forelegs and breast, corpuscles which burst and streamed milky fluids across its hide. It snorted and kicked wildly, smashing up the petrified thicket around it.

The rider had been thrown clear – but not clear of the thicket. He managed to stand, and then to stumble back out of the branches, shards of broken twigs protruding from his naked arms. He managed five steps before the poisons began to change him. Yellow-and-peach-coloured welts bloomed on both his arms, spreading across his skin more rapidly than Caulker would have believed possible. He gasped and fell forwards into the sand, clutching his throat as he struggled to breathe.

A bulky warrior with long black hair dismounted and rushed to aid his fallen comrade, but Ramnir barked a command: 'Don't touch him! His skin is coated with poison.'

The warrior hesitated.

Ramnir wheeled his own mount and took up his bow. He loaded an arrow, aiming it down at the gasping horseman. Strangled screams came from the poisoned man. A black, swollen tongue lolled amidst the yellow froth in his mouth. The skin on his arms hardened and began to split like cracked leather, revealing white nodules in the open wounds beneath.

Ramnir loosed his arrow, which pierced the fallen man's neck. The young Heshette gave a pitiful gurgle, then went still.

The glade fell silent, but for the nervous snorting of the warriors' horses. The poisoned man's mount lay dead among the broken thicket, its corpse still steaming in the cold fog. Hard black blisters covered its hide, like rook's eyes.

'Don't touch the corpses,' Ramnir warned.

John Anchor turned to him. 'This place is no good for your horses. A man might still avoid the trees, but the animals are skittish and unpredictable – it is not so easy to warn them of the dangers, I think.'

The Heshette leader shook his head. 'Our animals stay with us.'

'Then we must hurry.' Anchor pointed to where a faintly glowing bank of dense yellow cloud was drifting through the glassy trees towards them. 'A mist approaches.'

With Anchor leading, the party of warriors tightened their grips on their reins and urged their horses deeper into Cinderbark Wood.

A soft growl greeted Rachel as she swung open the circus wagon's door. There, on an empty sleeping cot, sat a small dog: a pathetic little creature with a scabrous coat and ragged, chewed ears. He glared up at Rachel with tiny black eyes.

'Poor thing.' Rachel scooped the dog up.

He tried to bite her, but lacked the strength to do any harm.

'Where's your mistress?' Rachel ruffled the pup's ears. 'Has she abandoned you, eh?'

Of the puppeteer herself there was no sign, yet all of her possessions remained undisturbed within the gaudy carriage, which was much more spacious than it had appeared from outside. The front half had been given over to living space: the narrow cot, some wall-mounted cabinets full of clothes and books and pots and pans, a small sink and a bucket, and even a neat little potbelly stove for heating and cooking. Beyond this, a door opened into a storage space at the rear where Mina Greene kept the treasures of her trade. Rachel moved towards it.

Trench took one look inside and said, 'Check for provisions. There's nothing to be gained by searching through *that* junk.'

'I saw this circus in Sandport,' Rachel said. 'I just need to check on something.' She squeezed into a narrow aisle between a wall of packing crates on the right-hand side and shelves on the left. The shelves were crammed with all manner of strange objects: hound skulls and monkey paws, beads and carved wooden figurines, glass spheres and bottles, and bell-jars in which floated bizarrely misshapen creatures. On display were dead fish with jaws full of needle-like teeth, tiny skeletons, and grotesque creatures with too many eyes or limbs. Some of them even looked partly human.

'Even in my day,' Trench observed from his seat on the cot, 'Deepgate received its fair share of showmen and tricksters. These are nothing but the foetuses of camels and other beasts. There's no magic here.'

'This wagon came to Sandport,' Rachel persisted, 'and the show-woman displayed something . . .' She shrugged. 'Something I've never seen before. It looked like a living demon.'

'Unlikely.' Trench shook his head. 'Hell's creatures can survive as shades for a while, only if they keep themselves in darkness, but for them to physically walk upon the Earth they require another source of power. That's why I required your friend Dill's body to carry my soul beyond Deepgate, and why the Mesmerists must now spread their Veil over the lands they plan to conquer.' He hesitated, as though considering another option, and then finally said, 'No, this show-woman was simply duping the crowd.'

Rachel continued to search through the packing crates, looking for the one Greene had displayed to the Sandporters. And then she saw it, stacked at the very top of the pile. 'Help me down with this one, will you?'

Between them, they lowered the crate, and carried it back outside where they set it down upon the white sands. Rachel pried the lid off with her knife, to reveal the wretched creature cowering within.

Trench hissed when he saw the contents of the crate. 'I had hoped never to see one of these things here.' He rubbed a hand across his furrowed brow. 'And I would advise killing it quickly, but that won't be easy.'

The creature in the crate was breathing in wet gasps. It had reassumed the same form Rachel had first seen in Sandport: a knot of flesh and muscle and wood combined. White eyes peered up at them from a bulbous lump which might have been a head. It made a pitiful whimpering sound.

'Then it *is* a demon?' Rachel asked.

'The term "demon" is meaningless – it applies to all of Hell's creatures. All demons are simply physical incarnations of souls on Earth.' His eyes narrowed on the creature. 'By rights they require a bloodmist to survive in this realm, but this thing . . . no, not this.'

'What is it?'

'An abomination. A Mesmerist experiment. King Menoa has long been trying to construct a form for his warriors which could survive on Earth without relying on the Veil. He had limited success with shape-shifters, such as this one – part living and part dead. However, they lack the will to maintain a single physical shape for long because they are unable to resist persuasion.'

'Greene turned it into a chair before the mob.'

The angel grunted. 'It will assume any shape you order it to, within certain limits. Smaller objects must be denser, larger ones less substantial, as it can only stretch its flesh so far.' He inclined his head at the thing. 'Try it and see.'

'No,' the creature wailed. 'It hurts. Send me back to Hell.'

'Mesmerist filth,' Trench spat. 'Menoa sent you here to spy.'

The thing's bulbous head shook. 'No,' it moaned, 'I have been the victim of sorcery. The mortal woman who owns this wagon summoned me here. I was powerless to resist.'

'Mina Greene is a thaumaturge?' Rachel asked.

'One of the greatest.'

Rachel cast an instinctive glance around the forest. 'And where is she now?'

The demon's many muscles flexed and glistened. 'She left six days ago to look for a door into Hell. This forest is riddled with them: old doors through which many phantasms have passed.'

Trench scoffed. 'Yes, *phantasms*. Portals like those are useless to anything except ghosts. No human could pass through such a vaporous gate.'

'But she has help,' the demon said.

The puppy in Rachel's arms gave a low growl.

The shape-shifter's eyes widened momentarily. 'I have said too much,' it said. 'Please command me to change into something small and quick – a hare, perhaps, or a bat. Let me flee from here.'

Rachel studied the puppeteer's dog. Its growl had been . . . *opportune*, if nothing else. Could this mangy creature *also* be a shape-shifter? But the pup ignored her stare, lapping at the assassin's thumb instead. Rachel sighed. This forest was making her paranoid.

Cinderbark Wood remained deathly still. Nothing moved amongst the painted boles and soft sands except a few wisps of fog creeping in from the north.

Fog?

In the desert?

'Ignore everything it says,' Trench said. 'Menoa's creatures can't help but lie. If you don't wish to kill the thing now, I propose we put it to use.' He leaned over the crate.

The demon cried out again.

Before Rachel could stop him, Trench had whispered a word into the demon's ear. The thing in the crate screamed just as its shape began to change. Its bones folded inwards with cracking sounds, and its flesh turned from pink and red to the colour of raw steel. With every heartbeat it grew smaller, and its cries became more distant.

'What are you doing to it?' Rachel cried.

'We've walked far enough without a decent weapon,' Trench growled. He reached inside the crate, and then withdrew his hand.

He was holding a sword: a shining steel weapon with a plain leather-bound hilt and copper-coloured pommel. Rainbow colours swept across the blade as the angel examined it by the light of phosphorescent branches. 'This is an example of one of King Menoa's first experiments to fuse the souls of the dead with corporeal materials,' he said.

Rachel stared in horror. 'Is the demon conscious? Does it still feel?'

'It does,' Trench replied. 'But do not pity it. It is more deceitful and cunning than it appears. It has intimate knowledge of the shapes of many weapons and can change between them in a heartbeat. Such creatures were once given to Pandemerian nobles as gifts – they can be far stronger than normal steel or glass, and are capable of adapting to any combat situation. "Shiftblades" we call them in the Maze.'

Rachel dragged her eyes away from the strange sword. A thought occurred to her. 'Menoa's *first* experiments?'

Trench grunted. 'He moved on.'

Rachel was about to ask him to expound, but she suddenly noticed that the fog had grown much denser. Whorls of mist drifted through the trees like the tentacles of some creeping monster. She could barely see ten yards to the north of them. A sudden chill gripped her. 'We'd better get going,' she said.

But Trench didn't move. He was staring intently into the grey pall which seemed to roll through the trees towards them. 'Is such weather normal for this time of year?' he asked.

'Not this deep in the Deadsands,' she replied. 'I've never seen anything like this before.' And then she noticed an odd briny odour in the air. 'That smell . . .' she whispered, suddenly on edge. Her senses were tingling. 'Trench, this is a *sea* mist.'

The angel grinned, and for a heartbeat Rachel could almost believe that this was Dill. Despite his ruined hands and missing wings, Trench's expression was so unexpected and natural that it seemed to Rachel that her old friend was back before her.

'Cospinol,' Trench murmured.

Throughout the trek through Cinderbark Wood Jack Caulker prayed for another accident – a fetlock brushing against a protruding root, a poison cache cracked open by a clumsy hoof, a rider failing to duck in time below overhanging branches – *anything* to make these heathens appreciate the utter insanity of this current adventure.

He dwelled on the vision Anchor's soulpearl had given him – that terrifying plummet from those airy heights into the mist-chilled valley below – and he shuddered. Caulker had experienced that old woman's death. He had been punished for *her* crimes, and each time Caulker slept, the tethered giant would become his judge and executioner once more.

Up ahead, John Anchor laughed at something Ramnir had said. Despite the dangers of this hideous stone forest and the stench of these heathen riders and great weight of the skyship he dragged behind him – and the countless souls he had eaten – the tethered man had *laughed*. What terrors did those consumed souls bring to Anchor's slumber? If the giant relived the deaths of those he had murdered, then how could he *laugh*?

Caulker felt small and weak and bitter, and he hated Anchor for that feeling.

He considered the Mesmerists, imagining himself striding through the halls of some glorious castle in Hell. And why should Hell not have castles as grand as any of those in Heaven? Ayen had spurned mankind, but now Hell sought to embrace it. He pictured John Anchor in chains, and, for the first time in days, the cut-throat smiled.

The horse lurched, bringing him back to the here and now. The Heshette horseman sharing Caulker's saddle had pulled sharply on the reins to steer his beast around a clutch of violet branches. Caulker then realized he had been staring at Anchor's pouch of soulpearls.

All those dreams of death. These were ghosts trapped in glass – every one of them murdered by Anchor. Caulker recalled the battle-archon's spirit he had released from its pearl amidst the ruins of the Widow's Hook, and now he began to understand why that apparition had attacked the tethered man so vehemently.

What would happen if *all* of those soulpearls were broken at once?

The woodland thinned as they crested a shallow rise. Ancient trees loomed at the limits of the fog like gaudy harlequins, their painted claws reaching out to each other, as though frozen in dance. Anchor took advantage of wider gaps between these poisoned boles, steering his rope so that he avoided the worst of the overhead branches. Behind him the rest of the party moved in silence but for the rustle of tackle and the clinking of the horse-men's fetishes. The air filled with the steaming breaths of their mounts, and the occasional snort.

Anchor halted and raised his hand. The Heshette reined in

their horses behind him. A moment passed, in which every man strained to see through the fog.

Caulker stared into the grey gloom, moistening his lips. Had Anchor spotted the scarred angel, or one of her companions? Perhaps even a Spine patrol? He failed to suppress a smile. A diversion might prove fruitful.

And then a cheerful voice emerged from the mists. 'The Adamantine Man! By the Seven Gods, I am glad to see you.'

Caulker watched in disbelief as a figure in tattered mail approached them through the coloured trees. He held before him a naked sword, but slackly, without any apparent intention of using the weapon. A second figure – a female Spine assassin – followed behind him.

Caulker ground his teeth and spat. He could not believe this turn of events. It seemed that even Anchor's supposed enemies, the very companions of those he was here to kill, were welcoming him.

14

REVELATIONS

With his rope and harness, his night-hued skin, and arms and shoulders that looked powerful enough to crush an ox, he was certainly the strangest man Rachel had ever seen. Yet he beamed at Trench and herself with such open delight that she felt herself relaxing, despite the crowd of mounted Heshette warriors hovering in his wake.

'The very people I look for,' the giant boomed. 'Yes? The boy angel and his assassin friend from Sandport? Good, good – we have much to discuss.'

Rachel frowned. The very people he was *looking for*? Her unease began to creep back. She clutched the puppeteer's dog to her breast. It gave a gentle growl.

Trench clasped hands with the big man. 'I must speak with Cospinol at once,' he said. 'I have an urgent message to deliver.'

Now Anchor's brow creased. 'You have the right body but . . . the wrong soul,' he remarked, staring down at the angel. 'Very strange.' He flicked his eyes to Rachel, and studied her dog for a moment, before returning his attention to Trench. 'It is just you with the wrong-shape soul. Wrong-shape sword, too. A shiftblade, yes?'

'That's not important,' Trench replied. 'Tell Cospinol—'

'It is important,' Anchor persisted. 'You were dead, yes? Dead souls should not be moving the living like puppets. Dead souls should not carry demons around with them.' He turned to Rachel and pointed at the pup she carried. 'And you . . . where did you find this creature?'

'The *dog*?'

'It is not just a dog.'

Rachel hesitated. 'It belonged to a thaumaturge.'

Anchor grinned. 'Belonged? No, I think it is the other way around. Basilis is much older than he appears. Older than John Anchor even.'

A soft sound came from the animal's throat.

Rachel looked closely at the pup. It nuzzled her fingers. She could feel its heart beating, the warmth of its tiny body against her palm. It weighed nothing, a harmless ball of fur.

Basilis?

Trench was becoming agitated. He quickly told the giant all about his ascent from Hell, his possession of Dill's body, and their escape from Deepgate. As his story unfolded, the Heshette were edging their horses nearer. Soon Rachel felt their dark eyes slide to her Spine armour. She held the puppy close to her chest. Quietly she began to note their various weapons.

As Trench and Anchor continued to converse, Rachel learned that the giant had come here in response to the Mesmerist threat against his own land. At Anchor's talk of gods and skyships, the assassin found her eyes lift in awe to follow that huge rope up into the foggy skies. *The god of brine and fog?* Trench refused to relay his message to Cospinol via Anchor, insisting instead on an audience with this sea god himself. The tethered giant thought about this for a long moment, then agreed. 'Cospinol will hear you,' he said. 'But you must leave the shiftblade down here. He fears assassination.'

Behind him, the rope trembled.

'He does not fear assassination,' Anchor corrected himself, 'but leave the shiftblade anyway.' His gaze lingered on Mina Greene's dog, but then he peered up and studied the poisonous canopy. 'I fear to bring Cospinol's ship all the way down through these branches,' he announced. 'But there are gaps between the trees through which it may be possible to lower a rope, if the ship is near enough to the ground.'

He reached behind his back and began to heave the rope down towards him.

Rachel, it seemed, was not the only one here to be witnessing this spectacle for the first time, for all the Heshette turned their gazes upwards and began to mutter among themselves and point at the heavens in nervous expectation. She wondered how Anchor had come to be travelling with such a ragged crew, but then her attention snapped quickly up to the sky.

The shadow of something massive was descending upon Cinderbark Wood.

As Anchor pulled the rope down, hand over fist, he called out, 'So you stay with your friend's body, Rachel Hael? Even though his soul is gone to Hell?'

Rachel realized he had spoken to her. 'I . . .' she began. The object above seemed impossibly vast; it was difficult to pull her eyes away from it. 'We made a deal. I help Trench deliver his message, and then he gives up Dill's body.'

'And where is your other companion – the scarred one?'

'She . . .' But then Rachel's instincts shouted a warning. How did this stranger know about *Carnival*? How had he known how to find them? *The very people I look for.* The answer dawned on her at once. Cospinol was the god Ulcis's brother.

Oh shit.

'I haven't seen her in weeks,' she replied quickly. 'She abandoned us before we reached Sandport.' Rachel dared not tell the man about her suspicions that Carnival had been shadowing them. A clash between the scarred angel and this stranger would certainly not help their situation.

Anchor grinned as he continued to drag span after span of rope down from the sky. 'Not such a good friend then, eh?' The stench of brine intensified as the fog above the canopy grew ever darker. 'A friend does not leave her companions behind.'

'I wouldn't exactly call her a friend.' Rachel could hear chilling sounds issuing from above now. *Distant howling?* She kept her gaze pinned to the heavens. The dog in her arms barked, and she began stroking its coat to calm the little thing. 'What do you want with her?'

The big man beamed. 'I bear her no grudge.'

Great spars of timber appeared through the gloom over their heads, thousands of them. Like the upturned masts and yards of a whole flotilla of ships, they formed a vast, cluttered mass of wood which stretched as far up as Rachel could see. There were armoured figures hanging everywhere among this construction – the source, the assassin now realized, of the growing clamour. She gave an involuntary gasp.

The horses reared in panic. Curses went up as their riders struggled to control them. Anchor kept pulling on the rope, inching the whole skyship earthwards. 'If her death can save the world,' he said to Rachel, 'would you give her up?'

'I don't think very much of Carnival,' Rachel admitted. 'But I don't think much of the world either.'

Anchor laughed, but then a mighty crash came from somewhere nearby, as the lowest parts of descending gallows collided with the canopy of Cinderbark Wood. A short distance to the east, several wooden beams had sliced down through the poisoned trees. Stone branches fell in bright showers, raising puffs of sand where they struck the ground. The howling in the skies grew suddenly louder as Anchor's captives fought against their nooses – an entire army of dead men.

'Sorry,' Anchor boomed. 'I was not paying attention. Cospinol's ship is low enough, I think.' He stopped hauling on the rope, leaving the bulk of the skyship floating a few yards above the forest canopy.

Rachel felt as though she had been trapped between two worlds. Cospinol's incredible vessel and Cinderbark Wood had clamped together like the teeth of Heaven and Earth, and now, impossibly, the assassin found herself staring up at an army of damned souls. Hundreds of warriors hung from their gins, moaning or crying out in unknown languages. Their voices echoed through the fog.

'Always complaining,' Anchor muttered, with irritation. He pinned the rope under his foot, then turned to Trench. 'Cospinol sends down a rope now. You hold on tight. They pull you up. Is better to ascend this way.' He nodded. 'The other way is, eh . . . not so good for living bodies.'

'I'm going with *him*,' Rachel announced. She had looked after Dill's body since Deepgate, and she wasn't about to let it out of her sight now.

'As you wish.' Anchor shrugged. 'You go up, you come back down later. Afterwards we speak about your scarred friend. I have many questions.'

A derisive snort came from somewhere close behind Rachel. 'Then put them to me, assassin.' Rachel recognized the voice at once – the very sound of it filled her with a sense of impending violence.

Carnival moved quickly out of the fog, her wings half-outstretched as though ready for battle, her dark eyes fixed on the tethered giant. 'You are an assassin, aren't you?'

'It is not personal,' Anchor said. 'Cospinol needs your blood.'

Rachel's thoughts raced. She had seen Carnival fight. She had witnessed the scarred angel cut through an army and murder a god, and she knew that Anchor stood no chance against this foe.

Yet if the giant had come here to fight the Mesmerists, then Rachel could not afford to let Carnival kill him. She looked at Trench for support, but was dismayed to see the hatred boiling in his eyes. His fist tightened on his strange demon-blade, and it let loose a pitiful wail in response.

Carnival murdered me. I trained every day for twenty years, yet she still defeated me.

Silister Trench had been another of the scarred angel's victims. But now it was Dill's fist clutching the sword, and Dill's blood that would be spilled in a fight.

'Get out of here,' Rachel hissed at Carnival. 'Please . . . just go.'

The scarred angel growled, 'You didn't complain when I cut you loose from a Spine trap in Deepgate. I didn't hear you complain when I brought down a fleet of airships to aid your escape.'

Yet Carnival had remained hidden all this time, watching and listening from afar, and now she was going to ruin everything. Cinderbark Wood was about to become a battlefield. The Heshette were urging their horses into a semicircle behind Anchor. Steel rasped as blades were unsheathed. Bowstrings tightened.

Carnival's full attention remained fixed on Anchor. 'Your master wants my blood?'

'He does,' Anchor replied.

'Then let him try and take it.'

But it was Trench who attacked first. Rachel caught movement at the edge of her vision, and she wheeled to see the wingless archon charge. He was muttering something under his breath. The shiftblade thrust forward, aimed at Carnival's neck.

'Wait!' Rachel cried.

The scarred angel danced back from the blow. She would have avoided it easily had the shiftblade not *changed* form. Halfway through Trench's strike, his sword turned into a pike. This sudden alteration caught Carnival by surprise, but not Trench himself, who wielded the iron-sheathed weapon with consummate ease.

The pike had a much longer reach, and its curved iron blade had nicked the scarred angel's larynx, drawing blood.

Carnival clutched her bloody neck and backed away.

Trench swung the pike in a circle over his head, his hands turning the shaft, then again brought the point down to bear on his opponent. Still whispering to himself, he thrust the weapon forward.

When Carnival lashed a fist out to grab the shaft, her fingers closed on nothing but air. The shiftblade had altered its shape again, from a pike into a rapier. Its steel tip pierced Carnival's hand just behind her thumb.

She shrieked in fury, and leapt back, turning to face the archon once more. Her eyes thinned to murderous slits.

Trench came at her fast – in a series of rapid strikes. Handling the rapier with as much mastery as the pike, he strove forward, shifting his hind foot with each lunge to keep every blow just in reach.

Carnival was forced to retreat again.

Now Trench moved to a broadward stance, seemingly leaving himself open to attack. He waited, the rapier tip aimed at a point above his opponent's heart.

Anchor had folded his arms across his huge chest and was watching the battle with interest.

Carnival pounced with frightening speed, her body flexing under the projected path of the blade, her hands reaching for the other angel's neck.

The shiftblade changed again. Trench's rapier became an iron shield, which he smashed into the scarred angel's face. She tumbled backwards, blood slicing from her nose, as a metallic *clang* resounded through the stone forest.

'Raw fury cannot match skill,' Anchor commented to the Heshette leader, a thin man with black hair and cynical eyes. 'The First

Citadel champion has some experience, I think.' He paused. 'But maybe not so much stamina. The fight ends soon, eh?'

Trench was already breathing hard, clearly struggling with the weight of the shield. Evidently Dill's untrained muscles were not used to such exertions.

The scarred angel's rage, meanwhile, gave her almost limitless endurance. She was snarling and spitting blood, already crouching in order to hurl herself back into the battle.

'Carnival!' Rachel cried.

But the scarred angel ignored her. She flung herself at Trench's shield like a force of nature: a storm of teeth and fists intent on ripping him apart.

Trench was driven back by the concentrated fury of her attack. He staggered and fell, but as he dropped to the ground he hissed another frantic word. Razor-sharp spikes burst out of his shield, shredding his opponent's hands. Blood flew in arcs from Carnival's flailing fists, but she did not stop.

'Too much blood,' Anchor said. 'I stop this now.' He looped a coil of loose rope around his huge bicep and strode forward, cracking his knuckles.

Trench was pinned under his shield, desperately trying to keep it between him and the scarred angel's frenzied blows. Carnival seemed oblivious to her own wounds, however, and continued her assault without pause. Skin now hung in shreds from her lacerated fists.

'Angel,' Anchor roared, 'leave the poor boy. It is time for you to face *me* now.'

Carnival wheeled on him, her face riven with blood and scars and strands of her own black hair. The lights of Cinderbark Wood glimmered faintly in her eyes. 'Assassins,' she hissed. 'I've killed so many now.'

'Don't do this,' Rachel warned. 'Carnival, please.'

The giant gave Rachel a sad smile. 'I make the end painless for your friend. You must not fear for her.'

Carnival rose slowly away from Trench's battered and cowering body. The rage seemed to have drained out of her abruptly. She glanced at Rachel, then back at Anchor. 'You're unarmed,' she said.

'I prefer fists and feet to using steel. It is best for both of us, eh?'

Carnival nodded. 'Then I'll kill you quickly.'

Rachel cried out a warning.

But the scarred angel moved like the shadow of a gale-torn cloud, a dark shape across the white sands.

Rachel *focused*. She had no clear idea of how to stop this bloodshed, but she needed at least a chance to try. Time expanded around her. The warriors hanging from Cospinol's skyship settled silently into their nooses. The Heshette horsemen froze in their saddles. Trench's ragged breathing stopped.

But Carnival did not. Moving as fast as any focused Spine, the scarred angel reached for Anchor's throat. Had Rachel's senses not been pushed beyond their normal limits, she might have missed the attack altogether.

But then John Anchor did something astonishing.

He seized Carnival's outstretched hand and jerked it aside. Even at this increased speed, his fist had been a blur. Rachel knew that she'd just seen something impossible – the force of air alone should have shattered the big man's bones.

Yet Anchor now lifted his other fist and punched Carnival hard against the side of her head. The scarred angel went limp, slowly, and began to collapse at the giant's feet.

Rachel dragged herself back to her normal state, her muscles already cramping from that one *focused* instant. Her heart felt like it was racing, although it was actually slowing. She watched Anchor pick up Carnival's body and sling it over his shoulder.

'It is done,' he said wearily. 'Another warrior for the *Rotsward*'s gins.' Then he plucked a reed from his breeches and blew into it.

The Heshette were hard-pressed to keep their mounts from bolting when the clattering, clicking mass of shells and pincers descended from Cospinol's ship. The crabs surged over the scarred angel, and then bore her body up Anchor's rope. Rachel stared at the spectacle like a woman observing her own nightmare from the fringes of sleep. Was Carnival still alive?

Conflicting emotions plucked at her. She had been through so much with the scarred angel – as bitter opponents, and then allies. Carnival had saved Rachel, and also once tried to kill her. Now watching her former companion's body ascending to the skyship, Rachel could not totally reconcile her divided feelings.

High above her, the disparate warriors suspended from the *Rotsward*'s yards suddenly howled and roared with greater agitation. To Rachel's ears, these cries evinced a profound madness. Was this what awaited the scarred angel?

Carnival had disappeared by now, borne rapidly up the great rope. Trench turned his eyes from the sky, a look of grim satisfaction on his face, then addressed Anchor. 'If I'm to meet your master,' he remarked, 'I'd rather reach his skyship in a more traditional way.'

Anchor laughed. 'Rope and basket?' he suggested. 'Same way we lift the fish and grain and fowl. Only John Anchor stays down here.' He stamped a foot on the ground. 'John Anchor stays with the beasts.'

Evidently the basket had carried up a great deal more fish than grain or fowl, for the stench brought tears to Rachel's eyes. Supported by a much thinner and frailer rope than the one Anchor used to pull the skyship, the wicker container plummeted quickly out of the fog and thumped against the sandy ground. Trench climbed in first, and was hoisted up out of sight by unknown handlers.

Several minutes later, the basket creaked down out of the fog. It was empty again. Rachel placed the puppy into the sour-smelling makeshift lift, and then hopped in beside it. She brushed her greasy hands on her breeches and wondered if the god she was about to meet would be likely to offer her a bath.

The rope drew taut, and with a jerk the basket began to ascend into the fog, up among the moaning warriors hanging in their nooses. Basilis sniffed around her feet and then peed against the wicker side. The softly glowing colours of Cinderbark Wood receded below her, the branches blurring into streaks of purple, green and yellow. From up here Rachel could see the hanging figures more clearly. They were dressed in queerly exotic armour, and while each of their suits was different from the next, they all shared the same pallid complexion of men long dead. Howling stares turned to follow Rachel as she rose among them. These warriors were suspended from a matrix of damp spars and masts, like a vast scaffold built from the bones of ships. It seemed end-less.

Up through the fog the basket climbed, its wicker lattice creak-ing under Rachel's boots. She could smell the brine strongly now; the taste of salt lingered on her lips. White crusts, like hoarfrost, laced the yards and ropes in places. Overhead loomed a shadow denser than the surrounding network of timbers.

And then she saw Cospinol's great skyship itself: the huge tat-tered hull of dark oak, the sleekly tapered bow, and the sheer bulk of the stern rising like the ramparts of a castle. Amidst this impos-sible scaffold, the vessel reminded Rachel of a spider at the centre of its web.

The basket rose until it clunked against the side of the mid-ships' balustrade and halted. Four slack-fleshed crewmen rested against their winch handles and fixed their vacant gazes upon the deck. There was no sign of Trench or of Carnival's body.

Warily, Rachel picked up the dog and climbed out of the

basket. No sooner had she set foot upon Cospinol's deck than a booming voice came from an open doorway in the stern of the vessel. 'If this message is truly from Hasp, then my brother Rys is behind it by proxy!'

'Rys knows nothing, I swear.'

The second voice Rachel recognized as Trench's. She ducked through the open doorway.

Trench was pleading with an ancient battle-archon, a greybeard clad in crab-shell armour. The god of brine and fog? Cospinol was bedraggled, pigeon-winged and wild of hair, and yet his blue eyes burned with feverish ferocity. 'Twelve of them!' he roared, striding across the gloomy cabin. The floor dipped dangerously under his weight. '*One* arconite was dire news. But *twelve* . . .? Where did King Menoa find the *power* to construct so many?'

'A piece of the shattered god burns within each arconite, thus granting them immortality.' Trench lowered his head. 'But the souls inside these creatures were taken from the First Citadel. We have suffered losses during this siege.'

Cospinol hissed. He glanced at Rachel, but his gaze then dropped to the pup in her arms. He continued to pace his cabin again. 'Twelve arconites,' he muttered. 'This world is finished if Menoa can spill enough blood to release them all from Hell.'

'He will butcher everything in his path to facilitate their release from the Maze. We must bargain with him, Cospinol.'

'*Bargain?*' The god snorted. 'Oh, Rys will like *that*.'

Rachel said, 'Trench, what's going on?'

'Who *is* this woman?' Cospinol cried. His outstretched finger shook as he pointed at the tiny dog. 'And why did she bring that bloody *hound* aboard my vessel?'

The pup growled.

Cospinol eyed the mangy creature warily. 'What is your interest in all of this, Basilis? Since when did you meddle in the affairs of the gods?' When the dog made no sound, Cospinol lifted his gaze to Rachel. 'Speak for your master, then, thaumaturge.'

Rachel gaped at him. 'I'm no thaumaturge,' she replied. 'I don't know what you're talking about. This pup belongs to someone else. We . . .' She had been about to say, *we rescued it*, but in light of these new events, she now began to wonder otherwise.

What exactly *was* Basilis?

Cospinol regarded her darkly for a long moment. 'This is a conspiracy,' he growled. 'Rys sends me to the other side of the world – to avenge our brother's death, *he says*. To gather power for myself, *he says*. To seal a portal and halt a second incursion.' His chest rose and fell under the crab-shell plate. 'All lies. Now that I'm here, what do I find? A messenger from Hell who insists we must abandon this land to the Mesmerists. And now a demon and his lying thaumaturge.'

'*Abandon* this land?' Rachel placed a hand on Trench's arm. 'What does he mean? Who are these arconites you spoke of?'

Trench was looking at Basilis, his brow creased in thought, but he now raised his eyes to meet the assassin's own. 'I'm sorry, Rachel. This has always been my message. King Menoa is assembling a new force of warriors: twelve giants who are able to walk on unblooded ground – who can travel freely beyond the Mesmerist Veil.' His shoulders slumped. 'Just *one* of these arconites destroyed the bulk of Rys's army at Skirl before they managed to subdue it. And even then they could not kill the thing. It lies chained in the ruins of a flooded city. But the gods on Earth now lack the strength to fight a second arconite. Cospinol and his brothers must surrender to the ruler of Hell and beg for his mercy, or they will perish.'

'But what about Deepgate?'

'There's no hope for Deepgate,' he replied, 'and no hope for Pandemeria either. The gods must now act to save themselves. I'm afraid there's no hope for mankind at all.'

★

The Heshette wouldn't desert their horses. Caulker had hoped to be rid of at least some of them by now. He had expected them to take up Anchor's offer of sanctuary aboard Cospinol's skyship, but they remained down here – as firmly entrenched in the giant's company as lice on a crone's scalp.

Anchor himself had become subdued. For a while he kept one ear to the skies above as though eavesdropping upon a secret conversation, but then announced, 'We go soon, I think. Bad news.'

'I'll be glad to get out of this wood,' Caulker muttered. He had already dismounted and was pacing back and forth between the boles of two poisoned trees. 'Although the path out of here is likely to be just as treacherous. The skyship must have brought down half a hundred branches from the canopy.'

Yet, despite his misgivings, Caulker was beginning to feel more comfortable. Anchor had dealt with the scarred angel with consummate ease. Any Spine they encountered on the road to Deepgate would not pose a threat to him. It seemed that they had survived the worst of it.

The tethered man took a soulpearl from his pouch and swallowed it. Then he rolled his huge shoulders and gave a great sigh. 'War always benefits Hell,' he said. 'Death and bloodshed makes it stronger. Menoa knows this. It is why he wants war. The gods know this too, but they cannot be slaves to Menoa.' He shook his head. 'I do not think there will ever be peace between them.'

'You think Hell is bound to win?' Caulker asked.

'It is likely,' Anchor admitted.

Caulker had suspected as much. All souls flowed to the Maze eventually. And with Iril shattered and powerless, no one could stop Menoa from claiming those souls. The King's Mesmerists would inevitably rise to consume this earth, and all who stood against them would die.

It made no sense to Caulker to be on the losing side.

John Anchor remained distracted. Absently, he consumed

another soulpearl. This time, when he swallowed the glass bead, he grimaced and looked like he was about to spit. An incautious choice of soul, perhaps?

The cut-throat eyed the bag of soulpearls. A single strike with the flat of a sword – or even a stick – would shatter most of them, releasing the furious spirits inside. Despite Anchor's great strength and speed, the wrath of one spectral archon had drawn the big man's blood. What damage could a horde of such ghosts accomplish? And what if they were released during the heat of battle? King Menoa would surely reward such cunning.

'How do you plan to deal with the Mesmerists?' Caulker asked. 'Deepgate must be crawling with them by now.'

'No doubt,' Anchor replied. 'But we do not meet Menoa's forces there.'

'No? But I thought—'

'We go east.'

'East?' Caulker gaped at him. 'But Deepgate lies to the west.'

'Cospinol changed plan,' Anchor said. 'We leave Deepgate to the Mesmerists and go back across the sea to Pandemeria. All are welcome. Even you, Jack Caulker. There is no more debt between us.'

The ember of Caulker's own plan faded. If he was to gain favour with the Mesmerists, he needed something with which to bargain. The cut-throat needed to show King Menoa where his loyalties lay. 'You mean to *abandon* Deepgate to the enemy?' he asked.

'Yes. We go to sea.'

A sea journey?

With the Heshette *as companions?* Muttering curses to himself, Jack Caulker slouched further into his fog-damp jacket. What other choice remained? He could hardly remain *here*. His vision of plummeting from Rockwall's battlements returned to him, and now it seemed apt – for he felt like a man who had stepped off a precipice, abandoning his destiny to the hands of the gods.

Anchor was consulting Ramnir now. Caulker could not hear their hushed conversation, but the big man's hand gestures were urgent. Finally the pair clasped arms.

And so Caulker found himself once more sharing the saddle with a Heshette horseman, as the group picked their way east now through Cinderbark Wood. They reached the edge of the petrified woodland without incident and stopped to camp a short distance out from the colourful boles, while they waited for the rest of the original party to bring their livestock down the eastern edge of the wood to join them. The tribesmen built a dismal fire from their supplies of dried dung, boiling strips of tough meat in a small iron pot – which they insisted on sharing with both Anchor and Caulker.

Caulker chewed the meat without tasting it. He was exhausted. Sleep tugged at him, but his fears of reliving that nightmare fall from Rockwall's battlements forced him to resist.

The tethered giant accepted the meal graciously enough, but he insisted on allowing his master Cospinol to improve their fare. Again the same basket was lowered from the skyship, now loaded with flagons of water, wine and salted fish. Anchor and Ramnir continued to converse in hushed tones while they ate. Ramnir seemed disturbed, often shaking his head or gazing thoughtfully into the fire.

Finally Caulker could no longer remain awake. He curled up on a foul-smelling Heshette blanket and closed his eyes. And in his dreams he fell a thousand times. Again and again he found himself peering down into that deep, fog-shrouded valley. He smelled the fresh mountain pines and he watched the eagles soaring through the mists below the high battlements. The cut-throat had no wings to save him. Each time Anchor pushed him, he fell screaming to his death.

He woke to the sound of his own cries. Sweat plastered his hair and face, his muscles ached, and for a heartbeat he feared that his plummet from the fortress battlements had been real, that his body now lay broken in the gloom beneath that faraway fortress. But then he became aware of the early-morning sun shining through the fog like beaten gold. Horses were snorting and goatbells tinkling nearby. He could smell livestock and dung fires.

The whole camp was already full of life. Heshette riders were cinching saddles and tackle, and strapping packs and weapons to their mounts. Women were milking goats, and chattering in their heathen language. Those greybeards and family descendants who had driven their livestock around the northern edge of Cinderbark Wood had finally caught up with the rest of the party.

Ramnir gathered the Heshette together and addressed them: 'Most of you have already seen the red mists rising from Deepgate,' he cried. 'This pestilence is the breath of Hell, and it has been brought upon us by the chained city's own priests.' He raised his hands to quell the murmuring crowd. 'Iril was shattered in the War Against Heaven, and now Hell has a new king. This bloody Veil heralds the approach of his armies. It is already spreading beyond the abyss, poisoning the lands all around Deepgate.'

One of the older greybeards yelled out, 'We'll pray for rain!'

'Rain will not wash this away,' Ramnir explained, 'nor will Ayen lower Heaven's barricades to help us. We cannot stop this thing. The Deadsands will be consumed.'

'The Heshette do not flee,' the old man muttered.

'Hear me out, old man,' Ramnir said. 'That abyss below Deepgate is one of two doors into Hell. The other lies across the sea in the lands which border John Anchor's country, and it is already the focus of a great war.' He paused to look at each of the surrounding group in turn. 'But who will stand and fight against Hell *here*? The chained city is in ruins, its people tempered and reduced to slavery. There are no armies to hold back the Maze

King's forces, and those tatters which remain will resist, at every step, our approach to the abyss.'

'We don't need an army,' the old man said. 'We need faith.'

But Ramnir shook his head. 'Our friend Anchor has offered us passage across the Yellow Sea to join his own people in the battle against Hell. We have the chance to start again, to fight with those who would welcome our efforts against a common foe. But if we remain here, we die.'

The sight of these withered men on their ill-fed beasts, considering war, almost tore a laugh from Caulker's gut, but he managed to clench the outburst in his throat as Ramnir's thin dark eyes turned on him. The Heshette had indeed no choice but to flee. Deepgate's armies had decimated the tribes during decades of war, King Menoa would now crush the survivors like lice.

After some discussion, the Heshette came to realize this, just as Caulker knew they would. They would be ferried to Pandemeria, taken in there as refugees, and then pitied and scorned by the locals. Caulker had seen it happen many times before: the beggar cups of nomads clacked around half the street corners in Sandport and Clune; tribal children raked through the refuse heaps like dogs. Anchor must have known this too. Surely the tethered giant didn't expect these weak old men to fight?

It was all in the blood, of course. Jack Caulker's own ancestors had been great river men, smugglers and infamous profiteers, thus he came from good stock. But these heathens were different: they hadn't crawled very far from the caves their ancestors had burrowed into Hollowhill. To think of them as human required a generous imagination.

But Caulker had little time to consider the matter further, since the group had now come to a decision. The Heshette would accompany Anchor to the continent of Pandemeria, abandoning forever the poisoned desert which had so long been their home.

'Do you expect to carry all of them on your back?' Caulker asked Anchor harshly. 'What about the elderly and crippled? And the beasts? Will your master really allow his skyship to become a menagerie?'

'All are welcome,' Anchor replied.

The cut-throat cursed – and then continued to curse throughout the sixteen-day march southeast towards the Pocked Delta. The Heshette led Anchor along an old nomad route, disused since the wells had been poisoned by Deepgate's armies. Now, at last, with a ready supply of food and water from Cospinol's skyship, the trail became passable once more. They travelled in haste, for outriders brought grim news from beyond their shroud of fog. The Mesmerist Veil was growing with each passing day, staining the western skies like a bloody gauze. Caulker's bones grated in the saddle. Sand stung his eyes. And the flies! A buzzing cloud of insects kept pace with the party, as if they too were fleeing the crimson pall.

Ramnir sent riders out far and wide to spread news of the exodus, and soon other tribes came along to join the group. By the time the party reached the sea their numbers had swelled to more than eight hundred: streams of refugees, including women and children, mingled with herds of thin goats and ranks of leather-faced horsemen. Warriors from a score of tribes gathered on Longlizard Point, a long low peninsula stubbled with tough ochre grasses. Beyond here, the Coyle emptied into the Yellow Sea, carving dozens of channels through the Pocked Delta mud. It was low tide, and birds strutted across the grey expanse, plucking at tube-worms.

Waves rushed and crashed against the rocks on the seaward side of the peninsula, lifting flecks of spume into the air.

Caulker dismounted on the lower slopes of the peninsula and wandered up the cracked rocks to join Anchor and Ramnir. The two men stood staring out across the fog-heavy sea.

'. . . are you confident?' Ramnir was saying.

'Yes,' Anchor replied. 'Easy.'

'Confident?' Caulker enquired. 'About what?'

The Heshette leader spat, and said nothing.

'Ramnir is interested to see how we will cross,' Anchor said. 'It is a long way to Pandemeria from here.'

'And how exactly *do* we cross?' Caulker asked. 'You can hoist all the goats and their keepers up to the skyship, but I fail to see how *you'll* manage. You've no boat. Don't tell me you intend to swim?'

'Swim?' The giant shook his head. 'John Anchor does not know how to swim.'

'Then *how* . . .?'

Anchor beamed. 'Confidence!' he exclaimed, striding back towards his followers.

For the rest of that day, the Heshette and their animals were hoisted up into the *Rotsward*. Humans and livestock travelled up by basket, but stout leather-and-rope harnesses had to be fashioned for the horses. The Heshette women wrapped cloth around the animals' eyes to prevent them panicking – a tactic which was only moderately successful. By dusk only Ramnir and Caulker remained on the ground with Anchor, although the leader's horse had already been stowed aboard Cospinol's ship.

Ramnir indicated that the cut-throat should go next in the basket, but Caulker wouldn't hear of it.

'I've been with Anchor since the start,' he said, 'and I'll stay until the end. You have goats waiting.'

The Heshette leader angrily reached for his knife, but Anchor stopped him. 'Go and look after your people,' he said. He grinned and slapped his belly. 'And we all need goats. Meat is more important than insults, yes?'

The other man smiled. 'See you in Pandemeria, John Anchor.'

Once Ramnir had been taken up to the foggy skies, Caulker was left all alone with the tethered giant.

'Why do you hate these people so much?' Anchor asked. 'It is bad for you. Enemies creep up behind your back with a knife.' He made a stabbing motion. 'Friends watch your back. Why make enemies and not friends?'

Caulker snorted. 'I know what these people are like. Had you spent more time in Sandport, you would have seen them for yourself. They wallow in filth and lethargy, poor as dirt. Their children run through the streets like rats.'

'Rats are clever. They know when to leave a sinking ship.'

'Animal cunning! You shouldn't have offered to take them with you.' He watched the foaming waves break against the base of the peninsula, inhaling the scent of them. How did Anchor plan to cross? He could only think of one way. 'That water's deep,' he muttered, 'and cold.'

'Here is your basket,' Anchor said.

The cut-throat climbed inside the wicker frame and clutched the rope. 'Don't trust them, Anchor,' he called out as he ascended into the fog.

Down below, the giant merely laughed. He rolled his massive shoulders, and then hopped down the rocks towards the shore. Then he leaned back and sucked in a long, long breath.

From up inside his basket, Caulker watched the Adamantine Man leap into the sea. He disappeared beneath the dark blue waters, with only the huge rope above water to reveal his progress.

Till the fog closed under him, Caulker saw that rope cut a path through the waves, moving slowly and steadily away from land.

PART TWO

THE MAZE

15

MENOA

Only top-ranking metaphysical engineers were permitted to ascend to the highest level of the Ninth Citadel. The House of Faces, as it had come to be known among the Icarates, had many separate rooms, but not one single window or doorway intervening between them.

Alice Harper stood before an entire wall of Mesmerist constructs. The creatures looked like thin grey men half-buried in the stone and mortar, a scrum of naked bodies reaching from floor to ceiling, yet Harper knew that this scene was deceiving. There was no stone or mortar in the House of Faces, only the flesh of incarnate souls. Their arms reached out towards the engineer, beckoning her closer to their yawning mouths. This particular wall was composed of more than three score of living creatures, but it was hard to be sure, since constructs often shared limbs with each other. Harper suspected the way through this wall would undoubtedly be painful.

'Let me pass,' she said. 'I have business with King Menoa.'

The wall writhed. Many voices hissed, 'Step forward.'

'Open a doorway, then. Let me walk through.'

'No. Step forward.'

Harper shivered. She really hated the process of moving from one room to the next within the House of Faces. Nevertheless, the wall seemed unlikely to cooperate, and she did not wish to make her regent wait. She stepped up to the wall, allowing those sharp fingers to drag her closer to its scores of waiting teeth.

The constructs ripped her to shreds. Harper tried not to scream – the agony would pass momentarily, she knew – but she could not help herself. The wall took delight in her cries, tearing at her flesh more vigorously as it continued stuffing pieces of the engineer into its countless mouths.

For a brief moment she was lost in a red haze, her displaced soul drifting through a dark space. Was it the inside of the wall? She felt other consciousnesses jostling with her own, older and more savage minds trying to reshape her from their own desires or memories. Harper shunned these alien influences, fighting to remember who she was and why she was here.

Alice Ellis Harper. Metaphysical Engineer First Class. Two arms, two legs, two hands, two feet, ten fingers, ten toes. One head. Red hair and grey eyes. I am here to give my report to King Menoa, Lord of the Ninth Citadel. I have one head. One head only.

And then she was through.

She found herself standing in a grey chamber on the opposite side of the wall. Her blurred vision came into focus, and she quickly examined her own body – checking herself thoroughly. Nothing seemed to have changed; even the grey cuffs of her Mesmerist uniform appeared to be identical to before. She clamped her hands against the sides of her head and breathed a sigh of relief. *Just one head this time.*

The chamber before her was almost identical to the last one, a grey cube fifty paces to each side. Mesmerist constructs writhed in all of the four walls, their hungry gazes even now turning towards her. Only the ideogram in the floor was different, the geometric shapes and numerals referring to the second of the Mesmerist Laws of Foundation. These esoteric patterns encircled a solitary blue-lipped mouth, no larger than any human's maw. It was licking its lips.

Harper approached it as it called out: 'In the seventh faction of the first third. Elevation one ninety, moving from blue to red.'

'Where is Menoa, Speaker?'

'King Menoa, to you. Be silent, soul. I am attempting to configure the third parallel into the third bank, moving three hundred armoured suits and associated worms from Cog Island Portal to the Middle Green Nine Line out with the fringes of the Red Road. How much blood must be infused into the Pandemerian earth? How much has already been *absorbed*? King Menoa wishes to know these things.'

'Since when do Speakers think?'

'The war effort presses us all. I have assumed additional functions to further serve our Lord.'

'Then don't neglect your primary function. Tell me where our ruler is, or I'll let him know you delayed an important message.'

'What message? I will relay it through the walls and floors to him now.'

Harper snorted. 'It won't make any difference. Menoa won't turn you into anything else. You'll stay a floor forever.' She smacked the heel of her boot against the outer circle of the ideogram. 'How does it feel to have people walking over you?'

The floor's voice rose to a shrill cry. 'I support the Ninth Citadel and those who dwell within it!'

'Then tell me where Menoa is!'

Its blue lips pinched together. 'Our Great Lord, Creator of All in Hell, is now pacing across the Thirtieth Balcony on the canal side of his glorious citadel. He maintains his most recent, most beautiful form of black glass and jewels and—'

'The *thirtieth* balcony?' Harper gave a huge sigh, then put her hands on her hips and stared at the countless hands and teeth of those constructs embedded in the nearest wall. The thirtieth balcony was close to the very top of the citadel. 'This is going to hurt like hell.'

'An inappropriate metaphor,' said the floor. 'This *is* Hell, and so . . .'

She ground the toe of her left boot into its mouth to shut it up, leaving it gasping and bleeding, then wandered over to the hands outstretched from the nearest wall.

Two arms, two legs, two hands, two feet, ten fingers, ten toes. One head.

Harper passed through sixty-two rooms and climbed one hundred and four stairwells to reach the king's balcony. She counted every step, trying to burn her progress firmly into her memory lest the Citadel trick her on the way back out. It enjoyed visitors too much, she feared, and was inclined to keep them here for longer than was strictly necessary. The long journey tired her, and she found that her concentration waned somewhat in the upper chambers. By the time she located Menoa, she had lost two fingernails and developed a curious grating sensation in her left knee, as though the joint had been subtly altered.

These were small changes, however, easy to remedy after she had enjoyed some rest. Most importantly, her uniform remained precisely the way it should be.

The Mesmerist Ruler stood beside the parapet of the sweeping red balcony, gazing out across Hell. The crimson sky smouldered behind him, casting liquid shadows across the smooth ridges and indentations of his black glass helmet. He stood about nine feet tall today, more or less the same height he had always been since Harper had been in his service, yet his glass armour warped gradually as light and shade passed over it. Even as Harper watched, Menoa's breastplate *flowed*, changing from the face of a cat-like beast to the grimacing visage of a hanged man. Spikes grew out of his shoulder plates, and then shrunk back again, as though following the rhythm of his breathing. His gauntlets rested on the parapet before him, like huge dark claws.

Harper could see bloodmists rising through the air behind him, those great fuming funnels of vapour exuded by the King's Processors. The balcony itself glistened in this living mist and, part flesh and part mechanical, the whole floor beneath them throbbed with mute pleasure. Evidently this part of the Ninth Citadel was drawing power directly from the bloodmists. From somewhere below came the sound of machinery and screams, all mingled with the low, rhythmic chanting of the Icarates.

The king's glass mask did not turn to face his servant, as he spoke in a low, distant voice. 'You have located the angel?'

'The dogcatchers picked up his scent briefly,' she replied. 'He manifested somewhere west of the Lower Blaise Canal Area, but then vanished beneath one of the Soul Middens.' Most of the souls from Deepgate were falling into the Middens, and she had instructed the Icarates and their packs to search that area first. 'It's only a matter of time until we find him.'

'The First Citadel knows he is here. His ancestors will be searching for him.'

'We've seen no trace of any other archons in the area,' Harper said. 'Perhaps the ongoing siege has restricted their influence so far from their own fortress?'

'No.' King Menoa turned abruptly and, for a heartbeat, Harper thought she glimpsed the face behind his mask – soft golden eyes, high arching cheeks, like those of a porcelain doll, and beautiful blood-red lips. But then the glass turned as black as an Icarate's throat.

'He is much too valuable to our enemies,' Menoa said. 'The First Citadel is determined to unravel the mechanism by which the angel escaped Hell. There was no portal open when he first died, nothing but a rotting body for him to return to, and yet he somehow returned to the *same* flesh.' The king traced a claw across the chin of his mask. 'He is the last of them, and yet he is somehow different from them, and they will risk everything to understand him.' The mask's glassy eyes stared through her, revealing nothing of the real eyes behind. 'Look for their warriors below the Middens. These archons have been growing castles in unlikely places.'

She bowed. 'I will seed the area with screamers to detect unnatural vibrations. The packs will assuredly flush him out.'

'The packs have failed me before.'

'And you altered them, my Lord' – she swallowed – 'severely. They will not dare to fail you again.'

Menoa must have noticed the quiver of repulsion in her voice, for he then turned sharply to face her. 'You yourself are from Pandemeria, aren't you?' he said.

The king's question startled her. He had never acknowledged her past before. 'I am,' she said. 'I mean, I was—'

'And you wish to return to the living world?'

She hesitated. 'If it pleases you to send me there, my Lord.'

The king was silent a moment. 'Do you enjoy the form you now occupy?'

Harper chose her words carefully. 'It allows me to serve you better.'

The king made a sign in the air with his gauntlet. At this unvoiced command, a witchsphere rumbled out onto the balcony from one of the citadel archways, its metal panels shining dully under the bloody skies. It rolled across the floor towards the king, then stopped and began to turn itself inside-out.

Harper looked away, but she heard the click of panels opening, followed by a hiss and then the brutal sound of snapping bones. When she glanced up again, the sphere had become a tangle of hags' skin and filthy hair, full of eager white eyes. 'King Menoa,' it said with a sigh.

'Consider the strengths of adaptation,' Menoa said to his

engineer. 'Your current form serves me well enough, yet another might serve me better. Take your own country for example.' He turned to the witchsphere and commanded, 'Show us Pandemeria, as it was.'

At once the sphere began to change again. The witches untangled themselves from each other, their withered bodies flowing together to form a single membrane. This membrane began to expand across the living balcony. Flesh bubbled and became earth, a representation in miniature of the fields, hills and mountains Harper had known so well. In other places the skin split apart to form arroyos, gullies and wide valleys. Clear fluid seeped from pores into these many hollows, defining the Moine lakes and Sill river. Tiny black trees sprouted like hairs. Lesions swelled and hardened to become boulders, or buildings, or runnels of glacial scree.

Harper identified the city of Cog, her home before the plague and the war and the great floods had transformed Pandemeria. She recognized a patchwork of streets and squares now forming before her eyes: Highcliffe and the Theatre District. She saw the Sill river, and where it split into two branches which curled around the city like a moat. And still the witchsphere grew around her, filling her vision. Revolution Plaza solidified before her eyes, the great white cathedral shining in the twilight – exactly as it had done before the Mesmerist Veil. She located Canary Street, Minnow Street and the Offal Quarter. And her own house – the house she had bought with Tom.

How long ago now?

Ten years, or a thousand? Involuntarily she clutched her chest. How much of this was real? The witches were clearly drawing on Harper's own memories to form this illusion. She was gazing straight into her own dream.

'Now show us Pandemeria as it is today,' the king said.

'No, please, my Lord.' Harper closed her eyes, but the scene before her did not change. She no longer had eyelids to shut out this changing vision. Menoa had made a simple alteration to her physical form. Now he was chuckling behind his mask. 'You want to see this,' he insisted.

Cog Island's skies began to darken with red mist: *the Mesmerist Veil*. It seemed to Harper that she was watching from a great height as the shades of Cog's plague victims rose from their mass graves out in Knuckletown Quarry and drifted towards the city in vast numbers. In moments they had crossed the Sill Bridge and were pouring into the city. Strange shadows flitted under the eaves of buildings, while from the east could be heard the braying of hounds.

'You remember this?' King Menoa asked. 'You recall the improvements my Icarates made?'

Harper remembered. Now unable to separate dreams from actual events, she saw the Icarates rise from the very ground itself. An army of warriors in queer ceramic armour, they moved from house to house, smashing down doors and dragging Cog's citizens out into the glistening streets. The Icarates slaughtered the weak and the elderly, and herded the rest out towards their flensing machine beyond Knuckletown, where a great red funnel of vapour was now twisting slowly above the plague graves.

The graves had crumbled inwards, leaving dark open pits in the red earth, and now the Mesmerists' Maze-forged hordes crawled out of them: men of flesh and iron and glass . . . witchspheres, Iolites and dogcatchers . . . Claws raked the wet soil, turning it into a bloody morass. White teeth flashed in the semidarkness.

Out they came in waves, and in impossible numbers, a seething tide which swept on into the doomed city. Time blurred. Days and weeks passed in mere moments and the scene changed again. New constructions now towered over the city: the Terminus, the Flensing Towers, and the Great Wheel through which ten thousand slaves supplied power to the new Highcliffe Laboratories. The Mesmerist Veil now covered Pandemeria as far as Harper could see. Recent rain showers had drenched the land, and now the crimson fields and furrows around the island city glistened like open wounds. The vanguard had moved out of sight, far across the Merian Basin to the north, yet hordes of reserve warriors continued to pour out of Cog City. They moved like rivers across the landscape, drawing power from the red earth.

Storm clouds were gathering in the north. Lightning flickered across the horizon among sheets of rain and great columns of black smoke.

Rys!

These fires heralded the approach of the god of flowers and knives. Rys had brought his armies down from the far north to meet the Mesmerist threat, and now the flames from his great war-machines lit up the horizon. The two armies had clashed on the northern shores of Lake Larnaig, outside the gates of Rys's own city, Coreollis. Here King Menoa's demons had been halted at last.

The witchsphere would not dare to display that battle for fear of enraging King Menoa. The Mesmerist leader had been soundly beaten at Coreollis. Instead the view remained focused on Cog: that skewed mound of blood-drenched houses and spires crouching upon Sill River Island. Four bridges connected the heart of Cog to its outlying suburbs on either side of the two river channels: Knuckletown to the east, Port Sellen to the west. A steam locomotive had been left abandoned on Opera Bridge, its empty wagons now half full of water.

For it was raining in torrents.

'Rys brought this rain to cleanse Pandemeria's blooded earth,' Menoa growled, his deep voice resounding like echoes in a cave. 'Yet he underestimated the Mesmerist power to adapt. His deluge merely changed blooded land into a blooded sea.'

Harper sensed time shift again in the scene before her. The Sill river swelled and quickly burst its banks. Both Knuckletown and Port Sellen disappeared under the rising waters. The river itself had become a raging, brown torrent, with floating detritus and corpses snagging on the underside of Opera Bridge. And still the floodwaters rose, drowning the low-lying streets and plazas, and the wide plains of the Merian Basin, until only the very highest city districts remained unaffected. Cog Island, once merely an outcrop of high rock between two branches of a river, had now become truly an island in the middle of a shallow sea.

The Mesmerists then made ships. Under the guidance of chanting Icarates, souls from the plague graves were allocated power from the Veil. These dead soon lost their own frail human forms. The Icarates changed them slowly, painfully, into great empty shells of bone, flesh and metal. Each new vessel cried out in agony and despair until the Icarates stifled its voice within the living steel.

And the troop deployment continued. Legions marched into the newly forged ships. Belching smoke and fire, the Mesmerist vessels sailed out over the flooded city and the plains beyond, while on the brooding horizon Rys's storm of war flashed and rumbled.

Menoa said, 'I have shown you this for a reason.' At another of the king's gestures, the witchsphere began to collapse and recover its former form, sucking in the Veil, the land and the waters like air inhaled.

'Here in the Maze, Form is merely a manifestation of Will,' the king went on. 'And yet you people choose to loll feebly in your own dreary memories, assuming the forms you are used to, rather than exploring the unknown. There has been a glut of power in the Maze recently, and yet Hell itself has grown stagnant despite this potential.' The glass mask continued to flux in the crimson light, the features changing, always changing. 'Your kind has no vision,' Menoa said. 'So I must impose *my* vision upon you and, by doing so, set you free.'

'Yes, my Lord.' Fear crept up Harper's spine. She had seen the frightening things Menoa had constructed to take his war into the world of men.

'Your fingers, for example,' Menoa said, 'are they suitably designed to fine-tune the mechanics of our ideas?'

'I . . .' Before Harper could properly respond, her hands began to change. Her fingers stretched and thinned and turned to silver. She cried out as she felt her nerves die in painful spasms. Crystals formed on each of her fingertips: mesmeric devices to measure and alter the soul harmonics of Menoa's warrior machines. Her knuckles swelled into irregular metal lumps, then ticked and whirred as clockwork mechanisms began to move inside them. Her wrists hardened and began to turn black. 'Please . . .' she gasped. 'Stop this.'

But Menoa did not stop. He stooped over her, his claw-like fingers directing the changes in her physical form. A hundred faces seemed to move behind his black glass mask. 'Understand that you will become anything I desire,' he said. 'If it suits my plans to alter any soul in my domain, then I shall do so without hesitation.' He frowned at her and made another sweeping movement with his gauntlet. The devices on her fingers began to retract and change shape once more.

Harper heard the witchsphere hissing with pleasure, but she could no longer see it. Menoa was changing the composition of her eyes: her vision became suddenly fragmented, like the view through the facets of a gemstone. She felt her back crimp and buckle, before she sensed something hard and flexible growing out of her spine. This protrusion split and then divided again and again.

What was he changing her into?

The world around her seemed to expand. Menoa's mask

loomed over her, black against the seething crimson clouds, as though peering down at her from a great height.

'You are nothing but an insect,' King Menoa announced.

A sound of buzzing filled Harper's ears. She glanced down at herself to see a clutch of chitinous shards protruding from her newly developed thorax. Her limbs had gone, replaced by bushels of wire-like tendrils. Sparks of agony shot through her freshly altered nerves.

Menoa scooped up his servant in one gauntlet and carried her to the balustrade. 'Fly to the Processor,' he said, 'and tell the Prime to prepare the Forming Ovens for another archon. I will delay the first strike until this angel has been suitably reinforced. Do this quickly and I might consider returning your arms and legs.'

He then cast Harper out into the skies over Hell.

She was flying, buzzing, clicking – a whirlwind of new pains and perceptions, yet Harper no longer possessed lungs with which to scream. She was trapped in a thin shell, carried by wings frail as paper. The Maze reeled around her; she witnessed it as a dozen subtly different views of the same terrible landscape. Behind her the towers of the Ninth Citadel rose up like a flayed figure, glistening and seething with transmuted souls. Canals looped around its base like red ribbons, through which Icarates plied their heavy black barges.

In awkward fits, her fragile wings carried her through a blood-mist above one of the Icarates' flensing machines. Harper felt a sudden surge of energy as her newly forged body drank in countless fractured souls. Thus enriched, she banked around Menoa's citadel and made for the Processor.

The great building at the heart of the Mesmerist war effort towered over the surrounding canals, ziggurats and creeping machines. It was an inverted pyramid, said to be built from more than a million souls transformed into black stone. Harper could well believe it, for, to facilitate the arcane processes within its living walls, the Icarates had not removed the voices from these souls.

The Processor howled and screamed. Even the steady chanting of countless Icarates and the sound of the forges and bellows inside could not mask those unholy cries. Steam billowed from the open hatch into one of the Forming Ovens, while a stream of rock and ore rained down from the heavens and was collected in the Processor's central depression. Evidently the Icarates were still gathering raw materials from the world of the living.

As Harper flew nearer, she saw the Mesmerist warrior priests backing away from the open oven. They hobbled across the smooth surface with their backs hunched under the weight of the white enamel armour that both shielded and powered their ancient bodies. Blue sparks dripped from mushroom-shaped protrusions on their heavy shoulder guards and back plates, striking the ground around their white boots in explosive bursts.

Now Harper could see why the Icarates were retreating from the steaming hatch.

Something was climbing out of it.

Two skeletal hands rose first out of the Forming Oven. Fashioned to resemble the hands of dead men, and yet larger than the mightiest of oak trees, the bony fingers clamped on to the lip of the building's summit with enough force to make the entire Processor howl.

Harper was about to witness the birth of an arconite: an iron- and bone-forged automaton built around an angel's soul.

Plumes of smoke hissed from the Processor's innards as the skeletal giant continued to clamber out of the Forming Oven. Its skull and wings towered over the pit, the creature's newly forged bones and tendons glistening with oil and plasma. Engines thumped heavily in its rib cage as they pumped arcane chemicals and blood through the network of pipes intertwined throughout the whole of its massive body. It was dragging hundreds of chains behind it, their links still glowing red from the heat of the ovens in which they had been forged.

Now free of the Forming Oven, the arconite stood on the Processor summit, unfurled its vast wings, and roared.

Even from up here, Harper could see that those wings were useless, naught but tattered grey flesh – an affectation the Icarates had created to help bind the archon's soul into this mechanical body. Even months of torture could not entirely cleanse an angel of the memory of its living body. Of all Hell's creatures, only an angel could not be altered by the sheer force of Menoa's will. In death, they retained something more than ordinary mortals, something which resisted even the king's formidable powers of persuasion.

And so the Mesmerist leader had resorted to this barbarism, this fusion of the physical and the metaphysical that bound an archon's soul to metal and bone.

The Icarates took up the automaton's chains and guided it to the edge of the Processor and down a ramp to join its eleven brothers in the vast holding area. This pen formed an open quadrangle amid the Mesmerist city, among those great black ziggurats and towers, rising like shards of obsidian, which stretched for as far as the eye could see. Red mists rose from a thousand flensing machines, while Menoa's queer mix of slaves, warriors and priests plied the deep canals in barges or crawled, limped and rolled along thoroughfares. A pack of liver-skinned dogcatchers left a Ziggurat of Worship and splashed through one of the shallower canals, howling and clicking their teeth as their masters drove them onwards. Many such packs had been dispatched lately as King Menoa increased his hunt not just for archons, but for pieces of the shattered god, Iril.

Harper flew to the top of the Processor and down through one of the smaller of the Icarates' doorways. She passed through corridors of blue wires and sulphurous pools from which hands reached up to clutch at her. Yet in this current shape she was quick enough to elude their grasp.

In time she came to the Bastion of Voices.

It was a high chamber constructed of translucent lozenges, each one forged from a soul of rare insight. In the centre of the room the king's twelve Prime Icarates sat motionless in a circle of thrones arranged upon a dais, listening solemnly to the whispers from the glass. Tubes ran from valves in their bone-coloured armour and disappeared into the black glass floor, where further ancient seals had been engraved. Unlike most Icarates, these lords did not wear helmets. Their ancient faces had the pallor and texture of dead fish-flesh, while their eyes and mouths had been sewn up with copper wire.

Harper could not understand the whispers all around her, yet the voices became still more subdued as she approached. Her presence here had clearly not gone unnoticed.

The engineer tried to find her own voice, but her current shape was still new to her. She merely made a startled clicking sound, and then settled on the floor immediately before the dais.

The arconites now equal the Prime, the voices of the chamber announced. *We have achieved everything Menoa has commanded. Twelve giants will walk upon unblooded ground, each of them as powerful as a mortal army. Our thoughts are their thoughts. Relay the king's message and retreat, insect. War is at hand.*

Harper tried to speak again, but no sound came out except a fibrillating scratch. Her bristled limbs twitched in frustration. Her carapace made a noise like dry paper rustling. Why had Menoa not issued her with a throat to declare his demands?

He neglected to provide you with a throat, the chamber explained, *to prevent you from lying to us. Your mind is like a mirror to us, sufficient to reflect Menoa's conversation with you.*

So Harper remembered her audience on the king's balcony,

and through her mere thoughts the Bastion of Voices came to understand what Menoa expected it to do.

At last the chamber said, *Tell the king we will construct a body for another iron angel, but warn him that there is much to do. Ore must be gathered from Pandemeria in abundance, and a thousand souls will need to be re-formed. It will be necessary to harvest blood and bone from the flensing machines.*

Leaving the silent Icarates upon their thrones, Harper took to the air again and retraced her path through the Processor. Outside, the newly forged arconite, still glistening and steaming from the Forming Ovens, was being chained to the floor of the holding area among the rest of its kin. These twelve giants squatted on the ground, their bony arms wrapped around their knees, in complete subservience to their Icarate masters. Flocks of airborne shades had already come to feed upon their great tattered wings, attracted by the living blood within them.

As Harper's own translucent wings buzzed like those of a dragonfly, she wondered how she had allowed herself to become a part of all this madness. After all, she had come to Hell for another reason entirely.

The king was waiting for her again on his balcony. He stared at her, and for a moment Harper felt his presence scour the inside of her mind. Then that feeling was suddenly gone, leaving her empty and shaken. He said, 'You wish me to restore you to your original shape?'

She didn't have to answer him. He already knew.

Menoa scraped one of his glass claws across the top of the balustrade, and Harper felt her nerves flare as her body began to change again. Her exoskeleton crackled with energy, then burst apart, spilling out convulsing innards which swelled and took on new forms. All around her the world seemed to shrink as she grew in size. Multiple views blurred together into one solid image. She sensed her wings dissolve and the tiny fibrous limbs re-forming into human flesh. She knew Menoa had returned her voice when an agonized scream finally burst from her throat.

But then the king raised a hand, halting abruptly the transformation process.

She cowered before him, a thing of shivering misshapen flesh, and tried to keep hold of her sanity.

'Perhaps I should place you inside a witchsphere,' Menoa said evenly, 'to share eternity with eight mortal sisters. You would see . . . wonderful sights.'

'I've done . . . everything you've ever asked of me,' she gasped. Something on her shoulder burst, drenching her twisted back. 'Has my service displeased you?'

He chuckled. 'No, but stasis bores me. You have the potential to be ever so much more than you are.' He strode towards her, his claws extended like a brace of scalpels. 'On your world, am I regarded as a butcher or a visionary?'

Despite her crippling agony, the king's question was absurd enough to make Harper suppress a laugh. *This monster cares about how others perceive him?* The thought occurred to her before she had a chance to stop it, and yet Menoa did not appear to have read her mind. He was still waiting for her reply.

'My Lord,' she said at last, trying to control both the pain and the cynicism in her voice, 'perceptions of you change frequently.'

Evidently this pleased the king, for he made another gesture which restarted Harper's transmutation. She cried out again as her limbs contorted into new shapes.

'Good,' Menoa said, satisfied. 'To confound our enemies we must never cease to adapt.' His black glass mask shone in the bruised light. 'While your service to me has occasionally been reluctant, Alice Harper, it has nevertheless been satisfactory. You Pandemerians have grown used to stagnation, yet you understand the traps and dangers of the living world so much better than my Icarates. Now I require even more from you.'

As Harper's body continued to change, she realized that something was wrong. Her arms and legs felt . . . unusual. She was already a foot taller than she ought to be, and this transformation showed no signs of halting. What was King Menoa doing to her? What was she *becoming*?

The king turned away again to stare out across the Maze. 'Your new form will surprise and delight you,' he said.

16

DİLL

In Dill's dream he was fighting amid a whole crowd of people. Men and women of all ages jostled him and yelled and brawled with each other. Fists flailed all around him. Boots kicked him in the shins and stomach. Greasy fingers grabbed his hair and yanked him down towards wet red earth. He broke free for an instant and found himself staring up at a featureless grey sky. Then someone stumbled against his wings, and Dill fell back under the crowd. A knee struck him on the temple, driving him deeper into the morass. He clutched at a ragged, sweat-soaked shirt, but its owner tore the shirt away and stamped on the angel's face. Dill looked beyond the boot up to a grizzled, grinning face, and a broad white chest muscled like an ox.

Then powerful hands hauled him upright.

'The trick of surviving a portal,' roared a deep voice from behind the angel, 'is not to let the other bastards smell your fear. That, and to smash their poxy faces in at any chance you get. Hah!'

A metal gauntlet lashed out across Dill's left shoulder and punched the grizzled brawler in the face, shattering the big man's nose.

His rescuer was a huge angel clad in old, battered steel armour. A giant, he towered over everyone else, including the man he'd just struck. Wild grey hair flew about his shoulders as he lifted his now limp quarry and then threw him far into the crowd.

The battle-archon laughed. 'We're all ghosts here, lad, trapped in the same lousy dream. The battle is merely a contest of will. Now watch this! You can find weapons if you use your wits.'

He stooped and grabbed the ankle of an old woman who had fallen. She wasn't moving. Grinning, the archon swung her round like a club, smashing a path through the terrified crowd. Spatters of blood flew everywhere. 'You see?' he boomed. 'Easy as you like.' Then he tossed the old woman's bloody corpse away like a soiled rag and said, 'Aye aye, there's a better one.' Now he picked up a soldier, dressed in rusty chain mail, and proceeded to use him similarly like a mace.

'The armoured ones are best,' the archon yelled. 'It nips a bit when you get hit in the face by a body wearing a hauberk.'

Dill paused to catch his breath. 'Who *are* you?'

'Just an old dead god,' he said, 'sent to watch your back and make sure you reach Hell in one piece. Look at that fellow! Fancies himself as a pugilist, I reckon.' He pointed to a scrawny man who had one arm wrapped around a young woman's neck and was desperately beating her in the face. 'Think you can manage him on your own?'

Dill's first punch split the thin man's lip. His target looked up, dazed, then he saw the two angels, dropped his victim, and tried to force his way back through the crowd. A haggard greybeard with feverish eyes took him down before Dill could get another blow in. The battle-archon's laughter roared out across the panicked scrum. There was space around them both now. The archon's blue eyes, full of humour, looked down at Dill. 'You don't get dreams like this in Heaven,' he said, 'which is why I never liked the fucking place. Come on, we'll be through the portal soon. It would be a shame to waste another moment.'

And so they fought together. Or rather, the battle-archon

smashed through the crowd like a bull through barley, and Dill kept close behind him, kicking and punching whenever the opportunity arose. Everyone became a target; fists pummelled flesh on all sides. Blood and sweat soaked the young angel's tattered mail shirt. Elbows shoved him this way and that as the crowd ebbed and surged, but he kept on fighting.

It was a battle without the clash of weapons or war cries or curses, an oddly silent brawl save for the occasional grunt or moan. Overhead the sky darkened to the colour of lead, and then of onyx. The participants were by now exhausted, yet they remained determined. Something drove them to fight, and none would readily yield, because there was nowhere for them to go, no space to retreat to.

Dill fought on. He fought breathlessly in the growing darkness, wanting to impress his new companion. He broke noses and pulled at lank, stinking hair, and delighted in the thrill of it.

Men pushed past or fell and disappeared. He punched leering faces until he could no longer tell one from another. The crowd became a blur, a single beast with ten thousand eyes and teeth and sweating limbs. He kicked and kicked at it, and broke its bones. But it had so many bones: it was endless.

And it never stopped fighting back.

The young angel received as many blows as he dealt, and bruises soon throbbed on his chest and arms. His knuckles bled. He saw his own loose feathers being stamped into the mire underfoot. Sweat poured freely from his brow till it filled his eyes. He could not say how long he battled . . .

Abruptly, he woke up.

Dill realized he had arrived in Hell again. Nothing was different except, perhaps, that this time there was less space.

He found himself trapped in a vice-like gap between two encroaching walls. Rough stone pressed his cheek, his ribs and his wings, pinning him in place. He could not turn his head. He wiggled his boots, but sensed nothing but air underneath him. Had the gap between the walls been a few inches wider, he might have plummeted.

To what?

His death?

But he was already dead. He remembered this clearly from the first time: the gloom, the wait, and then the transformation. Dill couldn't see anything but the wall just an inch from his face, its scarred stone surface illuminated by a peculiar grey light. Whenever he moved his eyes, that light moved too. His own gaze was the source of the illumination.

Memories crawled through the back of his mind like flies.

Trapped between walls . . .

And a *smell*?

The scent reminded him of beeswax. The more he thought about it, the surer he became. All at once the smell seemed to intensify, growing stronger until he was absolutely certain: it was the scent of polished wood.

He recalled this from before.

And a surge of panic came over him.

Dill struggled wildly against his prison, bucking and shifting his shoulders. He failed to free his body, but he managed to lift an arm.

There, at the end of his index finger, grew a tiny white shoot.

Dill's place within the Maze would grow from his own body. He was about to re-experience the tortuous process that had haunted his dreams since his last return to the world of the living.

It would mean unbearable pain.

As soon as he thought about the pain, he felt it. The shoot atop his finger began to nip like a wasp sting. Dill cried out. He scraped the white stem against the wall, and gasped. He could feel the roughness of the wall through the shoot. It had now become a living, sensitive extension of his body.

This sensation brought with it a flood of darker memories.

He yelled in frustration, then pushed the stem against the wall, bending it back on itself.

It broke off and fell away into the darkness below, leaving a bleeding stub on his finger. Dill shivered at the pain and sucked his finger until the bleeding ceased. Even the wound tasted of beeswax.

He felt more shoots now growing from his toes, pressing into the inside of his boots, but he couldn't reach these. All he could do was wait.

Time passed.

At some point Dill must have fallen asleep, because he was suddenly aware of opening his eyes and realizing that some sort of change had occurred. His body felt strange, awash with odd sensations. The previous pressure on his wings and chest had gone.

The walls had moved backwards a yard or so. He was standing on the solid wooden floor of a tiny stone cell.

Or rather, he was attached to the floor. A mass of slender white tendrils had grown out of his boots, bursting through the leather like the roots of a tree. These shoots had buried themselves in the wooden floorboards on which he stood, fixing him to the spot.

A flash of memories returned.

Dill moaned. The floorboards had not been punctured after all. They were extensions of the roots themselves. Each tendril had hardened and flattened as it had grown outwards, turning from white to the colour of deeply polished oak. He had grown a floor under his feet.

He could not move his trapped feet, and so he collapsed forwards on to his knees with a wail of utter despair. And then a curious thing happened. It felt as though he had struck a part of his own body. He could feel the pressure of his own knees through the wooden floorboards, the weight of his body pushing down. The grain of the wood was as tactile as his own skin.

Dill knelt on the floorboards that were not floorboards, and gazed feverishly around the tiny space. Where the planks met the wall, a skirting board had partially formed. He could sense the texture of the stonework behind it.

The angel was turning into a room.

This was all too much for Dill. He sobbed and smashed his fists against the floorboards, then winced at the pain it caused him. He tried to pull his feet free, but they would not shift. Eventually he lay down and wept.

At some point he slept again.

This time he woke up to find himself lying on the floor of an elegant wood-panelled chamber. Tall shutters covered the windows. A crimson and black patterned rug lay upon the waxed floorboards. There was a bed, a heavily carved four-poster draped with dark blue velvet, a poppywood sideboard supporting a vase of white flowers, and a dresser with three oval mirrors. On the dark panelled walls hung a dozen or so portraits of people Dill did not recognize. They were young men and women dressed as Deepgate commoners: maids and potboys and labourers. They were all staring at him. Dill found their gazes unnerving, and he looked away. From his position on the floor, he spied a tall doorway leading to another room – as large and richly furnished as this one.

A strange sensation crept over him, the same queer feeling he remembered from before. He could feel the grain of the floorboards under his palms, while at the same time he felt his own hands pressing down, as though he now had four hands, each pair pushing against the other.

In desperate panic he glanced back round. The tendrils that had grown from his heels and toes had thinned and darkened, becoming as hard and black as reeds. They still connected him to the floorboards. This opulent chamber was still a part of his body. It had simply grown around him.

Tentatively, Dill tried to move his feet. At first they would not budge, but then, after some effort, two of the brittle shoots snapped. Dill winced as blood leaked from the sheared roots, spilling out of both his heel and the floor. He paused, gasping for breath, before shifting his foot again. Three more of the weird shoots cracked, spattering the floor with further spots of blood. Now he had freed his left foot entirely. He stared in horror and fascination at the woody growths that sprouted like talons from his toes and heel.

He reached out and touched the place where the broken roots protruded from the floorboards. As his fingers brushed the stems, a shiver of pain coursed through him. The wood remained as tactile as his own tender flesh. He could feel the dull throb of blood leaching out from the floor, and the touch of his own fingers against the wounded roots. This sensation filled him with revulsion.

With a sharp jerk of his leg, he freed his other foot.

The pain came from everywhere: from Dill's bones and teeth and from the drapes hanging from the four-poster bed, stretched taut like veils of hot skin. He felt the tightness of the oval mirrors in their frames and wanted to shut them like eyes. But he couldn't. He couldn't move any part of this environment, yet he could feel every inch of it. The room was alive around him. It *was* him. He sensed an ache take root behind the lowest drawer of the poppywood sideboard, and then spread through each dovetailed joint in turn. The chamber's tall shutters cramped like the angel's own muscles. He felt the flowers tremble in their vase, and then he sensed the vase itself – a brittle curve of porcelain more delicate than any of his other bones.

The floorboards continued to bleed under him where he had torn his feet free. Warm iron-scented blood soaked into the rug.

He glanced up to see the wood panels in the walls expand outwards and then contract, just as though they were breathing. The spars between them itched and grated against each other – hurting him too.

And then he became aware of other chambers beyond this apartment he had grown around himself. Other rooms all around him, pressing close against Dill's own.

The Maze, he realized, was not just a place where dead souls went, for the damned created Hell around themselves. Every last brick and nail was sensate, a part of someone's living soul.

The Maze of Blood had been aptly named.

A sudden pounding headache struck Dill, as though a hammer was striking his skull repeatedly. He gasped and squeezed his temples before he realized the pain was coming from somewhere else. He could hear the sound of knocking. Someone was thumping on the door to his apartment.

He had a guest.

17

Transformation

King Menoa had turned Harper into a machine, a combination of interconnected tools for hunting, trapping and torturing errant souls. He had provided her with a cowl so that she might hide the potential of her vast and hideous crystal skeleton from the particular soul she was supposed to pursue. Yet there was no way to hide the knowledge of what she'd now become from herself.

All resemblance to a human had been stripped away. Now she towered over her own king, at least five or six times Menoa's height. Her increased stature would allow her to gaze far across the landscape of Hell, and yet she could not lift her eyes from the sight of her own body. Conjoined transparent sections now curled down all the way from her waist, like the tail of a serpent sculpted from glass. Crystal gears moved inside her pelvis and midriff, sending vibrations up through her ribs and chest. To replace her arms Menoa had given her three long, thin, glass limbs, each of which culminated in a different object: a spear, a sceptre and a mirrored shield. Intricate Mesmerist machinery turned inside the sceptre, emitting occasional pulses of white light.

'I have improved you,' the king explained. 'The sceptre acts as both an Oracle and a Locator, while the remaining limbs are designed merely for combat. Your spear can induce pain on many levels, and will inflict visions upon any creature you confront. Of course the shield offers physical protection, and yet much more . . . it is a rather special device.'

Harper lifted the shield and gazed down at her own reflection in the mirrored glass. 'My face . . .' she cried aghast, in a voice which sounded like crystal bells chiming.

'Beautiful, is it not? You wished to keep your original form, and so I have obliged. Now you exist as a combination of old and new.'

Harper's new skull was a bulb of clear glass moulded to resemble her face. The transparent eyes, cheeks, nose and mouth were fixed in an immovable expression of rage – a frightening grimace, yet not nearly as terrifying as the object trapped *within* the glass.

It was a manikin, the tiny shivering figure of a woman in a Mesmerist uniform. She was curled up very tight, with her arms wrapped around her legs and her head buried between her knees. Harper lifted her shield for a closer view. She could not see the little woman's face, but she recognized her nevertheless.

'She represents the core of your soul,' Menoa said, 'and yet I have given her the human weaknesses you still yearn for in Hell. Hunger and thirst will slowly kill her while she remains trapped.' He turned suddenly and walked away from Harper. 'Go find the angel and bring him to the Processor,' he called back. 'For your own sake, I suggest you do it quickly.'

Dill opened the door. Already standing there with his hands on his hips and clad in his old metal armour was the battle-archon from Dill's dream. The big angel frowned merrily down at him, his huge grey wings folded behind his back. A series of connected stone chambers stretched far into the gloom behind him. Each room appeared to be full of weapons, shields and training blocks, like an enfilading sequence of soldiers' barracks.

'Stay right where you are,' the archon demanded. 'We'll talk here at the door, if you don't mind. You just stay on your side, and I'll stay on mine. For either of us to cross this threshold would be improper, at least, and probably obscene. The castle behind me is the incarnation of my own soul, just as the rooms on your side of this door are the incarnation of yours.'

'Who are you?' Dill asked.

'I'm Hasp,' said the angel, grinning.

'Hasp?' Dill gave him a blank look.

The archon's frown deepened. 'You don't know who I am?' Dill shook his head.

'Hasp, youngest of Ayen's seven sons, Lord of the First Citadel. Is your mind addled?'

The young angel said nothing.

The god looked incredulous. 'Light and Life, lad! What have Ulcis's priests been teaching their temple archons? I'm his bloody brother – your own god's brother.'

'I didn't even know he had one.'

Hasp shook his head. 'I should have expected this. Your ancestors were not any wiser than you. It's the same every time we find another Deepgate angel down here.' He sighed. 'My brother liked to keep his little secrets, see? Stifling knowledge to keep the humans under their yokes. Anyway, it hardly matters. Ulcis was my brother, and Callis was one of his sons. So you must be my great-, great-nephew or something like that. Welcome back to Hell.'

'My body was stolen,' Dill said. 'By a shade, an archon. He said he was from the First Citadel.'

Hasp looked uncomfortable. 'Sorry about that, but we saw a chance to get a message out when the portal opened. A lot of shades were pouring out of Hell, and we felt desperate enough to attempt to send out one of our own. You'll get your body back sometime. As soon as Trench delivers his message, your body will be free of him again.'

'But I'll be down *here*!'

'It didn't stop you before,' Hasp said. 'The last time you arrived

in Hell, you vanished again before any one of us could reach you.'
The god chuckled. '*That* made us sit up, I can tell you. We were
hoping you could explain that little trick to us.'

Dill recalled his last time here in the Maze. He had been
trapped in a tiny cramped cell, without room to extend his wings.
He remembered the agony whenever he tried to move, and the
terrible dreams which had haunted his sleep. Each time he had
woken, it was to discover that the same cell had changed in some
subtle way. Finally he'd opened his eyes to see Rachel . . . who
had brought him back to life with Devon's angelwine.

Still, the young angel didn't feel comfortable divulging too
much to this strange god. He glanced behind the armoured
archon at the vast network of chambers, the tapestries and racks
of ancient weapons. This was a part of Hell new to him. 'It's so
different from before,' he said.

Hasp nodded. 'The Maze changes all the time. Your immediate environment is only a manifestation of your eternal consciousness – your soul, if you like. Handy if you learn how to
manipulate it, and so long as you keep your chin up.' He laughed.
'Just don't get any suicidal thoughts, however, or the walls of your
prison are likely to grow knives.'

Now the god was peering into Dill's own chamber over his
shoulder. 'Those portraits on your walls . . .' he said quietly.
'They . . . they actually seem to be looking at me.'

Dill turned. 'They do that.'

'Who are they?'

'I don't know.'

'You must know. This is your soul.'

Dill shrugged. 'I've never seen those faces before.'

Hasp stared for a minute longer, his expression growing darker.
'Well, ask them.'

The young angel felt suddenly reluctant to comply. Something about the portraits frightened him. 'They're just paintings,' he muttered.

But Hasp clearly wasn't convinced. He moved closer, until his armoured bulk filled the doorway, and Dill sensed the god's presence as a pressure building against his soul.

'Speak, if you have the wits to do so,' Hasp demanded of the paintings. 'Who are you?'

Thirteen voices whispered together. 'A Cutter by . . . Lisa, a maid . . . I don't . . . hop-keeper . . . My name . . . potboy . . . where is this? Why? Daniel Crook . . . Who are you? The pain . . .' And on it went: a torrent of hissed statements and queries.

'Enough!'

The paintings fell silent.

Hasp stepped back from the doorway. 'Those portraits are other souls bound to your own,' he said to Dill. 'You're sharing this small part of Hell with *thirteen* other people.' He shook his head. 'I've never seen anything like it before.'

The angelwine! Devon's elixir had contained thirteen souls, power enough to resurrect Dill. But now that the angel had died again, these same thirteen had accompanied him back to the Maze. Dill looked up in horror at the painted faces. Each one of them gazed down at him with a different expression ranging from curiosity to evident anger.

Hasp frowned. 'I need to get you out of here,' he said. 'If the Mesmerists get one whiff of this – and believe me, they will – they'll roll through here like a mountain of bones to capture you.'

'Out of here? Where?'

The god's face remained grim. 'We need to reach the First Citadel. If we're to have any chance of success, I'm going to have to start training you.'

Harper moved through the Blaise Canal Area, a maze of channels divided by walls of mirror-black rock. The faces of reconstructed souls glared from the smooth surfaces to the left and right as they watched the engineer pass. The fluids here were too shallow for Mesmerist barges, yet Harper's newly forged glass tail propelled her along rapidly. This was, of course, why Menoa had gifted her with it. Her sceptre flickered and hummed, indicating the presence of Icarates nearby. Soon enough she heard them.

The Icarate pack had gathered in a basin between the Soul Middens, those low hills where a thousand transformed souls piled one upon the other like heaped houses. Some of the dwellings, Harper noted, had fused with each other to form teetering castles and unlikely towers. These delicate structures would not survive for long, however, as Icarates continued to smash through the sensate brick and mortar to get at the souls within.

Overhead, the heavens smouldered like a dying hearth. In places flashes of darkness pulsed behind the rising crimson mists where bodies or pieces of detritus passed through the Deepgate portal and fell from the skies. Crackling sounds accompanied this hail of debris. Blooms of white light flashed less frequently, but fell like shooting stars wherever the souls of the living entered the Maze.

So many bones.

Icarates moved through the canals, and between the Soul Middens, collecting human remains and piling them into the hoppers of flensing machines. These vast slow-moving constructs resembled huge wagons with metal wheels and bone axles. When full, they would be dragged back to Menoa's Processor so that their contents could be used in the construction of arconites.

Her glass body clicking, Harper slithered over to the group of Icarates. There were six of them, powerfully built but hobbled like old men beneath the sheer weight of their ceramic armour. Knee-deep in the red mire, they wielded huge hammers in an effort to break through one of the walls at the base of a Midden. Holes had already been smashed into nearby dwellings; the occupants dragged out and locked inside cages in the centre of the basin. Dogcatchers moved lithely across the mounds above them, sniffing at windows and doors. One of the Mesmerists' most enduring creations, the dogcatchers had the look of skinless men with long white teeth, constantly tasting the air as they toiled for their Icarate masters.

One of the Icarates lowered his hammer and turned his pale helmet towards the approaching engineer.

'Menoa sent me,' Harper said.

He replied with a buzzing sound. Blue sparks cascaded from the protrusions on his back and shoulders. His crooked body even dipped in what might have been an attempt at a bow.

'We should move to high ground,' Harper went on. 'The king has equipped me with the tools to locate metaphysical disturb-ances. Archons from the First Citadel are likely to be hiding nearby. The pack must be ready to move quickly.'

Again the Icarate bowed. This time his thoughts murmured inside Harper's glass skull. *The First Citadel has no power here. We do not sense their archons' presence.*

'They may have buried themselves deep in the Soul Middens,' Harper indicated with a gesture of her glass spear. Death lights swarmed within the weapon's shaft. 'You must dig deeper.'

A sudden scream grabbed Harper's attention. The remaining five Icarates had finally broken through the outer wall of the near-est Midden and were now pushing through the cavity they had made. Those in the lead carried tridents crackling with black wisps of energy and stepped forward as a man cried out from within.

The Icarates dragged their captive out of the gap and threw him to his knees in the basin. He was young, dressed in rough hemp labourer's clothes – the most memorable of his earthly raiment, Harper knew, for his whole presence here was nought but a manifestation of his own soul's memories. Now devoid of the shelter he had grown around himself, his body rapidly began to fade, turning ghost-like.

A recollection chimed inside Harper's glass thorax, and for a moment it was not the shade of a Deepgate labourer kneeling on the ground before her, but her own husband Tom.

One of the Icarates drove his trident into the man's back, and his ghostly form became solid again. All likeness to Harper's husband instantly disappeared. A trick of the light? Or had the engineer's own thoughts intruded upon this man's soul? Out here he was as vulnerable to external influences as he was to complete dissolution. The Mesmerist priests must force power into the soul to prevent his physical form from becoming a shade. They herded the man off to the waiting cages.

This is what awaits the angel, Harper realized. *At least until Menoa bestows his new body.*

'Things were fine before the War Against Heaven,' Hasp called over to Dill. The god was searching through one of the many trunks set along the edges of his chamber. 'Balance was sustained. Iril got the wicked souls, Ayen got the good ones. But since the goddess of light and life shut the doors into Heaven, it's become overcrowded down here. Too many souls for even the Mesmerists to gather.'

Dill watched him from the doorway. 'But Ulcis took Deepgate's dead for himself.'

'We all did,' Hasp admitted. 'Each of Ayen's sons harvested souls. We needed to keep as many as possible out of Hell and away from the Mesmerists. Aha!' He pulled something out of the chest, an orb of brass clockwork with glowing crystals inside. 'And we needed the power for ourselves,' he went on, examining the strange globe. 'The War Against Heaven left us weak.'

How many people had been brought to Deepgate's temple and cast into the abyss, shrouded with promises of redemption and Heaven? In reality they'd been nothing but fodder for Ulcis. The young angel felt his eyes darken. 'How did *you* end up here?'

Hasp was silent for a long moment. Finally he rose, still holding the globe in his hand, and approached the doorway. 'My brother Rys decided that one of us should go and fight the Mesmerists in Hell.' He sighed. 'And I was chosen for that honour. Put your anger aside, Dill. If you want to survive down here, you'll need the help of the First Citadel. And you need me to prepare you for the journey out there.' He looked back over Dill's shoulder into the apartment the young angel had grown from his own body. His gaze lingered on the thirteen portraits on the wall, then moved quickly away. 'Ideally, you'd have time to familiarize yourself with your new environment.' He waved his hand at the rooms behind Dill's doorway. 'It is important for you to know every inch of your soul.'

'Why?'

'So we can detach you from it.' He rolled his shoulders, causing the armoured plates there to rasp together; then he lifted his globe. Crystals gleamed behind the brass filigree. 'But we don't have time to acclimatize you, and less time to train you, so we'll cheat.'

Dill stared at the orb in Hasp's hand. 'What is that thing?'

'It's a tool for creating voids: neutral spaces between the crush of souls in Hell. It will allow us two to meet without damage to either of our souls, but it exerts pressure on all those around us. Open your window shutters. We need to know who's nearby.'

The young angel strode back across his apartment. He *felt* his bare feet pad across the floor as though he was walking on his own skin. And in a sense he was. He was standing on his own soul.

The shutters towered over him, six feet high and three feet wide. A weird sensation ran through his flesh as he unlatched one of them and pulled it back to reveal a window composed of multiple small panes.

Through the glass he saw another chamber, much grander and gaudier than his own, shrouded in gloom. Shadows cloaked dim marble walls and pillars that retreated into deeper darkness. In the half-light, Dill could just make out a cupola overhead painted with scenes in which angels hunted queer pig-like beasts through a forest. Yet the shallow alcoves set in the walls boasted a still stranger display. The shelves within these alcoves were laden with the skulls of long-toothed creatures.

Dill strained to see.

Wolves or hounds?

In the centre of the room, a young woman sat at a desk. Dark brown twists of hair tumbled over the shoulders of her rainbow-coloured dress as she leaned forward to scribble in a journal. For a moment Dill stared at her slender wrists, as smooth as honey, and then noticed the swell of her bosom against the fabric of her dress.

Suddenly she looked up at him and smiled.

The wallpaper, curtains and rugs in Dill's room turned a sudden bright shade of pink. He looked away quickly.

'Who is it?' the god called from the doorway. 'Who do you see?'

'A girl,' Dill said. He glanced back through the window, but his neighbour had resumed writing in her book. 'I can't see her very clearly.'

'What size of room?'

'What? It's . . .' He thought for a moment. 'It looks expensive.'

Hasp grunted. 'Then she has an overly inflated ego. Most of these poor bastards are lucky if they can grow hovels around themselves. But does she appear human to you?'

He nodded.

'Then she's no threat. She probably got near us when we fought the crowds in the portal, or I might have been using her

242

as a club. I can't honestly remember. Close the shutters. She won't cause us trouble.'

Dill returned to the doorway, but he didn't close the shutters. The other room had no lanterns, no source of light. He couldn't bring himself to shut the girl in the dark. 'She can't see the doorway from her desk,' he explained. 'It's so dark in there.'

The armoured god shook his head. 'This is Hell, Dill. Do someone a favour and they'll just turn against you.' He flipped the orb, and snatched it out of the air. It glowed with renewed brilliance. Hasp set it down at the base of the doorway where the two chambers met.

Light burst from the device, and it began to swell, quickly increasing in size. The air around it shimmered and blurred like frosted glass. A bubble was forming. Dill backed away as the sphere grew larger than the doorway itself, *pushing* the walls outwards on each side. Now voices were issuing from this expanding ball of light, strange whispers in a language the young angel did not recognize.

'Step inside it,' Hasp said.

Dill hesitated. The space before him writhed with threads of light and hissing voices.

'Do it!' Hasp demanded.

The young angel stepped into the sphere. A feeling of terrible disorientation instantly came over him, and for a heartbeat he lost all sense of connection to the world around him. It was like he was floating in a sea of light.

And then his feet struck solid ground with a resounding boom. The swarm of lights faded, revealing a spherical glass chamber as large as a planetarium. Opaque walls curved up over the young angel's head, full of scintillations. Standing right before him was the god, Hasp.

But Hasp's armour had changed. Instead of old battered steel, he wore a suit of silvered metal. His grey wings and hair had turned as white as starlight, but his eyes held the same wry humour. 'We're standing inside a fragment of Iril,' he said, 'the god of death and darkness himself.'

'*Iril?*'

'Our father was shattered during the War Against Heaven. The Mesmerists constructed this tool from one of the pieces of him they managed to recover.' He grinned. 'Then we stole it from them.'

Dill gazed up at the swarms of stars. 'It's . . . beautiful.'

'Here we can meet safely without setting foot in each other's souls.' Hasp clasped Dill's shoulder. 'You must learn how to adapt and control your environment, and how to arm and armour yourself properly. Just look at your current armour . . .'

Dill's tattered mail shirt hung like curtains of rust from his shoulders. It was an identical manifestation of the armoured garment he had worn since leaving Deepgate, the one he had died in.

'You're only dressed in that sack of rust because you remember wearing it when you died. So change it by visualizing yourself in something stronger and finer.'

The young angel envisioned himself wearing a suit of silvered plate, like Hasp's own armour. Nothing happened; he was still standing there in his old rusty mail.

'So far, so bad,' Hasp grunted. 'Try on that suit behind you.'

Dill turned. A few feet behind him stood a wooden mannequin dressed in shining new armour. '*You* made this?'

'There's enough power left in this sphere to create armour and weapons for ten thousand archons. But it's only one of two pieces of the shattered god we possess, so we daren't drain it too much.' Hasp helped Dill into the suit, strapping the light plates together. 'The other fragment of the god is all that keeps the Mesmerists from storming the First Citadel.'

The suit felt as light as silk, and yet the hardened plates were as tough as steel. Dill flexed his wings then lifted his arms; the metal gleamed under the swirling lights.

'Now a sword,' Hasp said.

Dill turned again, expecting to see a weapon beside the now empty mannequin, but he was disappointed.

'Create it yourself,' Hasp said. 'Simply will it to appear in your hand.'

Dill concentrated. He felt the grip swell inside his closed fist and watched the air solidify into a long heavy blade. A gold guard extended over his hand. And suddenly he was holding his old sword again, the very weapon he had inherited from his fore-bears.

'Hmm . . .' The god frowned. 'That blade is too fragile and unwieldy. Try again.'

And so Dill focused his thoughts on the weapon again. The steel flowed like liquid silver, the blade shortened, and the guard retracted to form a simple cross-piece.

'Much better,' Hasp said. 'Now defend yourself. Show me what you can do.' A blade suddenly appeared in the god's hand and he lunged at Dill.

Dill had never been combat-trained, and his inexperience was soon evident. Hasp disarmed him in a heartbeat. Dill's newly manifested sword clattered across the glass floor.

'This is not good, lad,' the god said darkly. 'Ulcis's priests have been woefully lax in their duties. They ought to have shown you how to take care of yourself.'

'I'm sorry.'

'Pick up your sword. We have a lot of work to do.'

Training lasted until long after Dill was exhausted – and then it began again. Hasp showed him how to shrug off his weariness by the force of will alone. Fatigue meant nothing in Hell, where the body was simply a manifestation of the soul.

'Souls,' Hasp explained, 'do not tire.'

Days seemed to pass easily within that sphere, but the shimmering lights kept the same level of brilliance. Dill thought about nothing except the next attack and how to foil it. And Hasp attacked him relentlessly. The battle-archon did not waver or spare his opponent once. If Dill made a mistake, he suffered for it.

'Souls,' Hasp said, 'do not feel pain.'

Dill winced up at him from the floor of the sphere, and clutched two bleeding fingers in his other fist. This particular soul was feeling a lot of pain.

'Bah!' Hasp gestured with his sword. 'It's all in your mind, lad, and yet your mind isn't strong enough to let go of it. If I plunged this weapon through your heart right now, you'd die.' He frowned. 'If we can't detach you from this fiction with which you've surrounded yourself, then we can't take you back to the First Citadel. Do you want to be trapped here? No? Then stop whining about spilled blood that does not exist, and *get up*!'

Dill rose, but the blood on his hands still felt warm and slick.

Time passed in endless dazzling coruscations: weeks or years, he could not say. Dill parried and lunged, made feints, ducked and wove around the god's blade, until Hasp was suddenly grinning.

'Drop the sword,' Hasp said.

The young angel tried to comply, but he couldn't. The weapon's hilt had fused with his hand. Welds had appeared where his fingers touched the metal. In panic, he flailed his arm to separate himself from the sword. It would not budge.

'Good,' Hasp said. 'Now it's time to rest.'

'Do souls need rest?'

'Ha! Perhaps I should have said *ponder*. You need to remember who you were before you stepped inside this sphere. And then we'll begin again.'

★

Blood now soaked the ground between the Soul Middens; it flowed from broken masonry and woodwork and it gathered in pools. The Icarates had smashed through a full third of the nearest Midden, ripping out the consciousnesses and loading them into cages which now crackled with mesmeric energy.

Bones and debris continued to fall from the sky, scattering across a wide area. And this was the problem. There was no way to tell exactly where the temple angel had fallen. He might already be buried somewhere deep inside one of those great, growing buildings. So far Harper's sceptre had not been able to locate him or any battle-archon.

The souls in this particular Midden had sensed the Icarates' attack on their outer reaches. Now this mountainous building, this composite of individual manifested souls, had begun to change. The stubs of rude battlements and defensive towers were forming in places. Doors were growing reinforced iron bands across their planks, or simply shrinking and becoming stouter.

It was an unconscious reaction to the perceived threat. None of these souls had been in Hell long enough to learn how to adapt their surroundings with any skill. These battlements and towers would not be effective – they were merely affectations, a reflex display. And yet some of the souls were now working together in an altogether stranger way.

Three hundred yards away, one of the older Soul Middens had begun to creep away. This hill-sized mass of houses, balconies and towers was moving, slug-like, across the bloody ground. Somehow, the thousands of souls within the Midden had contrived a way to flee.

Harper watched with fascination. Those dwellings at ground level had sheared away from the souls trapped below. Mortar crumbled and wood split as the Midden inched further away, leaving behind a nest of rooms without ceilings . . . and a trail of

blood. The souls at the base of the Midden were sacrificing themselves for the good of those above them. They were *screaming*.

And yet this painful separation and flight was still doomed to
fail. This cluttered mound of buildings could not move fast
enough. The Icarates paid it no heed, aware that whenever they
decided to take their hammers to the shifting edifice, it would be
nearby for the taking.

While those souls trapped inside the Icarate cages moaned, the
dogcatchers had returned to the basin to feed and to wallow. Like
most creatures in Hell they drew energy from the red mire, the
endless pools, canals and gurgling channels within the Maze.
Here they were feasting on fresher fare than normal.

Harper's sceptre hummed suddenly, and the lights within the
glass orb pulsed. Icarates paused, amid their destruction, to turn
and stare.

Something . . .?

The engineer swept her sceptre across the scene before her. A
ghostlike figure appeared within the glass: a powerful battle-
archon. The image was vague, but the angel appeared to be clad
in armour. He was striding through a long stone vault. He slot-
ted a sword into a weapon rack, and then stooped to place a small
glowing object inside a chest. The sceptre purred, and then the
scene faded once more.

'An archon,' Harper said, pointing one of her glass limbs
towards the ripped-open rooms left by the creeping Soul Midden.
'He's deep underground.'

'The ability to change,' Hasp said to Dill, 'is everything in Hell.
King Menoa has exploited the uncanny nature of this realm to
forge demons. A soul can be persuaded to assume any shape and
to serve any master, and the Mesmerists are *very* good at persuasion.'

They were facing each other through the open doorway

between their chambers. Hasp had deemed Dill's progress with the sword to be 'satisfactory', although the young angel suspected that the god was secretly more than pleased.

'These chambers are a part of you,' Hasp said. 'So you ought to be able to change them. When the Mesmerists remove the core of a soul from rooms like these, they must bolster that soul with external energy or else it withers and becomes a shade. The rooms are then left without the will to do anything but bleed.' He paused to gesture again at the paintings on Dill's walls, the thirteen souls from Devon's elixir who had taken refuge within the young angel. 'Your chambers here are different, for most of the energy in this place comes from these interlopers. That ought to simplify the process of extracting you.'

'Extracting me?'

'Time is running out, lad. It would be better if you're strong enough to move your environment along with you, but if the Mesmerists find you before then, you'll have to run for it.'

Dill's nerves were threaded through the very floorboards and walls, and the room's stone and timber were his very bones. The thought of leaving this place terrified him. 'Show me how to change the rooms,' he said.

Hasp grunted. 'You just need to concentrate. You want something? Then think it into existence.'

So Dill concentrated. He imagined a stack of parchment and some charcoals, much like the ones his father Gaine had given him as a child.

A vague white shape appeared on the floor. It looked rather like one of the temple candles. The moment this thought occurred to him, the shape solidified till it was indeed a candle, exactly like the one he had just imagined. He picked it up, unnerved as ever by that odd sensation of his own fingers pressing into this newly created manifestation of self.

Hasp called over from the door, 'I advise you not to try lighting that. Don't even *imagine* that candlewick on fire.'

Dill couldn't help it. Hasp's own words planted the image of a burning wick in the young angel's mind, and suddenly the candle flared into life. He dropped it at once, but the pain did not diminish. He too was burning.

'Get out of the rain!' the god yelled.

And Dill's pain stopped as a sudden downpour of water engulfed him. Droplets of water cascaded from the ceiling, spattering against every solid surface. The candle flame had gone out. Dill *felt* the rain strike the floorboards and the furniture; he sensed it trickling down the walls and windows like sweat down his own neck.

The god laughed. 'Forgive me for putting that suggestion in your head, but it's better than the sensation of burning alive, is it not? I'll leave you to figure out how to stop the rain by yourself. If you don't you'll drown.' Still chuckling, he wandered back into his own castle.

Dill stood in the downpour, feeling miserable. The water had already risen past his toes. He imagined himself turning off a tap, but it didn't work. He pictured the Deadsands on a hot summer day.

But still the rain continued.

And then someone tapped him on the back of the head. Startled, Dill whirled round. There was nobody there. Water splashed off his fine furnishings. Already the ceiling plaster had begun to bow, a sensation Dill experienced as a soft ache in his skull. But the room was empty.

Another tap to the back of his head.

Again Dill wheeled. At first he saw nobody, but then he noticed the young woman standing outside his window. The glass panes had partially misted, but he recognized the rainbow dress. His neighbour! Dripping wet, he walked over and unlatched the window.

She smiled, showing dimples. 'I'm sorry to disturb you,' she said brightly. 'But this wall is leaking. I'm getting flooded in here.'

'Oh.'

Her large dark eyes shone. 'I wouldn't mind so much, but this water is . . .' She hesitated. 'Well, the water is an incarnation of your soul. I'm afraid it's giving me some odd thoughts.'

'Odd thoughts?'

She laughed. '*Your* thoughts. They're very nice, but they're spoiling my rugs.' She leaned closer, until her body brushed the window frame. 'Dill, would you like me to put a suggestion in your head? One which might stop this silly downpour?'

Dill smelled perfume.

The rain ceased abruptly.

'That's better,' the young woman said. 'I'm Mina Greene.'

'I'm . . .' But clearly she already knew his name. How much *else* did she know about him?

'Of course I know who you are,' she admitted. 'You're the whole reason I'm here. I have something for you – wait there.' She hurried back into her gloomy chamber, splashing through puddles. 'I had to wait until that bothersome old god had gone. I doubt he'd approve of this.'

'Approve of what?'

'Just wait!' She rummaged among shelves of skulls in one of the alcoves. After a moment she withdrew a sword and brought it over to the window.

Dill frowned. 'You're here to give me a sword? Who *are* you? How do you know me?'

'I'm Mina Greene,' she repeated. 'And I know as much about you as anyone from Deepgate. More, probably. It's my job to know a lot of things.' She weighed the sword in her hand. 'But no, I can't give you this. It's from the Forest of War. Basilis would be furious if I just handed it over.' Instead, she placed the edge of the sword against her own chamber's window ledge. Then she grimaced and slid the blade sideways, cutting loose a sliver of wood. Blood welled from the gouge she'd made.

Mina gasped. She hopped about on the spot, her hands clamped together against her breast until the pain subsided. 'Blood magic doesn't work in Hell,' she said in a strained voice. 'So we'll have to do this a different way.'

'I don't understand.'

'The Mesmerists want you,' she said. 'Why else do you think Hasp risked his soul in that portal to find you and bring you here?' Her brows rose, and she smiled again. 'And if what I've been told about King Menoa is true, he'll find a way to get you. Old Hasp isn't as strong as he used to be. I wouldn't put *all* your faith in his ability to protect you.' Now she held up the splinter of wood she'd cut from her window ledge. 'So I'm going to give you *this*.'

'A bit of wood?'

'A bit of *me*!' She managed to look cross and absurdly beautiful at the same time. 'How else will I be able to find you if I need to? This is what I came here to give you.' She huffed. 'Do you think we should just sit back while Menoa brings his version of Hell out into the world? We're not all as weak and foolish as the gods think we are. Cohl's Shades have come to Pandemeria, and John Anchor's stomping about somewhere.'

Rachel?

'And there are others too.' She smiled. 'Like me. Now hold out your hand.'

Dill reached for the splinter.

'No, not like that,' she said. 'Like *this*.' She grabbed his hand and slid the thin needle of wood into his wrist.

When the pain and shock of what Mina Greene had done to him finally subsided, Dill found himself lying curled up and shivering on the floor. Someone had closed and locked the shutters, and three vases of fresh flowers had appeared on the sideboard, but otherwise his room looked unchanged.

At least it was now dry.

His wrist throbbed, and he could see a faint red mark where the young woman had inserted the splinter. He rose groggily, and threw back the shutters.

But the view beyond the window had changed. A second set of closed shutters now prevented him from looking into Mina's room – these ones on the inside of *her* windows.

It seemed she no longer wanted to speak.

Dill sat on his bed, brooding. He thought he could still smell a whiff of perfume. He closed his eyes and pictured her: her soft dark eyes, her honey-coloured skin, and the deep curves of her dress. A creak startled him. The base of the bed, he noticed, had raised itself a little higher from the floor.

Should he knock on her window?

And embarrass himself? She clearly wanted privacy. Perhaps she was feeling awkward. The bond they now shared was unusually intimate. He decided to wait until she was ready to talk.

Living inside an incarnation of one's soul had a certain appeal, Dill continued to discover. As long as he didn't damage himself – by dropping a vase, for example, or accidentally slamming the dresser door too hard. He quickly learned to change his environment by simply willing those changes to happen.

In time he learned how to control the pain, and he began to experiment by conjuring flames. If he wanted a fire in the hearth, he simply thought about it, and it sprung into being. Only afterwards did he realize that there had never been a hearth in the room. That had appeared simultaneously too. At first the leaping flames sent jolts of pain through the chimneystack, but by degrees he managed to overcome this discomfort. He fireproofed himself, and the pain dwindled. It was an odd feeling, sitting there on a rug while part of your soul burned before your eyes.

But was it really burning?

Other things happened without his conscious thought. The window drapes often changed colour to match his mood. When he felt frustrated, he noticed they had turned orange. This observation filled him with awe, which then changed the curtains to gold. They stayed gold for a long time. The window panes became larger, while the shutters on this side of the glass diminished, creeping back into the surrounding walls. Eventually they disappeared altogether.

Mina Greene kept herself sealed in the darkness of her own room.

Time passed.

Hasp never closed his door, although he had made Dill swear not to step through it under any circumstances. From the god's castle came the constant thud of arrows striking wood. He had taken to practising with a bow.

Dill studied the paintings: those thirteen people who now shared his soul. They watched him soundlessly. Sometimes their expressions changed, but only when Dill wasn't looking. He thought he recognized a few of them: two of the younger lads from the temple kitchens, and a girl in a scullery apron. Of them all, only the assassin unnerved him. The man bore marks tattooed on his neck – the sign of a failed tempering procedure – and his painted eyes smouldered with madness.

Could Dill conjure up his own painting?

He successfully created a blank canvas surrounded by a heavy gold frame. But the painting itself eluded him. Should it be a scene from the Codex? The Battle of the Tooth? Perhaps he should just paint himself painting himself?

Too self-indulgent. He dismissed the idea.

He tried to clear his mind and think of nothing at all. The lights in the room went out.

Dill hissed in exasperation. *I'm thinking too small.* Everything in his environment was malleable. He could create anything he desired.

So what did he actually want?

When the lights came on again, he found himself looking up at a painting of Mina Greene.

18

THE LEGION OF THE BLIND

Harper's towering new form afforded her a good view of the open foundations below. She watched the scene through glass eyes. The great castle that was the upper section of the Soul Midden had crawled away, leaving a large open wound in the Maze itself. Blood from broken dwellings had leached into the chambers below, partially flooding them. The men and women in that pit, now fully exposed to the skies above, gazed up in horror.

'Clear them out of there,' Harper said. 'And ask King Menoa to send us a Worm.'

Most of the Icarates hobbled down into the labyrinth of walled spaces, their pale armour crackling with blue fire. Instead of hammers they carried tridents, for there would be no further need to smash down walls. What followed now would be a simple matter of collection.

Only the Icarate high priest remained: a stooped figure clad in ill-fitting white plates. The protrusions on his back were larger than those of his warrior comrades, like the pale fungi found on the boles of dead trees. Verdigris crusted his copper mouth grille, but he did not require it, or even a mouth, to speak.

It is done. Menoa will send a Worm.

The Worm came as soon as Menoa's armoured warriors had cleared the souls from the bleeding pit. It appeared as a black thread, snaking higher and higher up above the far horizon, and then rushed nearer until it was weaving through the hot red mists towards them. Massive and uncertain, this conduit of souls looped above Harper's head and then plunged down into the pit before her.

It was not one demon, but many linked together for one purpose. Their black scales rippled, serpent-like, across the Worm's skin, but all the claws and teeth were within. Waves of peristalsis flowed back along its length as it fed on the remains of the Midden and burrowed itself deeper into the ground.

Harper studied her sceptre, searching for a psychic disturbance in the ground below. If the archon felt the presence of the Worm, then he might panic, trying to flee. And then she would know exactly where he was.

But as she watched the Worm feed, a sensation of dizziness came over her, as though something inside her own body had shifted momentarily, throwing her off balance. She heard a weak tapping sound.

Harper raised her mirrored shield and gazed at her reflection.

The manikin peered back from inside Harper's own glass skull. This tiny manifestation of her former self already looked much frailer than it had been. It swayed unsteadily on its feet. Shadows had appeared under its eyes. It cupped one hand into the shape of a bowl, made a spooning gesture with the other.

The manikin was starving.

Mina Greene's shutters remained firmly closed. To Dill's horror, the wood had begun to deteriorate. Damp had softened and warped the lowest edges, and the shutters now appeared to sit crookedly in their frame. He spied patches of white mould and rust on the hinges.

'Something's wrong,' Dill told Hasp.

'Something's wrong with most of the people down here,' Hasp

replied. 'She's bound to be miserable. She's in Hell. And souls get worn thin over time. It takes great force of will to maintain one's surroundings. Ignore her, she'll be gone soon.'

'Gone where?'

'Nowhere. She'll just slip between the gaps and become a shade. Her room will eventually bleed to death and drain into the Mesmerist canals. Happens all the time. Some people just aren't strong enough to survive here.'

'Then she needs help.'

'What she needs,' the god said, 'is oblivion – the Veil. That's the best thing for her now, and that's where she's headed. Trust me, I've seen it a billion times before. Don't get involved.'

Dill rubbed his wrist where Mina had inserted a tiny splinter of her soul. He imagined her sitting alone in the darkness surrounded by those dusty shelves of skulls. He pictured her chamber rotting around her as she lost the will to maintain it. Perhaps he should just check that she was all right?

He knocked on her window.

It was a queer sensation. As his knuckles struck the glass, a vision flashed in his mind.

– *A crowd of Sandporters cheered and clapped in a wide town square* –

He knocked again.

– *A brightly painted wagon stood in a sandy glade, surrounded by colourful trees* –

'I told you to leave her be,' Hasp said.

'There's no response,' Dill replied. 'I'm going to open the window.'

'Not a good idea, lad. How would *you* feel if a stranger broke into your soul?'

But Dill was already searching for something to break the window with. And then he realized that he didn't *have* to search at all – this little part of Hell was entirely malleable. He glanced down to find that a crowbar had already appeared in his fist.

Hasp growled. 'Don't do it. That kind of contact sends tremors through the whole damn Maze. You're not just risking *her* soul.'

Dill hooked the crowbar under the window sash and pushed down on it.

– A mangy little pup sniffed around the deck of a ship –

The sash sprang open. He hoisted it up. Now only the closed shutters stood between him and Mina's room. Behind him, Hasp threw up his arms in frustration and stormed back inside his castle.

Dill pounded his fist repeatedly against the shutters.

– Something padded through darkness, a powerful hunched shape. Blood dribbled from a sword into a clay bowl. A wild beast howled –

The rotten wood had split where Dill had struck it. One of the shutters was already coming away from its hinges. Dill pressed both hands against the wood and shoved hard. The shutters flew open.

– An odour of loam and bark . . . and of freshly butchered meat –

Dill stared. The room beyond the open window bore no resemblance to Mina Greene's opulent chambers: this chamber was much smaller – a dull brick-walled space with an earthen floor. To the left, a single doorway led to another, similarly gloomy, cell. There were no pillars, no grand cupola, and no furnishings except for a long wooden box sitting in the middle of the floor. It looked big enough to contain a corpse.

'Mina!'

Dill climbed up onto the window ledge and was about to step through, when he heard a scraping sound. Mina backed through the doorway, dragging a second – much smaller – wooden trunk behind her. When she reached the long box, she paused to catch her breath.

'That's far enough, Dill,' she said without looking up.

'What are you doing?'

'Packing.' Mina opened the small chest. Then she tilted the

long box up, standing it on one end. It was almost as tall as she was. With some effort, she lifted it up, and then lowered it down again so that its narrow base rested inside the open chest on the floor.

Dill watched in astonishment as the tall container slid down until it had disappeared completely inside the smaller one. Mina went back through to the other room. In a moment she returned with yet another chest, smaller again than the one remaining on the floor. She repeated the whole process. By placing the narrow end of one container inside the wider mouth of the next, she eventually managed to reduce her luggage to the size of a jewellery box.

'Where are you going?' Dill asked.

'I thought I'd have a wander around,' she replied cheerfully. She made comical bug eyes at him. 'See some demons. Catch some ghosts.'

'That's not normal,' Dill said.

Her dark eyes gleamed. 'It is for me.'

'But what happened to your room? Where *is* everything?'

She wandered over to him, holding up the little jewellery box. 'All the important stuff is in here,' she said. 'Iril's canals can drink the rest after I've gone.'

'But . . .' A hollow ache had taken root in Dill's stomach. He didn't want her to leave. Absurdly, a loose thread hanging from a seam on the side of her dress caught his eye. Why did he find this tiny imperfection so suddenly endearing? She was so close he could smell her perfume: the warm scent of desert spice on her skin. Without thinking, he shifted his position on the window ledge.

'Dill!' she warned.

Dill reached up to grip the sash above, but the window *flinched* away from him. Suddenly he was gripping nothing, and overbalanced. He fell forward into the girl's room.

A moment of extreme disorientation overwhelmed him, as though he had stepped outside of himself, and was looking back at his own face. It was the oddest sensation, both familiar and utterly strange to him. He saw the wings of an archon, *his* wings, with a plush room behind, but he was also staring at a dark brick-walled space and a screaming girl in a rainbow-coloured dress.

He saw, or felt, Mina shudder; Dill couldn't be sure. His senses were reeling now, confusing him. He heard the savage howling of a wild animal. He reached out to Mina, or thought he was, because suddenly he was reaching out to himself, a young angel standing in a dismal cell. A girl stood over by the window, her arms outstretched.

His fingers brushed another hand. The touch sent a powerful shock through him. Nausea cloyed in his throat. He heard continued shrieking, followed by the deep growl of a hound. Perfume mingled with the thick stench of animals. It was too much to bear. He staggered back from the angel, from the girl in the bright dress. His hands gripped something. A window frame?

He fell backwards.

'Fool!' Hasp's voice roared somewhere behind him. 'Close that window now! You'd better hope the Mesmerists didn't feel that commotion.'

Dill's thoughts still spun. 'What? I don't understand . . .'

'You stepped inside her soul,' Hasp growled. 'Did you think her reaction to an intrusion like that would be subtle? You just violated that girl in the worst possible way.'

'I'm sorry,' Dill stammered. 'I'm sorry. I didn't . . .'

But he was cut off by a sound like an earthquake. His whole apartment – his whole soul – groaned and shook.

'Light and Life,' Hasp said. 'Get back from that window!'

Dill rose unsteadily. Through the open window he could still see Mina. She was wailing uncontrollably, clutching the jewellery box to her chest. Dust shuddered free of the walls and clouded the air around her.

'Get back! Don't make me come in there.'

But how could Dill leave her in such distress? Whatever was happening was his fault. By setting foot in her room, he had triggered this.

He shouted back to Hasp. 'What's happening?'

'Menoa's hordes are coming.' The god smiled coldly. 'And it sounds like they've brought a Worm.'

The rear wall in Mina's room suddenly cracked and then burst inward. Chunks of brick and mortar showered the earthen floor. Something smashed through, and then pulled away again, leaving a ragged gap.

Claws?

Mina screamed again.

Bricks exploded to dust behind her. In one heartbeat the entire rear wall of the room disappeared. In its place Dill saw what appeared to be a wide tunnel, sloping upwards at a shallow angle. The interior of this space was moving, seething like a swarm of insects.

Demons? They were crowded together in the darkness, a crush of anthracite-like bones and curved claws and teeth all woven together by strands of red muscle. This moving mass continued as far as the eye could see. The leading rim of the tunnel had pressed firmly up against the edge of Mina's room, while the nearest limbs reached in and tore away more sections of wall, passing the debris back to ranks of snapping teeth. A gale blew in from the tunnel, as heavy and dank as stale rainwater. The edges of the room had already begun to bleed.

Dill gasped. Further back among the tunnel's connective tissues, the crowd of demons were passing objects forward through their ranks towards those in front. These looked like pale gelatinous spheres, and the demons handled them with particular care. The objects, he realized, were eyes: thousands of them all staring back at the young angel.

Still screaming, Mina dropped to her knees and pressed her palms over her ears.

'Take my hand,' Dill cried. He reached back through the window. 'Come with me, quickly!'

She didn't look up at him.

'Get away from there, lad!' Hasp roared from the doorway.

The tunnel consumed more and more of Mina's room, chewing through the walls as though they were paper. Cracks shot through the earthen floor. Fragments crumbled away only to be plucked up by the howling wind.

Dill scrambled back into Mina's room, where her agony hit him like the blast from a furnace. He staggered but managed to grab her and drag her back towards the window.

Hasp pounded on the doorframe. 'Leave her!'

Somehow Dill bundled them both over the window ledge. With the encroaching tunnel of claws and teeth mere yards behind them, the pair collapsed in a crumpled heap on Dill's floor.

Or was it a floor? For a confusing moment Dill glimpsed forest all around him – dark, ancient oaks crowding his vision. The rich perfume of soil and mulch filled his lungs. He heard Mina give a gasp . . .

. . . Then silence.

Dill's vision faded abruptly; he was sprawled on the floor of his room again. Groggily, he shook his head and looked around.

Mina still clutched her jewellery box, but her eyes now stared vacantly into a faraway place.

'What's wrong with her?'

The god grunted. 'Shock,' he said. 'Watching the shell of your soul being consumed by demons can have that effect. It's a wonder she hasn't already become a shade. Look behind you!'

There was almost nothing left of Mina's room; it had been

swallowed up, the fragments carried back inside the Worm's end-less gullet. The rim of the tunnel had finally reached Dill's window. But then it came to a sudden halt, and those demons closest to the window held up their fists so that the eyes they clutched could peer into the angel's room.

Dill dragged Mina to her feet.

'What do I do now?' he cried.

'Get in here.' The god stepped aside.

'But, you said . . .'

'I know what I said. Get in here! The Mesmerists have *seen* us now.'

Dill took a final desperate look at his surroundings. The walls and furnishings were losing their colour, turning as white as his own eyes. The room was *afraid*. Only the portraits on the walls kept their colour – those thirteen souls who had shared his blood on Earth and now shared his space in Hell. Why should he leave them to be consumed? Frantically he yanked down the canvases from the walls. With frames stuffed clumsily under each arm, he urged Mina towards the doorway to Hasp's castle.

'Not the girl,' Hasp said.

'She can't stay here!'

The god spoke through his teeth. 'You had no business bring-ing her inside your soul, and you are not going to bring her into mine. Leave her!'

Dill didn't move. Something strange was happening within the tunnel now. The demons parted, jostling and snapping at each other as they cleared a path right through their ranks. The tunnel itself writhed and flexed, its muscles contracting. And soon a wide avenue had appeared among the hordes; it stretched upwards to follow the tunnel's inside curve. In the far distance Dill spotted some sort of procession marching down this newly cleared road: it was composed of a group of pale, armoured figures and several great brown beasts like oxen.

'Mesmerists?' Dill whispered urgently.

'Icarates,' Hasp growled. 'The Mesmerists manufactured them to enforce their laws. But they have been forced to bend the structure of Hell to facilitate their progress down here. See how their armour sparks? Their power is temporarily depleted.' His mouth set in a grim line, he beckoned Dill towards his own warren of chambers. 'Come with me now if you want to survive this. Quickly! Before I change my mind.'

'I'm not leaving Mina.'

Hasp gnashed his teeth in anger. And then he reached in, grabbed Dill and Mina, and pulled them both through the doorway into his castle.

The sudden sense of dissociation Dill felt when he set foot inside the god's soul nearly drove him to his knees. He dropped the paintings and heard them strike the floor. He saw Hasp's face looming over him, grey and sweating, his eyes a hard blue under his creased brow. And yet Dill felt power all around him, ancient and immensely powerful. It was staggering: memories of ten thousand battles assailed him. His skin crawled with countless pains. He heard the clash of steel and the war cries of armies, smelled blood and death. He sensed the pounding heart of a god in his own chest, and struggled desperately to cling to his own identity. Mina slumped against the wall, slack-faced and staring at nothing.

'My home,' Hasp said through his teeth.

'Your soul,' Dill replied.

Hasp grunted. 'Try not to break it.'

The procession in the tunnel was nearer now. Huge beasts like the gods of oxen snorted and steamed in the demon-crowded corridor, each harnessed to a wheeled cage. These prisons were full of people who gibbered and shrieked and rattled at the bars. Eyeless things with wet red skin and clickety teeth kept pace on either side, while banners of black and gold snapped in the gale above their heads. The white-armoured warriors hobbled like cripples, yet they wielded heavy hammers and tridents. They were merely yards away from Dill's room.

Hasp kicked Dill's dropped paintings aside, and then hurried the young couple along the long low chamber, past racks of swords and shields, bows and quivers of arrows. From behind them came the sound of splintering glass. The Icarates were smashing their way into Dill's soul. Pain clouded the young angel's vision, throwing up a barrage of colourful dazzling lights. He stumbled, but Hasp grabbed the collar of his steel shirt in one huge fist and dragged him onwards.

'Those rooms back there are just a manifestation of your soul,' said the god, 'like the body you think you now inhabit. That manifestation is now being destroyed, but the core of your soul remains here, under *my* protection. You can avoid the girl's fate if you have the will to do so. Remember your training. Ignore the pain or you'll end up as catatonic as this bitch.' He held up Mina like a rag doll in his other fist. 'You can avoid her fate if you have the will to do so.'

'I can't see clearly,' Dill gasped.

'Yes, you can.'

And Dill suddenly found that he *could* see. His eyes no longer stung, yet now the pain moved to his bones and almost crippled him. He heard the sound of crashing debris coming from behind, and then he felt it in his bruised and battered limbs. A second doorway loomed before him, this leading to an enormous banquet hall lit by golden chandeliers. The drone of a hunting horn vibrated the air.

Dill glanced back. The Icarates had now destroyed most of his apartment, and they were driving their procession through its remnants. As soon as Dill saw them, he sensed the beasts' hooves pressing down, the weight of their huge lumbering bodies on the floorboards. His vision blurred again. He felt like he was standing on the edge of an abyss – the darkness pulling him closer.

'Fight it!' Hasp shook the young angel. 'Don't lose your wits now.'

Still Hasp dragged the pair onwards, further into the banquet hall. Long tables had been arranged along three of the walls, each covered with platters of food. The god shoved Mina roughly to one side, and then snatched an apple from the nearest table. 'Eat this,' he said to Dill. 'It will give you the strength.'

'What about Mina?'

'Just do as I say,' the god growled. 'And don't even think about eating anything else.' Then he turned and charged back the way they had come.

As the Lord of the First Citadel ran, the chamber changed around him, reflecting his rage. The walls darkened, turning from rough grey stone to hard black glass. Over his head the ceiling began to crack. Ahead of him, the doorway expanded until its cavity filled the entire wall.

Dill could sense that the Icarates had destroyed most of his own soul. Through the throbbing of his blood he felt his room's agony: the split skirting, the broken furniture and the shattered bed with its torn drapes trampled under the hooves of those stinking beasts. Dizzying, disparate sensations crowded his exhausted nerves. Fighting unconsciousness, he took a bite of the apple. Abruptly, the pain diminished; his heartbeat steadied, then pounded with renewed vigour.

He took the apple over to Mina.

At the far end of the corridor Hasp roared. He had reached the open doorway, a portal now as large as a fortress portcullis. The Icarates had finished consuming Dill's room and now stood at the entrance to Hasp's own castle.

Here, they hesitated.

Either the Lord of the First Citadel had grown in size, or the passageway had constricted around him. In his old, battered armour, he towered before the intruders. From somewhere he had acquired a massive stone sword, which he held up effortlessly before him. The Icarates clicked and buzzed in apparent agitation, sparks fizzing from their awkward white suits.

Hasp flexed his shoulders. 'Should I break your souls?' he boomed. 'Or armour mine?'

A heavy iron grate crashed down across the doorway to his castle, separating him from the would-be invaders. Metal panels appeared from out of nowhere, then slammed and bolted themselves against the interior walls. Girders slid in from the walls on either side, meeting each other with a series of loud clangs. 'Would that stop your hammers?' he asked with a shrug. The metal defences wavered for a moment, and then dissolved like smoke.

'Or should I forge an army of my own?' the god went on.

The floor around him bubbled. The bubbles swelled and changed, forming black glass creatures like crude sculptures of men and beasts: club-footed golems and sleek, powerful cats. Their claws raked the floor of the passageway.

'Or should I simply move?' Hasp said.

Dill could not persuade Mina to eat. She stared through him, oblivious to her surroundings. He took another bite of the apple, and then offered it to her again, but she remained as slack and witless as a puppet.

The floor gave an unexpected jolt.

The passageway in which Hasp stood suddenly contracted, bringing the god and his glass-forged figures careening back towards the young angel, until he was immediately outside the entrance to the banquet hall. What had been a long corridor until a moment ago had now compressed into a short hallway.

But beyond Hasp's front door now lay a chasm. The Icarates and their tunnel had remained in one place while the castle had retracted from them. Now their procession was trapped on the other side of a wide gap. They were gazing out through a ragged hole in the wall of a vast and strange building.

Dill saw that his own little apartment had been one among countless others. Oddly shaped windows and doors clustered around the gaping rent where the Icarates stood. More and more apartments came into view – a thousand dwellings stacked one upon the other – even as Hasp's castle retreated. The facade looked like a cliff of stone, steel, glass and metal, all entangled as if an epic struggle between different builders had taken place. And in a sense that was exactly what had happened, for each apartment was the manifestation of someone's individual soul. The carved marble, brick and dark-stained timber was living.

This, then, was Hell.

But now the whole facade was broken and bleeding. Streams of blood poured from the fractured walls, spattered off timbers and girders, and formed a fine red mist. Debris cascaded past the portcullis, till a sweet, copper-rich scent filled the air. Then Hasp's castle picked up speed. Now the god's stronghold was burrowing through Hell itself, leaving its own ragged tunnel behind. By now the Icarates were left far behind.

Hasp wore a grim expression. Sweat lined his brow and his hard blue eyes were tense with concentration. 'This flight will cost me dearly,' he muttered. 'And it will destroy many of the other souls around us. I doubt I can keep this up for long. Did you consume the apple?'

Dill nodded.

'Good. Technically, I suppose that was cannibalism.' He shrugged. 'Better that than have you fade away completely. Now' – he turned away – 'our cover is gone. We must surface and draw what power we can from the bloodmists. Otherwise we'll be grounded.'

The living ghetto of souls existed on all sides of Hasp's

stronghold and, from the bloody passage the castle had already ripped through it, it looked impossibly vast. Hasp clenched his fists and the whole castle rumbled and began to rise, cleaving a path upwards.

'Leave the girl.' The god beckoned towards the corner of the banquet hall. 'She's safe enough here. I want to show you something. Follow me into the cage.'

'What cage?' Dill asked.

A folding metal gate appeared in the corner of the room, and then opened with a clatter and a clunk.

'That cage,' Hasp indicated.

It was an elevator much like the one Dill had used every day to descend through the heart of Deepgate's temple – a metal cage suspended by chains and pulleys. The god closed the folding gate behind them. 'While you remain in my castle, you're under my protection,' he said, 'and your soul will recover from the damage it sustained. Just don't start growing any walls in here.'

With a rattle of chains the cage began to rise. It jolted, and suddenly picked up speed. Before Dill had time to breathe, another jolt quickened their ascent again. And another. Soon they were racing upwards through a glass-walled shaft through which Dill spied luxurious suites full of plush furniture and golden, sparkling chandeliers. Rooms passed in a blur, scores of them, and still the metal elevator rose higher and higher.

They arrived eventually in a glass conservatory which glowed like a multi-faceted lantern. Lush green plants writhed around them on all sides, curling their slender leaves around each other in the golden glow from a swarm of fireflies. Vines crept up the windows, sprouted yellow flowers, and then withered and fell away again. As Dill watched, this process repeated itself again and again: plants grew, and died, then struggled up from the earth again.

Overhead, buildings smashed against the conservatory panes.

Hasp's castle was still rising up through Hell, still demolishing everything in its path. Dill could only wonder why the glass ceiling did not shatter and rain down upon them. Evidently the god's soul was tougher than it first seemed.

And then suddenly the heavens appeared above them. Chunks of masonry fell away from the windowpanes to reveal an angry red sky. Darker whorls of crimson and black drifted slowly across this vista like scum floating in a cauldron. But the conservatory continued to rise until they were looking out across the landscape from a great height.

A maze of canals etched the ground for as far as Dill could see, their mirror-black walls confining loops and narrow twisted runnels of dark red liquid. Above these channels towered high, sharply tapering hills crowded with houses as queer and disparate in their architecture as those left underground.

The shells of living souls?

But the skyline was dominated by a monstrous black worm – the exterior of the tunnel they had seen below, Dill realized. One end of it plunged into the ground a few hundred yards away from the walls of Hasp's castle, yet it stretched right to the far horizon.

Hasp said, 'Menoa must have expended a great deal of his power to send that Worm. We can only hope it takes time for him to recover.' He shook his head wearily. 'I had hoped to move my castle and your chambers slowly beneath the earth, where we might remain undetected. But now, we must run. I'll push this building as fast and as far as I can, but I fear it won't be far enough to reach the First Citadel. When that happens, you'll need to get out and walk.'

The castle halted its ascent, shuddered again, and then began to move away across the surface of Hell.

Harper watched the archon's castle burst from the bleeding ground and hover no more than twenty feet above the surrounding

271

Middens. The canals had already begun to drain into the hole it had made. Meanwhile her Icarates remained underground, still caught inside the great black Worm.

My Icarates?

When had she started to think of these warriors as her own? The thought repulsed her – Menoa's Icarates had been the cause of her husband's suffering, after all. But the threat of King Menoa's rage at the loss of the angel spurred her into action. Through her sceptre, she planted a vision in the Worm's collective mind, urging it to rise to the surface once more. The sheer force of King Menoa's will had kept the Worm together, but it would not last much longer in this form. And the loosing of those demons that comprised its exoskeleton and teeth would provide her with an army.

Harper intended to pursue her quarry.

Judging by the size and grandeur of the castle, its occupant was a powerful angel, perhaps even Lord Hasp himself. Had the Lord of the First Citadel come to claim the young angel? It was possible, Harper conceded. It made no difference. No amount of will could carry that vast fortress far enough across the leagues of Hell. Free of the ground, the castle's battlements and spires now towered over the Soul Middens, the maroon rock plated with thick iron on the lower walls, and occasionally festooned with glass. The pinnacles were capped by pointed roofs of deep blue slate. Flowering ivy veined its facades. Only the underside of the building was tattered and untidy where it had broken away from the souls below.

Blood fell like rain from those foundations and dripped soundlessly into the huge pit below. The archon's soul had already begun to die.

The stronghold hovered for a further moment, then moved away. Its heavy iron plates snagged against one slope of a Midden, and then it smashed through the dwellings and freed itself.

By now the Worm had extracted itself from the rendered foundations and laid its maw on level ground to expel both the Icarates and their retinue of beasts and soul-cages.

Harper used her sceptre to plant another vision within the Worm's many minds, one which would travel back to the Ninth Citadel itself. King Menoa would understand her plan, and hopefully sanction it. She *envisioned* the Worm breaking apart.

Evidence of the king's approval came back at once, for the Worm burst apart into all its component demons. A wave travelled from the horizon all the way to the Worm's maw as countless numbers of the black scaly creatures untangled themselves from their neighbours and leapt clear. This was Menoa's Legion of the Blind, the oldest and most primitive of his warrior clans. Long claws thrashing at the air and teeth clashing, the Blind dropped one by one to the ground. Of a similar size, though varying in shape, each possessed between four and six skeletal limbs. A hard turtle-like shell protected their backs, and served to link them together, when necessary, to form a Phalanx or a Worm. They had no eyes of their own, but many clutched the Eyes of the Old Worm – the parasite monster Menoa had butchered three thousand years ago.

Legend told how he had discovered the creature in a deep burrow, feasting on unclaimed souls. Menoa had persuaded the creature to ally with him by the simple offer of food, and then he had betrayed it. Now its eyes gave sight to the Legion of the Blind, while the Blind assumed the beast's former shape as if to torment it.

King Menoa's punishments often had no end.

The blind demons parted like a dark tide around Harper. Tens of thousands of them clambered over the Middens and across the walls between canals, or merely sloshed through the red mire. Some of them had not managed to extricate themselves from their neighbours and now walked in clusters of two or more, their shells still fused together.

But it was a considerable force, and fast, for the Blind moved surprisingly quickly. The perfect legion for hunting with.

The strain of his efforts pinched Hasp's expression, and yet the Lord of the First Citadel demanded that Dill accompany him to the training sphere. 'While you're a resident in my soul,' he said, with a sweep of his hand to indicate the great flying stronghold around him, 'you will abide by my rules. And that means learning to use battle-archon weapons. The short sword you know. But you must master the pike, rapier, bow, shield, spear, axe and mace. Once you've learned how to use those, I will teach you about more exotic weapons.'

The god had gone on to explain that they would train inside Iril's sphere so as to allow Dill to continue to fashion his own blades and armour. 'Remember, any sword you attempt to manifest in this castle would be forged from *my* spirit. Weapons made inside the sphere, however, draw upon the life-force of the shattered god. Iril's sphere is a void, and while we are inside it, our souls are not intertwined.'

Dill had been wondering how his continued presence inside Hasp's castle would affect the god. It was, after all, a parasitic relationship, for Hasp provided the shelter and strength the young angel required for his survival. The apple Dill had eaten was a manifest part of the god's soul.

Mina remained insensate. She stood in the banquet hall, clutching her jewellery box. Hasp ignored her, but he put up with her presence here for Dill's sake.

'I'm already sharing my fortress with an angel and his thirteen painted ghosts,' the god grumbled. 'Another human soul makes little difference.'

Dill trained. Hasp taught him how to will weapons into existence. And then he taught Dill how to alter them mid-strike to surprise an enemy. A sword could be transformed into a spear, a bow into a shield. Dill learned how to shoot an arrow and how to change that arrow so that it veered during flight, or looped and circled a target before contact.

Combat in Hell had few rules.

When he wasn't training, Dill spent his time with Mina. He talked about his former life in the temple, and about Rachel and how she'd save him from Hell once before. He even offered her food from Hasp's table, when the god wasn't looking. But nothing roused her from her catatonia.

One day Hasp came into the banquet hall and frowned at them. 'She ought to be shade by now,' he remarked. 'Human souls don't last for long down here without their shells.'

Dill rubbed at the splinter of wood she had placed under his skin, but said nothing.

All this time Hasp kept his castle floating across the Maze. Sometimes Dill took the elevator up to the glass house at the top of the fortress from where he could gaze out across the landscape. The Maze was endless, scarred with canals and stippled with Middens. Very occasionally Dill spied an unusual black structure in the distance – like the bones of some alien temple or monolith. He asked Hasp what these were.

'We don't know,' the god conceded. 'They've been here in Hell since long before we archons arrived. The Icarates use them for some purpose, places of pilgrimage perhaps. Occasionally those temples simply disappear. They may therefore be merely the dreams of ghosts.'

The skies darkened after dusk and grew brighter with the dawn, but each night lasted a different span of time. Some nights seemed to pass in mere moments, while others dragged on for much longer. Seemingly no pattern regulated the ebb and flow of light in this place.

'It is Hell's heartbeat,' Hasp explained. 'A result of the conflicting expectations of a hundred billion souls. Time runs at many different speeds in the Maze – it is constantly in dispute.' He grimaced and rubbed his temples, then gave a deep sigh. 'Lots of things have changed here since Iril was shattered. We are in a constant state of war.'

Hasp had been showing more evident signs of the strain he was under. His skin had become grey and slack, his shoulders stooped, and he moved with the weariness of an old man. Even his armour had dulled and rusted rust. Often the god stood in the glass house for hours, brooding, and staring back along the castle's wake. A dark smudge covered the landscape there, like an encroaching sea of tar. When Dill pointed it out, Hasp shrugged and refused to comment. Instead he ordered Dill back down to the sphere for combat training.

Dill retrieved the paintings from the lower hall and set them up in a room Hasp had allocated him. The thirteen spirits in Devon's elixir gazed out miserably from their canvases at their new surroundings. Sometimes when Dill listened outside the door he heard them speaking to each other in hushed voices, but they always fell silent when he entered.

He began to suspect they were plotting something.

After the twentieth span of darkness, the castle slowed. It seemed to Dill that the building had let loose a great sigh, and that it was giving up. Every mirror in Hasp's fortress grew dull. The floors sagged. The fruit in the banquet hall began to moulder. Even the stones seemed to glisten under a patina of sweat.

Hasp thereupon led him up a narrow spiral stair to the summit of the castle, the god himself pausing many times to rest. The stairwell took them to a small balcony encircling a tower, very much like the one Dill had grown up in. Like the one in Deepgate, ivy engulfed one side. If he climbed it, Dill wondered, would he find a weathervane on top?

'Yes you would,' Hasp confirmed.

Dill blinked. Did Hasp just read his mind?

'Our souls have shared space for so long now,' Hasp explained, 'that I've been dreaming your dreams. This tower, as you surmised, is similar to your former abode in Deepgate's temple. You are unconsciously affecting this environment. As my will fades, your own steps in to take over.'

'But I . . .'

'I know,' Hasp said. 'I know you don't intend it. Nevertheless it is happening.' He leaned on the parapet and pointed far across Hell to the black sea which had been constantly following them. It seemed much closer than before. 'You know what *that* is,' Hasp said, 'because *I* know what it is. And you understand what its approach means to us.'

'You can't go on any further,' Dill said.

The god nodded. 'I have exhausted all but the last shreds of my power. And we have still not covered a half of the journey to the First Citadel. You will have to continue on foot.'

'What about you?'

'I'll stay, hold them off a bit if I can.'

Dill was silent.

'You will be harder to find on foot, but you must take strength for the journey ahead. This landscape is dread, hopelessness: it saps the will. Yet you must not let it consume you before you reach the First Citadel.'

'What about Mina?' Dill asked.

'They're after *us*, not her. I'll try to hide her before the Legion of the Blind get here. She's only human, and therefore of little interest to Menoa. There's a chance she might escape their attention.'

'What do I do?' he asked.

'It's mostly done,' Hasp said. 'The sphere we fought in has been nourishing you from the beginning, giving up its strength to you.

It, not I, taught you how to fight, and that fragment of Iril is now inside you.'

Dill remembered the apple. *A part of you is also inside me.*

And Mina's splinter? Like Hasp, she had given up a part of herself.

'But there's something else I've been thinking about,' Hasp went on, 'another way we might tip the scales in your favour.' He scratched his stubble. 'You arrived in this place with thirteen souls. Your mind made paintings of them to hang on your walls, and yet they have never really been connected to you down here. Some part of you kept them at bay, and I propose we change that.'

'How?'

'I have an idea.' The god shrugged. 'I'm afraid it's rather grisly.'

Harper flexed her glass tail, propelling herself up the slope of a toppled black-stone monolith. Many such ancient structures dotted the Maze, and the Icarates considered them to be holy places. Harper had seen one of the rituals Menoa's priests performed inside these relics, and she had no desire to witness another one. Right now she just wanted a vantage point.

The Legion of the Blind flowed around the monolith, a tide of chitinous black scales, claws and teeth. Those demons in the forward ranks squabbled over the supply of eyes, snatching the precious artefacts from each other so that they might be the ones to see what lay ahead. Countless more followed behind with nothing to guide them but the relentless forward pressure of the horde. They moved like a tsunami, covering the landscape of Hell for as far as the engineer could see. She stared ahead of this army to the maroon castle in the distance. It had finally stopped moving.

An Icarate hunting horn sounded.

Arrrrrooooo.

And the Blind surged forward, eager for the opportunity to attack.

★

Dill was appalled at the hideous scheme Hasp suggested. To allow the young angel to absorb the souls inside the thirteen paintings, the Lord of the First Citadel had proposed they make a broth.

'This is about survival,' Hasp insisted. He looked exhausted, a shadow of his former self. 'Just as the Poisoner made an elixir on Earth, so we can make another here in Hell. You need the strength of these souls to bolster your own.'

'I'll survive without them.' Dill looked away from the portraits. The painted expressions glared down at him in rage and fear, clearly aware of their present situation.

Hasp shook his head. 'I can't guarantee that. My castle is grounded and you have drained the only fragment of the Shattered God in my possession.'

'But these are *people*, not meat to be eaten.'

'No . . . no longer people. This is the Maze, Dill. They have become nothing but ghosts trapped in paintings. What sort of existence is that? Do you think the Mesmerists will offer them a better deal?' From somewhere Hasp had found a source of anger, and his voice boomed through the low vaulted passageway. 'They were part of your life, so now make them part of your death. Take them with you to the First Citadel or leave them to Menoa's infernal imagination. The choice is yours.'

Hasp spoke the truth. Dill's fate was bound to that of these painted ghosts. It was evident that this fate did not appeal to them, but necessity gave him no choice.

'Do it, then,' Dill said.

For the procedure Hasp located a chest containing Mesmerist equipment: an iron tripod, an etched glass retort, and a reeking black candle composed of demon fat and a concoction of bitter herbs. Unlike the sphere, these seemed to possess little, if any, arcane power. As the candle burned, the tripod supported the retort, which was soon bubbling with a thinned solution of the young angel's own blood. One by one, Hasp saturated the paintings with this foul-smelling steam until the faces faded from the canvases.

In silence he continued to boil steam from the solution. Once he had reduced the liquid to a thicker consistency, he decanted it into a small bottle. 'Now drink.'

Dill swallowed the souls. It cloyed at his throat, making him cough, but he managed to force it down.

'I don't feel any different,' he said.

Hasp took the empty bottle back. 'Your own soul recognizes these others. But you must never consume another soul down here. Don't drink the blood in the canals, for it will lead to madness.'

'I must leave now?'

The god extinguished the candle. He clasped Dill's shoulders and tried to smile. But all energy and conviction had disappeared from his eyes. 'Stay low,' he said. 'The Mesmerists have a million spies who will see you if you attempt to fly. And take this . . .' From a pouch in his belt he took out something and pressed it into Dill's hand. It was an old brown apple, its flesh as wrinkled as Hasp's own now was.

Dill left Hasp's castle without ceremony. The god willed a small door to appear in the lower battlements and a narrow set of steps to take the young angel down to the surface of Hell. The skies churned like poison overhead, lending a ruby hue to the obsidian walls below. These partitions divided the Maze into a nest of devious veins, interspersed with rooms and corridors and houses and castles: the living incarnations of the souls who dwelt within them. There were archways and oddly shaped portals, and steps that sank down to bubbling sumps or drowned quadrangles, or rose up to nowhere. Standing beside Hasp at the top of the stairs, Dill noticed that the stonework of the Maze was rotten in places: mirror-black where it hadn't yet crumbled, but porous and dull where the constant flow of those red waters had eroded it.

Half a league away the canals opened into a wider space, a quadrangle where the alien remains of an Icarate temple loomed above the crimson slough, and where hexagonal pillars rose amidst mounds of polished white bones. The air was muggy and warped, buzzing with flies and larger, winged shapes which circled through the haze. Everywhere could be heard the sound of fluids leaking from broken walls and windows, gurgling and trickling into deep stone throats.

Hasp warned him to stay clear of the deeper channels, for living barges plied these thoroughfares: heavy wooden vessels with iron funnels and heaps of cages upon their narrow decks. These were called the Wailing Ships, for each vessel was a soul reshaped by Menoa's will – their captains could never leave their vessels because each captain *was* the vessel. And yet on their upper decks Mesmerist soul traders moved freely: dark figures fused to metal stilts, watching while stout-armed slaves pushed tillers or fed coal into screaming furnaces.

'Avoid those barges,' the god explained. 'Soul traders will try to capture you and sell you on to the Icarates. Stay away from locks too, indeed from anywhere where the canals change level. The machinery that operates the lock gates was once human, and it is notoriously deceitful.'

'Can I trust anything down there?'

'Trust the walls which separate the canals. Trust steps and wells. They will not betray you because they have no memory. But do not trust doorways. Menoa deliberately constructed them from the bricks of broken minds. Many don't realize that they are now doorways and will be angered by your passage through them.'

From the steps of Hasp's castle, Dill could see hills composed of these canals and walls, rising in tiers like ziggurats. He decided to avoid them. There would be locks between each level and he saw no point in even trying to reach higher ground. And yet the plains looked equally dangerous, a great wet labyrinth of narrow channels and rotting temples.

'Where do I go from here?' he asked. 'How do I reach the First Citadel?'

Hasp lifted his hand and pointed to a spot on the horizon where the red mists appeared thickest. 'There,' he said. 'To the place where every soul catcher in Hell brings his goods. The First Citadel is now under siege, encircled by Menoa's armies. That is where you must go.'

At another blast from the hunting horn, the Legion of the Blind came to a halt two hundred yards back from the battlements of Hasp's castle. The demons passed around their borrowed eyes among their ranks to survey the scene. Standing on the summit of a low ziggurat, Harper let her gaze travel up across the building's pitted stone and rusted armour plating. It had settled in the centre of a wide quadrangle encompassing a morass ankle-deep in blood. Little power could be drawn from this shallow lake.

Cracks zigzagged across the castle's facades, and even the spires appeared to slump. The Lord of the First Citadel was evidently exhausted. A consultation with King Menoa, by way of her sceptre, had confirmed the engineer's suspicions as to the castle's occupant. This particular archon could only be the god Hasp, youngest of Ayen's seven sons. No other entity within the Maze possessed enough power to move such a vast building so far across Hell at such speeds. Even the Blind had been unable to gain ground on the castle until it had finally slowed down.

Now Hasp was stranded here, and the Mesmerist hordes faced a much weakened foe. Unease still roiled in Harper's gut, however: the coming battle would not be easy. Hasp had proved himself to be a brilliant tactician, and his campaigns of terror had been a thorn in King Menoa's side for thousands of years.

Yet the Blind, however ferocious, fought with nothing but a

savage instinct to destroy. One could not marshal or direct them in any complex way. One merely set them loose.

A flash in the sky grabbed the engineer's attention. A great glass lizard, surely the largest of Menoa's Iolite spies, shimmered and blurred against the seething clouds. Crimson light washed through veins in its transparent wings and skull, so that it appeared to merge partly with the sky, fading and reappearing at will. In its invisible phase, only the tiny red heart in its breast betrayed its position to careful observers.

The winged lizard swooped low over the Blind, and then thrashed its wings to slow itself. With a sound like the wind blowing through crystal chimes, it settled on the ground beside Harper.

Call me Forgotten, it said. *The King has sent me to direct this battle and supply him with visions of our victory.*

'He sent a *spy* to do that?'

Forgotten clicked its beak. *A spy who has seen much conflict. I carried the news of Broken Peak skirmish to Menoa, and of the destruction of the Third and Fourth Citadels. I have observed Hasp on many battlefields, the Lake of Temples, the Garden of Bones.*

'Then you're a harbinger of ill luck.'

Luck is meaningless. I have Menoa's authority, engineer. He required a leader with combat experience. You have none. The great glass lizard then turned its long head towards the doomed castle, momentarily turning a deep shade of red as a surge of blood passed through its clear veins. Then it sent a vision to the waiting demons.

Harper registered the unvoiced command in her mind. Forgotten had conjured an image of a battlefield – *this* very same battlefield – in which the Legion of the Blind rushed forward to tear Hasp's castle into fragments. They would assault the god's soul in one powerful strike, relying on brute savagery to bring its manifested defences down.

And the Blind obeyed without question. As one, they charged across the open quadrangle, their claws reaching out towards the castle's tired stone and battered iron facades.

The castle shimmered and changed.

Hundreds of doorways appeared along the base of its walls: stone portals leading into the bowels of the building. Hasp had dismissed his defences with one sweep of thought, leaving his own soul exposed to the advancing horde.

But why? Harper suspected a trap. What horrors were waiting to greet the attackers in those dark passages?

But Forgotten's thoughts still shrilled loudly in every mind able to receive them. *Hasp has relented. He hopes for a quick death.* He sent another vision to the Blind, urging them to pour inside and rip out the heart of the building.

The demons streamed into the castle at a furious pace, hacking the living masonry apart as they went.

'Wait!' Harper shouted to Forgotten. This reckless assault was foolish. Hasp must have preserved *something* of his power. What traps did he have hidden within that battered old castle? What could possibly repel so many surging invaders?

A heartbeat later she received her answer. The Lord of the First Citadel possessed no secret legion, no manifested warriors to fight for his cause. All that remained of his power – of his very soul – now stood naked before them. Hasp had absolutely nothing left but his own tired castle.

And he used it.

The nest of passages he had conjured under his battlements now gave way under the sheer weight of the building. With a riotous crack and rumble of stone, the entire foundations of the castle crumpled. The whole fortress trembled and lurched, and plunged thirty feet into the rubble of its lowest floors, crushing the Blind who had already ventured inside. Clouds of red dust erupted and rolled over the remaining demon hordes.

He has diminished himself.

Harper recognized an aura of astonishment in the lizard's thoughts. What Hasp had just done was incomprehensible. He had destroyed a substantial part of his manifested soul. By doing so, he had crippled himself.

All this just to destroy a fraction of the demon horde? Hasp's actions would only quicken his inevitable defeat. Perhaps Forgotten had been correct after all? The god had simply chosen to die.

The demons who had escaped this partial collapse now rushed forward with renewed vigour, as if they had suddenly tasted promised blood.

The castle changed again.

A second line of doorways appeared under the battlements, occupying what had formerly been the second storey of the building but had now sunk to ground level. He was trying the same trick twice.

Forgotten sent a warning vision to the horde. There was no need to sacrifice more of the Blind. They must ignore this trap and remain outside. The winged Iolite ordered his army to attack the facing wall directly, thus denying Hasp the oblivion he sought.

Harper stared at these new doorways. They were as numerous as the ones before, apparently identical, and yet there was *something* different about them – something odd about the shadows within them.

Suddenly it dawned on her what the god had done, but by then it was too late.

This time Hasp had not simply conjured more passages into the heart of his fortress. He had willed away the bulk of the building's remaining foundations. The facade had only appeared solid; in reality it had acted as a disguise to conceal what lay behind. Now the thin outer walls collapsed, revealing nothing but a vast cavern underneath the facade of the castle. It looked as though a huge bite had been taken out of the lowest part of the building.

With fully half of its foundations gone the castle tilted, precariously, towards its attackers. It balanced there for two heartbeats, its vast shadow looming over the Legion of the Blind. And then the whole building fell forward like a toppled tree. It slammed into the demon army, crushing innumerable enemy to dust.

Perhaps ten or twenty thousand of the Blind now lay beneath that rubble, while Hasp's castle had received little damage beyond what the god had already done to it himself.

Forgotten's glass wings clashed. Its breast blushed red. *This god is killing himself*, it said. *He would rather die by his own hand than let the Blind cut the core of his soul out from within.*

The dramatic changes Hasp had been making to his manifested soul required a great deal of will, but, by diminishing himself each time, he had conserved his energy for each attack. Each transformation reduced the size of Hasp's fortress, and thereby reduced the amount of power required to hold the remains of the structure together. But this tactic was self-defeating: like the serpent who ate its own tail, Hasp was gradually consuming himself.

To confuse his opponents? Or to delay them – to keep them here while the younger angel escapes?

Forgotten now rose into the air with a mighty swoop of its wings, its beak snapping at the scattering demons to maintain some order. The Blind had lost some of their eyes in the collapse of the fortress, and now the survivors were fighting over those that remained. The toppled building in their midst had been temporarily forgotten.

The glass lizard reacted with fury, assaulting the horde with images of torture and punishment so savage that Harper recoiled and raised her shield to ward them off. The terrible vision worked as intended, quelling the riot among the Blind.

Hasp would die now, Harper was sure. His castle lay on its side in ruins. Its spires had sheared off and crumbled to the ground; the very backbone of the building had snapped. The trapped god could not hope to instigate another successful collapse from these shattered remains. To do so now would not postpone his inevitable death, for millions of the demons still waited behind the vanguard.

And yet the castle changed again.

More doorways appeared along its buckled walls, scores of them. Was this simply *arrogance* or *pride*? Or was this a final desperate attempt to diminish the last of his soul and thus end his life?

Destroy it! Forgotten raged. It showed Menoa's flocking army a vision of a single bloody heart surrounded by a circle of teeth.

The Legion of the Blind responded with savage lust.

But this time they met resistance.

Harper hissed, 'Oh god.'

From out of the castle doorways poured those demons who had been trapped by the building's collapse. Somehow, Hasp had protected them within his castle walls and, by enveloping these fallen creatures within his own soul, he had temporarily consumed them. Their simple minds had become a part of *his* mind, and therefore subject to his will. The god needed no power to create a legion of his own. He had simply stolen part of King Menoa's army.

And now these briefly buried demons, compelled by the mind of a cunning god, set upon their simple-minded comrades. However, it was twenty thousand against a million – a battle Hasp could not win.

And yet he almost did. Those of the Blind under the god's influence sought out the eyes of their former comrades. They attacked in organized packs while their opponents brawled for dominance among their own peers. Within moments Hasp's demons had taken one eye, and then a second, and a third. With each new acquisition their foes grew weaker and more disorganized. Soon they began to panic.

Forgotten flew overhead, flinging down desperate visions of furnaces and boiling lakes of poison at the Blind who fled or who turned in confusion to fight against their own side. But Hasp's demons were immune to such onslaughts, and the god's sheer force of will kept them firmly bound to his desires. After all, they were now a part of his soul.

Twenty thousand against a million. They cut a path through Menoa's army like a river of liquid obsidian across a field of cool rock. By now they had stolen almost all of the Blind's eyes, and the bulk of the opposing army was in chaos.

Menoa was losing the fight.

Harper flexed her glass tail and slithered down into the quadrangle, using her shield to push her way through the panicked throng. Menoa had given her a spear, yet she lacked the skill to use it. In Pandemeria she had served the Mesmerists as a metaphysical engineer. She had never been a warrior.

But she did understand the Mesmerists' arcane technology better than anyone except Menoa himself. To control his stolen legion, Hasp needed to maintain a psychic link with them. This required a great deal of concentration. If the link could be broken . . .

Her sceptre could be turned towards this purpose. The Mesmerists had developed *Screamers*, powerful psychic weapons designed to disrupt a soul's grip on its manifested reality. Icarates sometimes used them to shatter Middens and reach powerful souls hiding inside. Such force would not be nearly enough to destroy an archon's grip of his reality – she could not damage Hasp's castle even in its current state – yet she might be able to disrupt the god's link to his hijacked demons.

As Harper neared the fallen fortress, she raised her sceptre and let the device taste the souls around it. Crystal lights sparkled within the glass orb, and she saw a vision of the god deep inside his castle.

– Alone, seated in a chair with his eyes closed, his breathing shallow, his face lined with exertion – a young woman standing nearby. His woman? No visible sign of the second angel. On his way to the First Citadel?

Harper activated the Screamer. At the high frequency to which she had coaxed it, it emitted a blast of psychic energy so powerful as to compress the air around it. There was a flash, and the engineer's own thoughts blanked out.

Silence.

It took Menoa's army a heartbeat to recover from the shock, but much longer for Forgotten to force them back into battle. Hasp's demons no longer reacted to anything. They simply stood motionless and died under the claws of their former comrades.

Harper surveyed the battlefield. Menoa's army had been mostly destroyed, with fully eight-tenths of the Legion of the Blind wounded or killed. Their corpses filled the quadrangle and all the surrounding canals. The survivors, perhaps no more than two hundred thousand demons, waded through the flooded channels, groping in the waters for lost eyes.

Forgotten flashed a sudden warning at Harper, and she wheeled.

The Lord of the First Citadel stood in one of the doorways of his ruined castle. Sword in hand, and clad in old battered armour, he gazed at the scene of devastation with an expression of weary sadness. Behind him, the remains of his fortress began to fade. In some places the fallen battlements and spires were already as thin as gas. In a nearby corner of the quadrangle a pack of twenty or so Blind sniffed the air, and then started to creep towards him. Hasp ignored them.

He addressed Harper. 'You set off the Screamer?'

Slowly, the engineer tilted her glass head.

'Then you saved me some honour,' Hasp remarked. 'We archons generally like to fight our own battles. How many of the Blind remain for me to kill?'

'Two hundred thousand.'

The god grunted. 'Enough to make a good song of this day.'

'You know they won't kill you.' Hasp would suffer a far worse fate than death. 'Where is the angel who fell from Deepgate?'

'I slew him. His soul gave me the strength to rattle this little army of Menoa's.'

She knew he was lying, but said nothing. Her sceptre would soon locate her quarry.

The god extended his wings, now thin and ragged and clogged with grime. He took a step forward on trembling legs. He could hardly stand upright. Then he scratched the tip of his sword through the pile of rubble on which he stood, sketching a line in the dust.

His eyes narrowed on Harper again. 'I see a starving woman trapped inside that Mesmerist thing,' he said. 'She wears the uniform of a Pandemerian engineer, but she doesn't look happy to be in there.' With some effort he raised his sword. 'Come here and I'll set her free.'

Harper didn't move. All around her the Legion of the Blind clambered over piles of their dead comrades as they crept nearer to the diminishing castle and the solitary archon standing in its doorway.

'Two hundred thousand!' Hasp yelled. Wincing in pain, he hefted his blade high over his head, spun it, and brought it crashing down through the skull of the nearest demon.

Then he staggered back and leaned against the doorway, sucking in desperate gulps of air. 'That's one,' he cried.

Clutching their rescued eyes, Menoa's horde crawled closer.

19

THE SOUL COLLECTORS

Dill's feathers were sodden and clogged with gore. He couldn't now have flown even if he dared to risk it. He was slumped in a shallow pool, gasping for breath and gazing up at a black shape flitting across the sky.

Another one of Menoa's spies?

Walls hemmed him on three sides. He had found an alcove off one of the Maze's countless canals. But there was no shade here. And no sanctuary. Faces peered out at him from the stonework.

Trust the walls, Hasp had said.

Dill found it hard to follow that advice. The Mesmerist dog-catchers seemed to pursue him wherever he hid. Most often they came when the mists grew dark, the time Dill had taken to calling night. He'd hear their clickety-clack teeth and he'd be forced to flee again, dragging his leaden legs through the sucking red fluid. It flowed always from the broken buildings, the ones the Icarates had smashed through.

Sometimes Dill crawled through the rooms the Mesmerists had destroyed and left empty, the shattered, bleeding houses and apartments – but the memories he had inside those places weren't his own, and they frightened him.

Where was Hasp now?

In the seven days since he'd fled, there had been no sign of the god or his castle. Had it only been seven days? Time had no meaning here. Often the days lasted much longer than they should do, so he might have been running for a month, or a thousand years. The Legion of the Blind had not pursued him. Had they captured Hasp, or presumed Dill to be dead?

Either way, there were other dangers.

A doorway was following him.

He had encountered it that morning. A rectangular gap between two square columns, it had seemed to offer a way through a wall separating two parallel canals. Pits in the stone lintel had the appearance of tiny eyes, while longer gouges opened and grinned like mouths. It had whispered to him as he passed.

Step through. Quickly, little crow.

Dill *had* stepped through only to find himself back where he had started. Somehow the doorway had turned him around. In his confusion, Dill had splashed a hundred yards along the canal before he realized he was retracing his own path. The doorway had laughed and slid along the wall until it was out of sight.

But now, as the shadow in the sky moved out of sight, he heard the doorway's voice again. And it wasn't speaking to him.

It's up ahead. A hundred yards on the left. A bird, a little white crow of some description. But it chooses not to fly. Certainly afraid of spies. Follow me, hurry.

Dill peered out of the alcove. Three Icarates flanked a sphere of human bones which they rolled through the shallow waters between them. They were hurrying along the canal towards Dill's hiding place. Their anaemic armour fizzed and lit up faces in the surrounding dark stones, forcing ghosts to blink and look away. The doorway moved ahead of them, revealing flooded rooms and passages as it slid along the wall. Fluid gushed over its threshold like water over a weir.

There he is!

Returning to the open canal terrified Dill, yet there was no other way out. He fled the alcove and ran from the Mesmerist priests and their sphere, thick fluids sucking at his feet.

The doorway raced ahead of the Icarates, zipping along the canal boundary wall until it reached Dill. It kept pace with him, and through it Dill saw yet more roofless ruins, canals and sumps beyond the wall.

Step through me – I'll help you to escape, it teased.

'Leave me alone.'

The doorway cackled wildly, then slid back along the wall the way it had come. Dill glanced over his shoulder. The Icarates were gaining on him.

The canal opened into a wide circular space. From here, dozens of narrower channels branched out in every direction. Dill chose one at random and hurried down it. The channel split in two; he took the right fork. A hundred paces further the passage divided again. Now Dill turned left. He tried to vary his route but keep his progress in the general direction of the First Citadel. Although he could not see the great building itself, the skies over it were dark with the smoke from King Menoa's war machines.

Finally deep inside this labyrinth of channels, Dill ducked into another alcove, and slumped against the far wall, exhausted. For a long time he listened hard for the voice of the errant doorway.

Nothing.

But then he heard other sounds. From the other side of the wall came the rumble and splash of something rolling through shallow water, followed by the aether-like crackle of Icarate armour.

Dill had taken a long and twisted route only to end up mere yards from his pursuers. Now only a foot of stonework separated him from the Mesmerist priests and their cage of bones. He heard them pause on the other side of the wall.

Dill froze.

Where was the doorway?

Something metal clicked. There was another pause. A low hum. And then Dill heard the bone-cage move on again. He breathed.

He turned around to find the doorway facing him. It occupied one of the side walls of the alcove, and its tiny dark eyes all seemed to be fixed on the angel. As soon as Dill saw it, it cried out:

Back here! The white crow is hiding here!

The doorway slid around the alcove, moving to the rear wall where it now formed an opening between the angel and the channel in which his pursuers were approaching.

They came through the doorway with tridents.

Dill backed away as two Icarates stepped into the alcove. Sparks burst from their armour and showered the waters around their boots, raising a smell like scorched meat. Their iron weapons hummed; their eye lenses and copper mouth-wires shone. The remaining pursuer rolled the bone-cage up close to the doorway, but that hideous sphere was much too large to pass through this narrow gap.

The doorway giggled.

The first Icarate raised his trident.

But Hasp had taught Dill how to fight. He had shown Dill how to manipulate his soul to create weapons and armour. And Dill used his new skills now.

He willed himself a shield. A light steel buckler flashed into existence, already strapped to his knuckles.

The angel punched, slamming the shield into the trident before the Icarate could complete his lunge. The buckler deflected the heavy iron weapon, forcing it wide. One of its forks connected with the shaft of the second Icarate's trident.

And a concussion shook the air.

Dill took a step back as both tridents sparked violently. The Mesmerist priests' bodies jerked once and suddenly became rigid. Smoke hissed from their armour.

Wicked crow! You've ruined their armour.

The doorway was shrieking, shuttling rapidly back and forth along the wall in agitation.

Dill studied the two Icarates. They remained completely immobile. *They can't move without their armour?* He grinned and stepped closer to the doorway. 'Let the other one through.'

The doorway hesitated, but then it began to race back and forth along the wall with an even greater urgency than before. *No!*

Dill changed his shield to a sturdy iron pike. He clutched the shaft in both fists and drove the weapon downwards through the moving doorway, forcing the point hard against the ground opposite.

With a loud *clang*, the doorway came to an abrupt halt against the shaft of the pike. It slid left, and then right, but it could not move its side columns past this new obstruction. Dill had skewered it. He beckoned to the remaining Icarate.

It approached the doorway with a hammer.

Dill felt pressure mounting on his pike as the doorway struggled to free itself. It was pushed hard to the left, trying to move the pike. Dill maintained his grip, using every ounce of his strength to hold the weapon firmly in place. The tip of the pike scraped across the ground, but he gasped and held on. *Just a moment longer.* His arms were shaking. The doorway shuddered and heaved against the pike.

The last Icarate ducked inside the doorway.

When the Mesmerist priest was halfway through, Dill willed his pike to disappear. Faced with a complete and immediate lack of resistance to its enormous efforts, the doorway abruptly shot away along the wall, carrying the hapless Icarate with it. Unable to shed its momentum, it struck the adjoining wall at tremendous speed. But while the doorway could pass through solid stone, Menoa's priest could not.

Pieces of the crushed Icarate fell to the floor of the alcove, sparking briefly before they died.

Dill moved on.

The doorway continued to hound his every step. Enraged at being tricked, it shrieked and yelled and announced the angel's presence to anyone who might have been around to hear it.

Dill couldn't escape it, so he needed to find a way to destroy it. As far as he could tell, the Mesmerist creation consisted of nothing more than two upright stone columns with a lintel across the top. Yet it moved through the solid walls of the Maze like a bubble of air through water.

It seemed indestructible.

White crow, it yelled. *Icarate slayer.* It remained a few paces behind Dill, tracing the wall of yet another long, curving canal.

What would Hasp have done? Dill reached into his pocket and took out the apple the god had given him before they'd parted. The fruit looked even smaller and more rotten than before, but tasted surprisingly sweet. It boosted his energy and confidence.

And it gave him an idea.

During his journey through Hell, Dill had passed several ruined temples, quadrangles full of monoliths and arches and rotting black stonework. Icarate holy sites, Hasp had once told him – their ancient fly-infested facades rose higher than the surrounding canals and ziggurats.

A short distance away, Dill could see one of these structures now. Red light bled through the gaping windows of a crumbling black tower – a fang-like silhouette against the hot skies.

Dill changed his course towards the ruin.

As he drew nearer, the Maze began to show obvious signs of deterioration. The walls between canals were older here, much more dilapidated. In some places they had collapsed entirely, forming ragged gaps between the channels. Steps sank down into deep wells or spiralled up around fingers of dark stone with no apparent purpose. The ghostly faces within the walls looked different too – something odd, almost inhuman about their eyes.

The doorway grew suspicious. Each time it came up against a broken wall, it was forced to turn back and find an alternative route.

You won't lose me in this decaying labyrinth, it crooned. *The Maze has countless walls. There is always a way through.*

Finally Dill reached the ruined tower. It rose from the centre of a spacious quadrangle full of spikes of black rock. A ring of gallows had been built around the building's foundations, although none of the nooses were currently occupied. Several walls extended inwards from the quadrangle perimeter, like the teeth of a mantrap, but none of them reached the tower itself. Each ended in a pile of rubble, yards from the building.

Dill examined one of these partitions. The stonework was wet, rotting; it crumbled away under his hand. He set off again, following the wall towards the tower.

The doorway kept up with him. *You won't escape by hiding in that tower,* it said. *The Icarates perform their rituals in such places. Dangerous things lie within.*

Dill reached the end of the wall, and stopped. The doorway could go no further.

You are still surrounded by walls, it snarled. *Run and hide. I can wait forever for you to reappear. I'll tell Menoa's priests where you are.*

But Dill had no intention of hiding. He stared at the tower for a long moment, frowning, as he pretended to weigh up his options. Then he strolled a few paces back the way he had come, halted, and regarded the tower once more. The doorway was waiting, watching him to see what he would do.

Dill willed himself a hammer – an enormous iron brute of a war-hammer. He swung it hard at the wall. The fragile stonework crumpled under the blow. The top third of the wall teetered, then fell forward and crashed to the ground. He raised the weapon again.

By now the doorway had realized what was happening. It screeched and raced back towards the angel.

A second hammer-blow took out another two feet of stonework. Dill had made a jagged rift in the top half of the wall.

It was enough to stop the doorway. The Mesmerist creation could move through stone, but not air. When it reached the gap Dill had made, it came to an abrupt halt, now trapped in an isolated section of wall – an island in the Maze.

Don't leave me, it said urgently. *Don't leave me trapped here.*

But Dill was already walking away.

Rebuild the wall, the doorway howled after him. *Don't you understand? I can't stay here forever. I can't die! I don't know how to die!*

'You don't know how to shut up either,' Dill called back.

The sound of splashing brought Dill sharply to his feet. Weeks – by his estimation of time here – had passed since he'd rid himself of the howling doorway. Glutinous liquid pulled at his shins as he waded across the pool. The walls felt sticky where he pressed his palm against them for support. Eyes opened deep within the glossy stone, like reflections in a mirror, and glared at him. *Trust the walls.*

Hasp had been right. No walls or steps had betrayed him. Sometimes when he listened closely to the stonework he could hear it whispering advice. *Go left here . . . Avoid the three-tiered ziggurat . . . A Mesmerist vessel approaches . . .* Dill wondered if they had begun to recognize the part of Iril he harboured inside. Or had the Shattered God himself found a way to communicate with the angel? Maybe it was simply that rumours had been spreading through the walls of the Maze?

Even those doorways he'd met since the Icarate's temple had been strangely quiet and obedient.

One such doorway now led to the canal beyond the roofless room where Dill was hiding. He forced himself to stop and take a breath before peering through.

More soul collectors were coming.

A caravan was moving through one of the canals. Great steaming oxen-like beasts dragged a train of huge wagons and cages along the shallow waterway. In deeper waters the Mesmerists used barges, but caravans ploughed these shallower channels. Strange machines and lurching wooden towers rumbled along behind. Wheels creaked and hooves churned the red slurry into froth. Banners and flags of many colours bobbed among the throng. From somewhere behind came a riotous tumult: the sound of lashing whips, the clicking of stilts and the howls of men. Over it all sounded the deep, sonorous groan of horns.

There was nowhere for Dill to escape to, so he slunk back into his hiding place, crouching down low, and waited for the caravan to pass him by. Silently, he willed a short-sword to appear in his left hand, and a punching-shield in his right.

The first cages were full of partially altered souls: hot-eyed louts who screamed and rattled their metal limbs across the bars; cackling hags with oddly shaped skulls; huge warriors clad in plate and helms of exotic design, sitting quietly, sharpening the blades on their fingers. These were escapees of some kind, Dill surmised, for their transformations had not yet been completed. A column of box-wagons followed behind, sending thick waves through Dill's doorway. Queer hieroglyphs drenched their slatted sides; the running boards below were chipped and scraped. Next came one of the Mesmerists' living machines: a spherical metal device crammed with chains, wheels and needles. After this, a cage full of dogcatchers.

Dill slid lower into the bloody pool to mask his own scent. Dogcatchers had keen noses.

The demons resembled cadaverous men, and indeed they had

once been men, but now their skin glistened as red as the canal beneath their coop. They turned their eyeless heads this way and that, sniffing the air, gnashing their long white teeth. They could not speak, Dill knew, but they could howl, and the one who shifted his blind gaze towards the young angel howled now.

With many creaks and bellows, the procession grumbled to a halt.

Dill readied himself for battle.

They came for him. Anaemic and gibbous, these Icarate soul collectors wore stained ceramic armour spattered with black corruption. Pale discs mushroomed from their hunched backs, crackling and dripping blue sparks. Dill presumed these creatures to be a lower caste than the Icarates he had seen before, for there were subtle differences in their appearance. Fractured reflections glinted in their cracked eye-lenses when they turned their heads, and when they grinned, the copper wires in their mouths showed verdigris. They were larger, bulkier, than the Mesmerist priests he had seen before, but they wore similar ill-fitting armour and carried the same hammers and tridents.

And Dill was getting used to dealing with those.

He stepped out into the canal, and ducked as a whip lashed out at his head. The tip of the whip struck a prisoner who had been gripping the bars of his cage, severing the tip of the man's finger. The prisoner howled and flinched away.

Dill stared at the owner of the whip – an obese Icarate in badly rotted armour. He was hunched over like a cripple, seemingly barely able to stand at all. Rust covered half of the priest's face, obscuring one of his eye lenses, while a green crust had obliterated the wires in his mouth entirely. The ceramic obtrusions on his back looked like stained teeth. The angel's heartbeat quickened. That attack had been *fast*.

The prisoners started to chant in their cages. 'Fadder Carpal, Fadder Carpal, Fadder Carpal.' One man whooped and cried out:

'That was the testing stroke, boy. The next one will take your fucking head off.'

The Icarate swept his whip back again.

Dill willed himself a suit of spider-silk armour – a hauberk, chausses and a camail to protect his neck. He considered expanding his punching shield to cover his entire forearm, but decided not to encumber himself any further. He needed to be fast.

The lash struck out again.

Dill simultaneously raised his buckler to block and his sword to sever through the whip. But the thin leather cord *twisted* in mid-air and changed direction. It folded around the edge of the tiny shield and struck Dill's knuckle. The tip of the lash bit into the angel's flesh and stuck there.

A flash of pain surged up Dill's arm. He cried out, shaking his fist and shield madly, but the lash would not release him. He swiped at the leather cord with his sword – again and again – but the whip danced around his blows like a living thing.

The caged prisoners were chanting faster now: 'Fadder Carpal . . . Fadder Carpal . . .'

The tip of the whip began to *burrow* into Dill's knuckle. He felt it crawling through his flesh like an insect – a sensation that made him freeze and stare at his hand in shock. A lump had appeared on the back of his finger; it was moving rapidly under his skin towards his wrist. Dill beat at it with the pommel of his sword, but it continued to push into him.

Half in panic, and half in desperate rage, Dill charged at the Icarate. The Mesmerist priest made a motion with his hand – the whip sang between them, formed loops in the air, and then coiled around the angel's neck.

Darkness crowded Dill's vision as his camail compressed around his throat. The Icarate's rusted face and broken lenses loomed before him – a dreamlike mess of rotting metal. Dill fell forward, lashed out wildly with his punching-shield. His buckler connected with *something*.

He remembered struggling, gasping . . .

. . . the blare of horns, a lurch, and creaking wheels.

He was locked up in a cage near the rear of the caravan with a drooling hag and a dwarf with hooks and needles for fingers. The dwarf sniggered and tried to pluck handfuls of feathers from Dill's wings. He claimed to be the only thief in Hell. 'I stole from egoists,' he said, 'until Fadder Carpal caught me.'

'Fadder Carpal?'

'You hit him with your shield. It was his impotent master that stung you, his Penny Devil. Not a bad fight, considering.' He leaned closer and crooned. 'You lasted longer than those gladiators did. Even longer than that scabrous thing we caught grazing in the Garden of Bones.' He grinned. 'But nobody escapes Fadder Carpal.'

'The Icarate with the whip?'

The dwarf snorted. 'Fadder Carpal is the greatest soul collector in the Maze. And that was no whip. You felt the insect at the end of it, eh? The kiss of a Penny Devil?'

Dill's knuckle still throbbed. 'It burrowed *into* me,' he said. 'Like a—'

'Hookflea?' The dwarf chuckled. '*That* was one of Ayen's debased. Liria, they used to call her on Earth, the Queen of Fleas. If you think Ayen gave her lover and her sons a hard time . . .' He paused to pick at his misshapen teeth with one hooked finger. 'Consider what she did to the angels she really feared: Orus, Basilis and Liria – all royally fucked for eternity.'

'The *whip* was Liria?'

'Liria was the sting at the tip. And Fadder Carpal is her guardian, at least—' He broke off as the old woman beside him suddenly began to convulse.

'Look lively,' the dwarf said to Dill, 'the madwoman is fading again. You'll see the Icarates revive her.'

'Cruelty!' the hag wailed. 'Flesh is the stuff of memories. I can't recall fat and skin.' The fiery light that sloped through the enclosure bars seemed to find little resistance in her body, but rather pass through it as though through a mist. 'Nobody here helps me to remember. They might as well have locked me in with the blistermen.' She pointed to the cage in front of them and snarled, 'See where the flies lay their eggs.'

Dill recoiled.

'She's mad,' the dwarf said. 'Menoa can't do much with woozy minds like hers. She's bound for the flensing machines and the Veil, if she makes it to the portal at all.' His dark eyes glittered; he shuffled his crooked bones away from her. 'Either she'll fade completely and join the ghosts in the walls, or one day soon we'll all be breathing her.'

The hag licked her gums and said, 'They promised me a parrot.'

One of Carpal's Icarates appeared outside the cage, and thrust his trident into the old woman's side. The weapon crackled; the hag gibbered and slavered. But soon enough, her phantasmal form solidified again. She became corporeal once more. The Soul Collector peered in at the other two captives for a moment, his rotten mouth-grille buzzing, and then returned the way he had come.

The sky grew dark and the strange caravan lumbered on. Dill could not sleep. He lay curled in a bed of wet straw, and thought about Mina. Had she escaped the Legion of the Blind? Where was she now? When he finally closed his eyes he imagined he could smell her perfume oozing from the splinter in his wrist.

The caravan did not halt for three days. Axles rumbling ceaselessly, the wagon train meandered through the Maze, sloshing along one red canal after another, creeping up the slippery rises and plunging into flooded depressions. The ghost-mists darkened again.

Dawn brought plumes of crimson steam and a metal taste to the air. The madwoman displayed her gums and cackled. The dwarf thief sniggered and rattled his needle fingers against his teeth.

'I stole pieces of souls,' he said, 'and devoured them in Icarate temples. It kept me busy. You have to keep busy in Hell or you fade away.' He picked his nose. 'Do you know what lies underneath those temples?'

Dill shook his head.

'The failed experiments, the things that didn't function but didn't die either. There are rivers and pools full of them. And something else . . .' He leaned his damp face closer to Dill and whispered, 'A *presence* that blows across the Rivers of the Failed like a cold breeze. All that anguish is incubating something nasty down there. The Mesmerists are afraid of it.'

'Iril?'

The thief shook his head. 'Iril is almost burned out. His archons sit on the brink of defeat.' He pointed to the smoke-darkened horizon. 'See where Menoa's armies have besieged the First Citadel? Icarates, Non Morai, Iolites and demons born from a thousand of the king's dreams. You should hear the machines. You know how the Mesmerists make them, don't you? Persuasion.'

Suddenly the thief made a frantic gesture. 'Shush! The soul collectors are coming back.'

Icarates filed past the cage, their armour dribbling blue sparks. The stench of burned metal followed them. By now Dill had learned not to look at them directly. Their tridents crackled and stung whenever they shoved them through the bars into his face. They would punish him until he thanked them for it. Better to simply lie still and hope they wouldn't notice him.

One red day turned into another. Their passage through the Maze became dreamlike, as if seen through a veil. Dill viewed the world in glimpses of barges moving in the deeper canals, the steaming oxen and the crack of Carpal's whip, the hag lolling in wild dementia, and warriors in other cages scraping stones along the edges of their fingers. The old woman faded and was revived three more times. They rolled past walls of ghosts and broken temples, and bulky machines that breathed out plumes of vapour.

One day they passed a vast square pool in which floated three tall metal ships. Deep, forlorn moans resounded within the hulls.

'From Pandemeria,' the thief explained. 'These vessels are the commanders who led Menoa's fleet against Rys.'

'What are they doing there?' Dill asked.

'Watching eternity go by.'

The endless trek began to take its toll on Dill. Most of the time he lacked the energy to rise, and instead lay wheezing helplessly in his bed of straw. He woke regularly without realizing that he had been asleep. At night the prisoners gibbered and howled. The dogcatchers' flesh glistened; they snapped their teeth. Flies swarmed over the blistermen and laid their eggs in appalling places.

And on and on the procession crept.

Many days later the dwarf beat his head against the bars of their cage and cried out, 'I'm weary, I'm bored. Where can I find something to steal?'

'Steal this!' yelled a man in the next cage. He whirled a sling over his head, then released it.

A pebble shot between the bars. It ricocheted off the dwarf's skull and pinged away.

Those captives in the nearest cages shrieked with laughter. The soul collectors silenced everyone with a flurry of burning touches.

Although Dill could not share the good humour, he had begun to appreciate his surroundings more. The Maze was as beautiful as it was complex. This crimson playground which had at first driven him to such despair had become, by degrees, less threatening. There were so many marvels to behold: the chuckle of fluids behind the cage wheels; the bright chunks that clung to the spokes like rubies; the madwoman's scrawl of white hair. He relished these sights. Once he spied silver-robed figures floating high in the sky, and he felt his dead heart soar with wonder.

'Don't look at them,' the thief warned. 'Dangerous, dangerous creatures.'

How much time had passed, Dill did not know. The soul collectors found new prisoners for their caravan, and they threw them into the cages behind. There was a naked man without teeth or eyes and a bruised shapeless thing that could not stand unaided, a thin pale woman who never made a sound but just gaped at her darkly stained hands, and an old, old angel with a tin hat and only one wing. Most of the other captives laughed at this last find, but Dill only smiled.

He thanked the Icarates daily.

A year passed, or maybe a hundred years. Dill's skin crawled with the memory of burns, yet these sensations were important to him. In those moments when he forgot the pain of the Icarates' tridents a desperate panic came over him. The agony anchored him; without it, he feared he might forget who he was and start to fade like the hag. The soul collectors' tridents gave him vigour; the burns he received kept him focused.

He couldn't stop smiling. His friend, the thief, was always there to encourage him. 'Fadder Carpal knows his business well,' he said. 'He takes good care of us, of his family. He won't let us become like *them*.' He inclined his head towards the faces in the walls.

The phantasms gazed out at Dill from the stonework. Their lips were moving, but he could not hear their words, only the sound of Fadder Carpal's whip.

One evening soon afterwards, the caravan finally reached its destination. Dill had been dreaming, and he didn't notice the grey towers at first. Instead he first became aware of crowds of strange creatures around his cage. A few of them resembled humans, but most had been changed. There were the usual Icarates and dog-catchers, and even a tall cloaked figure with a blisterman on a leash. Other figures moved with metal limbs or wheels and leaked foul-smelling smoke from their lips. Two women with crystal skulls paused to peer into Dill's cage. A constant hubbub of chatter and mechanical clunks filled the canal through which they were passing. This avenue was different from those they had passed along before. The walls on either side were taller, full of windows and doorways that crept slowly past one another.

'We are *here*,' the dwarf said. 'Here for show and then sale to the king's captains. Look! Over there you can see the First Citadel.'

They had arrived in a great city. Monolithic black buildings lined the canals here, their flat roofs bristling with needle-like protrusions and slowly turning wheels. Smoke and fresh red mist wheezed from valves set in walls, but the waters in this shallow avenue were tinged with green and smelled of fuel.

Over all this towered a group of six stone towers, each supporting a flat platform at its summit. On each such platform grew a tree. Arched bridges between linked the platforms together – although three of these had collapsed. Blue windows shone in the tower walls below each platform – as though reflecting a different sky.

'The trees repel shades,' the thief explained. 'And it's said that the roots grow all the way down through the towers themselves.' He gazed up at the fortress hungrily. 'There's no way in from the ground. I would trade my hands for wings to sneak in there.'

Dill nodded his head woozily. Sleep beckoned him, but he resisted.

On through the streets the soul collectors' procession sloshed. The dwellings lining the canals became sparser, replaced by arrays of chattering mechanical towers. Eventually these gave way to low ziggurats that exhaled white fumes and groaned as if packed with people.

Now the procession rolled into a wide circular arena hemmed by tiered stone steps and wound around itself in an expanding spiral. Dill at last staggered to his feet and pressed his face against the bars to get a better look. The soul collectors were unharnessing their kine. Between the wagons, the great beasts bellowed and bulled and reeked of dung. For the first time, Dill saw the entire procession at close quarters. Wagons were being unloaded, structures erected all around: huge spiked wheels and gaudy towers, and metal huts, each with a single puffing chimney and its walls etched with hieroglyphs. Hammers pounded, ropes skreaked in pulleys. Thin metal boxes, as long as a man, were carried from one flat cart and stacked upon the sodden ground. Gladiators clashed their swords against their shields and whooped. Everywhere, men were shouting and thumping their cages.

'Now the Mesmerist captains will see what we can do!' the dwarf cried. 'They will witness a dance of steel the like of which has not been seen since Hasp met Ayen's bodyguards in the War Against Heaven. We'll cut through dead men and demons and beasts from nameless worlds and give them wounds that will amaze them even as they sink into the mire.' He grabbed Dill and shook him. 'Here is our chance to bathe Fadder Carpal in glory.'

Dill's heart surged with joy.

The Icarates took three days to assemble their market. They beat Dill until he felt alive again. On the evening of the third night a heavy silence settled over the arena and the ad-hoc collection of structures which had sprung up within its boundaries. The sky brooded, dark as a velvet shroud. Green and yellow lights bobbed on ropes between the cluttered towers, wheels and huts, bathing all in harsh and sickly radiance. Soul collectors glided between the gladiator cages, their queer armour sparking brightly, their eye-lenses gleaming.

Dill was curled up on the floor of the cage, imagining the battles to come. He would shine for Fadder Carpal and fetch him a good price at the warriors' market.

A strange crystal voice sounded nearby, like the chiming of tiny glass bells: 'A thorough job as always, Fadder, although the process took much longer than the king expected.'

Silence.

'I understand, Fadder, but we cannot delay any longer. Menoa has already constructed the thirteenth arconite. His surgeons have now finished with Hasp and his woman. There are plans in motion. He needs the angel's soul *now*.'

Another moment of silence.

'Of course we know about the splinter. The king is satisfied. It is time to bring Dill to the Processor.'

PART THREE

PANDEMERIA

20

ALICE ELLIS HARPER

The train to Coreollis rumbled along a narrow slag embankment above Upper Cog City, dragging mountains of smoke behind it. The lower districts remained flooded, but here the waters had receded some fifteen yards below the raised steel tracks, leaving streets clogged with silt and rusting warships. From the embankment's slopes to the horizon, ten thousand vessels had been left to rot among the waterlogged shops and houses. Mangled heaps of gunboats and destroyers filled the plazas of Highcliffe and the Theatre District, while the cries of these adapted souls rose higher still. Battleships loomed like great red headlands above rows of townhouse roofs, their hulls scarred by cannon-fire or scraped and dented by rubble from collapsed buildings, their groans of pain long and low. A Mesmerist-adapted war-barge had come to rest against the roof of the cathedral in Revolution Square, her bow pointing skywards, her stern deep amid café tables and mud. The late-evening sun gave a molten edge to those funnels, decks and gun-batteries which rose above the chimneystacks, and bathed the brickwork between ships in soft amber light.

South of the terminus the embankment sank with the surrounding streets towards Sill river, and here the waters rose to within a foot of the newly laid railway sleepers. Flooded lanes looped around the Offal Quarter factories like a giant fingerprint, or like the canals of Hell, all choked with flotsam, furniture and corpses. Nacreous swirls of oil and yellow, aquamarine and ochre froths revolved between hull, keel and lamppost. Cannon-boats drifted in the deep square pools of old Workhouse Yards or lay beached on tenement roofs, their lines fouled in weathervanes. The bloodied waters in Emerald Street, Minster Street and Canary Row were clogged with steam-yachts and with painted dolls from the Low Cog Puppet Workshop. A breeze came up from the city: bitter, engine-scented air full of hot dust and strange metallic cries.

To Harper it seemed that the ships were singing laments she understood. These iron voices were no longer human, and yet they evinced human suffering clearly. The Mesmerist Veil had thinned over this old battleground, though blood could still be seen on the townhouse walls and in stagnant pools across the city. The train, however, had not been adapted metaphysically, but mechanically. Pumps wheezed out clouds of crimson vapours behind the engineer.

King Menoa had granted her a human shape for this trip to the front. She had become a pale woman wearing a stiff, ash-coloured uniform, and now she stood on the hunting platform at the very rear of the train, idly fingering the tool belt slung at her hip. She had taken her cap off and her hair tumbled like red smoke. Up ahead, a whistle sounded. The train shuddered, then smacked across a bridge where the ruby-bright waters had eaten through the bank below. Shaken from her reverie, Harper turned away, dimly aware that she had been reading the names Menoa's reservists had painted on the ship's hulls – searching for one in particular.

The sun sank lower in the west until it slipped behind the vast silhouettes of the Mesmerist war-behemoths and god-smashers on the outskirts of the city. The train thundered on, building speed, cleaving through the river districts towards New Sill

Bridge and Knuckletown. Before the war, her engine had been nickel-plated and inlaid with silver filigree. But four years ago she was stripped of her decoration, re-bored for power, and from that day forth the exhaust from her stack had stained her skin a deeper, more honest black than the hulls of her saltwater cousins.

Harper had loved the train the moment she'd first set eyes on her in the yards at Cog Island Terminus. The *Pride of Eleanor Damask* had seemed proud and unforgiving: eighteen coupled driving wheels powered by eight high-pressure cylinders. For four years now she had dragged shale, steel and machinery for the railway reconstruction project. She had pushed the newly raised tracks closer to Coreollis and the front lines while Harper rotted in Hell. The *Eleanor* had once been a worker, a symbol of mankind's determination to overcome impossible odds. For Harper, the train had once represented the entire human struggle. To look at the old engine now inspired nothing but pathos.

Tonight the *Eleanor* was transformed. Her new glass carriages were all aglow and sparkling in a celebration of light and gold: the observation cars crowned with multifaceted domes; a dining carriage of crystal geminate panes and spars of beech; two frost-walled sleeping wagons, and a music car in which chandeliers trembled over artfully etched mirrors. Even the hunting platform had been constructed from crushed-composite glass and festooned with aether bulbs. All human work, and paid for with looted gold, for the King of the Maze had found allies in Pandemeria.

From this height Harper could see through the glass roofs immediately ahead of her. Mesmerist resonance muskets and shiftblades packed the racks in the train's armoury. In the music car beyond, she spied fractured glimpses of revelry: gentlemen and ladies dancing, laughing and chatting. Through the confusion of glass, three men in the same plum-red suit appeared to be playing a white piano at different angles, although she could not hear the music above the pounding wheels and rushing air.

These were Cog's elite, those men and women who had backed the Mesmerist campaign against Rys and his brothers. Tonight they were having a party at Menoa's expense, and tomorrow morning the god of flowers and knives would kneel at their feet.

She spotted Jan Carrick. The Chief Liaison Officer was untangling himself from the revellers, nodding greetings and heading this way, and so Harper shook out her hair and gathered it up to tie back. By the time he opened the armoury door below the hunting deck, she had replaced her cap.

'Glorious, they assure me,' Carrick said happily, climbing the narrow steps to join her on the platform. 'The lights, mirrors, glass. Menoa has surpassed himself.' He was a solid man, hard-faced but not ugly. One hand tugged, as always, at the neat viridian collar of his new uniform, where Harper glimpsed a length of the pewter chain he wore with such pride. It had been given to him by the same Pandemerian Railroad Company financiers he had just been entertaining below. 'It's fitting, I suppose,' he said, 'if a trifle ostentatious. Must have cost a fortune. They're burning enough aether back there to light up Heaven.'

He reached her and put an arm around her waist and pulled her close. His hand slipped inside her jacket and found her breast. His skin was hot; hers cold and dead. She breathed in a lungful of Mesmerist mist. Harper had learned not to flinch, but she couldn't hide the way her jaw tensed, and she couldn't smile for him.

'How can you be so cold?' Carrick said. 'This is what you wanted, isn't it? To be among the living again . . .' He squeezed her flesh hard enough to make her gasp, before releasing his grip. 'Now why don't you just loosen up and enjoy the party?'

Harper said nothing. She gazed across Cog City and, when she narrowed her eyes, the sea of roofs and funnels became a different sea: of towering grey and black waves, vigorous and storm-lashed and angry. But then this vision faded and she was looking once more at the drowned ruins and rusting graveyard. Half a mile away, a pale blue rag, snared on a cable, snapped and fluttered. It might once have been part of a naval uniform.

'I already bought salvage rights,' Carrick said, inclining his head towards the piles of rotting steel and iron scattered throughout the city. 'When Menoa issues claim edicts, I'll have money, Alice, lots of it. I could buy you a house of your own in the city, a private place—'

'Out of sight of your friends.'

He didn't look at her. 'I'm offering you a comfortable life. You could get back your old job at Special Engineering. Keene would have to rehire you. You wouldn't need to return to the Readjustment Centre.'

Harper gave his offer serious consideration. In the month since her departure from Hell, she had felt like a leaf tossed about in a storm. She had not been spared the Readjustment Centre: the examinations, the mountains of paperwork and the endless interviews with social integration officers.

Just another few days, Miss Harper. There are some more questions we need to ask you. If you'd be kind enough to look at this list and tell me the names you recognize . . .

Cog's Readjustment Centre had been built to accommodate a hundred and fifty citizens, but Harper's room had been the only one occupied. The curtains, towels and bed linen had all been brand new.

Those souls before her had left the Maze via a different route.

Carrick was still gazing at the derelict ships. 'That's a gold mine,' he said. 'It would be a shame to let it all go to waste.'

The ships had been forged in response to Rys's rain: paddle steamers created for the Supply Effort; cruisers and pickets, cannon-boats and destroyers, all built from the souls of Cog's dead. Some wit had since named this place the Sea of Invention. Harper remembered when there had been nothing here but shops and taverns and homes.

Cog Island had changed so much in her life and deathtime: from urban sprawl to boiling sea to this weeping landscape of scrap. The god Rys had conjured the endless rain, in his promise to wash away the Mesmerist Veil and restore human rule to Pandemeria. But his plan had failed. The waters were now draining; the pools and canals – poisoned and starkly beautiful in the failing light – sinking back into the earth, or perhaps back into whichever pocket of that god's imagination they had come from. But wherever they went, they left in their wake a thick red scum.

And for all their present glory *The Pride of Eleanor Damask*'s pretty carriages would one day dull and shatter. The human passengers didn't care, of course. They would be gone by then, dancing at some other venue. Tonight they were burning enough aether to light up Heaven.

'Tomorrow will mark a turning point in history,' Carrick said. 'No god has ever knelt at the feet of humans before. It's a new beginning for us all. After Rys signs the treaty, you'll see great changes around here. King Menoa has promised to reward his most loyal servants. He's going to release two thousand souls in the first year. You won't be alone much longer, Alice.'

Metal winds moaned in the distance.

'I'm not alone,' she said. 'Can't you hear the ships singing?'

'You know that's not what I meant. I'm talking about the *unaltered*: the families of those people who stood by Menoa throughout this war.'

Harper moved a hand to her chest, feeling for the empty soulpearl she wore on a cord inside her blouse. For a breathless moment she couldn't find it, and then her hand closed on the familiar jewel and she breathed. The pearl was there, close to her heart, cold against her cold skin.

Carrick was gazing back along the ever-lengthening curve of steel track behind the train, back to where the Mesmerist Eye towered over the concrete terminus building. Its twin wheels, set back-to-back on opposing axles, revolved gradually in opposite directions. Even from this distance, the hourly shift-change klaxons could be heard blaring out across the drowned city. Crowds of administrators would be disembarking from the lowest of the twelve Workwheel office gondolas, their own weight having helped to drag the mighty steel spokes through another 180 degrees. Now they would receive their food parcels and begin the long climb up the central scaffold to the uppermost gondola of the Sleepwheel. Other workers, their satchels full of paperwork and candles, were already leaving the bottom of the Sleepwheel to join them on the scaffold for their own ascent to the top of the Workwheel. In this manner the Pandemerian Railroad Company powered the machines in their Highcliffe laboratories, while maximizing return from the food issued to their staff.

'Another one jumped last week,' Carrick said. 'I'll never understand these people. They're given a good job, decent food and soft bunks. They get plenty of exercise, and the best damn view on Cog Island. And what do they do? Spit it all back in the company's face, and take the big leap.'

'Their lives are a constant uphill struggle,' Harper said. 'Don't *you* ever feel like that?'

Carrick pulled away from her suddenly. 'Only with you,' he said, turning to face the bright curve of glass carriages stretching ahead of them. The train was now thumping across the New Sill Bridge above what had once been Knuckletown Port District. Down below, the former bridge could still be seen below the murky waters, its stanchions and girders now furred with red weeds. 'I need you back inside now,' he said. 'We've had complaints of something dead aboard the train. God-awful gibbering noises coming from the heating ducts in car C, down near the slave holds. Likely it's just a ghost one of the passengers brought aboard, so be gentle with it. If you send it screaming back to the Maze, I won't be the one who has to tell them.'

Harper nodded and turned to go.

'Alice,' Carrick added, his teeth looking strangely bright in the uneasy light, 'you will be gentle with it, won't you?'

To reach car C, Harper had no choice but to walk through the crowd gathered in the music carriage. The party was in full swing and most of the guests appeared to be drunk or well on the way. The pianist noticed her and broke off abruptly from the waltz he was playing into a crescendo of notes that reached towards a climax as she approached, halting abruptly the moment she reached him.

'A toast,' he said loudly, for the benefit of the room, 'to the first woman to return from Hell still wearing lipstick. I give you Cog City's most beautiful corpse.'

The crowd closed in on Harper and she found herself pinned by the attention of a roomful of well-dressed gentlemen and ladies: the frocks all puffs of almond-, orange- and rose-coloured silk, the suits in rich dark hues of plum and whalehide. The men wore snub-nosed pistols or Mesmeric rapiers at their belts, the blades sheathed in white leather, as had been the fashion since Adelere's adaptation of *Cohl's Shades* had become the most talked about play in Highcliffe. Glasses were raised, as was a voice from the back of the room: 'Did you say most *beautiful*, Ersimmin? Which among the dead do you rate second to her?'

The pianist played a dramatic flurry of notes. 'Perhaps I should have said most *human*,' he said. 'Our resurrected dead have lacked that quality until now. But you shouldn't dismiss all of them out of hand, Mr Lovich. Menoa's hordes aren't *all* blisters and fangs. In fact, there's a pretty little sloop lying on its side in Covenant Square. I've had my eye on it for a while.'

'I do wish you wouldn't play that tune every time I speak,' the other man said.

Ersimmin said, 'It's from a famous play, you know.'

The other man sighed.

A young woman in a puffy peach dress and black elbow-length gloves sauntered up to Harper. A fat necklace of soulpearls looped her powdered neck. 'I think it's disgusting,' she said. 'Do we really need to plunder Hell for workers? Aren't there any living people who can do *her* job just as well? No offence, dear, I'm sure the Maze was lovely.'

This elicited a chorus of stifled shrieks and giggles from the younger ladies present, a collected frown from the older women, and a unanimous expression of bemused innocence from the gentlemen, each affected with various degrees of skill.

Harper realized she was staring at the woman's soulpearls, and lowered her eyes. The speaker had half a hundred of them there, on display like ordinary jewellery for anyone to see.

A collector, then. King Menoa had already rewarded this one well.

'Excuse me.' Harper moved to push on through the crowd.

An elderly, white-whiskered man in a crimson suit extended an arm, blocking her way. He wore an extraordinarily fine Mesmeric sword at his hip, its pommel an exquisite knot of silace and crystal, the sheath an alabaster spike to match his moustache. 'Please . . . Miss Harper, isn't it? Won't you stay and join us for a drink? My name is Duncan Jones.' He gave a curt bow. 'I served with your husband in the king's reservists. Damn fine young man. We fought together at Larnaig.' He paused a moment, his cheeks flushing. 'I'm sorry about what happened. This must be a difficult journey for you.'

'How can it be difficult?' said the woman in the peach dress. 'Demons don't have feelings, Mr Jones.'

'She's not a demon, Edith.'

'Why? Because she still has breasts?'

Another flurry of giggles swept through the younger ladies. Jones's face reddened further; his whiskers twitched. Several of the other gentlemen had the decency to look embarrassed, but not, Harper noted, Ersimmin. The pianist was grinning.

'As far as I'm concerned,' Edith went on, 'if she's come from Hell then she's earned that title.' She eyed the heavy flask and rubber bulb attached to Harper's belt. 'Don't let her appearance deceive you. This woman breathes human blood, just like the rest of those foul creatures.'

Harper was already beginning to feel woozy. The mist pumps had not been switched on in here, and the air in this carriage was too thin for her dead lungs. But the young lady's words had stung her, and she resisted inhaling a breath of mist from her bulb.

'Please let me pass,' she said.

'Feeling faint, dear?'

'Leave her be, Edith,' Jones said. 'She doesn't look well.'

The young lady raised her chin and gave the old reservist a supercilious glance, but she stepped aside to let the engineer pass.

Harper didn't meet her eyes for more than an instant. She'd possessed a temper once, but it had dried up long ago. She left the music car just as Ersimmin began to play a new tune, each note perfectly timed to match her rapidly retreating footsteps.

Car C boasted a lounge of gilt-edged pastel furniture, plush recliners and low tables, and scattered reading lamps fashioned like jellyfish. It was currently deserted. Reflections of the room bounced back from the etched-glass walls and gave the impression of a multitude of identical lounges placed side by side, but behind those phantom reduplications Harper spied the dark shapes of the buildings and abandoned demon ships in Knuckletown slipping past. She didn't have much time. The train would soon be pulling in to its first stop.

The human passengers were about to meet their Hellish leader in the flesh.

Harper felt dizzy. She slipped the rubber bulb from her tool belt, raised it to her lips and inhaled deeply. The dense mist cloyed in her throat, but it cleared her head and brought some colour back to her skin. She replenished the bulb with a trickle of liquid from her flask, and then considered the job ahead.

The lounge had a glass floor. Harper did her best to ignore the upturned faces in the slave pens below, but their stares burned into the soles of her feet. She didn't know which was worse, the gaunt, pleading looks from the slaves or the baleful glare from the god imprisoned along with them.

She unscrewed a copper grille set low on the interior frosted-glass wall, and slipped her Mesmeric locator from its pouch on her belt. In nature it resembled the sceptre she had once carried across Hell, but this device had been manufactured in the laboratories in Highcliffe – a physical tool with a metaphysical core.

Warm perfumed air blew up through the exposed vent. After she had wound the crystal device, Harper set it resonating. A range of ninety to one hundred and twenty Bael cycles would pick up all unauthorized soul traffic, with angel or demon emotae at the higher end of the spectrum. Most likely, one of the passengers had broken a soulpearl, and they now had a human ghost aboard.

While Harper waited for the locator to react, she checked the mist-pump feeder tubes and pressure gauges inside the vent. Everything seemed to be in order for the king's arrival. It gave her a certain amount of pleasure to think of the living passengers breathing the same foul air as their master while he remained aboard.

The tiny needle wavered from one ideograph to another before it settled in the centre of the plate.

Then it went off the scale.

Harper stared at the locator in astonishment, not quite com-prehending. She shook the locator, then stopped herself. It was operating perfectly correctly. She'd calibrated it against stored ghosts at the Pandemerian Railroad Company terminus on Cog Island, so this reading was not at fault. Quickly, her hands trem-bling, she reset the device and broadened the spectrum, from ninety to one hundred and sixty Baels – the range required to detect gods. Once more she set the locator resonating, watched the needle waver, settle and then leap.

The needle went off the scale again.

Impossible.

Either the device was malfunctioning, or the intruder was something she had never seen before – which meant that it could not have come from Earth or Hell.

She did not, however, get the chance to speculate further. From the direction of the music car came a loud bang, followed by the sound of women screaming.

A restaurant and two accommodation wagons separated the lounge from the music carriage. Harper stormed through the restaurant, shouldered curious and apprehensive stewards aside, bumped against tables and chairs and slammed through the door to the first accommodation car only to find her way blocked by a fat little boy trailing along a dog in a bag. She would have jumped right over the lad had he been a few inches shorter. As it was, she was forced to slow down and sidle by him, her back brushing the wall of the glass corridor. She stepped over the dog: a tiny thing, zipped tightly into a richly woven travel bag so that only its head was visible.

'Do you work here?' the boy said.

'Don't have time, son, sorry.' She took off down the corridor at a run.

'I heard screams,' he said. 'Is it a ghost? Aunt Edith said I can hunt them at Coreollis. Got my own gun and everything.'

'Not a ghost,' Harper called back. She was already halfway along the corridor. 'Something else.'

'A demon, then?' He ran after her, pulling his imprisoned dog after him. Apparently the bag had wheels underneath. 'Aunt Edith said I can hunt them when I grow up. Should I get my gun? Can I let Wolf-thunder out of his bag? I want to train him to hunt demons, but they won't let him wander about in case he poos.'

She had reached the end of the corridor. 'I don't know what it is, but stay here, it might be dangerous.' Without pausing, she slammed into the far door and plunged on through. The rapid squeaking of wheels came from somewhere behind.

Wolf-thunder yipped.

The music car was in chaos. Three of the ladies had swooned and now lay on recliners where they were being attended to by several of the gentlemen. The piano had been smashed into what looked like a pile of heavily lacquered kindling wrapped in a confusion of wire. Ivory keys and small hammers were strewn everywhere. The white-whiskered reservist, Jones, was busy brushing most of it into the corner with his foot, while Ersimmin the pianist watched him with a look of amused befuddlement on his face. A strange odour lingered: the earthy scent of a forest or a swamp mingled with something else – something bestial. Harper inhaled it deeply, trying to identify it.

Carrick stood in the centre of the room, reeling, seemingly unsure of where to turn or who to speak to. He still had a flute of wine in his hand.

Edith was shrieking. The colour seemed to have drained from her face to her thin chest, which heaved against the confines of her peach bodice. She had removed one of her gloves and clutched a bloody handkerchief in her naked fingers. A handsome man and his young wife, in matching raven-dark suit and frock, were attending to her. Harper now recognized the man as Edgar Lovich, an actor who'd made his fortune tramping the boards of Cog's theatres before the war. Lovich was holding the young lady's uninjured hand while his wife sought to inspect her wound. 'Please, Edith,' she said. 'I can't help you unless you let me look at it.'

'It took my finger off,' Edith cried. 'It took my finger off!'

'Let me see, then.'

'What happened?' Harper demanded.

Carrick wheeled to face her. 'Where in Hell have you been? While you've been off slacking, we've had a manifestation. Miss Bainbridge has been injured.'

'What kind?' Harper made a point of staring at the drink in Carrick's hand.

'What?' The chief gaped at her.

'What *kind*?' she repeated. 'A dogcatcher? An Icarate? Was it one of the Non Morai? If I'm going to get rid of it, it would help if I knew what it was.'

'What are you talking about?' Carrick said. 'It manifested itself. *Here*. It smashed up the piano.'

The actor's wife had succeeded in extracting the handkerchief from Edith's hand. Now she was examining the young woman's bloody fingers. 'It's fine,' she said. 'Just a cut. One of the piano wires must have caught your knuckle just here.'

'The finger's gone,' Edith moaned.

'No, dear, look.' She counted the fingers. 'One, two, three, four and five. All digits present and correct, see?'

'It's gone!' The young woman turned tear-filled eyes on Harper. 'And it's *her* fault. She's supposed to prevent things like this from happening on this train!'

Harper let out a long sigh. 'Would somebody please tell me exactly what happened?'

'Ersimmin was playing one of his new compositions,' Lovich explained, 'when this thing appeared from nowhere, destroyed the piano and then vanished. Just like that!' He made a flamboyant gesture with his hands. 'The whole incident was over in a heartbeat.'

'What did it look like?'

'Hideous, utterly hideous. It was quite dark and . . .' he frowned, 'chunky.'

'Seven Hells, Edgar!' Jones exclaimed. 'You make it sound like one of your wife's muffins.' The former reservist approached Harper, his expression grave. 'It was about five feet tall,' he said, 'but bulky, powerful. Damn thing had muscles like the biggest navvy you've ever seen . . . and it was hairless, all covered in grey blisters.' He thought for a moment. 'I don't recall that it had a face as such . . . just blistered skin.'

Harper frowned. 'A blisterman?'

'Bugger was armed too,' Jones went on. 'But not with a Mesmeric weapon. Only a plain stone hammer.' He lowered his voice. 'It seems to have taken violent exception to Ersimmin's playing.'

'It had taste, at least,' Lovich muttered.

Harper frowned. Such manifestations had become more common since the Cog Portal had opened. Demons could sometimes materialize in places where a lot of blood had been shed – the Cog Island plague pits, or in old temples to Iril – but this train was supposed to be clean. They hadn't yet switched on the interior mist pumps.

And why had it targeted the passengers? These people were King Menoa's human delegates. They were under his protection, and they would remain so until he betrayed them.

And then there was her locator reading. For an instant she had detected something far more powerful than a simple blisterman. There were obviously gods at work here.

'If it's still onboard, it will probably be hiding in the train's blood tank,' she said. 'I'll go there now. I can set off a Screamer and force it out.'

'Splendid.' Ersimmin the pianist clapped his hands. 'To the armoury, gentlemen. What do you say . . . ten spindles apiece, eh? The prize goes to the fellow who bags the thing?' He began to stride in the direction of the train's arsenal.

Harper called after him. 'I'm sorry, sir, you can't fire weapons in here. The carriages are made of glass. One shot could shatter a wall.'

'Who cares about the carriages?' Edith howled. 'Just shoot the damn thing!'

Jones stepped forward. 'She's right, Edith. You must think of our other guests. How would it look if we arrived at Cog Portal with a shattered train? The king would not look very kindly upon us. Even you can see that, Ersimmin.'

Edith buried her nose in the handkerchief.

Ersimmin looked disappointed too. 'Hellish waste,' he muttered. 'I can get a thousand spindles for a blisterman soul on the collectors' market. But no, you're right. It would be foolish to risk damaging the train.'

Edith stamped her foot. 'I demand that you turn this train around immediately. I require medical attention.'

'It's barely a scratch, Edith,' Jones said. 'Just let Miss Harper do her work. She'll locate the thing and send it back to the Maze before you know it.'

'Don't hush me, old man,' the young lady retorted. 'And don't tell me to put my faith in this corpse. She did nothing to prevent the creature from appearing in the first place. Any *living* engineer would have caught it long before it had a chance to wreak havoc.'

'Edith . . .'

'No! I will not be patronized or belittled by you or anybody. I am not a child.' She spun to face Carrick, who still seemed to be in shock, and said, 'Turn the train around this instant.'

Carrick raised his hands. 'Miss Bainbridge, please, if you—'

'I will not be coddled by you either, Chief Carrick. Do not forget your position here. My family could make life very difficult for you.' Suddenly she seemed to be on the verge of tears. 'Why do you all have to be so cruel?'

Lovich's wife gave her a gentle hug.

Ersimmin was frowning at his pocket watch. 'Well, if we can't shoot the damn thing, might I suggest a quick and practical alternative?'

'Sir?' the chief asked.

'Let Hasp out,' the other man said. 'Let him dispatch it for us.'

'That's not a good idea, sir,' Carrick said.

'Why not?' the pianist demanded. 'He can't harm *us* without a direct order. Menoa's surgeons made quite sure of that. And I seem to recall that *you* gave us your personal assurance before we even stepped aboard the train.'

Carrick fidgeted. 'Impossible,' he said at last. 'If Hasp was killed before the handover, his brother Rys would refuse to sign the treaty. Any chance of peace between Coreollis and Pandemeria would vanish.'

'*Killed?*' Ersimmin said. 'But this is the god who single-handedly slew thousands of the Blind. *Tens* of thousands. And you're worried about *one* demon? Hasp could kill this thing in his sleep.'

'I'm sorry, sir, there's too much at risk. I don't have the authority to sanction this.'

The pianist's expression clouded. 'I am *giving* you the authority, Mr Carrick. We are due to arrive at the portal in less than twenty minutes – at which point our king will hand over the peace treaty and entrust *us*, his chosen Pandemerian ambassadors, with its safe delivery. How would it look if we turn up to greet His Majesty with a violent intruder already loose aboard this train?'

Carrick looked even more uncomfortable. 'I don't know,' he muttered.

Ersimmin said, 'Chief Carrick, I will take full responsibility for Hasp's release. The king will know that it was *my* decision. And I will of course compensate you handsomely for the inconvenience.'

Harper was shaking her head. 'Sir,' she said, 'I strongly advise against this. Company regulations require us to repel intruders by normal means.'

Jones agreed. 'One monster on the loose is bad enough,' he said. 'There's no sense in upsetting the ladies any more by releasing a second one. Let me trade my pistol for a steel sword and I'll help Miss Harper deal with our uninvited guest.'

Ersimmin laughed. 'Company regulations? Miss Harper, may I remind you that I own a twenty per cent share in the Pandemerian Railroad Company?' He turned back to Carrick. 'What do you say, Chief? Shall we have a bit of sport to liven up the party? Would a thousand spindles make it worth your while?'

Now Carrick had a gleam in his eye. For the first time since the manifestation, he seemed composed. 'Do it,' he said to Harper. 'Let the glass bastard out of his cage.'

21

THE GOD IN GLASS

The constant clickety-clack of steel wheels on the rails below had begun to sound like a chorus of insistent voices endlessly repeating the train's destination: *Coreollis, Coreollis, Coreollis*. Mina Greene shuddered, pulled her thin blanket more tightly around her glass-plated shoulders, and looked down at the floor of the slave pen. It was as hard and transparent as the brittle scales the Mesmerists had given her in place of her old skin. Wheels and axles whirred in the gloom beneath the train. Sleepers, slag and gravel blurred past.

The other slaves refused to move for fear of shattering their own transparent skins, and so she sat alone in the centre of the low-ceilinged space. They seemed to be afraid of talking too, as if words could shatter glass! More likely, they were wary of her proximity to the Lord of the First Citadel, which made Mina smile. They had a right to be nervous, she decided. He was a fearsome type.

'Hasp,' she said.

The god looked up, and a wheezing, clicking sound issued from the metal-and-bone mechanism clamped to the back of his skull. He frowned, then lowered his gaze and went back to whatever he was sketching. To keep the wounded god happy, the Pandemerian Railroad Company had given him some paper and pencils.

Despite his current appearance, she still preferred to think of him as an angel. Menoa's Icarates had removed his wings completely, cutting out the bones, muscles and tendons from his shoulders, so that now he almost looked like a man: an old buccaneer slumped on the floor, all drooping jowls, patchy stubble and a paunch. But the image of Hasp as a man was difficult to sustain, for his eyes constantly shifted colour. Sometimes to the colour of verdigris or gold; sometimes to the colour of the blood that flowed through his own ghastly armour.

Mina watched the god's blood pulse through glass veins in his breastplate and shoulder-guards, out through the flexible, transparent pipes into his arm- and leg-bracers. She marvelled at the blood looping around his neck, where it branched into thin channels within his cheek-guards and half-helm, and she wondered how the Mesmerists could have engineered something so hideous and yet so beautiful: those cold-forged, metameric plates, spikes and tubes were as magnificent as any sculpture to be found in a Dalamooran vizier's palace.

The angel's armour was much grander than the other slaves' glass scales, and yet it was just as brittle. One hard tap with a sword would shatter it as easily as a wine flute. And it would be shattered soon, she suspected. The proposed handover, the peace treaty – all just more of Menoa's lies. Their blood would stain the ground around Coreollis before the sun set tomorrow.

'Lighten up,' she said to him.

Hasp didn't even look at her. His brow crinkled and he spoke slowly: 'I preferred you when you were catatonic in Hell. You talked less.'

Mina giggled and shifted closer to him. The curved panels on her legs and ankles clacked against the floor, but she didn't care. 'Kill me then,' she said. She snatched up two of his pencils and rattled them against his glass-sheathed shin.

Hasp moved his leg away. 'What's wrong with you?' he growled.

'If you want to die so badly then stand up and hurl yourself against the floor. I guarantee the fall will break your fragile skin.'

'But I want *you* to do it,' she cooed.

'Only because you know I can't.' Tiny gears skrittered somewhere inside the god's neck, or perhaps in his brain. A smell of burning wires and scorched blood came from the implanted Mesmerist device at the back of his skull. He twitched, and his cracked lips contorted into a grimace beneath his transparent helm. 'But keep annoying me and I might even try. This is a dangerous game you're playing, lass.'

Mina examined one of the pencils, turning it over in her grubby hands. 'It's not a game.'

Hasp's jaw tightened. His irises pulsed through a spectrum of colours, and his hands clenched to fists. 'Bastard Menoa,' he hissed. 'I think he put a spiteful demon in my skull.'

'I like it when your eyes do that,' she said.

'Same thing happens to all angels on earth.'

'Do it again.'

'I'm not your pet, Mina.'

She sighed and dropped the pencil. 'You're so boring.'

'Then leave me alone.'

'Only if you help me break this.' She placed her hands against her chest.

A growling sound came from Hasp's skull. His eyes shifted colour – grey to black to blue to red. 'I can feel its teeth now,' he said. 'You're making the damn thing bite.'

Pumps sounded overhead, blowing more mist through valves into the slave pen.

Mina stifled a laugh.

'Enough,' he growled, then clamped his teeth together and went back to his sketch. 'You are tormenting me simply because you can. What have I done to you? I sheltered you from the Icarates. I tried to defend you.'

'Yes, you did.'

'Then what more do you want from me?'

'I want you to kill me.'

The god hissed again. 'So you can go back to Hell? You'll end up back there soon enough without *my* help. What do you think will happen to you in Coreollis? Do you think Rys *wants* to be reminded of his failure?' He grunted. 'My brother will sign Menoa's treaty and then butcher us all.'

'Not you.'

'Especially me,' Hasp said. 'I'm no use to him like *this*.' He turned his glassy hands palm up. 'Rys will feed me to his garden and grow roses from my blood. He'll do it just to spite Menoa, because he can't fight back at the king in any other way. This war was over as soon as my brother learned about the arconites. His memories of Skirl still haunt him.'

'I disagree. You're more important to Rys than you think you are.'

He scowled. '*You* don't know him.'

'What are you drawing?' She craned her neck to see, but Hasp turned away from her to hide his work. She pouted and smacked him gently. 'Go on,' she said. 'Just break my arm, a finger even. You wouldn't even need to use your shiftblade.'

'Right now, I'd break your neck if I could,' he said.

But Mina knew that was a lie. The parasite in Hasp's skull only protected Menoa's servants. It did not care which of the king's enemies the god killed. Hasp could have slain her easily, and yet he chose not to. And that was exactly why Mina persisted. The defeated god had been so horribly debased that she needed to keep reminding him who he really was. She couldn't let him simply give up, for it would be too easy for him to end his own life.

Hasp was gazing at the shiftblade on the floor beside him, a weapon which could change its shape into any other. King Menoa himself had given it to him as a display of his absolute power over the Lord of the First Citadel. Shreds of muscle still clung to the steel blade, showing that someone in the king's army had used it recently.

A sudden tremor ran through the god. His neck jerked violently, before he was able to still himself, and the pencil in his hand had snapped in two. He let out a long sigh and tossed the broken fragments away. 'Two hundred thousand,' he muttered. 'And I managed to slay less than thirty.'

'You gave up too easily.'

He grunted.

Mina slouched back from him. The other slaves remained motionless, breathing gently. She recognized none of them, and none would meet her eye. Crystal chandeliers trembled in the lounge above them, illuminating the thin glass scales covering their faces and necks. Perhaps she ought to have spoken with them before this? But what was the point now? They had accepted whatever fate would befall them. Now they simply sat there and counted their own breaths. So she thought about her father instead, bumbling about their house in Lye Street, chattering about the badlands north of Deepgate and all the gold he hadn't found and all the lead that he had. He had been a big man, like Hasp, and in all his life she had never seen him give up.

She let her gaze roam over the fine furnishings on the opposite side of the glass ceiling: the soft gold curlicues of a table, an opaque blue vase, the leaves etched into a mirror. Beautiful, she supposed, and yet cold. She could not enjoy such objects. Mina imagined she could hear soft music over the insistent thump of the train, and she strained to see through the carriage roof to the stars beyond. Hasp had supposedly once been one of those stars – Ulcis and Rys too. But the heavens were invisible from down here, obscured by a hundred aether lights. Wasn't it funny how the most transient things could outshine the timeless?

She slid her body even closer to the angel's, and then rattled another of his pencils repeatedly against his shoulder guard, trying to time each tap to the pulse-rate of his blood inside the glass veins. Hasp blew through his teeth, then hunched further over his sketch, evidently trying his best to ignore her. But had his heartbeat quickened? Mina fancied that it had. 'Please,' she whined, 'I'll make it worth your while.' Now *there* was something to think about. Could Hasp still . . .?

'Get away from him!' The new voice had come from behind. Mina twisted round to see a female engineer unlocking the door to the slave pen. Beyond the woman, a gloomy corridor ran the entire length of the carriage, through whose outer wall Mina glimpsed dark brickwork and steel blurring past.

'He's not some animal to be prodded,' Harper continued. She briefly inhaled mist from a rubber bulb. 'And he's dangerous. Carrick should never have put him in here with the rest of you.'

'He's *not* dangerous.' Mina laid a hand upon the angel's arm; his armour felt surprisingly hot. 'Are you?'

'Leave . . .' Hasp jerked his arm away from her. 'I have warned you . . .'

Harper ducked inside the slave pen. 'They want you upstairs,' she said to Hasp. 'Bring your shiftblade, let's go.'

The blood pulsing within the angel's glass armour seemed to quicken even more. He trembled, his eyes blackened, and he snatched up his weapon. 'Odd,' he growled, frowning at the blade with an expression of distaste and confusion, as though he'd just picked up a river snake and was trying to work out why. 'Odd that I should recognize your voice.' He stared up at her. 'Menoa has changed your form since the last time we met.'

The engineer nodded. 'Alice Harper.'

'You were a serpent?'

Harper studied him a moment, then said, 'I order you to drop the weapon.'

At once, Hasp released the shiftblade. The sword cracked against the glassy floor. Most of the slaves flinched away from the sound – all except Mina, who was watching intently.

Hasp winced. 'I see nothing has changed.'

'The parasite in your skull,' Harper said slowly, 'will obey *any* of King Menoa's servants. Even the weakest of them could order you to slay yourself' – she inclined her head – 'or your woman there, and you would be forced to comply without hesitation.'

Hasp glanced at Mina, but said nothing.

'If you try to resist it,' Harper said, 'it will eventually kill you.'

The god's massive shoulders bunched under two dozen plates of overlapping glass; tubes flexed; cords in his neck pushed against his transparent collar. 'Before or after I reach Coreollis?' he asked.

The engineer looked away. 'It's agitated because it has been removed from Hell. That's why it's causing you so much pain. I can stop that from happening.'

'My thanks.'

'Then you'll come upstairs with me?'

Hasp snorted a laugh. 'As long as you don't order me to.'

The engineer crouched down beside him. She rummaged in her tool-belt and, after a brief moment, brought out a slender silver device about the size of a pencil, which she twisted at various points along its length. The tool crackled and then made a high-pitched whining sound. 'Lean forward,' she said.

Hasp obeyed, and Harper inserted the device into a tiny slot at the back of his skull. 'Tell me if this hurts,' she said, 'or if you begin to feel dizzy.' She inhaled from her bulb again and then, gently, blew into the device. After a moment she paused and said, 'You may experience a brief moment of confusion, some bright flashes of colour at the edges of your vision, unusual sounds or smells. If you think you're going to pass out, tell me at once.'

The god gasped, and then bared his teeth, 'Get that . . . thing out of my mind!'

Harper withdrew the device, and stood up. 'It's done,' she said. 'The demon is calmer now. But you're going to have to stop resisting it.'

'Stop resisting it?' Hasp pressed his fist against his breastplate, at the place where the blood spread from his heart in a crimson web across his chest, and took several deep breaths. 'If I don't resist it, I'm dead anyway. When Rys learns that his own brother has become a tool, a weapon to be used by any of his enemies . . .' He shook his head. 'Tell me, Alice Harper, what would *you* do?'

The engineer looked down at him with an expression that might have been pity. She shrugged. 'I'd make friends with a Mesmerist.'

Hasp's grunt was almost a laugh. He reclaimed his shiftblade and stood up. 'You want me to kill something, I presume.'

From inside the slave pen, Mina Greene tried to follow the angel's progress along the corridor and up the stairs to the lounge, but she soon lost sight of him among the confusion of glints and glimmers within the train. She glanced down at Hasp's sketches, now strewn across the floor amidst the fragments of his broken pencil. She gathered up the sheets of paper, then flopped down and leafed through them.

Each sketch was different, but of a similar subject: stone keeps and towers of every shape and size, round or square, tall or stubby; each with battlements and high turrets, narrow windows and thick iron portcullises, deep moats and stout drawbridges. Mina tossed the drawings away. Ultimately they were all boring. Hasp sketched nothing but castles.

22

FLOWER

Hasp strode into the music carriage, and into the centre of a circle of cold stares. The humans fell silent as he entered. His armour shifted and clicked, the blood-filled plates rasping over each other and over his skin, splitting the light from chandeliers and reading lamps into a mirage of rainbows. Since Menoa had imprisoned him inside the suit, Hasp had learned to ignore the physical discomfort: his body had hardened and no longer pounded with infection. But he had yet to grow accustomed to the profound sense of vulnerability.

He hated the Mesmerists for that feeling, and hated those who assisted them. Without his parasitic conscience he would happily have murdered every one of these odious bastards. They knew it, of course; he could read it in their flushed faces and their ridiculous affected postures of ease; in the way they toyed with their jewellery, soulpearls or weapons. They were thrilled, frightened, entertained. The web of blood around the god's heart now seethed and boiled inside its glass prison.

These same people had sold their souls for power.

All five of the men had armed themselves, two with crystal Mesmeric blades, and the other three – including King Menoa's Chief Liaison Officer – with shiftblades similar to Hasp's own.

339

The women flocked behind them in a breathless hush of fruit-coloured silk. Fans wafted over jewels and powdered necks.

Easy enough for him to snap . . .

A furious buzzing behind the angel's ears sent spikes of agony deep into his cranium. Menoa's demon had sensed the direction of Hasp's anger. His left eye now flickered uncontrollably; his fist crushed the grip of his shiftblade. In a hot blur he saw the women back away, pressing themselves closer to their own reflections in the walls of the music carriage. Harper approached, an apprehensive frown creasing her brow.

The Chief Liaison Officer, Carrick, gripped his shiftblade like a man who wanted people to think he knew how to use it. But Hasp had never met a human with any real talent with the blade. It took a long time in Hell to master the necessary mental skills to use such a weapon.

Carrick raised his chin. 'Hasp,' he said, and then paused to moisten his lips. 'Kneel.'

Hasp fought to resist the man's instruction. He bit down hard, summoned every shred of willpower, pushed back, struggled like a man trapped beneath a rock fall . . .

. . . and found himself kneeling on the floor, gasping.

'You see?' Carrick gave a theatrical wave to the assembled guests. 'You are perfectly safe. Menoa's parasite is irresistible.'

A handsome man in a dark suit spoke up: 'He doesn't look particularly dangerous to me. He's wearing slave skin, for god's sake. One prod with a sword would crack that wide open.'

'That's true, Mr Lovich, and yet the king was good enough to exhibit him at the Highcliffe Fair. Not one of the reservists who sparred with the archon survived the encounter. He showed remarkable skill with a shiftblade.'

'This is a foolish idea.' This came from an older, more heavily built man with white whiskers. 'We'll reach the Portal in minutes.

Let's put this monster back in his cage and let Menoa decide what to do with the intruder.'

From somewhere Hasp found strength. He surged to his feet, his fist taut as iron on the hilt of his shiftblade, and bared his teeth at Carrick. 'Try that again and I'll rip your head off, reach inside your throat, pull your insides out and stuff them back into your empty skull.'

Carrick staggered backwards, fumbling for his pistol. 'Get away!' he cried. 'That's an order, an order!'

Hasp halted, growling. He felt the demon's teeth clench inside his skull. Pain like molten metal ran through his jaw. He tasted brass.

The whiskered man's brow furrowed. 'He appears to be resisting his implanted conscience, and I rather suspect that the puff of smoke which has just issued from the mechanism in his head was not an intentionally engineered effect. Take him back to the slave pens, Chief Carrick, before you lose the ability to control him altogether. I have no desire to cross swords with an angry god' – he gave the slightest nod of his head – 'when there are so many ladies present.'

Hasp studied the old man. This human had not glanced once at Carrick during his short speech. He was getting on in years, certainly, and portly, but he stood lightly on the balls of his feet, his hands resting just-so on his hips. A good-quality rapier hung from a sash wrapped around his midriff, the blade sheathed in worn white leather. Hasp had no doubt that the old man well knew how to wield it.

'He cannot harm us,' Carrick stammered. 'He *cannot*. The parasite *knows* we serve its master.'

Hasp noticed with a kind of derisive pleasure that the Chief Liaison Officer's shiftblade had turned the same colour as his suit. Its steel edges had already softened. Under Carrick's ownership, the shape-shifting demon could not even maintain the guise of a sword.

'Very well,' Jones said. 'But let's dispense with the showmanship and be about this business quickly. We are running out of time.'

Carrick faced the angel again. 'We've had a manifestation,' he said. 'We require you to kill it.'

'Kill it yourself.'

Carrick fingered the grip of his shiftblade, still apparently unaware of the weapon's degradation. The sword's guard was now wilting like butter in the sun. He said formally: 'As the Chief Liaison Officer between the Pandemerian Railroad Company and Hell, I order you to locate the intruder aboard this locomotive and destroy it.'

Hasp could not stop himself from flinching. How could words cause so much pain? Each syllable felt like a drop of acid inside his skull. Before he knew what he was doing, he found himself marching towards the front of the train, clutching his skull, dimly aware of Harper following behind him. She was whispering, 'Don't fight it, Hasp . . . go with it, please.'

But just as they reached the door to the accommodation section, it opened, and a small boy towing a travel bag along the floor behind him came through. A small dog poked his head out of one end of this bag – the pup had been zipped up inside.

'Out of the way, son,' Harper said.

The child stopped, and gaped up at the battle-archon. Behind him, his trapped pup growled. The rear end of the leather and cloth satchel oscillated wildly. 'I wanted to see the angel,' the boy said. 'Aunt Edith promised I could watch it kill something.'

Hasp halted, still reeling, and looked down at the boy and his pet. 'You want to see me kill?' he muttered. 'Then order me to do so. You're all Menoa's fucking people on this train.'

The boy brightened. 'Do it!' he said. 'Kill something now.'

'As you wish.' Hasp kicked the dog with all of the strength he could muster.

Had the animal been made of tougher stuff than flesh and bone, or had its bag been composed of something more substantial than woven thread, it might have made an impact hard enough to shatter the glass wall at the end of the corridor sixty feet away. Instead, the creature and the torn remains of its embroidered travel-bag spattered against the opposite end of the passage in a series of wet smacks, more like a shower of red rain than anything resembling the corpse of a dog.

The boy screamed.

Hasp cricked his neck, then shoved the child aside and stomped away, his transparent armour swimming with rainbows.

Harper paused, hardly able to believe what she'd just witnessed. In under a heartbeat, the entire accommodation-section corridor had been transformed from neat opulence into a scene from a slaughterhouse. Gore covered everything: the lights, the walls, the floor. Somewhere behind her a child was screaming, men were yelling, women shrieking. Hasp did not halt; he stormed ahead like some demonic vision, an anatomical nightmare composed of surgery and sculpted glass.

The engineer closed the door behind her, mindlessly hoping it might hide the gory scene from the passengers in the adjacent carriage. But it was useless: the corridor door was as transparent as the walls and ceilings. She ran after the angel, grabbed his arm and tried to stop him. 'Hold on.'

Hasp shrugged her off.

'Why did you do that?' Harper insisted. 'What possible reason could you have had for killing that animal?' She felt suddenly woozy, and sucked in a breath from her rubber bulb.

'I couldn't resist,' Hasp snapped. He threw open the blood-spattered door at the far end of the passageway, and ducked into the second accommodation car.

Harper followed. 'You pressed that boy into giving you an order.'

'Did I?'

'You must have known what would happen. You must have—'

'No!' He wheeled on her, his eyes black with rage. 'I didn't. I was ordered to kill something, and it was either the pup or one of you. Don't you see what Menoa's arrogance has accomplished? He's turned me into a sword, a weapon for any of his own people to use at will. Is there really no one you would like to see killed? Ask that question to the next man and the next, and you'll soon find out how dangerous this situation is.' He touched his breast-plate. 'This armour makes me vulnerable. Order me to punch my own chest, and I will happily oblige. But command me to slay another man and he'd better be damn quick to get out of the way. And that makes me a desirable commodity. Do you think those power-hungry bastards back there aren't also thinking about that right now?'

Harper understood. Hasp's presence on this world now posed a threat to every man, woman and child. All it would take was a word in his ear.

'And what about you, Alice Harper?' The battle-archon grinned savagely. 'Who hurt you?'

Instinctively, Harper grabbed for the soulpearl hidden inside her blouse, then quickly dropped her hand. She could feel the empty jewel against her rapidly beating heart. Had Hasp noticed the gesture?

He simply turned and marched ahead, whirring, clacking and leaking smoke from the mechanism behind his head like some ghastly automaton. His shiftblade scraped the carriage floor.

'This parasite Menoa put in my skull is such a fickle thing,' he snarled. 'So fickle.'

He threw open the door at the end of the corridor, ducked through and stormed along the next carriage. No one had told him where to hunt for the demon, but Hasp had evidently decided to start the hunt as far away from the passengers as he could get.

The night outside smelled of rotting engines and old blood. Stars jostled with torrents of embers from the locomotive's stack. Aether lights illuminated the embankment ahead of the train, exposing swathes of the black mud and wrecked shacks which had once been Knuckletown. To the south Harper could make out the shadow of Sill Wood, a low dark mass against a dark purple sky. She stood with Hasp on a narrow scaffold at the rear of the coal tender, buffeted by wind and noise: the rasping shovels of engineers feeding coal into the firebox; the *Eleanor*'s wheels drumming the tracks; the shuddering glass of the wagons curving away behind the engine like a string of jewel boxes.

Harper aimed her locator back along the length of the train, and wound its frequency range to its broadest setting. She didn't know exactly what she was looking for. More worryingly, her *locator* didn't know. The soul trapped within the device now appeared to be agitated – its needle oscillated wildly between ideographs, until Harper whispered to it to calm it down. Then the needle became still. 'Nothing,' she shouted to Hasp over the thumping engine. 'We'll have to get closer to the source, or get lucky. I doubt I'll measure a reading until we're right on top of it.'

Hasp was watching the dark scenery rush past. 'Promise me something,' he said.

'What?'

'Don't ever let that girl in the slave pen become a Mesmerist.'

'I think that's unlikely to happen. Let's walk back slowly. Be ready.'

'Is that an order?' he asked, dryly.

'If you like,' she replied.

They worked their way back from the coal tender through the staff-accommodation cars. The coal-shovellers, pressure engineer and driver who made up the midnight shift were still asleep in their cots on either side of the central passageway, snoring like bulls. Harper swept her locator over the men, but registered nothing unusual here. Two stewards and a cook were playing cards at a low table in the second of the bunk-wagons. Harper nodded a greeting to them, but didn't linger.

Beyond this, they came to Carrick's private quarters, where a frost-glass wall divided the Chief Liaison Officer's suite from the sixty-foot-long corridor. Harper slipped inside the room she shared with her new boss.

Hasp followed close behind.

Dark opulence defined the suite. Gold thread fringed heavy wine-coloured drapes along the exterior wall. A tall Ellonese wardrobe stood at the far end of the room, beside a mirrored dresser with claw-shaped ivory handles. Shelves on the interior wall displayed Carrick's collection of melodiums, those sumptuous golden music boxes he had brought with him from his Highcliffe home. She knew every one of their tunes intimately.

Harper scanned the walls and finally the bed: a wide high-sided cot smothered in red silk and gold pillows. Her position in Hell had been determined by success or failure at given tasks. Now her rise through the ranks of the Pandemerian Railroad Company might be measured by the quality of bed linen on which she rested each night.

I could buy you a house of your own in the city, a private place.

Why *had* Carrick pursued her with such enthusiasm since her return from Hell? He'd never shown much interest in her while she'd been alive.

She sucked in a temporary breath of life from her bulb, thinking of the bed she'd once shared with Tom.

Hasp leaned on his shiftblade and glared around at the room with distaste. Harper noticed the frayed pile where the ragged tip of the angel's sword pressed into Carrick's ermine rug, and she couldn't suppress a smile. The chief would probably have a fit when he saw it.

'I'm reading something,' she said finally. 'But it's faint, a residual echo.'

The angel sniffed, and his forehead creased. 'This room smells rotten. Your demon has been here.' He picked up one of Carrick's melodiums and examined it.

Harper couldn't smell anything unusual. 'I don't think it's a demon,' she said. 'My locator didn't recognize it.'

Hasp grunted. 'It's a demon all right. Just not something your device has encountered before. Do you think you've witnessed everything there is to see in this world? There are old and powerful things lurking in places that the Mesmerists themselves never imagined. But those things stay away for a good reason – you know why?'

She shook her head.

'Because there's nothing for them here. They don't seek power, and they don't need to creep into this world like stray dogs to lap at spilled blood.'

'Then why is it here?'

'How should I know?' He gave her a humourless smile. 'Your Mesmerist toys aren't going to bother this thing much. You won't be able to damage it with a Screamer, I warn you. This intruder is a warrior.'

'Like you?' she said.

The smile left Hasp's face. His eyes darkened and the

mechanism behind his skull made a low crackling sound. He released the melodium, which clattered to the floor and began a chiming tune. Hasp glanced down at it for a moment, and then crushed it beneath his glass-sheathed heel.

'Careful,' Harper said. 'Your armour is more fragile than you think.'

Hasp kicked the broken pieces away.

The engineer gazed blankly at the scattered fragments of the music box, thinking hard. Beyond the Veil all known demons and shades haunted only those dark places of the world: the black city of Moine, Spire Nine back on Cog Island, the old whaling station down at Nigel's Folly before Rys's rain had flooded Pandemeria – places where battles had been fought and men had died. They came there like flies in the wake of murder. The Mesmerists had long known that portals into the Maze could be opened only with the blood of the dead. But what could have caused such a power-ful entity to manifest here? If it had no interest in blood . . .

'It was summoned?' she said at last.

Hasp's smile was almost warm. 'Clever girl, now you're begin-ning to understand. You have a saboteur aboard. Someone or *something* doesn't want us all to reach Coreollis alive.'

'But who would gain by disrupting the peace treaty?'

'Only those with no future to lose.'

A vision of Tom came to her then: as one of many sailors board-ing the tender that would take them out to the *Karlsbad*, the last god-smasher class warship to sail for Larnaig. Menoa had con-structed the huge vessel from a single archon's soul. The Mesmerist Veil had smothered the drowned city that was once their home. Crowds of onlookers had jostled on the temporary wharfs and pontoons built around the ever-shrinking islands of Highcliffe. Red waters sloshed against the piles under her feet. She remembered seeing the spire of Cog Cathedral, the only part of that great building which had remained above the rising waters. Somebody had contrived a way to make the bells ring, and they were clamouring now. Tom laughed, waving to her from the deck. He had called out to her above the noise: *If I end up dead, you better ask Menoa to return my ghost. I'm not spending eternity in Hell with all these bastards. You should hear their awful jokes.*

She had called back to Tom as the tender cast off: *You think I'm going to spend my life saving up for a soulpearl? She had laughed along with him. Don't you dare get yourself killed. We can't afford it.*

That had been the last time she'd seen her husband, and for all King Menoa's promises, the soulpearl next to Harper's heart remained empty.

The melodium lay in pieces scattered across the rug. Harper suddenly realized that Carrick would be furious at the loss of such a precious toy. She felt like destroying the rest of them then, snatching them off the shelves and hurling them against the wall. But she needed Carrick's help. She needed to stay firm.

They had a saboteur aboard the train?

'Can you kill this demon?' she said to Hasp.

'Perhaps. But I'd rather not be ordered to do so.'

'Fine.' She closed her eyes a moment, breathed deeply and focused on what she had to do. 'Just . . . please don't kill any more dogs.'

'Are there any more dogs aboard?'

'No.'

'Then there shouldn't be a problem.' The angel's gaze lingered on Harper's uniform, at the place where her hidden jewel rested against the hollow of her neck.

Harper shrugged off his stare and raised her locator again. 'Let's keep moving.'

Observation Car One was a misnomer, at least at night, for the transparent carriage shimmered like the inside of a Mesmer crystal, the myriad light blotting any view of the dark landscape rushing by outside. Aether lamps made twinkling constellations on the many glass facets, while a spiral staircase of clear composite triangles led up to a viewing dome and an open terrace where passengers might stroll and take the air, weather permitting. Red plush chairs surrounded tea tables on which vases of pink and white roses had been artfully arranged. But even the heady odour of flowers could not wholly disguise the smell of the Pandemerian Railroad Company's chemical antiseptic.

A twitch of movement on her locator brought Harper to a halt. She adjusted the device before sending two full-spectrum pulses out in opposite directions. Then she changed her position, and repeated the process. The needle fluctuated unevenly between both ends of the scale. 'The device is still confused,' she whispered. 'But I'm reading *something* . . . a local disturbance. It might be hiding in here.'

Hasp slouched over his shiftblade and looked bored. 'It smells like it's here.'

Harper altered her position, and went through the procedure one more time. Finally she halted to one side of the stairwell, and slipped a Screamer from her tool belt. The delicate skeletal globe murmured in her hand, its Mesmer crystals sensing the proximity of uncontained spiritual energy. She twisted one hemisphere of the Screamer against the other, engaging the clockwork timer.

'Eight seconds,' she said.

Hasp shrugged.

'Six seconds.' Quickly, she checked her locator. 'No change. If it's here, then it *should* manifest when I trigger the Screamer.'

The door opened and Carrick strolled in. 'Harper, for god's sake, I've been searching the whole damn train for you. We're pulling into the portal station now. The guests are furious. This' – he batted a fist in the direction of Hasp – 'glass-wrapped bastard killed a passenger's nephew's pet. They'll be discussing lawsuits as soon as they can figure out who to sue. And the mess . . .' He stopped when he realized her full attention was on the Screamer in her hand. 'What the hell are you doing? What's that thing? Haven't you caught this demon yet?'

'Almost,' Harper said.

'Almost isn't good enough,' he replied. 'Do you think the PRC pays you to *almost* do your job? You'd better find the fucking thing now, or you're finished.'

'Two seconds,' she said.

Carrick's temper reddened his face. 'Not two seconds,' he snarled. 'Now!'

'If you say so.'

The Screamer screamed. The interior of the observation car blazed with crimson luminance as furious bolts of Maze-light crackled and flashed between its glass-panelled walls. There was a sense of building atmospheric pressure, a violent snap, and then the air thickened with an earthy, rotten stench. The sphere in Harper's hand glowed white. She dropped it, wincing – its metal frame was burning-hot. Carrick stumbled backwards, shielding his eyes, and knocked over a tea table. Hasp hefted his shiftblade. Harper backed away, gagging at the dense odour, while loops of Maze-light whirled and pulsed and contracted into a bloody knot, and then vanished with a pop.

Something remained there in its place.

Shorter than Hasp, but twice his bulk, the demon hunched over a stone hammer which looked heavy enough to level a mountain. It looked rather like a blisterman, but bigger. Grey sacs of skin covered every inch of its naked body; they were inflating and con-tracting like lungs. It was wheezing loudly – but Harper could not discern a mouth or nose in its face, just pinprick eyes which stared out from that tumescent flesh. The enormous muscles on its shoulders and arms glistened and steamed with red fluids born of forced manifestation.

It turned to Hasp and said, 'I am in pain. Why have you done this to me, angel?'

'Not me, soldier,' the archon replied. 'I've no quarrel with you.' His eyes were fading to a sombre grey. 'You have been the victim of a clockwork incantation. Technology, these people call it.'

The demon cocked its head for a moment, as though trying to digest this unfamiliar word. The blisters on its skull puffed in and out, hissing faintly. Finally it said, 'I am named Flower. I am trapped in this place. I heard noises. This is not the Forest of War.'

'You are aboard a steam locomotive bound for Coreollis,' Hasp said, 'in the country of Pandemeria.'

'Those names are unfamiliar to me. What is a steam locomotive?'

'A vehicle propelled by burning the souls of old Earth spirits.' The demon nodded.

'Be wary, soldier.' Hasp indicated Harper and Carrick with a nod of his head. 'These people will order me to kill you, and I am compelled to obey them. If you are slain in this world, your soul will go to Hell.'

Flower turned its pinprick eyes on Harper. 'I do not wish this to happen. Send me home.'

'I can't,' she said. 'Not until we discover who summoned you. Tell us his name.'

'I do not know it.'

Carrick had retreated to the far end of the carriage. The chief's face was slack and bloodless, but he found his voice at last. 'Get rid of it, Harper.'

'Hold on,' she said. 'We need to know who brought it here.'

His expression soured. 'What are you gabbling on about? *You* brought it here.'

'No,' she snapped. Why could the chief engineer not understand the most fundamental concepts of soul traffic? 'I pulled it out of hiding, forced it to manifest. I didn't summon it. It was already onboard the train, remember?'

'Well, send it back to Hell before the passengers get a whiff of it.'

'It isn't *from* Hell! We don't know—'

'I don't care!' Chief Carrick yelled. 'I want it out of here, *now*. It's dangerous.' He turned to Hasp. 'Kill it.'

The angel flinched and his glass armour flashed with pools of reflected aether light. His eyes suddenly darkened. The sound of clockwork came from his neck. He gave a grunt of pain, raised his shiftblade and stepped forward.

'Wait,' Harper said. 'I order you to leave it alone.'

Hasp staggered, then hesitated, his sword wavering.

'Kill it,' Carrick snarled at him. 'Kill it now. That's an order.'

Blood surged in a red web through the angel's breastplate. The parasite trapped within the mechanism in his head chattered furiously, and then *shrieked*. Hasp hissed and took another step forward, eyes churning from black to red to black again. Teeth clenched, he lifted his weapon again.

'No,' Harper cried.

Carrick spat the order through his teeth, 'Kill it!'

'I do not wish this,' the demon said.

The angel took a ferocious swing at the blistered creature, but Flower leapt back easily, now whirling its great stone hammer above its head.

'Stop it,' Harper yelled at Hasp. 'That's an order.'

Carrick grabbed her and clamped his hand over her mouth. 'Kill it!' he yelled.

Hasp roared in pain. He brought his shiftblade back up, changing it from a sword to a heavy bone club, and then swept it down, aiming for the demon's skull. The demon parried the blow with the shaft of its hammer. Petrified bone struck stone with a sound like a detonation. The concussion blasted half of the carriage window panes into shards. Bright fragments of glass exploded outwards into the night. Wind rushed in.

The demon had twisted its hammer and driven the angel's club down, pinning it against the floor. 'I do not wish this,' it said.

'Gods!' Hasp hissed. 'I . . . don't . . .' He slammed the heel of his free hand into the creature's face, sending it hurtling backwards. Flower crashed into a cluster of chairs and a tea table, smashing them to fragments. A vase of roses fell and shattered.

'Watch the furniture!' Carrick roared. He had a manic grin on his face; his eyes shone with violent lust. 'Don't smash anything else, angel, or I'll make you pay for it. I'll make you suffer so badly you'll think this is a pleasant dream.'

Harper struggled to break free of his grip, but he was too strong for her.

Hasp reeled, screwing up his eyes, then snapped them open again and gasped. The blood quickened and seemed to glow like molten iron inside his glass armour. Rose petals skirling around him, the angel advanced again.

Flower had already risen. The blisters on its face had burst and now wept clear fluids over its chin, but the demon didn't appear to have been injured. It hunched low, twirling its hammer again, its tiny eyes locked on the approaching opponent.

Harper tried to grab Hasp as he passed, but her fingers found no purchase on his smooth arm-bracer. The armour felt red-hot where she touched him. She twisted away from Carrick. 'Hasp, I order—'

Carrick silenced her with a punch to her stomach and then wrestled her against him. Harper felt the wind go out of her. She tried to reach the bulb in her belt, but couldn't move her arms against the chief's grip.

The angel advanced.

Hasp swiped at Flower, and again the demon danced away – surprisingly quickly for such a bulky creature. The hammer shot out, but Hasp diverted the blow by changing his club into a shield. A second violent concussion shook the observation car. Facets shattered and rained down around them. Fresh torrents of wind screamed through the carriage. 'I do not wish this,' Flower said.

'Don't break the glass,' Carrick yelled at Hasp. 'I order you not to smash any more fucking windows!'

The angel groaned and staggered back, clawing at the metal-and-bone mechanism at the back of his skull. Streams of smoke unfurled through his fingers. The parasite howled like a wild beast. Hasp closed his eyes. 'You . . .' he gasped. 'I . . . don't . . .'

'Finish it,' Carrick snarled.

Hasp was still reeling as Flower stepped forward and swung its hammer hard at the angel's chest. But the god raised his shield in time. The blow connected with a terrible thud. Hasp stumbled back a step, yet remained on his feet.

Carrick threw Harper aside and snarled at Hasp, 'Kill it now, without that damned weapon. Use your bare hands.'

Abruptly the angel dropped his shield. He lunged at the demon, grabbed its head between both hands and pulled it close to his chest. Flower tried to swing its hammer, but it had no room to move. Hasp hunched over the blistered thing and squeezed.

The demon gasped. 'I do not . . . wish this.'

'Yes,' Carrick hissed. 'That's it. Break that skull.'

'I do . . . not . . .'

'Harder!'

'No, Jan, please. For god's sake don't make him do this. Order him to stop.'

'I do not wish . . .'

'Harder!'

'Hasp!'

'I . . .'

★

355

After it was done, Carrick ordered the angel to find a mop and bucket and clear up the mess. Hasp obeyed the Chief Liaison Officer without a word, but his eyes stayed black for a long time afterwards.

Mina Greene was bored. She had pressed her nose against the exterior glass wall for three minutes, looking for ghosts in the bloody desolation beyond, but she soon grew tired of that. She had gathered up the god's sketched castles, then set to work improving them, adding people in the windows and flowers and flags on the balustrades, until the last pencil-lead had snapped. Finally she had crumpled all of the sketches into pellets and flung them at the other captives. They were all broad-shouldered Northmen with wheat-coloured hair and hard blue eyes. Once strong and proud Coreollis soldiers, they now slouched like broken men. They grumbled weakly as Mina threw her paper missiles. One of the older men even had the temerity to demand that she sit still and stop annoying him, and behave like the god-damn human being she was supposed to be.

Now Mina ignored him. It wasn't difficult: he was hideously scarred – all hunched over under his blanket, with only his scorched hands visible. They looked like they'd been roasted in a steamship furnace before being plated with glass. She ignored all of the others, but she singled this one out for special indifference.

He had the cheek to feign relief.

The train's steel wheels clattered on the tracks below: *Coreollis, Coreollis, Coreollis*. She wondered how Rys would respond to the return of these glass-skin warriors, now that they had been so thoroughly disfigured by Menoa. Would the god make a show of executing them? Would he inflict a second death upon these soldiers to punish them for dying on the battlefield the first time around?

The pumps in the corners of the slave pen puffed suddenly,

blowing fine red mist into the air. The soldiers breathed it in deeply, but Mina just wrinkled her nose.

The Mesmerists' one weakness. They could not survive for long without drawing power from bloodied air or earth or water. And this was why Rys would not dare to kill his own brother, Hasp. The blood of a simple soldier might sustain an Icarate or dog-catcher for a while. But the blood of a god was a far more dangerous thing to shed.

Invigorated by the hellish air, the soldiers stretched and shifted like men aroused from a long sleep.

'The train's slowing,' one of them said. 'We're pulling in some-where.'

Another man opened his eyes. 'The Larnaig ferry? Can you see Coreollis?'

'No.' The first soldier was peering through the carriage wall into the darkness beyond. 'We're still in Pandemeria. This is the Cog Portal.'

The second man grunted. 'Then they're sending us back to Hell. Lord Rys must have changed his mind about the handover.'

'Not a chance. This is just a temporary stop. The Red King is coming to meet his ambassadors.'

'Traitorous fucks.'

The soldiers had gathered along one wall to watch the train pull in. Mina could hear the locomotive slowing now, the thump of its engine, the hiss of steam and the clack of rails under steel wheels.

Mina thought of her own painted wagon so far away in Cinder-bark Wood, and her eyes suddenly filled with tears. She turned and hid her face against the wall, ashamed to let the others see her like this, and found herself staring at her own grubby reflec-tion. A sob found its way out of her throat.

'Quiet, girl.'

The old burned man had spoken to her. 'I don't want to listen to your bleating all night,' he went on. With his bent black limbs and crooked spine, he looked more like a ghoulish puppet than a man. She might have felt pity for him, if his grin hadn't been so sardonic and cruel.

'Don't you dare speak to me like that!' she snapped. 'I'm Mina Greene. I'm older than you.'

'I'm Mina Greene,' he mimicked in a sing-song voice. 'I'm Mina Greene, I'm Mina Greene.' His eyes narrowed on her. 'Who is Mina Greene? Shall we take off your blanket and see?'

She exhaled sharply, composing herself.

He began to crawl towards her. 'We'll all be dead again in a couple of days anyway,' he said. 'Why not enjoy ourselves now?'

'You'd better stay back,' she said. 'I'm dangerous. I know spells.'

'Oh, yes?'

Mina looked to the other slaves for assistance, but none of them would even meet her eye. 'Get away from me,' she cried. 'I'll scream.'

The old cripple sniggered. 'I'll enjoy that too. I haven't heard a woman scream in months.' He reached for her foot.

She kicked out. The glass scales on her heel clicked against those on his hand.

'Careful,' he hissed.

'I'll kick you harder next time.'

He grinned. 'Bad news for one of us.' Again he approached.

Mina sighed. 'I did try to warn you.' She made a quick gesture with her hand, as if drawing a knot in the air. Then she bit her lip, drawing blood.

The cripple suddenly froze and stared at her uneasily. Beads of sweat appeared on his forehead, and he began to wheeze. 'What . . . did you just . . . do?'

'I didn't do anything. You're the one who got all hot.' It made her smile every time she used that line. 'And look at where it's got you now.'

The man let out a gasp. 'I . . .'

'Can't . . .' Mina said, mimicking him, '. . . breathe?'

Steam curled from the cripple's glass scales, yet he remained rooted to the spot. The other men looked on in shocked silence as his scales glowed red. The smell of burning skin wafted through the slave pen.

'I told you I know spells,' Mina said. 'This isn't even a hard one.' She made another hand gesture, and the crippled man collapsed on the floor before her. Even from here she could feel the heat radiating from him.

An hour later he had cooled enough to allow Mina to touch his scales. She pulled one of the glass plates off his shoulder and hid it inside the folds of her blanket. It would make a good addition to her collection.

23

IRON ANGEL

The Pride of Eleanor Damask arrived at Cog Portal station shortly after nightfall. Steam billowed along the platform and around the tall cloaked figure standing alone on the platform. Aether lights popped and flickered overhead, illuminating the message someone had scrawled across the wall of a metal storage shed.

PLATFORM TWO FOR HELL

But there was no Platform Two. Beyond the solitary tongue of concrete alongside the line, the land sloped away in a steep embankment. At the base of this lay the Pandemerian door to Hell.

Harper had seen this place twice before, once on her journey to the Maze, and once on her return. After Cog's great plague, the ground there had sunk underneath the burial pit to form a vast basin. Over subsequent years the steadily thickening Mesmerist Veil had turned this depression into a broad red lake.

Now, as she filed off the train with Carrick and the Pandemerian passengers, Harper glanced down towards the pit again. Sections of one of the original steel tracks could be seen running along the base of the embankment, although the old station itself had been buried somewhere under their feet. Extra rails swept out to an engine shed, where Menoa's old troop-supply train had lain since the rains drowned these lowlands. Shades of grey and black defined the landscape down there; the low dykes and woodlands were as scrapes and smudges of charcoal on slate. Even in this weak light the engineer spied Portal Lake. Dark masses of misshapen figures were waiting around it, peering into the greasy waters.

King Menoa stood on the platform. He had wrapped himself in a long dark robe and altered his mask to resemble the visage of an elderly man with a strong, proud jaw and kind eyes – exactly the sort of benevolent ruler he wished his human ambassadors to see. The hem of his robe blew raggedly behind him, although there was no wind.

By his side was a child – a thin, sad-eyed girl of about nine or ten wearing a grey dress. Lines of script had been tattooed in crimson ink into her arms and face. Her small hand clutched one of the king's glass claws.

'Chief Liaison Officer,' Menoa said to Carrick. 'How good to see you again.'

'The pleasure is mine, Your Highness.'

The king turned to Harper. 'And my engineer,' he said. 'Are you enjoying your new position with the Railroad Company?'

'It allows me to serve you, Your Highness.'

'Of course. I trust Chief Carrick has looked after you well?'

This civility was all for show, Harper knew. The king was presenting a human facade. Nevertheless she nodded.

The passengers had by now noticed the legions waiting around the Portal Lake, and the smiles they had prepared for the Lord of Hell were failing within a growing atmosphere of uncertainty. They shifted uncomfortably, their gazes returning again and again to the darkness below the embankment where the king's demons waited. The thick wet air was already beginning to stain their fine clothes.

Menoa reassured them. 'Reinforcements for the front lines,' he said. 'A display of our power. When Rys kneels before you, he will know that the whole Mesmerist army stands at your back.'

As Harper's eyes grew accustomed to the gloom she saw that this great dark horde stretched far across the fields beyond the portal. And she could hear them – the legions of beasts snuffling under the stars, the rumble of war machines moving in the distance. Reinforcements? This looked more like an invasion force.

'Friends,' said the king. 'Mr Lovich . . . Mr Ersimmin . . . Dear Edith. Between you, you own most of Cog City – the factories, the railroad, even the lives of the citizens themselves. Without your help, the process of change in Pandemeria would have been long and bloody.' He spilled a fist of soulpearls onto the platform and waited while the passengers scrambled after them. These would contain the lowest caste of demons and perhaps the odd human, worthless to anyone who used such trinkets for power, but they were scooped up by the guests like diamonds.

'You helped to shape this world in preparation for my coming,' the king went on, 'and I thank you for that. You assisted me throughout this long campaign and, again, I am grateful.

'Tomorrow you will reap the rewards I have promised. Once Rys abandons his foolish war against us, Pandemeria will become the centre of our new world.' He urged the little girl forward. 'Here is your treaty, an unspoiled soul. Her name, of course, is Peace.'

Jones and Lovich frowned. Clearly this was not what they had expected; Harper could see their minds working to unravel this unexpected twist.

But then the child looked up at Menoa, and the king nodded.

The girl began to change, shrinking rapidly until she was a fraction of her original size. Her hair whirled around her, and then her body itself began to spin. She became a blur of tattooed script.

Her flesh turned the colour of parchment. A sharp intake of breath came from one of the female passengers.

Carrick stooped and picked up the scroll that had appeared in the child's place.

'Bring Rys's signature back to me,' King Menoa said. 'And I will return the treaty to the Ninth Citadel. May it last forever.'

A great howl went up from the waiting armies, like the sudden onslaught of a storm. The platform shuddered as ten thousand boots, hooves and claws beat against the earth around Portal Lake. The passengers flinched. Mrs Lovich buried her head in her husband's shoulder as a cold gale tore across the platform.

King Menoa turned to face his horde.

Brands flared in the darkness below the embankment, tens of thousands of them, and Harper saw the king's army clearly at last. There were ranks of Icarates and glittering Iolites and other, bulkier creatures with hammers for fists and great curling horns. The Blind composed a large part of this army, along with packs of dogcatchers and phantasms and Non Morai, and beasts like oxen or huge boars, and winged lesser demons, and men-shaped gladiators in bronze plate. War machines waited on the hills beyond the main force: great spiked spheres and smoking iron towers, lumbering armoured beasts carrying upon their backs cannon towers or crystal globes full of corpse mites and yellow flies. And in the middle of the plague pit stood an arconite.

A collective gasp came from the human onlookers.

Harper's gaze roamed up from the creature's skeletal feet, and up past its pelvis, and up to where the arcane engines thundered in its ribs, and up again to the skull still glistening red from the Portal Lake. The creature was colossal; its tattered wings, out-stretched, could have enveloped a mountain. In one bony fist it clutched an oak tree pulled from the ground nearby. In the other hand it held a locomotive shed. It had lifted the building up close to its eyeless skull, and was peering inside the way a child might inspect a new toy.

King Menoa sounded like he was smiling, but his glass mask, of course, gave nothing away.

'His name is Dill,' he said.

24

MENOA'S ARMY

Dawn came: thin and grey and flecked with puffs of lead and pewter. The skies lightened, and *The Pride of Eleanor Damask* began to climb out of the Pandemerian Lowlands towards the Moine Massif. Wheels thumping, stack blowing, whistle screaming, she followed a long snaking route up through the black volcanic hills that bounded the edge of the plateau. King Menoa's reinforcements meanwhile followed the Red Road running two leagues to the southwest. A vast plume of smoke from the king's war machines bent its way across the sky, while the troops marched in a long line behind. From this distance they looked like a river of ink flowing uphill from the portal basin. Only the arconite itself could be seen with any clarity. The giant had moved far ahead of its smaller brethren, and now stood among the hills below the Moine Massif.

Even these highlands had not been immune to Rys's torrential rain. The valleys and gullies below remained flooded, so that it seemed like they were now weaving through a chain of lagoons. Crescents of basalt rose from steaming pools, linked by causeways of metallic slag and cruel iron bridges. Fuels and oils left by the railway reconstruction effort made rainbow patterns on the waters, colourful skins that unravelled wherever the currents mingled. New maps named this place Callar Wash, but on old

maps the land had been called Callowflower. The train followed
the rims of hot calderas or plunged, shuddering, through dark
defiles, or was carried between islands by spans of silt- and weed-
clogged girders.

She clattered across bridges: Cutlass Bridge and Broken
Temple Bridge where a thousand empty lanterns depended from
hooks, out over the drowned farmland beneath Spinney Crag.
Smudged by a shifting dawn haze, the summit of the crag itself
still sulked above the waterline, diminished now from an impos-
ing mountain to a meagre sketch of dolerite and black pines.
Other trees could be seen in the oily waters below, now dead and
rimed with furs of crystal.

Harper had moved out of Carrick's room into a spare bunk in
the stewards' quarters. Uncomfortable in the unfamiliar surroundings, she had woken early and been unable to get back to
sleep. Now she stood on the terrace of Observation Carriage Two
and gazed down into the pools between the islands. Sometimes
she thought she saw fish below: impossible black shapes, huge and
motionless. There seemed to be faint green glimmers where their
eyes ought to be, an ice-cream sheen underneath where the belly
would be, but these objects never moved.

'Pike.'

Harper turned.

'The fish,' Carrick said. 'They're pike.'

'Pike don't grow to that size.'

'They do now.' The chief joined her by the glass balustrade and
peered down. Yellow sunlight slanted through the carriage under
his feet. 'There – you see?' He pointed at a long shadow hanging
beneath the water. 'They've changed.'

'*You*'ve changed,' she muttered.

He ignored this, continuing, 'Nothing should be able to live in
that queer water, but some things do. Fish from the old rivers and
canals; animals from the woods. The trees still grow, but not in

the same way they did before. People, too, maybe. The combination of Rys's rain and the Mesmerist Veil did strange things to the land here.'

'People?'

'The engineers who raised and rerouted the track swear it. They say the farmers are still down there, alive . . . but altered.' He was silent a moment, then he shrugged. 'I've never seen anything like that. A lot of workers drowned during the reconstruction. I suppose the survivors are superstitious.'

She nodded.

The *Eleanor* rattled across another bridge. Far below, a clump of farm buildings huddled around an earthen courtyard, the scene apple-tinted and woozy under twenty fathoms of water. Dark windows looked out over submerged fields and dykes and scraps of queasy woodland. Harper spied an old steam-tractor, and the carcass of some large animal now soft with white eels, and shivered at the thought of anyone still living down there.

What did they farm?

'I brought you a refill.' Carrick held out a flask of blood. 'I noticed you were getting low.'

She just stared at it.

'I'm sorry.' Carrick's smile looked ugly and desperate. 'That's what you wanted, isn't it? An apology. Well, there it is.'

'It's not enough, Jan.'

The lines around Carrick's eyes pinched. 'I'm asking for a second chance. You could do a lot worse than me. I was serious about the house in Highcliffe – a place of your own.'

'As your personal whore?' She snorted. 'I'll think about that offer if Menoa ever turns me away from Hell.'

Carrick spat into the water below.

Harper glanced back at Observation Carriage One. The *Eleanor* carried enough spare glass aboard for the midnight shift to repair most of the shattered windows, but many of the rest of the panes remained empty. Someone had suggested they cover these up with paper or squares of linen, but Carrick had insisted those patches would spoil the look of his train. Harper sighed: either way, the passengers would not be happy. They were bound to complain. 'Somebody summoned it,' she said. 'If you'd only let me interview the passengers, Jan.'

'I'm not getting into this again,' he replied. 'I've told you what I think.'

Carrick had refused to entertain the idea that the demon had been summoned. It had slipped out of Hell like countless other foul creatures had done, and now was dead – end of story, as far as he was concerned. He didn't want to bother his guests any more.

'The slaves at least . . .' Harper suggested.

'Out of bounds. We had one death already of suspected plague. You're not even to mingle with them.' She opened her mouth to argue (what proof did he have that the man had died of plague? He was old and crippled), but Carrick went on, 'And I don't want you going anywhere near that glass bastard until we arrive at Coreollis. I'm not having you tinkering with his goddamn head again. He's obstinate enough as it is.'

'What I did to the parasite has nothing to do with his behaviour. Hasp has been fighting the implant every step of the way. You're the one being stubborn here.'

'You admit he's dangerous?'

'Of course he's dangerous. I didn't want him released in the first place.'

The lines around Carrick's mouth tightened. 'You'd better go sweep the train again before the guests get up,' he said. 'I don't want any more surprises on this journey.'

Harper turned away from him. 'I was leaving anyway. The air stinks here; I don't want to breathe it too long.' She walked back towards the stairs which led down into the carriage below.

Carrick called after her: 'I'm not a bad man, Alice. You hear me? I'm not a bad man.'

The engineer quickened her pace. It scared her to think that he might be right.

'And I know why you're here,' he added.

She hesitated at the top step.

'I've seen the soulpearl you wear under your uniform,' he went on. 'Do you think I don't know why you hide it? Why you always clutch it when you're upset? Why you take it off at night before you come to bed?'

She turned slowly. 'A lot of people collect souls.'

'What soul?' Carrick chuckled. 'That pearl is empty. The holding patterns are there, but there's no glow, no ghost inside.' He studied her for a long moment before his eyes narrowed. 'Everyone knows what happened to your husband – the real story, not that bullshit the PRC put out.'

Harper made a dismissive gesture. 'I bought the jewel at the Garrison Market. It's fake,' she shrugged, 'but I liked it. I thought it looked pretty.'

'I've seen fakes before,' Carrick said, 'and that isn't one of them. You are wearing one hell of an expensive jewel, Alice. How many times did you have to open your legs before you could afford it?' He bared his teeth and his voice dropped to a whisper. 'Or did you just fuck Menoa himself? He certainly fucked you.'

'Don't . . .' She glanced over her shoulder as if expecting to find the king there. He had remained at Cog Portal, yet his presence still seemed to haunt the train.

Carrick's tone became contemptuous. 'You think I'm any worse than your husband?' he shouted. 'I survived the war, Alice, and Tom didn't – and there's nothing you can do about it. You should thank Menoa for keeping that coward in Hell.'

Harper stormed down the stairwell, her heart pounding like the train's own wheels. When she reached the observation lounge she

369

glanced up. Carrick was leering down at her through the transparent ceiling. She wanted to hide, but she couldn't think of anywhere to go. Her world was made of glass.

The train thundered on through the conical black hills, climbing steadily, crossing bridges and causeways between islands until the ground rose at last to meet the edge of the Moine Massif. From her viewpoint at the rear of the train, Harper watched the landscape unfold. White froth still clung to the rocks and grasses in places, a sour indicant of the extent of the water's retreat, but the landscape beyond remained untainted and naturally bleak. To the north, clear streams still chuckled and bounced down the slopes of Moine Mor. A dun heather moorland swept southwards towards Helmbog and the distant peaks of the Fossil Mountains, where the low sun could be seen gleaming like a copper penny in the pale sky. Ancient maps named that land Benecoir or Bencora. But most people knew it simply as Brownslough; Hafe's realm.

The king's army stayed on the Red Road, which had been regularly bloodied so as to maintain a direct road to the front lines. They could not dare leave that trail. Only the arconite wandered further afield. It had climbed right up onto the massif, and now paced the border of Brownslough.

During the war, the Pandemerian Railroad Company had posted pickets along the borders of Hafe's realm. King Menoa had been warring with Hafe's brother, Rys, after all. Harper rolled her empty soulpearl between her fingers as she recalled those early days: the incessant rain; the distant flashes across the horizon; the raging seas around the Highcliffe wharfs and pontoons. The wind had seemed to carry the booms of resonance cannon from halfway around the world. She closed her eyes, pressed the pearl against her chest.

But the god of dirt and poison had not retaliated. He'd killed those diplomats the PRC sent out to parley after the war, and yet he'd kept his own armies close. It seemed Hafe was quite content to let his brother Rys do all the fighting.

Gods were always difficult to predict. What devilry would they be up to now? Hafe sat in Brownslough and grew fatter. Cospinol's great skyship would be patrolling the seas beyond the Riot Coast, hunting any ships that ventured too close to his domain; while Sabor just watched the sand grains trickle through his castle in the Charrel Mountains. Mirith never strayed far from his elder brother, Rys, of course, following that handsome god like a loyal puppy. And Hasp brooded in the *Eleanor*'s slave pens even now.

Only Ulcis had been slain, murdered by an unknown assassin in Deepgate.

Harper clutched her soulpearl again.

If one god could die, why not two?

By midday the moor had become a blanket of cerise heather and white flowers rising towards the mountains all around. Pools of still water mirrored the vast blue sky, turning partially submerged boulders into islands hovering in their own pockets of air. The train pulled its banner of smoke in a long curve around Ialar Mor and through the Ialar Pass to where the coke-oven funnels of the town of Moine rose above the moorland beyond. Here the *Eleanor* stopped to refuel at the depot coal stage, where two strange things happened.

Edgar Lovich was butchered in his sleep. And the *Eleanor* picked up an unlikely passenger.

As much to stretch her legs as to avoid the clouds of coal dust which would inevitably descend around the train, Harper took a stroll out across the locomotive yard. She was careful not to stray too far from the train, and to take a full bulb of mist with her, for the sun would quickly sap her strength. Being dead had distinct disadvantages in the world of the living.

She envied the arconite Menoa had constructed from the angel Dill. Powered by a fragment of the Shattered God, it had been able to leave the Red Road, following the train across the plateau while the troops forced to march only on bloodied ground lagged far behind. The smoke from Menoa's war machines still stained the southeastern sky, but the distance between the *Eleanor* and the king's army had stretched. Now the arconite towered over the town of Moine, its vast wings covering most of the southern sky. The foul waters from the Portal Lake had now dried to a brown crust on its bones, but it did not need this blood or any mist or crimson earth to survive here.

Menoa had used a fragment of the Shattered God to create the arconite, and then butchered countless souls to widen the portal temporarily so that it could leave the Maze. He had unleashed a warrior capable of destroying entire cities and armies. Free from the confines of the Veil, this single great automaton was worth more to the king than his entire horde.

The rumble of coal came from behind as the *Eleanor*'s crew refilled her tender from the stage. Moine had been a mining set-tlement before the war, but Rys's rain had lifted the water table, swelling the town's tar pits past bursting. Now this noxious overflow had rendered the place uninhabitable. The PRC had cleaned up the yard itself, but the streets and lower walls of the workers' houses and coke factories had been abandoned to the viscid black liquid. Away from the train, an eerie silence blanketed the spoiled town, broken only by the sigh of a hot breeze and the occasional slap of a tin shutter against a brick wall. Moine, more so even than Cog Island, was a city for ghosts. Harper was startled when she heard a very human cry for help.

The shout had seemed to originate behind one of the old engine sheds which ran parallel to the main track. She stepped over the auxiliary rails and walked around the building to inves-tigate.

Parts of the yard's outer wall had collapsed, leaving only a chain of slender brick islands connected by rubble. This broken wall formed a promontory of sorts, jutting out across Moine's lake of tar to stop some five yards short of the cleaned concrete surface of the yard. A thin-faced man in a white suit was sitting here, waving a white parasol. Evidently he had reached the wall by climbing through the shell of one of the coke factories bordering the yard, and then walked along its uneven summit only to reach a place where he could not proceed any further without soiling his fine clothes on the thick black gloop all around. He wore a sheathed clockwork sword at his hip, and circular blue lenses over his eyes which now turned to face Harper.

'I require assistance,' he said. 'Would you be kind enough to help me?' He inclined his head at the tar separating him from the engineer. 'It's rather undignified, but I suppose I'll have to be carried.'

Harper folded her arms. 'Who are you? What are you doing out here?'

He gave a wan smile and a smooth bow. 'Isaac Pilby, renowned lepidopterist, published poet and lately an unwitting tourist. My guide, having reneged upon our deal in the field and demanded an additional – exorbitant – fee in order to have his entire village employed as porters, stole my luggage and my butterflies, before abandoning me over there.' He flapped a hand in the general direction of Ialar Mor. 'I walked all morning before I saw the smokestacks of this wretched place. With so much industry, one would have expected to find civilization.' He shook his parasol. 'Instead of cafés, I find a town knee-deep in some ghastly pollutant.'

'Tar,' Harper said. 'It stinks but you're safe enough. I doubt it's more than an inch deep. You might lose your shoes, but it won't do you much harm.'

'It may be shallow,' Pilby said, 'and it may be safe. But it is filthy. I have traversed this town from one side to the other in leaps and bounds to minimize the damage to my suit and shoes, and I have no intention of soiling them now. These brogues were hand-made in Skirl, you know?' He gave a small shrug, then adjusted his lenses. 'You'll just have to carry me over.'

Harper was about to reply, when she heard a clicking, whirring noise behind her and turned to see the glittering figure of Hasp approaching. Sunlight blurred through the extremities of the angel's transparent armour and gave him a flame-red halo. His brow crinkled beneath his glass half-helm, folding the tattoos above his brow. 'Refuelling is finished,' he growled, his gaze flitting between Harper and the stranded man. 'They sent me to find you.'

'Who did? Carrick?'

He nodded.

'An hour ago Carrick forbade me or anyone else from going anywhere near you.'

'Some of the ladies,' Hasp said, 'thought my armour would look splendid in the sunlight. So your boss obliged them, and then took the opportunity to demonstrate his power over me. Sadly, I remain compelled to obey the orders of Menoa's lackeys, so here I am. Who is this idiot on the wall?'

'Isaac Pilby,' Harper said. 'He collects butterflies.'

The angel studied the man for a moment. 'Let's get back then.'

'Excuse me,' Pilby called after them in a high voice. 'I say! Excuse me?'

The angel and the engineer kept walking.

'You can't leave me here,' the lepidopterist protested.

The *Eleanor*'s rear carriages came into view as Harper and Hasp neared the corner of the engine shed.

'Wait!' Pilby yelled after them. 'Listen! I have a magic stone.'

'Oh that's funny,' Harper muttered. She faced Hasp. 'How are you feeling now?' The angel's eyes had remained the same dark, brooding grey since she'd last seen him. 'Have you suffered any dizziness since . . .?' Since Carrick had forced him to murder.

'I'm fine,' Hasp said, in a tone that suggested he wasn't.

A shrill voice came from behind them. 'I can pay. That's what it's about, isn't it? You mercenaries! You're no better than Cohl's Shades. Very well, you've made your point, now name your fee.'

'The chief enjoys power,' Harper said to the glass-armoured god. 'That's why he orders you to do these things. But your resistance to his commands will kill you. If you obeyed without question, without thought, he'd lose interest and you might stand a better chance of reaching Coreollis alive.'

Hasp grunted. 'If I obeyed without question or thought, then I wouldn't deserve to live.'

Harper sucked in mist from her rubber bulb. 'What would you do if you *were* free?' she said, offering the bulb to Hasp.

Hasp glanced at her out of the corners of his eyes. 'I'd try to kill Menoa.' He shrugged. 'In this condition, I'd pose no threat to him, but it would be a worthy end.'

The engineer was silent for a while. 'I joined the Mesmerists for one reason,' she said at last. 'My husband Tom was an officer in the King's Reservists. After he died at Larnaig, I begged for an audience with Menoa. I wanted to convince him to give me Tom's soul.' She remembered the months of pleading with Carrick at the Cog Island Liaison Centre. 'I was rising quickly through the special engineering branch of the PRC, working on adapting Mesmerist technology to work in this world. It wasn't easy – we had to engineer solutions for metaphysical devices the king could simply will into existence in Hell. Carrick refused to pass on my requests to meet Menoa, but then, after I had a breakthrough with the first locators, the king actually asked to see me.'

'He thought you had potential?'

'The special engineering branch was crucial to the War Effort, and I was a crucial part of the branch. Once the king had heard my plea, he agreed to return Tom's soul in exchange for a guaranteed term of service.'

'And he reneged on that deal?'

'He applies his philosophy of change to everything, including his promises. I soon learned that I couldn't trust him.' She paused. What she was about to say, she had never told another person before. 'So I went to Hell myself to find my husband.'

Hasp nodded. 'You're not the first to try it.'

'But of course Menoa expected me to try just that. I ended up working for him in Hell instead.' She sucked in another long breath of mist from her bulb. 'And now I'm back here, and I'm dead, and I'd like someone to kill that bastard for me. Do you know anyone strong enough to accomplish such a feat?'

'I used to, but he's not the same god he was before. He's much more fragile now.'

Turning the corner, they stepped over the network of rusted steel tracks that led out from the engine shed. Harper glanced inside the building's wide door but there were no locomotives inside, just a vast cavernous space pierced by dusty shafts of sunlight. Weeds reached through glassless metal windows in the outer wall and spread out in green veins across tired brickwork. Ahead of them, the *Eleanor* waited on the main line behind the coal stage, her carriages aglow. A haze of fine black dust drifted from her tender and spread across the yard and the moor beyond.

The majority of the passengers had alighted and stood some distance from the train in groups of three or more, chatting or smoking clay pipes. Some carried porcelain cups of tea or flutes of white wine. Harper noticed Jan Carrick talking to a group of three ladies who were laughing and beating the air with their fans. Slightly closer, Ersimmin appeared to be engaged in a fierce debate with Jones. The pianist gesticulated wildly in Harper's direction, although he hadn't turned and thus could not be aware of her arrival on the scene. The older white-whiskered man shot a glance her way, and his face flushed.

'I should probably have helped him,' she said to Hasp, 'the man on the wall.'

The archon grunted. 'What kind of man asks a lady to carry him through a pool of sludge?'

'A lady?'

Hasp's neck buzzed. 'That was the demon talking,' he said.

A call came from behind them: 'I say!'

They turned.

Isaac Pilby had evidently resigned himself to the fact that he'd have to rescue himself. Shoeless and covered in tar up to his shins, the lepidopterist strode across the yard towards them, brandishing his folded parasol like a rapier, while his real sword swung in its white leather sheath at his side. He had been successful at keeping neither brolly nor blade entirely free of Moine's pollution, for the tips of both now sported six inches of black gloop.

'You,' he jabbed the parasol at Harper, 'abandoned me. And you,' now he jabbed the umbrella at the angel, 'are an abomination in glass. Now both of you are completely responsible for and deserving of whatever amercement the Pandemerian Railroad Company sees fit to extract from you as a result of this incident. I have powerful friends!'

'If someone ordered me to kill him,' Hasp muttered, 'I don't think I'd resist *too* much.'

Either Pilby didn't hear him, or he was choosing to ignore the angel. Chin thrust out, the little man strode on towards the train and her staring passengers, rocking his thin shoulders in an almost comical gait, as though desperate to squeeze every last shred of majesty from his sorely blemished appearance.

Jones was the first to approach him. 'My dear sir,' he said, eyeing the other man with what appeared to be a degree of suspicion, 'what on earth are you doing out here? Carrick, fetch a brandy for this gentleman at once.'

Carrick looked up from his audience, a line of annoyance creasing his brow – before he saw Pilby and the frown deepened.

'I do not require alcohol,' the shoeless lepidopterist said, 'merely a change of raiment and transport away from this foul place.' He planted the soiled tip of his parasol on the ground and raised his nose in an expression of haughty indifference. 'I will compensate you handsomely for the inconvenience of returning this locomotive to Cog City. But know that I fully intend to write a severe—'

'We'll take you with us,' Harper broke in, more to stop his endless prattling than from any great fear of reprisal. The sun was already making her feel nauseous and weak. 'But we're not heading back to Cog until the day after tomorrow. This train is bound for Coreollis.'

'Coreollis?' Pilby looked vaguely confused. 'But they closed the Larnaig ferry. There's no way to reach the city by train now. And Coreollis is *Rys's* stronghold.'

'The PRC have just reopened the ferry.'

'Well, that's bold,' said Edith Bainbridge, moving through the crowd of onlookers. She was wearing a different peach-coloured frock from the one she'd worn earlier. If anything it was peachier. 'You, sir, are interfering with a diplomatic mission,' she said to Pilby. 'Besides, why should you have a free ticket when we have financed this whole event? The idea is ridiculous. We've little enough room as it is.'

'Madame—' the lepidopterist began to object.

But Carrick broke in. 'Compensation, you say?'

Harper exhaled quietly through her teeth. Carrick had a familiar distant, calculating, look in his eyes. She half expected him to ask *How much?* but, given the present company, she doubted even Carrick would be so crass.

'Well, yes,' Pilby remarked. 'It's only fair. Return me to the terminus at Cog City and we'll discuss some payment for your services. I am a man of considerable means. Indeed, if I had known that the Pandemerian Railroad Company had reopened the route, I would undoubtedly have bought a ticket myself.'

Carrick grinned. 'Harper, find this gentleman some shoes, will you?'

But before the engineer could go and find Pilby some footwear, a cry came from one of the stewards. There had been a terrible accident. Edgar Lovich was dead. The passengers rushed back inside to discover the actor's body lying sprawled in one of the corridors. Lovich's wife, Yve, let out a shriek of horror and dropped to stem the flow of blood from her husband's body. But it was already too late. Edgar Lovich had died within the last hour. Someone had stabbed him in the chest.

Yet nobody, it seemed, had seen anything.

Harper gave instructions to the crew to mop up the spilled blood, and left the ladies to accompany the sobbing wife back to her bedroom. Then, ignoring Carrick's quarantine, she told Hasp to follow her back to the slave pens. As soon as they were out of earshot of the others, she asked the god, 'Did you kill Lovich?'

'Yes,' he replied without hesitation.

'Why?'

Hasp shrugged. 'I can't think of a plausible reason or motive.'

'Did someone order you to do it?'

'No.'

The engineer frowned. Not only was Hasp incapable of violence against any of Menoa's ambassadors without a direct order, but if someone had ordered him to slay the actor, then couldn't they also have ordered the god to lie so as not to implicate the real culprit?

She tried again. 'I order you to answer my next question truthfully. Did someone order you to kill Lovich?'

Hasp winced. He reeled, staggering against the carriage wall. And then he dropped to his knees on the floor, clutching his skull and moaning.

'Forget that order,' Harper said quickly. 'Hasp? Don't answer my question.'

The tension left the angel's face. 'No more questions,' he breathed. 'The parasite . . .'

Harper understood. Menoa's parasite was punishing Hasp for failing to answer her question. But it was also *preventing* him from answering that same question. The angel had been given two mutually opposing orders – he could not obey one without disobeying the other.

'If you were instructed not to reveal the identity of the murderer under any circumstances, then any question that threatened that order—'

'Might kill me,' Hasp finished in a despondent tone.

Harper was thinking hard. How could she ever get to the truth of this if Hasp could not speak?

If a passenger could get away with one murder, what else would they use the doomed god for? Would the engineer be at risk herself? She phrased her next question carefully. 'If I asked you to detail your exact movements since Carrick released you from the slave pen, would you wish to answer?'

'No,' the angel said.

Of course not. Even that information would implicate someone. 'Let's get you out of the passengers' way, then,' she said.

Back in the slave pen, Harper studied the remaining captives. After the cripple's death, eight of Rys's Northmen remained, together with Hasp's young female companion from his palace in Hell. The men sat apart from each other in silence, the scaly bodies wrapped in blankets. Not one of them would meet the engineer's eye. 'Did any of you see what happened?' she asked.

The girl spoke up. 'Why? What happened?'

'A passenger was killed.'

'Someone was killed in here too, but you don't seem so bothered about that.'

Harper shrugged. 'What do you expect me to do about it?' The truth was: Carrick had actually threatened to put her off the train for pursuing the matter. He cared nothing for these people. Ten slaves or nine, it made no difference to him. Harper doubted that it made much difference to Rys either. The handover was nothing more than a gesture of goodwill – intended to show the citizens of Coreollis that their new king was benign and just.

The presence of Menoa's vast and terrible army at their doorstep would merely reinforce the point.

A low sky and ceaseless drizzle shrouded *The Pride of Eleanor Damask*'s arrival at the southern end of the Ialar Pass. Smoke from her stack boiled up between wet granite cliffs on either side, rock faces which still bore the pick-axe scrapes of those slave labourers who had widened the natural ravine here in recent years. Overhead the clouds bunched together in clumps like dirty sheep's wool. The train slowed, the solid thump of her pistons reverberating in the narrower space. Then she sounded her whistle. Echoes bounced among the hidden, cloud-wrapped mountain peaks, before a horn-blast from the *Sally* outpost answered the call. The soldiers stationed ahead, just beyond the pass, would now be preparing to wake the ancient steamer which would carry them across Lake Larnaig to Coreollis.

Another voice answered the whistle, this one a long low roar which rumbled across the heavens. Menoa's arconite came into view, striding between the foothills at the base of Rael Canna Mor. Its skull and shoulders were lost above the clouds, giving it the appearance of a decapitated giant. Engines thundered behind its ribs, powered by some arcane system of blood and fuel the Mesmerists had developed in Hell. Its voice echoed like thunder over the hidden mountain peaks:

'I am ready to serve.'

It turned away and strode quickly into the mists ahead, shaking the ground under its feet.

To watch this spectacle of divine engineering, the passengers had gathered upon the viewing platform of Observation Car One. Rain dripped from colourful umbrellas as the party waited: the men in one group, smoking cigars while they discussed in layman's terms the mechanics, torque and forces about to be employed; the ladies in an excited huddle, whispering about some duke and his mistress and what she had revealed to so-and-so three months ago.

Harper stood back from the group in an attempt to avoid the occasional acerbic glances from both Isaac Pilby, who still blamed her for the loss of his brogues, and Edith Bainbridge, who held the engineer accountable for everything else that had gone wrong, including the weather. She inhaled mist from her bulb whenever she felt her strength begin to wane.

Jones had given the lepidopterist a pair of shoes from his own wardrobe, while Ersimmin, being of a closer size to the newcomer, had donated several of his own crimson suits. Both the pianist and the elderly reservist seemed to have taken a special interest in Pilby, for they rarely left the small man's side. The three of them together, in their dark red suits, reminded Harper of that fractured glimpse she'd first seen of the pianist through the music-car ceiling.

Did this trio have more in common than the white sword sheaths they each wore? She didn't dwell on the matter, for whatever common ground they shared would be cinched by the social circle in which they moved – a closed world to someone from Harper's working background.

Yet Jan Carrick seemingly remained unable to see the gulf of this class divide. Pilby had come to some financial arrangement with Menoa's Chief Liaison Officer, who evidently regarded this as the first rung of a ladder that would raise him to a position of equality with the very guests he fawned over. The passengers tolerated the chief, of course, but they would never welcome him into their fold. They smiled and chatted with him, but with a barely concealed contempt Carrick utterly failed to notice.

At a second horn-blast from beyond the gorge, Harper heard the hiss and squeal of the *Eleanor*'s brakes. Carriage linkages compressed beneath her, then took up the strain again with a series of clanking jolts. The mist pumps exhaled, turning the air momentarily red and coating the surrounding rocks. The rhythm of the train's pistons slowed. Through the billowing smoke ahead, Harper glimpsed the walls of a keep rising above a slope of black mud and quarried rocks. Flanked by two musketeers, a Company signalman stood behind the parapet on the roof of the building, waving a red flag.

The railway line branched here. The old line turned east and followed a sloping shelf cut from the rock of the Moine Massif, a gradual descent that took it down to the abandoned village of Larnaig at the water's edge four hundred feet below. The new line was much shorter, and more dangerous.

Harper couldn't drag her gaze from the signalman's red flag, which struck her as some dim portent of doom. They had a saboteur and a murderer aboard. Wouldn't the perilous descent to Lake Larnaig provide the perfect moment for foul play? Harper studied each of the passengers carefully, searching for any emotion or expression which might betray a hidden agenda.

She saw nothing suspicious.

While the murderer was most likely to be one of Menoa's own

ambassadors, the saboteur need not be a passenger at all. She glanced back along the train. Stewards were busy inside each of the carriages, wrapping up loose and breakable items and stowing them away in preparation for the descent. Those vague shapes moving inside the frost-walled accommodation cars would be more staff performing this same task with the passengers' belongings.

Finally the train huffed free of the ravine and out into the base of a quarry abutting the northern edge of the Moine Massif. Here the railway line which had brought them all the way from Cog Terminus finally came to an end, halted by a precipitous drop of four hundred feet down to Lake Larnaig itself. Crescent cliffs of ochre rock formed a basin between the slopes of Ialar Mor on one side and an ancient Arnic burial site in the shadow of Rael Canna Mor on the other. The unremarkable keep Harper had glimpsed earlier squatted to the left of the tracks among slopes of weather-worn scree, mud and great wet mounds of anthracite. Opposite this, the flooded imprints of boots marked paths between hummocks of crushed limestone and shale, and sumps where old steam-diggers had been left to corrode in pools of orange rain-water.

The last excavations undertaken here had undermined the burial site itself, exposing the tunnels and chambers that the ancients had burrowed in the clay subsoil. Someone had even packed these openings with lime to discourage Non Morai from gathering where the dead had once lain. Harper wondered vaguely what the workers had done with the bodies they'd already unearthed. The remains of four cairns squatted above the cliffs, their tumbled mounds of stone patched with white lichen.

Ahead, the smoke cleared to reveal the very end of the railway line. The Larnaig ferry had already built up a head of steam; her funnels were pumping cords of white and grey smoke into the clouds. A pre-revolution eight-decked paddle steamer, the *Sally*

Broom was a hulk of sepulchral metals. Ornate steel passenger decks clung to her superstructure like drapes of cobwebs, all lit by yellow oil lanterns which shuddered to the thump-thump-thump of her engines. Ten or so of her crewmen were busy at winches, lowering a wide gangway in the vessel's stern, which led into her hold. Chains rattled, and then the gangway boomed down, slamming neatly into an indentation in the quarry floor. The steel tracks now led all the way into the ferry's hold – a cavernous space large enough to swallow *The Pride of Eleanor Damask* and all of her carriages.

Harper's gaze travelled out beyond the lip of the quarry to where the bulk of the old steamship appeared to float, impossibly, in open air four hundred feet above Lake Larnaig. It took her several moments before she was able to reconcile her preconceptions of the landscape with the sight of the four enormous skeletal fingers gripping the hull.

The arconite held the steamship in one bony hand, her stern pressed against the uppermost edge of the cliff.

With its feet lost somewhere in the swollen lake four hundred feet below, and its skull hovering like a moon in the gauzy sky, the bone-and-metal colossus remained completely motionless, hunched low over the lip of the Moine Massif as though it had rusted solid while inspecting the connections between the railway line crossing the quarry floor and the steamship it held in its skeletal grip. Grease glistened on the cogs and pistons visible between its knuckles, and on the many shafts and hydraulic rams in its forearms and spine. Countless souls swam in its chemically altered blood. It had two engines: one engine, the size of a locomotive shed, occupied its skull and controlled the movement between vertebrae, and hence the flex of the spine; the second, much larger engine, was housed within the ribcage and gave power to the automaton's reinforced limbs. It had wings in proportion to its torso, yet they were tattered and useless, as thin as the clouds that now enveloped them.

There was a collective intake of breath from the passengers, and then Jones said, 'Good grief.' The old reservist had taken an abrupt step back. 'Up close it's so . . .' he shook his open brolly at the sky '. . . big.'

'The automaton is modelled on the form of the controlling soul,' Harper explained. 'It's less stressful for a spirit to accept a form it considers natural. Its size was merely dictated by what was possible. The larger the arconite, the more damage it can cause.'

'You mean this machine was once an angel?' Jones asked.

She nodded. 'Dill was one of the guardians of Ulcis's temple in Deepgate. We caught him in Hell.'

'Dill?' Jones laughed uneasily. 'It suits him, I suppose.'

A horn sounded inside the easternmost keep, drowning out the passengers' chatter. The signalman on the roof of the building lowered his red flag below the level of the parapet and *The Pride of Eleanor Damask* shuddered to a halt. Steam hissed from brake-piston pressure valves beneath her carriages.

'. . . until recently,' Carrick was answering a question from one of the group. 'And yet the king thought this way would be smoother. He feared the constant movement would shake the ship too much and damage our captives. It's only a short distance across the lake to Coreollis.'

'It's hideous for a reason,' Edith whispered to one of her companions. 'To strike terror into Rys's Northmen,' she explained, waiting until the other lady nodded, before adding, 'The king told me he might make more of them if this one is successful.'

Harper said nothing, knowing King Menoa had already constructed twelve other arconites. All he required now was enough blood to release them from Hell.

Carrick grinned. 'Even the gods cannot match our strength,'

he said. 'With warriors like this, Pandemeria will become the dominant world force. Menoa has given us a great future.'

A laugh from down in the quarry distracted Harper. The train driver had hopped down from the engine and was now chatting amicably with two Company officiators in slate-grey uniforms, who had strolled out from the keep to meet him. One of these men had apparently made a joke. After the officiators' release forms had been completed to their satisfaction, the driver tipped his cap to each of the two others in turn and then climbed back aboard the train. At a wave from one of the uniformed men, the signalman on the keep raised his red flag again. *The Pride of Eleanor Damask* jolted, and then huffed forwards, closer to the edge of the cliff where the Larnaig steamer waited in its cradle of bones.

Harper gazed up at the arconite as the train inched along. Rain slicked the broad expanse of cranium and dripped from ridges in the guano-spattered skull. The eye sockets were deep caves full of wheeling gulls and dark machinery. Hydraulic tubing veined naked bones everywhere, while metal vats, valves, ramrods and camshafts, all slick with black grease, crowded within the chest cavity.

A rumble shook the carriages. The glass train began to inch across the iron gangway into the hold of the *Sally Broom*.

'Condensers,' the driver shouted from the engine cab.

A locomotion engineer threw a switch on the control panel beside the driver, turning on the *Eleanor*'s condenser pumps. A furious clattering came from the train's engine; the clouds of steam above her stack dwindled to a wisp.

'We're rerouting the exhaust,' Carrick explained to the passengers, 'and condensing the steam back into water.'

'It's very noisy,' Edith complained.

'True,' the chief admitted, 'but preferable to venting so much hot vapour into an enclosed space. The mine trains in Moine and Cog use the same system.'

The arconite did not move even as the locomotive, the tender and then the leading carriages were swallowed by the steamship's cavernous hold. Three of the ship's crew appeared on the gangway, bending low to check the steel links where the sections of the Cog railway joined those of the *Sally Broom*'s deck. A dank, rusty darkness engulfed the passengers as the *Eleanor* rumbled further inside the vessel. The sound of the condensers became louder, rattling between bulkheads.

'Oh, this is awful.' Edith's exclamation had a hollow ring to it. 'How are we supposed to see anything at all? There aren't any windows!'

Carrick had to raise his voice above the booming engines and the clacking of the condenser pumps. 'We'll alight as soon as the train is fully aboard. The ship has a splendid observation deck, for which the cooks have prepared a buffet lunch.'

'It doesn't look very splendid from here,' Edith retorted, sweeping an angry gaze across the orange puddles on the floor. 'I don't want to spoil my dress.'

'I'll stay here with you.' Isaac Pilby thrust out his chest and gripped the hilt of his sheathed sword. 'We can avail ourselves of the *Eleanor*'s dining car.'

'You shouldn't even be here!' Edith cried. 'And if you're staying, I'm going.' She spun on her heels and stomped away across the glass carriage roof towards the stairwell.

'I rather think you put your foot in it there, old boy,' Jones muttered to Pilby.

The lepidopterist gave the old man a withering smile, yet Harper thought she saw an odd hint of satisfaction in this expression. Had the little man *wanted* to stay here alone?

When the hunting platform at the very rear of the train was finally aboard, the driver eased the locomotive to a stop. The

Eleanor's kitchen staff disembarked first. Guided by another two of the *Sally*'s crew, they carried oil lanterns and wicker hampers out across the hold towards a stairwell that would take them to the upper decks. Stewards mustered all of the passengers except Pilby – who had elected to stay – and then wasted no time in herding everybody off in the wake of the picnic baskets. Harper first refilled her bulb, then hopped down from the carriage as more men ran back to raise the ship's gangway and to chain the train's wheels and axles to steel hoops set in the deck.

The low drone of engines followed the guests up a carpeted stairwell, past boiler and crew decks. They emerged into a bright, if somewhat musty, saloon. The *Eleanor*'s stewards were already unpacking the buffet onto long tables set beneath the lines of portholes on either side of the spacious room. Orange flames puttered in the gasoliers overhead, casting a rich light over the tarred bulkheads and threadbare carpet. Hatches to port and starboard opened onto narrow grey-metal passenger decks and the mist-heavy skies beyond, while a set of double doors in the bow had been flung open, giving access to a wide, wooden hurricane deck. The scent of freshly baked bread from the lunch tables mingled with the odour of burning coal.

Harper wandered outside and peered over the hurricane-deck balustrade. Clouds of smoke from the *Sally*'s funnels blew across the edge of the Moine Massif, enveloping the arconite's forearm up to its elbow. The engineer spied intricate patterns of loops and whorls etched into its massive bones – similar to those found on Ayen's old construction machines. Seen to the starboard side of the steamship, a mass of heavy machinery filled the skeleton's ribs. At its heart, a dull red light glowed.

'Ladies and gentlemen,' Carrick called from the saloon, 'if you will follow me outside, we'll get a better view of the spectacle.'

The passengers assembled on the deck behind her, but Harper didn't turn away from the view. From this vantage point she could look far out across Lake Larnaig. Shafts of sunlight pierced the clouds to the west and dappled the silver waters far below. She leaned out and looked straight down the side of the steamer's hull. Four hundred feet below, the waters had risen above the old mine depot at the base of the plateau. A stone quay with its cranes and mooring stanchions was dimly visible under the surface of the lake and, clustered around the huge feet of the arconite, lay a great red-brown heap of sunken ships and steam locomotives.

'Carrick,' she muttered, 'what are those?'

The chief responded with an angry hiss, 'Don't make a fuss about them.'

'I'm not making a fuss. I'd like to know why there's a pile of wrecked ships and trains clustered around the arconite's feet.' She counted the hulls of five vessels, and as many locomotives, lying half-buried in the silt at the bottom of the lake. In each case, a section of the sunken trains had remained partially inside the hold of one of the ships, having apparently spilled out of it. 'And I'd like to know why two – no three – of the ships down there have the name *Sally Broom* painted on their hulls. I was under the impression that this was the only vessel to bear that name.'

'I'm rather curious about that, too,' Jones murmured. The old reservist had joined them and now stood beside Harper with his hand resting lightly on the grip of his rapier. He, too, was peering down intently at the submerged hulks. 'Those steamers look so badly damaged, one might assume that they'd been dropped from a great height.'

'No,' Carrick began, 'I can assure—'

'What's that, old boy?' Ersimmin now wandered over to stand beside Jones. He looked down. 'Oh, my!' he exclaimed. 'That's rather unnerving, isn't it? You know, I did hear a rumour that another arconite had been constructed before this one.'

'The Skirl demon,' Jones confirmed. 'I don't think it was an arconite though. Nobody in the Liaison Office will talk about it.'

Carrick shifted uncomfortably. 'There's no truth to those rumours.'

'What have you boys spotted now?' Edith Bainbridge's frock rustled towards them across the hurricane deck. She peered down and frowned. 'What are those?'

The Chief tried to guide her away, but she resisted, an expression of distrust now forming on her thin face.

'Sunken ships,' Ersimmin said, 'and locomotives.'

'Ships?' Edith was still frowning down at the wreckage. 'Why would so many ships sink there? Is there a reef?'

Ersimmin chuckled. 'No doubt that's it, Edith.'

'The stewards are now ready to serve,' Carrick announced.

But Edith Bainbridge, whose mind had finally grasped the implications of the scene below her, suddenly shrieked, 'Good grief! Stop the descent, stop the descent!' She reeled, turning the full extent of her wrath on Carrick. 'What in the name of Cog's Dungeons do you mean to do to us? Kill us all? Open the doors, I'm getting off this ship right now!'

The other guests rushed over.

'Miss Bainbridge,' Carrick said, 'there were some initial . . . teething problems with an earlier automaton. But I can assure you that these have now been fixed. There's really no danger at all.'

'So there *was* an arconite at Skirl,' Jones muttered to Ersimmin.

'And it would seem to have passed this way,' the pianist replied.

Edith stabbed a gloved finger at Carrick. 'Those are not teething problems.' Her shrill voice rose above the sound of the steamer's engines. 'That is a graveyard, and I am getting off before this vessel ends up down there too.'

At that moment a horn blared in the quarry behind them and, after a heartbeat, was answered by a blast from the *Sally*'s own foghorn. Harper felt a shudder run through the hurricane deck and looked up to see a forest of piston-shafts and wheels turning inside the arconite's ribcage. Gulls scattered, screaming, around the huge machine. The red light at the heart of the engines darkened, and started to pulse.

And then the bone-and-metal automaton raised its vast grinning skull above the quarry and straightened its spine. Its thin wings unfolded, extended and cut through the clouds, shedding sheets of water. The steamship trembled again, then lurched. Harper sensed her locator murmuring against her hip. She slipped the device from its holster, wound it quickly, and studied the wavering needle for a moment before relaxing. She had registered nothing more than a surge of power from the fragment of Iril inside the arconite's heart.

The sound of metal scraping on rock came from the rear of the *Sally Broom*, followed by the shouts of men.

'Lines clear!'

'Lock the gangway.'

Chains rattled; the steamship trembled. The huge engine inside the arconite's ribcage was churning furiously now, pumping chemically altered blood through its metal veins. Its red heart-light throbbed, brighter and faster. Dark walls of gears chattered. Piston-shafts moved in its arms; cam-shafts turned, quickening. A mighty hiss came from the skull, and Harper felt the air stir. She clutched the rail of the hurricane deck.

In one monstrous hand, the arconite lifted the steamship – locomotive, passengers and all – away from the edge of the Moine Massif plateau and out into the open air.

'Ladies and gentlemen,' Carrick shouted over the clamour of working metal, 'let us return inside where we can enjoy the descent in comfort.'

'I'm not going anywhere,' Jones exclaimed. 'This is too good a sight to have to watch through any porthole windows.'

The ship lurched violently and then halted. Her funnels gave a massive groan as they strained against the main deck of the ship.

Harper stumbled, but the old reservist grabbed her. 'Our gigantic friend needs to learn gentleness,' Jones remarked. 'Another movement like that could break this vessel in two.'

She caught her breath. 'I hope that didn't shatter some of the more fragile glass inside.'

'I'm sure the staff have wrapped up everything breakable.'

'Not the slaves.'

'Oh,' Jones's face fell, 'I see what you mean.'

Ersimmin had caught hold of Edith Bainbridge, who was now beating at the pianist with her fan. 'Get off me, you lout. It's going to drop us! I must find myself a life-preserver.'

For a few moments the ship remained motionless in the arconite's grip. Harper leaned out over the balustrade and peered back along the hull. Beyond the vessel's stern, the wet brown cliffs of the Moine Massif sank a sheer four hundred feet down to the calm waters below. A blizzard of gulls skirled around the ship. The arconite's skull turned slowly, then moved closer until its yellow grin filled the sky above them. Harper's locator gave out a sudden shrill tone.

'What is it?' Jones asked.

She stared hard at the device, with a growing sense of dread. Its fluctuating needle darted back and forth between either ends of the scale. Crystals pulsed fiercely inside.

'I don't know,' she admitted. 'The *locator* doesn't know. It's panicking again.'

The reservist kept one hand on the hilt of his sword. 'Another uninvited guest?'

She shook her head. 'It might just be the proximity of the—'

But just at that moment another massive jolt unbalanced the passengers. Still gripped in the automaton's skeletal hand, the ship began a sudden rapid descent.

'Cruel heavens!' Jones cried. The old man's long white hair

lashed about his face as the ship dropped closer to Larnaig's waters. 'Do we need to descend quite so briskly?'

'I expect that need has little to do with it,' Ersimmin replied. The pianist had extricated himself from Edith. Now, like his reservist colleague, he appeared to be quite relaxed – an observation which could not be extended to encompass the other guests. 'From the expression on our host's face,' Ersimmin went on, inclining his head towards Chief Carrick, 'it seems that we are currently experiencing yet another of his teething problems.'

Carrick was clutching the deck rail with both fists, his face a curdled off-white colour. Most of the passengers had found something to hang on to by now. The gentlemen had grabbed the saloon bulkheads or deck balustrades; the ladies clung to the gentlemen.

The steamship shuddered again, and then tilted sharply towards the bow. Several passengers stumbled. Plates toppled and smashed within the saloon.

Ersimmin's voice radiated calmness. 'I'm beginning to understand why the Mesmerists hired our railroad company to support the War Effort,' he said to Jones. 'They make terrifying soldiers, but they haven't quite got the hang of transportation matters.'

25

BASİLİS

The jolt had sent two Northmen crashing into each other, shattering their glass-scaled skins. Mina's feet slipped out from under her on the slick floor, and she struggled to push herself back up onto her hands and knees. Her hands were now wet and red. Oil lanterns stuttered in the deep gloom of the ship's hold, throwing lances of light through the transparent carriages.

'Wasn't this what you wanted?' Hasp cried. 'A quick return to Hell.'

'I asked *you* to kill me,' she replied. 'I didn't ask for this.'

'An unusually biased form of suicide. Still, there's a glut of fresh souls here. Time for some thaumaturgy, if I'm not mistaken?'

'How did you know?'

'I've known from the start.'

She wrinkled her nose.

The slave pen lurched again and another of Rys's former soldiers crashed against the wall. His glass scales cracked at the wrists, elbows and head; his life poured out of him.

Mina muttered a prayer: an appeal to her guardian, Basilis, the Hound Master of Ayen. She made sigils in the bloody floor:

One red soul for the Forest of Eyes,
A second for the Forest of Teeth,
The third to rot in the Forest of War,
If you'll aid your servant now.

Hasp grunted. 'It's been a while since I've witnessed blood thaumaturgy and longer since I've come across that bastard Basilis. This'll be fun.'

The stink from the Forest of War greeted Mina's nostrils as something moved within the red pool on the floor, then reached out roots and branches, growing until it filled the space before her. This was Basilis's heart tree, a manifestation of Ayen's Hound Master himself.

Those Northmen who were still alive to witness this apparition now scuttled away to the far corner of the chamber, their eyes wide with fear and horror.

A deep voice rolled out from the tree: 'These are weak souls, thaumaturge.' Basilis's arboreal manifestation dripped and shuddered. 'As thin as memories.'

'They're still souls,' she retorted, 'and I didn't have to kill them myself. I need your help again, Basilis. We need to do something about Dill.'

The Hound Master laughed. 'You always underestimate yourself, Mina,' he said. 'You summoned a guardian from the Forest of War without my help. You killed one of your fellow captives without my help. And didn't you place a piece of your soul inside the arconite without my help? All you have to do now is reach out to it.'

'I can't!' she protested. 'The Mesmerists changed me. My soul is all muddled up and . . . *sore.*' She almost stomped her foot down, but thought better of it. 'Besides, I'd feel more comfortable if you were there with me.'

Another laugh issued from the tree.

Hasp said, 'This is a new form for you, Basilis. Didn't you used to be a dog?'

'Hasp . . .' the tree sighed. 'Why are you not in Hell?'

The god grunted. 'The Mesmerists caught us both. They assumed *she* was my woman.'

'Your *woman*?' Basilis growled.

'Relax,' Hasp said. 'She's not my type.'

Mina felt suddenly cross. It wasn't that she *liked* the god – not in *that* way. But for him to have a type that didn't include her seemed desperately unfair. The floor lurched again and she slid a yard to the left. She reached out to grab the heart tree's roots, but Basilis withdrew them. A low snarl came from the demonic tree.

Oh no.

'Hasp and I both happened to be looking for Dill,' she said quickly. 'That's all. I'm sorry I left you alone in Cinderbark Wood, but I couldn't pass up the opportunity to sneak into Hell undetected. Deepgate's portal was already teeming with Mesmerist shades, so I didn't want to risk it. You know I'll come back for you just as soon as I can.'

The steamship plummeted. In the iron gloom of her belly, *The Pride of Eleanor Damask* heaved and groaned against the chains binding her wheels and axles to the hold's deck. Steel links stretched and warped. The glass carriages ground against each other, straining to be free of their shackles.

Basilis's voice sounded like thunder. 'I am no longer in that poisonous forest,' he rumbled. 'And I am no longer alone. A Spine woman and her companion found my physical form in Cinderbark Wood. They brought me to Cospinol, who has delivered us by skyship to Coreollis. While you were in Hell, Mina, I have travelled across the world. Now I am in Rys's own palace, not two leagues away from you. From here we can watch the arconite's approach across Lake Larnaig.'

'Woman?' Mina said. 'What *woman*?'

The demon chuckled. 'She is no thaumaturge, Mina.'

Another jolt sent blood sloshing against the slave-pen wall. Mina slipped, but one of Basilis's roots writhed across the floor, curled softly around her wrist, dragging her back towards the tree. Even Hasp was gripping the demon's roots. But the Northmen were still fearful of the apparition and would not approach it. They fell and hit the wall hard, cracking their scales. While these unfortunate soldiers tried in vain to stop their lives pouring out, Mina clung to her demonic master.

'Now reach out for the splinter,' Basilis said. 'Show these poor frightened gods what a Penny Devil and his guardian can do.'

'I need your help to see it clearly.'

'Very well.'

Mina envisioned herself in the Forest of Eyes – the first of her master's three aspects to survive his expulsion from Heaven. A scrawl of black trees surrounded her, as dense and tangled as a thicket of thorns. The twisted boles and branches glistened as countless eyes within the bark turned towards the thaumaturge.

Mina strolled up to the nearest tree and peered into one of its eyes. She frowned and then looked into another, and another, while millions more stared down at her.

'Help me, Basilis,' she cried.

But the eyes just mutely blinked.

Harper's knees struck the deck as the steamship hit the surface of Lake Larnaig with a boom. The hull pitched violently and a shower of icy water drenched the hurricane deck, soaking her and everyone else on it. Edith Bainbridge screamed and stumbled backwards, but Jones and Ersimmin, who had both somehow remained upright, caught her between them. The other passengers had fallen into an unseemly jumble of silk frills, fans and hankies.

Carrick remained to one side of the group, still cowering, with both of his arms wrapped around a wooden life preserver. The deck righted itself, groaning, then rolled over in the opposite direction. Water rushed up the hull below, and subsided in a sucking wave of froth as the steamship rocked to a gentle halt.

'I will sue, I will sue, I will sue.' Edith's hair hung in a limp black net across her face, framing dark tears of eyeliner beneath her shock-wide eyes.

'Calm yourself,' Jones said. 'It's not over yet. Listen!'

Harper tilted her head. An odd humming, crackling noise was beginning to build; it seemed to thrum along the ship's iron banisters and reverberate through the bulkheads. She checked her locator.

'A door opening?' Jones ventured.

Harper studied the device, trying to make sense of what she was reading. The silver needle shifted and bounced between ideographs, resisting her attempts to isolate the source of this burgeoning spiritual energy. 'It is the same thing as before,' she said. 'This energy isn't coming from Hell or Earth. There are portals opening and closing *everywhere*, but they don't lead to the Maze.'

'Is that *possible*?'

She clenched her teeth. 'It's as if something is searching the ship.' Her gaze travelled the length of the deck where green and black flames flickered and diminished, lingering around the iron nails in the planks. The cold fire leapt from the deck and licked the metal balustrades and fixtures, burning nothing but exuding an ancient and earthy odour.

'It smells like a *forest*,' Harper said.

The passengers were backing away from these weird fires, covering their noses against the stench, as the *Sally Broom* rocked back and forth on the surface of the lake. Harper watched as the flames poured between the rails of the balustrades and cascaded down the hull to where the submerged hand of the great bone automaton was slowly releasing its grip on the floating vessel.

Harper raced to the side of the ship. 'It's going for the arconite.'

Jones's whiskers twitched. 'Sabotage?'

'What else?'

'Please lower that device,' said a voice from behind.

The engineer turned to see Isaac Pilby standing inside the door to the saloon. He had unsheathed his sword and now held it out: a white weapon with a polyhedral crystal pommel set in a nest of silver. With a twitch of the blade he indicated that he meant for the engineer to stop what she was doing.

Harper complied.

'We'll wait here a few moments,' Pilby continued.

Harper noticed that the tip of the little man's blade was covered in fresh blood. 'What have you done?'

Pilby gave her an apologetic smile. 'There were too many staff aboard this vessel for my comfort. Doubtless many of them were agents of King Menoa.'

'Who the hell are you?' Harper demanded.

'Look at the colour of my blade,' he said. 'This weapon, unlike so many of the others present here, is not an affectation. I make no concessions to fashion. And my name is not Pilby.'

The sound of crackling came from the waters below as the arconite lifted its arm above the level of the deck. The bones of its hand and wrist were now wreathed in green and black flames.

The lepidopterist glanced up at the automaton, then back at Harper. 'I am the First of Cohl's Shades,' he said. 'I am the White Sword.'

'Damn mercenary!' Jones exclaimed. 'How much is Rys paying you to sabotage this mission?'

The White Sword shrugged. 'Stay down on your knees.'

'There are a hundred of these arrogant bastards out there,' Jones explained to Harper. 'Cohl's mercenaries fight with weapons coloured in shades anywhere between black and white. The Black Sword and his counterpart, the White Sword, are the most skilled warriors in each one of the two disciplines of Kiril and Yen, while those in-between kill each other to secure better weapons and thus better ranks.'

'I see you've watched Adelere's play?' the White Sword remarked.

'I watched Edgar Lovich play you on stage!'

'Badly, I fear.'

'And you killed him because of that?'

The small man shook his head. 'Alas, someone beat me to it.'

'What do you want?' Jones said.

'Just let the thaumaturgy work without interference.'

The flames had now risen up to the arconite's shoulder, and the great bone giant stood wreathed in green and black fire. In this unnatural light, Pilby's face seemed much harder than it had previously looked. His laconic smile evinced an utter lack of fear, a confidence in his own abilities that exceeded arrogance. 'Many entities, mortal and immortal, sought to prevent the release of this arconite into the world,' he said. 'That has failed, so now they must try to control it.'

'And which of them do you serve?' Jones said. 'Rys, I suppose?'

Pilby gave a brief nod.

Ersimmin the pianist had been watching all of this from a few yards further back along the passenger deck. 'Preposterous,' he called, walking over. 'Your weapon isn't even white. Ivory, I'd guess. Compare the shade of it to my own.' He drew his sword.

Pilby's eyes flicked to the other man's blade, then back to meet the pianist's gaze. 'Yours is a fake,' he declared.

'No,' Ersimmin said, 'it isn't.' He lunged at the smaller man. Steel clashed.

Pilby foiled one attack, then a second, but the third thrust took him in the neck.

The self-proclaimed First of Cohl's Shades gurgled once, then crumpled to the deck, his blood pouring out between the fingers now clamped over his throat.

Ersimmin picked up the fallen sword and compared it to his own, examining both weapons closely. Finally he nodded to himself. 'His blade is darker. Old Pilby was labouring under a misapprehension.' He slipped a handkerchief from his suit pocket and wiped his own sword clean of the other man's blood. 'This business can get confusing, what with so many weapons of a similar lustre in circulation. One can never really be sure that one has achieved true supremacy.'

'Then you're the White Sword?' Harper said.

The pianist gave a curt bow. 'I'm more confident of that title now, although I can't be absolutely certain until I have faced the remainder of Cohl's Shades. I've heard of one Kirillin warrior who has collected twenty-two blades already.' He shrugged, and appeared to stifle a smirk. 'Almost as many as myself.'

Jones helped Harper up. 'How many of you bloody mercenaries are on board?' he asked. 'I suppose Lovich was another one?'

'Hardly,' Ersimmin snorted. 'He was just a terrible actor with a painted blade – an embarrassment to all of Cohl's Shades. There was no need for me to challenge him to a fight.'

Harper inhaled deeply from her bulb. So this was the man who had ordered Hasp to kill Lovich? She was about to demand answers from him when her locator shrilled.

Ersimmin eyed the device in her hands. 'King Menoa foresaw difficulties, so he hired me to protect this mission and to allow you to do your job, Miss Harper. Can you stop this sabotage?'

'I don't know,' Harper admitted. And, truthfully, she didn't know if she wanted to stop this sabotage. The loss of an arconite would be a tremendous blow to Menoa. In a small way it would be revenge for what had happened to Tom. But if she failed Menoa now, she might never get close to him again. And she could not predict what the automaton might do if it were freed from the king's influence.

A whisper of steel. Jones had drawn his own rapier from its sheath and now swept it in an arc from his hip towards the pianist's neck. Ersimmin parried, before lashing out a fist at the side of the older man's head. Jones ducked, striking his opponent hard in the chest with his elbow. The pianist recoiled. Jones pushed his blade deep into the other man's heart.

Ersimmin's body slumped to the deck atop of Pilby's corpse.

'Arrogant bastard,' Jones muttered. He put one foot on Ersimmin's pelvis and heaved the bloody sword free of the other man's chest. 'Lovich wasn't *that* bad.'

For a moment Harper stared at him in shocked silence. 'Don't tell me *you*'re . . .'

'The White Sword?' Jones picked up the pianist's handkerchief and wiped his own blade clean. The metal shone with a dull stony colour. 'No. I suppose I'm actually somewhere in the mid-greys.' He grabbed both Ersimmin's and Pilby's discarded weapons and tossed them over the side of the ship into the lake below.

'Aren't you supposed to hold on to those?' Harper asked. 'In order to ascend the ranks?'

The old man grunted. 'I'm just in it for the money. The moment you possess a pure white or black sword, then every one of Cohl's shades comes after you. Besides,' he hefted his own grey blade, 'this one is just as sharp as the others.'

Edith Bainbridge stepped forward, raising her chin. 'Mid-grey!' she shrilled. 'This puts an entirely new perspective on our arrangement, Mr Jones.' Her eyes became small and hard. 'I was under the impression I had hired a grand master of Kiril, and yet you appear to be little better than a common cut-throat. Mid-grey indeed! You have misled me, sir.'

Jones shrugged. He glanced up at the automaton and then turned to face Harper. 'I'm sorry, Miss,' he said, 'but I can't let you stop this process. It seems that Pilby and I unwittingly shared the same contract. Had Ersimmin not slain him, there would have been no need to reveal my identity.'

'You're Rys's agent?'

He directed a nod to Edith Bainbridge.

'He works for me,' the small woman said. 'And I work for the god of flowers and knives.' She smiled. 'You Mesmerists think the human race exists to be used, moulded to any purpose that suits your warped ideology. Unlike you, dear, I chose not to abandon my own race.'

'We won't hurt you,' Jones said, 'provided you do not interfere with our plans.'

'You brought a thaumaturge aboard? Who is he?'

Jones looked peevish. 'Honestly, we don't know. If Rys is behind this sorcery, he didn't mention it to us.' He shrugged. 'But then he said nothing about Pilby either. It matters not. The thaumaturge's actions suit our purpose, and so we will not interfere.'

The *Sally Broom* had by now steamed some sixty yards out from the base of the cliffs and was heading in a wide curve away from the automaton. A ribbon of froth bobbed up and down in her wake, carried by the swell of the grey lake waters. High above them the arconite appeared to be in a state of great agitation. The castle-sized skull was staring down at the engine in its own chest, where the colourful fires now blazed. Flames of green and black danced deep within the machinery, illuminating gears, pistons and blood vats. With a mighty creak and thump of metal, the arconite raised one huge hand and beat it against its ribcage. Gulls burst from their nests within the titan's shoulders and neck, their alarm cries shrill and distant.

'You don't understand,' Harper said to Jones and Edith. 'If the arconite is released from Hell's influence, it will become independent, unpredictable. We'll be put in grave danger.'

'Carrick,' Jones said, 'would you be so kind as to inform the

Sally's captain of our predicament? I'd suggest to him he might want to increase our speed and move us directly away from that automaton.'

All this time, Chief Carrick had been sitting on the hurricane deck, slack-jawed, staring witlessly at the corpses of Ersimmin and Pilby. Now his glassy eyes darted up to meet Jones's. 'Yes, sir.' He scrambled to his feet and departed.

A great iron clamour fell from the clouds, like the clash of a hundred bells. The fires had contracted into a knot around the arconite's chest, and drawn from it a cry of anguish. The five-hundred-foot-tall mechanical archon shuddered, then threw its arms and wings wide. A cold blast of wind rippled the surface of Lake Larnaig, lifting rags of spume which blew across the steamship's deck. The *Sally* rocked on her belly, riding each swell, chugging steadily away from the bone giant and the base of the Moine Massif . . . but not fast enough, for as Harper ran inside to fetch Hasp, she glanced up to see the giant's skull turn slowly to fix its gaze upon the ship.

'Is it free?' Jones asked.

'Yes,' Harper replied. 'Iril help us!'

'Good. Then Menoa has been deprived of a weapon.'

The arconite raised its fists to the heavens and *roared*. And then it began to march towards the tiny fleeing vessel.

Down the stairwell the engineer raced. The smack of her boots on the metal floor seemed distant, as though a queer silence had filled the airspaces between bulkheads; a stillness that muffled the drum of the *Sally*'s own engines, the heave and slap of waves against her hull. It felt like an omen, a taste of death. Hasp could not slay the monster outside. The automaton need only lift the ship and cast her far across Lake Larnaig, or push her decks down into the chill waters. It would be the simplest thing. Harper plunged deeper into the vessel, though inside or outside, it made no difference; she would drown either way.

In the *Eleanor*'s slave pen she discovered a gruesome scene. Blood covered the floor of the cramped space. The corpses of most of the slaves lay heaped in one corner. Only two had survived: Hasp, and the young woman, whom the god held in his arms. She was unconscious but breathing.

'Our thaumaturge?' the engineer asked.

'Mina Greene, of Deepgate,' Hasp replied. 'But I fear she has exerted herself too much.'

'Come with me quickly.'

'More killing?'

Harper just stared at his glass skin and shuddered.

Back on the uppermost deck of the *Sally Broom*, she watched the arconite stride through the lake towards them. Huge waves, formed by the movement of its legs, rolled across the surface of the waters and pounded the side of the vessel. Gulls swarmed around it like confetti.

It halted, filling the entire scope of Harper's vision, and crouched beside the ship.

But rather than crushing the *Sally*'s hull, the bones of one vast hand curled, almost tenderly, around her bow, halting her forward movement.

And then it brought its skull closer to peer at its captives.

Deep inside the dead eye sockets, the engineer saw black crystals glittering. She heard the continuous clatter of engines from its cranium and ribs, the slow thump of weird chemical blood. She smelled rust and grease, and something else . . . the odour of bones and tombs. For a long, long moment the automaton seemed content just to watch its captives.

Dill?

Was there anything left of that young angel in there? Did he realize who or where he was? Could the Lord of the First Citadel now reason with him? She had to hope so.

But Chief Carrick had other ideas. 'Kill it,' he ordered.

And the words rewoke the parasite lodged in Hasp's mind.

The order had been given, and the glass-sheathed god remained compelled to obey it. He broke away from the group, vaulted over the balustrade towards the front of the ship. He tore a coil of rope free from one of the *Sally*'s lifeboats, and ran towards the bow, his shiftblade gripped in one huge fist.

Harper cried out for the angel to stop, but Hasp *ignored* her.

Jones called out his own command, but the angel still refused to halt. 'It seems the parasite no longer considers us to be loyal servants of the king,' the old reservist said. 'I daresay Menoa did not approve of what he saw through the arconite's eyes. We have been cut loose.'

Harper faced Carrick. 'Hasp can't kill that!' she said. 'But he knew the young angel in Hell. He helped him, protected him. Just let him try to talk to Dill.'

The Chief Liaison Officer glared at her with utter hatred in his eyes. 'You've chosen your side, Alice. You'll have to live with that decision for the rest of your . . . miserable existence.' He shot a glance at Jones's sword. 'The glass bastard's too far away to hear any more orders now.'

The automaton's grinning skull filled the dismal sky. Tiny white gulls wheeled in slow circles around it or settled, finding rude perches among so many acres of bone, dropping specks of shit. Still the machine made no move. Its eye sockets were caverns. In its stillness, it had once more become an inanimate thing: of ridges, cracks and hollows – dead spaces to be eroded by the wind, places where the rain might gather and pool. But Harper knew there would be anguish, even despair, boiling at the creature's core. The thaumaturge's strange fires had wrapped around its soul, like a fist squeezing the poison from its beating heart, and then they had retreated, freeing the creature from Menoa's grip. Now Dill's soul would be exposed to the agony of metal and bone and chemical blood, and to the knowledge of what he had become.

By now Hasp had reached the place where the automaton's hand gripped the ship. He leapt from the deck to the back of the creature's knuckle, then set off again, scrambling along the vines of steel hydraulic tubing that wrapped the forearm. The automaton, if it sensed his presence, paid him no more attention than it would have given to a fly. Clearly Hasp was too insignificant to be worth the effort of swatting. At the elbow joint, the god slipped between two pistons and began to climb the upper arm, into the shade of the clavicle.

The arconite chose this moment to unleash its fury. Its right hand remained pressed against the bow, while the left, a clawed fist, suddenly loomed overhead and smashed through the superstructure near the stern of the vessel. Metal buckled and tore. The concussion knocked Harper from her feet; her head struck the deck hard. When she looked up she saw a sky full of teeth, and then the clouds seemed to fall towards her.

The automaton had hefted the steamship airborne in its right fist. The deck lurched, sloped away at a dizzy angle. From inside the saloon came the sound of smashing crockery or glass, the thud of heavy objects breaking against interior bulkheads, the smell of burning lamp oil. A metal groan trembled through the wooden planks beneath her; cables stuttered and pinged. There was a series of snaps and one of the *Sally*'s two funnels toppled forward, ploughing through the ship's bridge with a jaw-breaking boom. Harper glimpsed heaving grey waters far below the bow of the vessel, with flecks of white foam. She clung on desperately. Pistons rumbling, the *Sally* plunged suddenly backwards through the air.

The automaton drew back its arm to throw the ship.

From somewhere Harper thought she heard the sound of battle.

The parasite chattered inside Hasp's skull, insisting on destruction even as the angel raged against the command he had been given. This giant was Dill, the very archon he had fought so hard to save in Hell. And now he had been ordered to slay him. A red mist blurred the god's vision, a veil his fury sought to cut through with his sword. He had tied his rope to a pipe near the automaton's scapula, the other end around his own midriff. Now he had reached the creature's shoulder.

Before him loomed the arconite's spine and skull. Hasp could see wires among the vertebrae. He ran across the plates of bone, his blade ready.

The skull turned.

For a heartbeat, something glimmered deep in the arconite's eye sockets – in the crystals which had replaced Dill's eyes. His huge jaws opened and closed with a crash.

'I have been ordered to slay you,' Hasp shouted, 'and I cannot resist this order.' His mind swam under the strain of speaking. 'Kill me and save yourself.'

A voice rolled out from the thing, as deep as an earthquake. 'Hasp . . .?'

'Slay me, Dill.' Hasp had reached the arconite's neck. He raised his shiftblade and plunged it into a nest of wires and crystals and cogs between two vertebrae, trying to hack it all to shreds. But he could not dent nor even scratch the machinery.

The arconite howled.

Its massive fist came up and closed around the glass-skinned archon, and Hasp did not flee. He could not stop himself from harming Dill, but he had been given no orders to protect himself.

A cage of bones now surrounded him, and Hasp felt himself

being suddenly carried out far across the waters of Lake Larnaig. The parasite in his skull demanded destruction. Before the god could stop himself, he turned his shiftblade into an axe, and began to hack at the skeletal fingers looming before him.

The fist opened.

And once more Hasp found himself staring up at that huge face. Dill's dead eyes lacked expression. His grin could not express whatever emotions he felt. Yet Hasp sensed turmoil within that skull. Dill could so easily have crushed the archon in his hand, and yet he hadn't.

Hasp raised his axe again.

A voice cried out somewhere below. The words eluded Hasp. He clove his axe into the arconite's wrist. No wound or gouge appeared under his blade, and yet the arconite cried out in agony. Hasp lifted his axe again.

'Stop . . . order . . . Hasp!'

This time Hasp recognized the voice. Chief Carrick was calling out from below. Had he just ordered Hasp to stop the attack? The glass-armoured god looked down.

Far down below on the deck of the steamship, Jones had a blade against Carrick's throat.

'Stop the attack,' Carrick shouted. 'That's an order.'

Harper was standing next to the pair, a look of vast relief on her face. Jones just looked up and grinned.

'When we saw how the arconite reacted to you,' Harper explained to Hasp a bit later, 'Jones persuaded Carrick to intervene.'

'I—' Carrick began.

Jones moved his sword closer to the Chief Liaison Officer's throat. 'Remember what we said about silence?' he reminded the other man.

Hasp had returned to the *Sally*'s deck without further incident. The arconite had then lowered the steamship back into the water and now towered over them, peering down. Hundreds of birds had settled on its great tattered wings. The other passengers had retired to the saloon for a stiff drink.

'His name is Dill,' Hasp said.

Harper could only nod. Of all of them, she had played the greatest part in his downfall.

Dill had woken from a terrible dream, and yet he found the reality of his present situation identical to the memories of that nightmare. His body felt strangely numb, disconnected, with no sensation of cold or warmth – only pain. The skeletal arms and legs he saw before him could not be his, and yet – disturbingly – they moved in correspondence to his own conscious movements. He heard engines pounding somewhere nearby, but he could not at first locate them. The sound of gusting wind reached his ears, yet he felt nothing.

He was standing up to his shins in a pool, peering down at a tiny ship. From its deck, tiny people stared back up at him. In his nightmare he had walked across a miniature landscape of small trees, grasses, desolate moors or stone-hemmed fields left to grow wild. He had come to a steep bank and stepped down into a shallow pool. Voices had compelled him to lift this tiny vessel down into the waters. And now that the voices had stopped, he found himself gazing down at the same vessel, and at an archon in glass armour whom he recognized.

'Hasp?'

His own voice sounded like a collapsing mountain. It seemed to echo back from the ends of time. Dill was suddenly afraid. He lifted his hands and gazed down at the hard dry bones. When he flexed his fingers, the bones moved.

'Hasp!'

The tiny archon was shouting, '. . . me up . . . your hand.'

Dill reached out towards the ship, and let the archon leap into his outstretched hand. The Lord of the First Citadel looked no larger than a glass bead. Dill lifted his hand up close to his face.

'Don't think about anything except my voice,' Hasp said. 'Just listen to what I have to say.'

Dill nodded.

'You've been dreaming,' Hasp continued. 'But your soul is now free. You're no longer in Hell. You don't have to fear the Icarates any more.'

'Hell?' Dill began. Memories of his time in the Processor assaulted him like a violent squall: the Icarates chanting, the screaming walls and sobbing, chattering machines, the knives and the blood. He stared in horror at his skeletal hand.

'A physical form is transient,' Hasp said. 'Only your soul is eternal. That's all that matters now.'

'Where am I? Where is Deepgate?'

'You're on the other side of the world, lad, and I don't even know if Deepgate still exists.' The Lord of the First Citadel gave a long sigh, and then pointed southwest. 'Do you see that stain on the horizon? That is Menoa's army. They have taken the Red Road out of Pandemeria.'

Dill spied a series of dark shapes – rough squares and oblongs – a short distance beyond the perimeter of the pool, following a crimson track. Smoke trailed from the rearmost of these.

Machines?

'Now look to the northern shore.'

The earth here was stained red in a thick line extending out to the east and west, beyond the shore of the pool. Masses of tiny black creatures crawled over this crimson landscape, and at first Dill took them to be insects. But then he realized the truth of it. An encampment had been erected there. It housed a second army – much smaller than the one approaching from the southeast, but a considerable force nevertheless. Beyond these legions the ground sloped gently up towards a pale city of slender minarets hedged by thick walls, all rising before a curious bank of mist which enveloped a large part of the northern skies. Earthen and timber barricades had been constructed on the open ground before the twin Gate towers, and flanking these were iron-banded ballistae.

'Coreollis,' Hasp explained, 'the fortress of the god of flowers and knives. King Menoa expects my brother, Rys, to bend the knee before Hell's ambassadors today – to sign away his soul to the Ninth Citadel. He must comply or face complete annihilation.'

'From that army?' The dark horde beyond the shore seemed so tiny and insignificant to Dill, but he began to understand the threat from Hasp's perspective.

'No,' Hasp said. 'From *you*.' He looked towards Coreollis. 'That fog yonder must mean that Cospinol has arrived to fight beside my brother. Rys's Northmen will use it to conceal their pitiful numbers.'

'Then they'll fight?'

'Now that Menoa has lost you, he knows Rys will not sign the treaty. He has no choice now but to throw his whole horde against Coreollis and try to break her.' The god looked back up at Dill. 'The forces of Hell and Earth will clash here today. If the Mesmerists win, King Menoa's form of living death will replace all life here. This country will become the stuff of Chaos.'

Dill watched tiny figures assembling along the shore. They were boarding low sleek boats and pushing them into the lake. Wherever these dark hulls met the water, they bled, leaving crimson trails behind them.

'They have realized that something is wrong,' Hasp said. 'Or King Menoa has already issued orders. They will attack us soon.'

Dill lowered Hasp to the deck of the ship. Then he reached a hand under the hull and lifted, hoisting the whole vessel clear of the waters.

With the *Sally Broom* safely in his grip, he set off to meet Menoa's bleeding ships.

26

COREOLLIS

Rachel left John Anchor laughing and drinking with one of Rys's commanders and walked through the streets of Coreollis along with Trench and Ramnir. They had arrived two days ago – and just in time, for the Mesmerist reinforcements had been spotted already approaching via the Red Road on the western shores of Lake Larnaig. But something else had unnerved the populace of Rys's city – something vast and terrible – and it was this that she had set off to witness.

Coreollis was now preparing for battle and Rys's Northmen were everywhere. Trained veterans well used to repelling attacks from the Mesmerist hordes, they filled the streets of the city. As Rachel and her companions walked down a narrow lane, they passed a unit of mounted soldiers. Like the god they followed, these men wore silver plate forged here in Coreollis. They were tall and golden-haired and broad of shoulder – a race descended from the Skarraf Northerners who had claimed this handsome city a thousand years ago. And yet Rachel had noticed an edge of cruelty to their ways. They were quick to show disapproval, and quicker to inflict punishment on the hapless locals.

Coreollis lay right in the shadow of the Mesmerists and yet it had never come under siege. Menoa's hordes, it seemed, required blooded ground to sustain them as they crept from one battlefield to the next, and Rys's soldiers had exploited this weakness to their advantage, keeping such threat away from supply lines open north of the city. They had effectively corralled the enemy to an area which had seen intense conflict over the last decade, refusing to let the Mesmerists ever encircle the city.

Now a sense of urgency filled the streets. Rachel, Trench and Ramnir passed a quadrangle full of shouting warriors engaged in combat practice, almost colliding with a runner who had been distracted by this melee. Wide steps led them down to an esplanade before the city Gate Towers, where soldiers would form ranks before marching out to positions outside the city walls. Commoners hurried about them, carrying supplies to the archers and pike-men on the battlements. As they reached the foot of the steps, the trio passed two soldiers of the Flower Guard, who were untying their horses' reins from a post.

'Hey, donkey man,' the first guard said to Ramnir. 'Fetch me some hay for my beast.'

His companion laughed.

The Heshette leader made no reply, but his hand went to the knife at his waist. Trench stopped him.

'That counts as a threat,' the guard growled. He stood a foot taller than the Heshette and was twice his width. Sunlight blazed on his breastplate. 'You don't reach for a weapon in the presence of the Flower Guard. Someone needs to teach you fucking heathens a lesson.'

The other guard, who was older, grunted. 'I think Anchor brought those bastards in to work in the stables. Have you seen their women? I'd rather sleep with my horse.'

'Don't let me stop you,' Ramnir replied.

The older guard paused, then straightened, frowning.

Rachel had already pulled Ramnir out of one fight since they'd arrived, and she didn't like the look of these two.

'Please, gentlemen,' she said, 'we're guests here. We mean no offence.' She pulled the Heshette leader past the two men and out between the Gate Towers. 'They're just nervous,' she said as the city walls fell behind and the landscape opened before them. 'Because they know they have to face *that*.'

They stood at the edge of the Larnaig Field, a gently sloping bank leading down to the lake shore, about half a league distant. Soldiers of the Flower Guard, the Knife Guard and the City Guard had gathered on several of the dirt embankments before the walls of Coreollis. To the west Rys's ballistae squatted on the rolling landscape. The city stables lay to the east, from where Rachel could hear the rhythmic metal clanks of a farrier working at his anvil.

King Menoa's armies now waited on blooded ground by the water's edge: a mass of queerly shaped figures and machines. There were ten thousand or more, and very few of them resembled men. Half a league away, a force ten times this size was moving north along Red Road to join them. From this legion rose a pall of greasy smoke.

But the giant standing in the lake took Rachel's breath away. 'The arconite?'

Trench nodded.

The skeletal figure towered over the ship floating close to its shins, which listed badly, black smoke pouring from its toppled funnels. A few of Menoa's troops had launched boats to rendezvous with the automaton and the ship. These sleek black craft ploughed through the still waters of the lake without oars or sails, leaving dark trails behind them.

Rachel hissed. 'How do we kill it?'

'With swords and axes,' Ramnir said.

Trench shook his head. 'The first arconite could not be killed. It still lies trapped in sapperbane chains amid the drowned city of Skirl. More than one hundred thousand warriors died trying to subdue the beast. I think this one' – he inclined his head towards the giant – 'is bigger.'

'Look!' Ramnir said. 'Something is happening.'

The arconite stooped and picked up the entire ship in one hand. Then it strode towards the shores of Lake Larnaig, as if to meet the Mesmerist craft.

It moved slowly, its bony legs propelling high waves before it. The afternoon sun glimmered on the lake behind it, and the vast expanse of water shone like silver. In the far distance rose the cliffs and misty mountains of the Moine Massif, appearing as thin as vapours.

Three of the five Mesmerist boats had drawn near to the approaching giant, but now hesitated, keeping a short distance back.

'Something is wrong,' Trench said.

Rachel sensed it too. Aboard the Mesmerist craft, figures were moving about hurriedly. She could imagine frantic orders being given. The boats began to retreat.

A warning horn sounded somewhere behind Rachel. Evidently the guards on the city walls had spotted the Mesmerists' unusual behaviour in the lake. She turned to see Rys's soldiers racing across the top of the city battlements, shouting down orders to their comrades within.

'It has begun,' Trench said.

Harper stood on the hurricane deck, battered by the wind, and three hundred feet above the surface of the lake, as Dill smashed his way through a flotilla of Mesmerist boats. The giant automaton did not require a weapon. His passage through the waters swamped the craft on either side. He stomped on those immediately ahead of him, reducing their living hulls to bleeding shards. Icarates fell into the lake, their weird armour pulsing with vivid blue flashes as they sank from sight.

But some of the craft fought back. Directed by Icarate priests, the boats began to change shape. Their gunwales flowed into new forms: metal contraptions with barbed spinning discs, multi-joined insectlike arms with claws, clusters of pipes and arm-thick whips designed to expel poisons. Clanks and whispers and whoomphs of air heralded these assaults. Fiery blue and red arcs of spitting fluid soared high above the lake and exploded against Dill's chest. The missiles screamed on contact, for these had been souls ingrained into the fabric of the boats.

Dill barely appeared to notice the assaults. He shrugged them off and kicked the boats aside, leaving a bloody wake behind him.

Now Menoa's encamped force was massing on the lake shore. Driven on by their Icarate priests and witchspheres, the demons swarmed over the bloody ground. A group of heavy-armoured boar-like beasts made up the vanguard. They gouged their tusks into the ground and bellowed, and threw up clods of wet red earth. Their segmented-plate hides bristled with spines and steamed in the sunshine like hot lead.

Dill reached the shore and crushed the first of them underfoot. Engines thundering in his chest, he kicked at a pack of the hapless beasts. Their broken corpses flew far across the Larnaig Field.

The shadow of the steamer now fell across ranks of seemingly more human figures – the brawlers, murderers and gladiators Menoa had left mostly unchanged but for sharpened metal limbs or patches of steel or iron skin. These attacked with hatchets, spears, knives and long curved blades, but Dill's ankles did not linger to receive their blows, and he left the field unscathed.

War machines continued to spit fire at the arconite, and at the steamship he carried over the heads of Menoa's forces. But Dill cleared the long thin battlefield in less than a dozen strides and set out across the upwardly sloping ground to meet Rys's waiting forces at Coreollis. Hunting horns sounded among the horde, but they did not pursue the giant.

Hasp watched grimly. 'The enemy will wait until all their rein-forcements arrive before marching forth,' he explained to Harper. 'They must first butcher slaves to bloody the battlefield in prepar-ation for the assault, and they must steep themselves in the living earth. But the attack will come soon.'

Menoa's main force was already pouring into the encampment on the lake shore. Harper had never seen such vast numbers arrayed against mortal men before. The ranks of adapted warriors and beasts stretched in a long dark curve around the eastern shore of the lake. Countless twisted metal weapons glinted in the late-morning sun. A vast pall of red vapour enshrouded them – the breath from their dead lungs, she realized. She heard their bones and armour clicking, and felt the ground tremble as boots and hooves and wheels churned the Red Road to bloody mud.

'So many,' she said. 'Can Dill possibly defeat them all?'

'Easily,' Hasp said.

'Then why would Menoa attack?'

'Because to flee now would be madness. The arconite would simply follow and crush them on the Red Road. The Lord of the Maze must try to cripple Rys while he still can, sacrificing his Mesmerists to slay as many as possible of my brother's sol-diers. Menoa cares nothing for these demons. He has all of Hell to harvest a new horde.'

Dill halted outside the city gates and set the steamship down upon the green grass. The *Sally Broom* sank partly into the earth, listed, and came to rest with a groan.

The vision of this giant had stunned the Northmen on the battlements to silence. But then, from within the city came a soft, thick fog; pushing through the gates and over the thick granite walls.

Jack Caulker felt that his moment was near. As an outsider, he'd found no solace amongst these cruel northern men, who jeered and spat at him. And despite his demands, Rys and the other gods had not seen fit to grant him an audience. Indeed, he'd spent most of the journey here cooped up like an animal below decks along with the Heshette hags and their livestock.

The nights had been torturous, for whenever the cut-throat slept, his nightmare returned. Night after night he would become that same old woman in her flimsy gown, standing on the battlements of Rockwall Fortress. And again and again he would plummet to his death in the valley below, pushed by John Anchor. Caulker slept in fits and bouts, always waking to the sound of his own screaming. His eyes were constantly red and sore. He itched and twitched and felt invisible insects crawling over his skin.

But he kept close to Anchor's side. The Adamantine Man remained jovial, laughing loudly at the news of the arconite's defection from Hell's armies. Caulker had been watching him carefully, keeping one eye always on the pouch of soulpearls tied to the giant's belt. Anchor consumed one soul each day at noon, when the sun had risen to its zenith. After examining the glass beads to find the strongest and most pure, he would swallow the imprisoned ghost and then slap his huge fists together and pull at the mighty rope to test his strength. Caulker had noticed that Anchor's great strength ebbed and flowed around these repasts. He was weakest just before he feasted.

That leather pouch of soulpearls never left the big man's side, and yet he made no effort to hide this treasure from the eyes of others. And Caulker's eyes feasted upon it. How many furious spirits resided within that bag? It would be so easy to smash their tiny glass prisons and release them. With the armies of the king of Hell so close by, it was time now, he decided, to make his move.

'These Northmen seem capable,' he remarked to Anchor as they passed between the Coreollis Gate Towers. Archers in light, stripped-down plate and boiled leathers patrolled the city walls above them.

'Capable, yes,' Anchor replied. 'Veterans of many battles with Hell, these men. But they are not good men. The poison they drink in order to wear such cruel armour . . . it makes them cruel also.' His expression wrinkled into one of distaste. 'I killed one of Rys's soldiers once, but the soul was tainted. Very bad.'

'What do you mean *cruel* armour?' By pretending to avoid a rut in the ground, Caulker moved to a position where he might best be able to reach the pouch of soulpearls at the big man's side.

'The breastplates,' Anchor explained. 'Wait, I'll show you.'

They were outside the city walls now, close beside the grounded steamship. Fog obscured the field sloping down to the lake, but Caulker could hear the howls and cries of King Menoa's army nearby. *So close!* He gazed up at the dented hull, and back along the length of the ship. Her rear gangway had been lowered and now soldiers of the Flower Guard were inspecting her interior. A small group had assembled beside the vessel: various nobles in odd rich raiment, an official-looking couple in matching grey uniforms, and a strange old man and a young woman – both wearing what appeared to be red glass armour.

A unit of cavalry thundering past distracted him. The horsemen disappeared into the mists to the west, heading in the direction of Rys's ballistae. Caulker could not imagine how such ranged weapons could be effective in this visibility, but he assumed they had acted as a line of defence long before the arrival of Cospinol's skyship. He looked about for the arconite but saw nothing.

How could something so vast remain hidden from view?

'You!' Anchor boomed at one of the Flower Guard. 'Yes you, man. Come here, please. I wish to show my friend how Rys makes such good warriors. You will help me, yes?'

The man grinned and came over to join them, clearly pleased to demonstrate whatever superiority Anchor had perceived him to possess. He was tall, and handsome, with cropped fair hair and an angular jaw, and he wore the same silvered breastplate and bracers as all his fellows. As he approached, he loosened the leather straps at his side that secured the metal plate across his chest. 'Has this heathen not heard of knife armour?'

Anchor shook his head. 'No, he is from another land. They do not know Menoa's forces like you.'

The soldier snorted. 'A soft breed then? Not trained to resist the Deceiver's persuasion as we have been.' He peeled away the breastplate, with a shudder.

Caulker felt instantly sick.

Beneath the soldier's armour, the man's chest was a red mess of scars. His skin had been punctured in half a hundred places. The metal plate, Caulker saw, was lined with four inch knives, each pointing inwards.

'You see?' Anchor said to Caulker. 'Rys's soldiers wear such armour since the age of seven years. The knives start small, then as the child grows, the armour plates are changed for ones with longer blades. The body adapts around the metal.'

Caulker turned away.

'Many die,' Anchor admitted.

The soldier laughed. 'But the survivors grow stronger.'

They left the soldier and walked west around the city walls, passing legions of assembled men preparing for battle behind earth and timber palisades. Caulker stared at their silver armour with dread, imagining the torsos within.

'The suffering makes them resilient,' Anchor said. 'King Menoa finds it hard to sway men like this. It takes many years in Hell to break them. Ah look, here is the iron angel now.'

It was vaster than Caulker expected. From where he stood he could see nothing but a pair of monstrous skeletal feet, under leg bones which disappeared high into the fog. A vague shadow filled the sky overhead.

'Big, yes?' Anchor chuckled. 'And strong. It has found a weapon.'

Caulker looked again. Something huge and metal hung in the mists above his head. He peered harder. He could just make out a long, bulky iron object with a funnel and rows of metal wheels connected by couplings. It moved suddenly, and a shower of black stones fell from it.

Coal?

'Perhaps we should return to the city,' he suggested to Anchor. 'The soldiers will not thank you for bringing this fog.'

'I help them in the fight,' Anchor replied, still staring up at the arconite. 'They put up with Cospinol's fog. Fair trade, eh?'

'I don't believe it,' Trench hissed.

Rachel turned to see the group of passengers who had disembarked from the steamship outside the city walls. Now Silister Trench, the archon who had accompanied her all the way from Deepgate, rushed over to greet one of them.

The old man clad in queer glass armour looked up as Trench approached, and grinned. 'You made it, then? And without wings I see.'

'You appear to have lost more than a few feathers yourself.' They clasped arms.

'Rachel, this is Hasp,' Trench said, 'the Lord of the First Citadel and commander of the Maze Archons. Ulcis's brother. Hasp, this is Rachel Hael, a friend of the angel who gave up this body for me.'

Rachel swallowed. How many more brothers of the dead god Ulcis was she likely to meet?

Hasp said to her, 'You knew Dill?'

She nodded. 'Trench told me you would search for him in Hell. I . . .' She hesitated. 'Did you find him?'

Hasp studied her for a moment. 'He exists still.'

Relief flooded her heart. If Dill's soul had not been destroyed, then there remained a chance to return it to his body. Trench had promised her as much. But then she had a sudden thought. What did it mean that the Lord of the First Citadel was here on Earth? Who, then, was looking after the young angel in the Maze?

'Menoa got to him,' Hasp said bluntly. 'I tried to protect him but I failed.'

'What do you mean? What's happened to him? Where is he?' And Hasp explained.

'We go to look at the enemy now.'

'*What?*'

John Anchor beamed. 'Cospinol's fog makes it difficult to see. Come . . .' He beckoned to Caulker. 'We will go and see what type of demons we are facing.' He started walking down the slope towards the hidden horde.

'Shouldn't you wait for the soldiers?' Caulker called after him.

Anchor glanced back over his shoulder. 'What for?' Then he laughed and set off again, dragging his massive rope behind him.

Caulker hesitated. He'd seen Anchor fight, and knew that the big man was probably more than a match for whatever pickets the demons had placed around their encampment. And he realized that this might be the one chance he'd have to betray the tethered giant to his enemies. But the thought of walking into that terrible unknown made him pause.

Anchor had almost disappeared into the fog ahead. It was now or never. He bolted after the big man.

'Jack Caulker,' Anchor said as the cut-throat drew alongside him. There was a hint of sadness in his tone. 'You once asked Cospinol to tell you how you will die. He did not know the answer then, but he knows it now.'

Caulker was stupefied. Now he wasn't sure that he wanted to know the answer to that question. He eyed the big man warily.

'You die trying to betray a friend,' Anchor said.

Caulker said nothing. A feeling of unease crept over him. How could Anchor possibly know his intentions? The big man was trying to trick him again, the same way he had tricked Caulker into swallowing the tainted soulpearl. And there was the truth of it, Caulker realized. The soul had somehow been rotten – that's why it gave him such horrible visions of death. As they marched on through the fog, down towards Menoa's horde, the cut-throat became angry.

'You betrayed *me*,' he said. 'You fed me a poisoned soul.'

'No.'

'You cursed me! Every night you return to murder me in my dreams.'

Anchor shrugged. 'It is the nature of Cospinol's soulpearls. These ghosts are angry. They live inside us, and give us strength, but they will try to hurt us too.'

'But *you* don't suffer.'

Anchor stopped abruptly. Dark shapes were shuffling at the limits of the fog ahead, while larger shadows sagged in the grey gloom behind. *Tents or banners?* Caulker smelled the dense odours of beasts and charnel. He heard the rasp of steel, the creak and rumble of an axle turning, and a thousand other low grunts and snuffles.

The tethered man whispered, 'I have the same dreams, Jack Caulker.'

'Liar!' Caulker reached for the leather pouch at Anchor's side, but the big man grabbed his wrist, stopping him.

'All of these souls are angry, rotten and bitter,' Anchor said quietly. 'The one you chose was more benevolent than most.'

'No.' Caulker hissed through his teeth. This damned giant was lying to him again. Had Anchor brought him here to *betray* him? Did he hope to gain King Menoa's favour *first*?

Anchor untied the pouch from his belt. 'If you don't believe me, then choose another. It will only add to your suffering.'

Caulker eyed the bag of pearls. How many dozens had the giant consumed since the Deadsands without suffering any ill effects? *The souls of warriors from a hundred distant lands, battle-archons and demigods.* And yet Anchor had tricked Caulker into consuming the rotting essence of a madwoman.

The cut-throat snatched the bag and ran.

He ran towards the armies of the King of Hell, and as he ran he gorged himself, stuffing the glass beads into his mouth. The shadows in the fog ahead became clearer. He sprinted past a barricade of bones and wicked crystal-tipped spears. Hobbled shapes flinched and grunted in the gloom all around, but still Caulker ran. And then suddenly he was past the pickets and leaving Anchor's fog. He could see the whole encampment spread out before him, the horde amassing on the crimson lakeshore. He glanced back, and noticed that the fog was flowing quickly back up the incline towards Coreollis. Anchor had decided not to pursue him.

Caulker grinned and ate more pearls. *These* were not rotten, for he was already growing stronger. With each new soul he consumed, he felt his fatigue lift. All of the hard years he had spent on Missionary cogs and in the streets of Sandport simply peeled away. He could have run forever.

Now he could make out individual groups amongst the throng: chained human slaves urged forward at spear point; tall figures on stilts and warriors in white armour following behind; red flayed things which crawled like beasts? Machines with human skin and faces crowded amongst their gears and chains?

Caulker slowed his step.

Where was the King of Hell? But, of course, these were merely minions, foot soldiers, slaves. No doubt the leader would be directing the battle from the rear. All Caulker had to do was find a way to get to speak to him.

He must offer a gift.

Alone at the encampment border, the cut-throat held up his stolen pouch. 'A gift!' he cried. 'Souls for your King Menoa. Let me speak to him.'

The demons advanced. They marched, crawled or slithered up the incline. Before them they drove a group of twenty or so chained humans. It had become a true killing field. Slaves cried out as Menoa's warriors cut them down to soak the earth before them. Wheeled machines belched smoke from hot pipes and crushed their bones. Savage howling things set about the slaves' flesh with claw and fang. The twenty slaves became ten, and then five.

Caulker swallowed another soulpearl for strength, and then another.

Grinning faces leered up towards him. Huge armoured men in bronze armour clicked metal fingers together. Steel grated steel. Teeth chattered and axes fell. Five slaves became four, and then three. Their bones crunched and their blood flew everywhere, soaking the advancing horde. Witchspheres rolled among the throng, whispering, gouging shallow trenches in the fresh red earth.

'A gift for your master,' Caulker cried. 'I seek an audience with him. I have important news.'

Nobody would answer him.

Somewhere distant he heard a hag scream and cackle. Caulker reached for another soulpearl, but the bag was empty. How many had he eaten? Twenty? Fifty? He could feel their power soaring inside him. It gave him confidence.

The king's army marched closer, glaring at the cut-throat the way a predator inspects food. The last slave fell before them, his scream echoing across the sunlit slope. Swords and spikes were raised. Mouths drooled and salivated.

'I demand an audience with your king,' he said. 'I demand—'

But the army had reached him now, and they had no more slaves left with which to bloody the ground.

From the fringes of Cospinol's fog, Harper watched the reinforcements join the main bulk of Menoa's army. And now she could see the human slaves among them. They had been harvesting the lands of Pandemeria en route to bloody the ground before Coreollis.

Part of Harper's heart urged her to abandon these humans and join the demon hordes. Her bulb of mist had almost dried up, and therefore her strength would soon fade. She was not one of the living, nor could she survive for long amongst them. Hell waited for her inevitably at the end of this day.

'There must be a hundred thousand souls in that army,' Jones muttered, 'without even counting the slaves.'

'More,' she said. 'Menoa uses souls as ammunition. Each acid bolt and ball of flame is someone's life. These weapons feel as much pain as the victims they burn.' She turned to face him. 'Why did Edith Bainbridge betray the Mesmerists? What did Rys offer her that Menoa couldn't?'

He smiled. 'The god of flowers and knives is very handsome.'

'That's it?'

'That's it.' He gave a shrug. 'She's vain and foolish, rich and arrogant and selfish. But she's still a woman.'

'How would Rys feel, I wonder, to know that his looks helped to turn the war?'

'It would appeal to him greatly,' Jones mused. 'But if Menoa unleashes the remainder of his arconites, this turn of events would seem to make little difference. We have only one giant.'

The reservist was right. Dill might slay every demon on the

field down there, but he would be hard-pressed to stand against even one of Menoa's twelve remaining arconites. She said, 'Can we hope for more aid from the thaumaturge?'

The old man shook his head. 'Mina Greene has been reunited with her pet, but that hound is nothing more than a Penny Devil. Basilis is crippled and debased, but I fear he has already over-stretched his powers.'

'Then we're doomed to fail.'

'I think so, yes,' he replied. 'But not today.'

Horns blared suddenly down by the lake shore. Menoa's armies began to stir. Now they herded hundreds of their human slaves onto the battlefield, slaughtering the stragglers even as they urged the remainder forwards. The king's war machines, more resilient to untainted earth, rolled out on either side to flank the main force.

An answering trumpet came from Rys's Northmen. His army bellowed and clashed swords against their shields. Then they marched on, a tide of silver flowing down the incline to meet the threat. Banners of yellow and white streamed over their heads. The sound of their boots resounded like the beat of a metal heart.

And Dill moved. He opened his wings to blanket the whole of the northern sky, disturbing low clouds. In one hand he gripped *The Pride of Eleanor Damask* like a club, the old locomotive shedding coal and oil upon the grass. He stooped to pick up the *Sally Broom* with his other hand. The empty steamship gave a mighty groan. Her hull buckled under his grip and her single remaining funnel collapsed.

Hasp stood alone on the city battlements, watching grimly. He had demanded that Rys allow him to fight, but his very skill as a warrior had stood against him. Even the weakest of Menoa's advancing hordes could have ordered the Lord of the First Citadel to turn against his fellows. And Rys would not risk that.

John Anchor's laughter could be heard above the sound of the marching troops. He clapped his big hands together and dragged his master's skyship down the hill where his fog lapped the heels of Rys's Northmen.

Armed with bows and axes, Ramnir and his Heshette warriors urged their tough little horses down the western flank.

And the battle began.

Dill hurled the *Sally Broom*.

That great iron steamship ploughed a furrow through Menoa's warriors. It sliced through the wet earth, throwing up a vast spray of red soil and corpses and machines. And then the hull struck a mound in the landscape and rolled, tumbling funnel over keel. Whole decks peeled away and spun out across the enemy forces. Metal debris rained down. Its superstructure now torn apart, the bulk of the hull jumped and crashed down again, burst into flames, and settled close to the lake shore in a cloud of grit and smoke.

The king's dogcatchers set upon Rys's Northmen. They moved like wild beasts, seeking to tear at exposed flesh, but Rys's warriors formed phalanxes. Spears shot out of the metal huddles, again and again, slaying demons on all sides. Once the attacks had been quelled, they lifted their shields and charged as one wall into a mass of Menoa's gladiators. Bronze-clad warriors fell under them, but the wall of Northmen pushed on, leaving the wounded to the swordsmen following behind the vanguard.

A pall of bloodmist had risen over the killing field. And now Harper watched as the king's war machines sent screaming missiles hurtling into the thick of the battle. Bright explosions flashed among the ranks of Coreollis troops, shredding whole units of them. A witchsphere burst into a cloud of pus. Hellish cries and moans pierced the air.

Silister Trench fought alone against seven Non Morai, his shift-blade changing constantly as it blurred between forms. The winged demons spun and howled around him. The Champion of the First Citadel made shields to protect himself from their claws, then suddenly altered the weapon to hack or cut or jab at their leathery wings. Corpses fell around him and he moved on to fresh pasture for his demonic weapon.

Dill's great skeletal body towered over the battlefield. He still wielded *The Pride of Eleanor Damask*. None of Menoa's forces were a match for his size and strength, and he slaughtered them like insects. He raised the iron locomotive and then brought it down again, pounding the ground, crushing Icarates and dog-catchers and war machines and everything else to mulch. The pistons in his joints hissed and leaked thin vapours. His engines growled like a forest of wolves. The very ground shook under him.

The Heshette were in trouble. Their mounts, unaccustomed to facing such creatures, reared and panicked. The horsemen strug-gled to control them, while firing arrows into a pack of fang-toothed giants. These creatures had been pushing the war machines, those spinning, shrilling wheels of knives and nests of flesh and chains. Two-thirds of Ramnir's men had already fallen, while the others were hard-pressed to retreat. Menoa's armoured giants seemed impervious to arrows. They tore the horses to shreds and feasted on the meat.

But John Anchor moved to help his friend.

To see him in battle was to see nothing. Wherever his veil of fog moved through the army, it left corpses in its wake. And as it reached the last Heshette survivors, Harper turned away.

'It's a slaughter.'

A young woman was standing beside Harper, gaunt and dressed in battered leathers. 'Rachel Hael,' she announced her-self.

'Alice Harper.'

'It's not often I meet another as pale as me,' Rachel said.

The engineer drained the last mist from her bulb. 'I'm dead,' she said. 'And by all accounts I should be down there with the rest of Menoa's freaks.'

Rachel shrugged. 'We're just as freakish on this side of the battlefield too, only prettier.' She smiled. 'And we're winning.'

Harper squeezed her empty bulb. 'Out of blood,' she said. 'When the battle's over, I'll have to wander through the butchered corpses to feed my soul.' She expected a look of shock or horror from the other woman, but what she got was an even broader smile.

'Sounds pleasant,' Rachel said. 'I think I'll join you. A friend of mine is down there now, someone I haven't spoken to in a long time. He's grown since I last saw him.'

'Dill?'

She nodded.

'It won't be long before it's over now.'

Rys's Northmen had driven the remnants of Menoa's army back into the waters of Lake Larnaig. Trench, finding room around him, had lowered his shiftblade. He was breathing hard, his tattered mail shirt drenched in gore. Down on the western fringes, Anchor's cloud of fog moved away from another field of corpses. And Dill now stood alone in the centre of the battlefield, gazing down at the destruction. Fresh blood plastered his shins; his monstrous club was dented and missing most of its wheels.

Rachel and Harper set off together down the slope.

Severed limbs and shards of metal littered the ground for half a league in every direction. Red steam rose from wet mounds of unidentifiable remains. The landscape had been battered and scarred, pocked with great holes and trenches where Dill's club had fallen. In places they were forced to wade through a crimson mire.

But Harper felt her strength return. 'They bloodied the Larnaig Field,' she muttered.

'What?'

'Menoa saturated the ground all the way to the gates of Coreollis,' she explained. 'After that arconite . . . Dill . . . had turned, he couldn't hope to win this battle. He sacrificed his entire army in vain.' She shrugged. 'It seems so senseless.'

'Simple rage?' Rachel asked.

Harper shook her head. 'That isn't like him. He plans everything in perfect detail. All his plans have plans within them. It's his nature to adapt to changing circumstances. He thrives upon it.'

Rachel dragged her heel out of a sucking pit. She shook blood from her boots. 'Perhaps he just couldn't adapt to face this threat. He had every living god ranged against him here, the most powerful warriors I've ever seen together in one place.'

Harper stopped suddenly. She swung her gaze around the battlefield, and the thousands upon thousands of dead, both human and demons, all piled together. Crows had already come out from the city to feed. They squawked and tore at strips of flesh, then fluttered away with their prizes. Crimson vapours rose from the newly slaughtered, so heady and sweet and rich that it made Harper shudder.

'All together in one place,' she whispered. 'Rys, Cospinol, Mirith and Hafe, the living gods. Hasp and his champion, both of the First Citadel. Human mercenaries and the Army of Flowers and Knives. A thaumaturge from Deepgate and her Penny Devil. Everyone who could have stopped Menoa made it to this battlefield.' Now she gazed up at Dill. 'And the only arconite who could have turned . . . Gods help us.'

'What do you mean?'

'The thaumaturge put a splinter of her soul in Dill. That's how she was able to reach him. But Menoa *knew* about the splinter.'

'I don't understand.'

'Menoa made twelve arconites. His Icarates have been feeding them all of these years, persuading them, torturing them into submission. But not Dill.' She threw her arms out. 'Don't you see? Dill was different. He was the only one who *could* betray Menoa. The King of Hell *expected* him to defect.'

'But why?'

'Because of all this,' Harper cried. 'This killing field! This graveyard! Enough blood has been shed here to open another portal.'

And even as she uttered the words, Harper felt a tremor run through the battlefield. The ground began to sink under her. Heaps of corpses tumbled inwards, consumed by the now pliant earth.

Dill stumbled and then staggered back from the collapsing field as flesh and bone and armour slid towards a widening depression. A new lake was forming between Larnaig and the walls of Coreollis, a pool of foul red water. Crows rose, shrieking, and flapped back towards the city. Harper recognized the stench of the Maze.

Hemispheres of bone appeared in the bubbling waters, rising as large as islands. They rose slowly to reveal scarred brows and deep depressions where Harper knew their eyes would be, and then jaws and teeth. Twelve sets of grinning teeth.

for

miss konkland

LOVE
you